THE BLEEDING STONE

Book One of the Spellbinders and the Gunslingers

Joseph John Lee

For Adam

PROLOGUE

A Beginning, and an End

The Year 1581 Anno Salvatoris
40 Years After the Settling

Sea winds abounded amidst an air rich upon Aritz's tongue with the taste of salt. As gulls called, circling the depths of the Ocean of Catelina in search of food, his magnificent galleon, draped with sails of Acrarian regalia, pulled into port. A host of attendants waited for him along the dock, lined in parallel rows of six apiece. The ship was a marvel of engineering, the auspices of the Years of Industry benefiting it greatly. Up close, it nearly resembled a fortress. Ten cannons jutted out from each side, promising hellfire with the slightest of provocations. The blue and white coat-of-arms of the royal family adorned the sails, though it was a lordly variant of that emblem. She sailed alone into the port, but that was hardly anything new. No sailor worth their salt dared challenge the might of the *Chariot* in open waters. Any man lacking the salt merely would find themselves returned to the salt in short order.

The *Chariot* was a symbol. Of power, of wealth, of status. And, of course, of Aritz himself.

Distantly, he could hear an exclamation of, "He has arrived!" from one of the attendants, a portly and aged man adorned in solid blue robes of dyed hides sporting a deep V-shape in the front to accommodate the warm southern air.

Aritz took a handful of steps forward along the creaking wooden dock, crystalline waves splashing in intermittent bursts. As his shoes soaked in the puddles of salt water, he watched as a servant aboard the *Chariot* pushed a ramp down to the walkway below, bowing out of the way to graciously allow Aritz passage.

"He has arrived!" the attendant said again. "Lord Aritz is returned!"

The pomp and circumstance were nothing new for Aritz. For over two decades, this was his charge, his reality. And to tell the truth? He was quite all right with that.

As he prepared to descend the ramp, he drew a deep breath and collected himself, fixing and straightening his adornments. He removed his cloak, far too peppered by the lingering aroma of ocean and fish from the three-month sea voyage, and, without a glance, handed it off to some unseen boy. They came in droves whenever they were needed. He liked that about them. Underneath the cloak lay one of his finest leather tunics, solid blue as was the custom. A white cape was draped over one shoulder, symbolizing a man of status and means. His trousers and shoes were of more simple taste, however. Simple for a Lord, at any rate.

With the plank groaning underneath his weight, Aritz descended to the level of the eager throng of attendants. To his eyes, they were always men of wealth, though only by virtue of their position as lecturers at the University. On this land, that was quite something. Back home in his native Acraria...not so much. Aritz looked them over individually, all gatekeepers, individuals holding the key to a higher realm of understanding, all of it hiding behind such odd and baseless smiles. *Sycophants and arse-kissers, the lot of them*, he thought. *Always eager for something.*

The first attendant greeted him heartily from the first half-step he took on the dock, reaching out and shaking his hand with the vigor of the mightiest of earthquakes. "Oh, Lord Aritz! Welcome! Welcome back to Ferranda! You are always missed here!"

Managing a half-hearted smile, Aritz removed his hand from the eager man. "A pleasure as always, Master Horatio," he said.

"Beg pardon, my Lord, but I am Master Hernan," the man said with a sheepish chuckle. "Master Horatio passed some years ago."

"Ah yes, of course," Aritz said, passing Hernan by with a pat on the shoulder. "My mistake, Master Herman."

Hernan did not make any further corrections. Unless inane blathering and stuttering counted for such. While the rows of silent scholars bowed their heads in respectful silence, the portly attendant shuffled quickly after the Lord, seemingly eager to continue the welcome. "It has been quite some time since you returned to Ferranda, my Lord, has it not?"

Surely, they're awaiting an opportunity for a boon to be granted them, as though my coming here was not enough, Aritz thought with a grunt. "Four, five years, I'd wager." The way Hernan walked behind him was frankly irritating. Hardly a plump step, just a shaky shuffle, almost like he was afraid his heavy footsteps would punch a hole through the dock. *I'd enjoy seeing that, honestly.*

"Such a long time, my Lord. You must miss your time here dearly."

"I spent the first half of my adult years here. Now I've a family." Aritz shrugged, the three months at sea suddenly bearing down upon his joints. He was no longer the spry man he was all those years ago. He *had* seen almost sixty years, after all. That was more than evident on his face. Wrinkles had long since set deeply in cavernous formations along his forehead and cheeks, and where his rows of curly hair once shimmered with shades of auburn-brown, they were now peppered with at least six shades of grey.

"And how *are* your lady wife and children, my Lord? They must live in wondrous comfort back in the homeland."

"They must, yes." *Am I even allowed a moment's rest and restoration, or is this braggart intent on following me to the privy, too?*

Hernan hummed an acknowledgment and shuffle-shuffle-shuffled quicker to maintain Aritz's pace. Savior Above, he was an unsightly man. Every orifice of his body just seemed to *drip* sweat.

I'm rather regretting shaking his hand now, Artiz thought.

"At any rate, my Lord," Hernan said, heartily clearing his throat as though to announce his intention to speak further, "it is a tremendous honor and privilege that you have come all this way. The students will be immensely thrilled."

Well, at least someone *is* thrilled I am here. "I'm delighted to hear so." *So long as we do not have a repeat of last time. Where* did *that girl get so many eggs?* "I trust they are still being instructed well." *And those that aren't are gaoled appropriately, I trust.* "Have they word of my arrival?"

"Ho-ho, oh no, my Lord. We wanted it to be a surprise for them."

"Oh, goody."

"Yes, yes, 'good-ee,' my Lord! 'Good-ee' for them that the Founder himself is about to provide a special guest lecture!" He sighed longingly, shades of hopefulness adorning his breath. Hopefulness smelled like shite coming out of him.

The Founder. Sometimes Aritz would forget that title. Strange thing, memory is. After all, he *had* been a Lord for some time now because of it. Everything he was, it was built upon Ferranda's foundation. That was always worth remembering.

The precipices of industry loomed over the horizon, heralding the arrival into view of Ferrand City, the capital of this island nation. The very tip of smokestacks spewing out production became visible as the wooden docks gave way to dry land.

It was always such a treat for Aritz to see how much further this island progressed in his absences, and after spending a quarter of a year on a ship, walking that much further on a rickety dock above water, with terra firma just barely in sight, was such a torturous tease. Aritz didn't think he could ever be so enthralled by the sight of stone-lain pathways, but they looked so enticing that he could kiss them.

His entourage-in-tow would probably have worshiped the very ground had he done so.

The satisfaction of that mental image wasn't worth the dirt and grime getting into his mouth, so he decided against it.

Relishing the solid ground beneath his feet, Aritz eyed the city of his own creation with satisfaction. A reminder of great days. Turning his gaze loosely to Hernan, whose piercing green eyes were ever-vigilant and ever-disturbing, he asked, "So, when am I expected to be at the University?" He looked up at the sky, the sun in a position to indicate high noon.

Nervously, Hernan coughed and ran his plump fingers through his diminishing hair. He was sweating even more profusely now, if that were possible. "Ah, well. It's near midday now, my Lord, so I would wager...ah, well..."

"Out with it, man," Aritz said impatiently.

"Ahem, well. Near on ten minutes from now."

"Ten *minutes*?!" His eyes widened, an untapped frustration burning in his irises. At that moment, he felt he could melt the sniveling Hernan to the ground with just a glare. If anything, that dampness in the scholar's trousers likely wasn't from sweat anymore. Didn't smell like it, either.

"A-a-ah, w-well, my Lord." Repeatedly, Hernan ran his hands through the thin strands of hair atop his head, such that half of the hair was sticking straight up and the other half was being pulled out in clumps. Maybe *that's* why he was half-bald. A nervous tick, apparently. "We had expected you a day or two past, and assumed that would be plenty of time for you to gain your bearings, relax, ah...*accommodate* yourself, and—"

"Well, beg pardon for the winds not playing to your favor, Master Berman!" Truthfully, Aritz was slightly annoyed but not as angry as he was making himself out to be. *It does my heart well to knock this man down a peg, though.* "It will take *fifteen* minutes just to walk to Ferrand City, for I see you've neglected to prepare a horse for my arrival. Is *this* how you welcome your Lord?!"

"No, no, *please*, my Lord! A thousand apologies! All fault belongs to me! Please, if I may—"

"What you *may* do, Master, is delay the day's lecture." Aritz eyed the retinue behind him, all averting their gazes to the vast and empty unknowns around them. *Fascinating discoveries, these scholars must be having. I wonder if they've at last learnt to see the wind.* "At the very least, gentlemen, I would like some time alone in my chambers. Allow me that time, and I shall ready myself within the hour." *And all the more to get this lecture over with.* "Is that satisfactory for you lot?"

Hernan looked nearly on the point of tears as he emphatically nodded his head in agreement. The nameless scholars—well, they had names, of course. Aritz just didn't care to know them—likewise voiced their gratitude in united measures, a choral harmony seeming to indicate appreciation to the Savior that they still had their necks.

"Wonderful. I know the rest of the way, gentlemen. I can show myself to my manor. I shall see you boys at the University." Aritz doubled his pace, wanting precious little to do with the group any further. With a final glance over his shoulder, he eyed Hernan, still trembling in shock, a stark contrast to the overbearing and undue confidence he had just a few moments ago.

Smiling at the sight, Aritz called out, "And be sure to change your trousers before class, pisspot!"

The sight of a warm bed not accompanied by the rank and odor of eighty other men-at-sea was immensely appealing. What Aritz wouldn't have given to just kick his feet up, sleep away the past three months, and call it a day. But the longer he put off this lecture, the longer it would take to be done with it. *Within the hour. Pheh, I should have said within the week.*

His chambers were more or less as he left them five years back, save for the routine maintenance the manor staff so kindly kept up with. How heart-warming it was that he could leave his treasures and trophies unattended for years at a time, and they would not mysteriously go missing. Something about *consequences*, surely.

A quick eye's glance confirmed that it was still the home away from home, the home *before* the home. A personal kingdom he had crafted and dwelt in for two decades, back when the Kingdom he served had yet to become the Kingdom he'd create.

Banners were draped along the walls, one of the blue-and-white heralding Acraria, another with the variant depicting the crest of his House, a red bear, fierce and proud.

Familiar sights remained in the middle: a large table displaying a map of Ferranda, from the southern shores of Ferrand City to the secluded peaks of the Northern Mountains, a cartographer's gift which once functioned as a war map; off by the large-paned windows, an ornate desk of the finest woods, carved delicately by the finest woodsmiths the Kingdom could offer; to the side, shelving housing treasures and trophies, memories of a time long past, all flanking his cherished flintlock pistol, an heirloom he'd no longer a need for, but came well in handy during the founding of Ferranda.

It was almost worth the voyage east just for the rekindling of memories. Almost. As enticing as nostalgia strove to be, Aritz did have a task to get out of the way.

Retreating to his wardrobe, he discarded the sea-tainted leathers of his journey and replaced them with identical—more or less—garments of similar grandeur, the only difference being the trims of white-gold fringe along the sleeves and collar. He was invited as something befitting royalty, and he intended to look the part.

Bidding a final glance to the glory days, Aritz barged out from his chambers, paying little regard to the attendants awaiting his intent to leave, and strode out of his manor and onto the streets of Ferrand City, the unheeded beckoning of his guards faintly following in his step.

The capital had come a long way since its first inception almost forty years past. Seeing the advent of progress made it hard to believe that this once was just an expanse of fields with hardly any development to its name. Parsing the panoramic view before him put a smile on his tired face.

Beyond the gate leading to his manor, stone streetways laid the path, sidewalks of smooth granite directing foot traffic. The pitter-patter of horseshoes clicked along the streets, leaving him to ponder whether they were carrying lovelorn hopefuls by carriage to what was probably their next coital activity at this time of day. A steady commotion littered the air as inquisitions of the day's coming attractions rang out, passive conversations about when to visit the open markets against aggressive arguments about Madame Whoever's philandering husband. Poetry to Aritz's ears. A modern society.

As he walked past the gates and turned the corner, still offering little mind to the attendants who were technically meant to be his bodyguards, Aritz breathed in the refreshing sea breeze, a remarkable change of pace from the urban stink of his homeland. Buildings of various compositions flanked his periphery, a sign of the early days when homes were haphazardly thrown together with whatever wood and stone they could salvage. There was a certain charm to it, at any rate. Puffs of smoke billowed out from atop chimney pipes, the subtle aroma of cooking coals wafting out from the assorted houses. It smelled like someone was charring a steak to perfection. *I'll have to come by afterwards for a bite. What are they going to say to me, "No?"*

The University stood tall at the end of the road on the right-hand side. Save for his own manor, it was the largest building in the city. That was by his own design. It needed to express its importance while not overshadowing *his* own grandeur.

Regardless, he was willing to allow some more expansive worship to be given to the factory, which acted as the University's cross-street neighbor. After all, without the factory, Ferrand City—and the whole of Ferranda, for that matter—would not be where it was. The advent of industry back home in Acraria allowed the development of this small nation to hit the ground running, with everything from the smallest of tools to the most intricate of engines holding some manner of inception within the walls of that place of creation. When Ferranda was but a mere stopover on a much larger trade route to the west, the building was vital for storing precious goods for barter. Soon enough, it became the *source* of those goods such that the entire island became sufficient on its own.

It didn't take long in Aritz's saunter of marveling at his own creations for citizens to take notice. Hushed whispers rumbled in growing excitement as more and more people came to realize just who was walking the streets of Ferrand City. Murmurs proclaiming the return of the Founder echoed through the city, and it would not be long before the entirety of the populace was in an uproar over his return. Any time Aritz showed his face was a momentous occasion, for one reason or another.

With the furor of excitement reaching a zenith, Aritz could only barely hear the warning cries from his attendants, however far behind him they were. He wasn't much concerned, regardless. So, people knew he was back in Ferranda? No bother. The whole lot of them would only stare and gawk. For a people so reverent of the teachings of the Savior, they certainly seemed to offer Aritz the same degree of platitude. He paid them no mind either way. In his peripheral vision, men pumped their fists in a bastardization of the Acrarian salute while women shrieked and swooned after him. Over the din of fanfare, Aritz could, at last, hear a discernible voice saying, "Sir, we should really be moving along." The concern that these upstart bodyguards elected to show was wonderful.

It matters very little, though, Aritz thought. *Here, I am untouchable.*

Leaving the roar of the crowd behind him, offering them nothing but a parting glance, Aritz at last arrived at the University, the hub of learning on this small island nation. Its architecture was gaudy, an embellishment of sculpted marble imported from the mainland and pristine stonework originating from the Mountains. The intent was to model the building after the arcane structures of the great philosophers to the south of Acraria. With this Age of Industry also came an Age of Knowledge, and suddenly looking back to the past and learning the obscure thoughts of men smarter than he was in vogue. More power to everyone, then.

The centerpiece to the University, however, in Aritz's most humble opinion, was the victorious statue in the middle of the courtyard depicting his image. Bearing a sword and pistol, a mantle atop his head, and a star across his chest, his was a caricature of how Ferranda was founded: through strength and progress, for Crown and Savior. The sword was a bit tacky, though. He had never used one before.

Once again eager to see Aritz was Master Hernan, at last removed from his streaks of sweat and soiled trousers. The portage to the Main Hall was wide open, the scholar extending an arm inwards as a means of welcome. "The uproar of the crowd was signal enough of your arrival, my Lord," he said, much more calmly than he had at the docks. "Please, follow me. I shall show you the way to the lecture hall."

With a shrug and a nod, Aritz allowed the shuffling feet to guide the way. The hallways were nothing short of impressive. Elaborate artwork adorned the walls, imports from some of the greatest artistic minds in the Acrarian Kingdom. Prominent voices resembling those sullen, murmuring tones of his welcoming party at the docks echoed through the corridor, doing their best to captivate a disinterested audience. *What a pity, that,* Aritz thought. *Those students will not be blessed by my presence.*

Upon reaching the lecture hall, Master Hernan humbly requested Aritz to stay put and await his introduction. Enough of a commotion was apparently drawn from the portly scholar's shuffle-steps that heads began to poke out from adjacent classrooms, intrigued by what could possibly have instilled in the man such fleetness of foot.

Listlessly, Aritz raised an acknowledging eyebrow to the passersby and glances of curiosity. Something to brighten their day, at the least.

Listening closely, Aritz quickly realized that Hernan's voice was muffled. Either that was a lecturing style unique to Ferrand City, or the man was just mumbling into his bouncing jowls again. Not intent on waiting for some dramatic pause or silence, the Acrarian Lord burst into the classroom, shades of regality glistening in the eyes of those present.

Hernan didn't seem to take notice of the grand entrance. Instead he was intent on going over some logistical gubbins about this or that. "—and as a reminder, the Feast of the Savior is slated for three days hence, *by invitation only*. I do not want a repeat of last...what is it? What the blazes are you all looking...oh."

Oh, indeed, Aritz thought. *Aren't I meant to be the man of the hour today?*

Nervously, the scholar began sweating again and aggressively rummaging through his hair.

Aritz barely skipped a beat and continued to descend the steps to the lecture podium, eager to remove Hernan from his *esteemed* duties.

"Ah, yes. Ladies and gentlemen, as promised, a special guest! I thank you all for your patience and flexibility in accommodating our *most* special guest. Here to speak, having just traveled this way all the way from Acraria, is Lord Aritz a Mata!"

Stunned gasps and exuberant faces were the only response with which Aritz was met. A smattering of claps rang out while various excited whispers rumbled through the room.

"The Founder? I can't believe it."

"I can't believe the Founder is here!"

"What do you think he's going to talk about?"

"It's about time. My father's paid an arm and a leg to send me here for stuff like this."

"My father paid my servant's arms and legs to send me here."

"Incredible! I can't believe it."

"Do you think he'll like my idea?"

"No, literally no one thinks catapulting gulls at people is a good idea."

"Shh, he's waiting to speak!"

Raising his arms to quell the mood, Hernan appeared to have regained his composure by the time Aritz reached the podium. "Now, now, everyone.

Please be silent. Lord Aritz has traveled for three months to be here. Please offer him the respect and gratitude deserving of him." Gesturing an arm to the Lord, he offered a polite nod, perhaps too aggressive a nod at that, given the beads of sweat that shot forward like bullets. *And I had just tidied up, too.*

"Lord Aritz, the floor is yours."

Taking his cue, Aritz strode before the eager faces, all with expressions of exuberance and hopefulness. Bright, youthful, naïve hopefulness. He remembered those days, long ago. "My thanks, Master Sherman." A handful of stifled scoffs and snickers whispered through the crowd. Hernan merely took it without objection. "Good afternoon, students. Thank you for your time and for granting me the wonderful privilege of speaking with you, the future of our fair nation, and of our great Kingdom." A smattering of polite applause. "I'm sure, as much as it is to your surprise and delight to have me here, it is equally a wonder as to why I have come. For what purpose am I here to speak with you?" He turned his gaze toward a still-nervous Hernan. "Master, would you please care to introduce today's topic of discussion?" *Because your request to "be a living history for our minds of the future" was both ambiguous and pompous.*

Clearing his throat and nodding briskly, Hernan shuffled forward. "Class, today, we will be discussing the call to adventure, service to the Crown, and the founding of our nation. And who better to discuss it than the living history of our nation, the man who built Ferranda from nothing and turned it into the wondrous community it is today?"

Aritz slowly blinked for one second, two seconds, three. *You asked me here for a bloody* history *lesson? Did you forget how to print a history book?* Too late to back out now, then. What was done was done. "Yes, who better, indeed, Master? Class, forgive me if this may seem duplicitous of the histories you have learned whilst growing up. I suppose this will be great practice for when I at last draft my memoirs." A few chuckles littered the room, a handful of smiles, and one stern, unamused expression upon a girl in the middle rows. Can't please them all, apparently.

"Right then, let's get on with it," Aritz began. "Growing up in Acraria, I lived in the shadow of a dream of my father, Lord Nofre a Mata, a dream to see the world and prove our family's worth to the Crown. We were a family of means, mind—my father was a spice trader, and we *had* possessed a small fortune by regional standards. But ah, that's neither here nor there." He paused, taking an extended moment to reflect on those halcyon days.

"At any rate, an opportunity arose when it was posited that lands far to the west of the Continent existed. The possibilities ran through my father's head. The opening of trade routes, of spice routes, a way to prove our family's worth to Their Royal Highnesses. My father entered a bidding war of sorts to lay claim to the route in the name of the Kingdom. Eventually, he won that war and was granted the opportunity to create a route before any of our neighbors did.

"Unfortunately, my Lord Father passed away before beginning his journey, but I refused to allow his dream to die with him." Aritz scanned the crowd, clenching his fist at chest height in a symbol of defiance. A few faces nodded intently at the sentiment.

With an embellished breath for the sake of composure he did not need to regain, Aritz continued. "I mourned my father the requisite two years, and boldly, as but a young man not much older than yourselves, still just a boy of twenty, truthfully, I embarked on the quest he so desperately wanted to undertake himself. In my travels, after a quarter of a year at sea, I stumbled upon this wonderful island. In my excitement, I admittedly mistook it for this mysterious West we had heard of." He raised his arms out to his side as though offering a sermon, a sly and amused grin creasing his lips. "Quick was I to discover my error," he added with a chuckle. Several students shared in the laughter.

"But at the same time, it seemed the most wonderful stopover for the larger trade routes. My men and I built makeshift ports and set out further west, and thank the Savior, we found that great West. Our route was established. We *succeeded*." Again, Aritz rose his fist to his chest. But this time, it was not in defiance but rather in victory.

"But, what to do with this small island?" He turned about the room as though presenting a grand landscape, even if he was merely at the front of a lavish lecture hall. "It seemed a pity to have it go by the wayside. It seemed a waste to allow the prospect of natural resources to go unused. And, most of all, it would have been a shame not to spread the blessings and teachings of our wonderful Savior to new territories. Why, He is responsible for all of us living, of course." Aritz caught a glance of a handful of students bowing their heads at the mention of the Savior. "But the thought that so few beyond our Continent potentially knew that? I couldn't allow that to pass, either.

"So, we did what seemed natural. We built. Our Age of Industry has treated us so magnificently, and within fifteen years, we had a model city, a precursor to our great Ferrand City. We were no longer just a stopover, a holding ground for resources meant to be sent one direction or another. We were *making* those resources. Suddenly, what would become our Ferranda became of *vital* importance."

Aritz took a moment to pause and sip at a glass of water that had at some point appeared before him. Wiping his damp lips with the back of his hand, his eyes continued to parse through the scattered faces before him. All enthralled by his words and deeds save for that one girl in the middle rows who remained unimpressed, not even pretending to take notes.

"Thanks to my forward-thinking," he continued, "the King and Queen were able to expand their reach far beyond simple trading posts in a foreign land. They have established full-fledged *colonies*, self-sufficient yet ever dedicated. What was once a Kingdom was on the verge of becoming an *Empire*. And in the name of the Savior, it was done. It all began on this island, a mere afterthought in the grand scheme of things, but a beginning, nonetheless. A beginning for an Empire, and an end for a Kingdom.

"But our scope on this island was limited in those early years. We maintained our territory to the lands south of the Mata Forest, but beyond that, those plains reaching to the Northern Mountains, those were precious resources that we had yet to claim for Crown and Savior. We felt comfortable in ourselves as a sufficient people to claim those lands. A unified land. A single nation. Under the light of the Savior and by the rule of King Ferrand and Queen Catelina. I had to credit this land in their name, and so I bequeathed upon it the name of Ferranda, and the ocean which carried us here the Ocean of Catelina.

"And in those ensuing years, the years so proudly served as a man of an empire, I was bestowed a Lordship, a sizable homestead, and *this*. Ferranda." *I would have expected nothing less for all that I did for the Kingdom,* Aritz thought.

"They dubbed me 'Founder' and sent me along to the history books. The very books from which you all learn." *And the very books written by my own hand, of course.*

Aritz sighed, taking an extended moment to appreciate all he had accomplished. He relished in the satisfaction. It did bring a smile to his face.

"I suppose that shall be lesson enough for today." Audible disappointment rose from a collective voice at the announcement. Smirking, Aritz pointed a finger to the crowd, ready to impart upon them golden words of wisdom to stew in their minds. "When the call to adventure rings in your ears, answer it. For Crown and Savior, answer it," he concluded, taking a final step backward and nodding his head.

Eagerly, Master Hernan led enthusiastic applause, which most of the students happily joined. *Most.* There was still that one unamused expression amidst the throng.

I may be opening up a box of horrors here, but I've run out of things to talk about. "I am happy to field any questions from the crowd. How about..."

A sea of excited hands rose, a wave of emotional beckons and pleas for undue attention cascading through the air. A gathering of young adults reduced to children in an instant.

Making a show of it, Aritz drifted a pointed finger along the perimeter of the crowd, before settling—as he had intended all along—on the face of that unamused girl. She'd barely registered a modicum of interest during his entire tangent. How dare she. "...you, Miss? Surely, the most silent voice is the most thoughtful."

The young girl raised her eyebrows with some degree of annoyance, arms crossed, a scowl settling onto her olive-skinned face. Reluctantly, she rose to her feet, as was the custom. "I suppose my question would be this: what became of the native population on this island whose land you stole?"

Where once there was a clamor of excitement, a din of stunned and shocked silence fell into place. It was deathly quiet, as though the most grievous of insults was spoken. Master Hernan was sweating profusely again, shuffling in place, apparently unsure in what direction he should move his feet. Rows of students clenched their teeth in fearful displays as though apprehensive of the public consequences of questioning *the Lord of Ferranda* directly to his *face*.

For his part, though, Aritz was calm and collected. It wasn't the first time he had been asked something like this before.

"And where, Miss, did you hear of such nonsense?"

The girl remained unfazed. Her arms stayed crossed about her chest, hair tied back in a braid draped over her shoulder. Aritz tried to discern some sort of tick to denote nerves—a trembling lip, a twitch of the eye, *something*. But she looked calm and collected. It was as though she had been waiting for this moment for a long time. "There *are* history books written by those *other* than the victors if you know where to find them."

"If they weren't victors, what's the point of even learning their history?" muttered one student under his breath.

"Now, now, permit her to speak," commanded Aritz to the disgruntled student. With grace, he extended his hand in front of him. "Now, as you were, Miss."

"There were entire tribes on this land once," she continued. "Entire cultures. Now there aren't. Yet we don't learn about them. Why?"

Aritz smiled. What harm could a couple kernels of truth do? "I will concede this to you, Miss. Upon our first arrival, we were shown great hospitality by a tribe along the eastern coast. They provided us food and lodging for our troubles, and though we were barred by the grips of language, we managed to communicate. We explained our purpose, our needs. We came as humble travelers, merchants, not conquerors, after all. Kindly, they showed us to open land where we may settle for our needs, which is where we are all standing now. As our needs grew, we expanded, as is the price of progress. But they understood, and they, too, felt the price of progress for themselves and expanded elsewhere."

She continued to stand, unblinking, unconvinced. "Progress. Expansion. Sounds like subjugation and elimination to my ears."

"Have a care, girl!" exclaimed a student from the back row. "You can't talk to Lord Aritz like that!"

"If you don't like Ferranda, you can get the hell out!" exclaimed another.

"Maybe think for yourselves, for once," the girl coldly retorted. Finally, inclinations of emotion were visible upon her face. Frustration. Annoyance. Anger. "Is it not strange that a small island nation comprising barely ten-thousand people became one of the crowning achievements of Acraria in a relative overnight? Where once there was nothing, suddenly there was *progress*?"

"Ugh, these are the idiots my father warned me about..." muttered a gruff voice from up front.

Aritz raised his arms, attempting (half-heartedly) to dissuade the furor beginning to take over the lecture hall. It helped. A little bit, anyway. "Now, Miss. I did say that the tribes were gracious. They helped us find suitable land for our needs, and yes, we did indeed receive their assistance. We could not have built Ferranda to what it is today without their help."

"Was it all of Ferranda, then?" she asked, eyebrow raised once again, arms still folded across her body. "You seemed to imply that it was only Ferrand City that they 'helped' with. And if they 'expanded' and went elsewhere...where was that? *I've* seen no trace of them."

"Because they retreated to the Mountains, *girl*." Aritz snapped at her a bit more fiercely than he had intended. But what were a bunch of students going to do about it, anyway?

"They 'retreated,' then. Not expansion. Retreat. Those seem different terms entirely."

"Yes, they retreated, off to the far reaches of who-knows-where!"

"How curious that they would up and leave like that." More and more, her expression was becoming *irritating*. "Curious still that there remain those who say you, yourself, led a tribal attack on this city, just so that you could play the role of heroic savior later."

The tumultuous din quieted to cautious silence. Any semblance of calmness was now bereft in Aritz. He didn't need to be questioned like this by some anonymous University student. He was the *Founder*. "Tell me, girl. What do *you* know of these tribal *people*?" The last word came out of his mouth with disgust, a poison escaping his tongue.

"Well, they—"

"Let *me* tell you all about them," he interrupted. "These tribes were a group of nomadic *spellbinders* who thought that animals bestowed upon them strength and wisdom. They worshiped animals like *gods*, despite being born under the Light of the Savior. They openly practiced in wicked rituals, killing people with but a single touch, seeing a hand offering life and offering only death in return. Would you feel safe in allowing such *savagery* to wander among us? These lands do not belong to them. They belong to the Savior, and any who would reject His light render themselves undeserving of his glow. But I am a kind man, just the same. Surely, there is the opportunity that they may see the errors of their ways, and so they still remain, far to the north, deep within the Mountains. If you're so inclined, perhaps you may wish to conduct your research there. If they don't slaughter you first."

The classroom burst into an uproar, the majority swayed by Aritz's words. The girl, still, appeared unconvinced. She had more to say. "Were they apt to 'slaughter,' as you say, because it was supposedly in their nature," she said, "or were they just defending their land from a foreign invader?"

Seeing an opportunity to raise himself in Aritz's eyes, Hernan stepped forward, a big step up from shuffling forward. "That's enough! Now, Miss, um…I'm sorry, I don't recall your name…but anyway. Are there any questions other than this…um, drivel and slander?"

Hands shot back up through the air, and the girl sat back down. She did not look dejected by any means.

If anything, Aritz had to respect that about her. In those brief moments between questions, they locked eyes with one another, verbal sparring foes wanting to duel on equal footing. But there was no such footing to be given on Aritz's part. He spent the remainder of class time fielding questions from various points of interest, from war stories to life as it was back in Acraria to a strange conversation about launching gulls via catapult because of reasons. From there, it was a thorough, clean, and engaging hour of discussion.

But all things must come to an end, and eventually, the students conceded the remainder of their time and filed out of the classroom, Master Hernan following closely behind, not wanting to be further embarrassed by Lord Aritz. Clearly, he had learned his lesson.

As the students cleared the lecture hall, Aritz had expected his sparring partner to remain, and so she did. She had yet to move from her seat, arms still crossed, a look of sullen satisfaction plastered across her face.

Aritz took a few steps toward her, hands locked behind his back, looking every bit the image of a regal man. "Are you quite pleased?" he said to her, softly.

A sly smile creased her lips. "Quite."

"Most would concede that they had lost a battle."

"That's true," she said. "Why haven't *you*, then?"

Aritz chuckled. "Look around you, girl. Does it appear that I have lost anything?"

"Maybe you haven't. But many did. And a people and culture do not cease to exist simply because your eyes have shut."

He furrowed his brow and looked away in silent consideration for a quick moment. *Profound words. But who's to say my eyes have shut? They have remained open all along.*

When he turned to face his opponent again, she was already gone. "Curious," he scoffed. "Very curious."

CHAPTER ONE

ABSENCE

The Year 1556 Anno Salvatoris
15 Years After the Invasion

Brin closed his eyes. And then they were open.

As pulses of warmth radiated from the center of his forehead, his vision adjusted to the ethereal landscape before him. The mountain range still extended far beyond where his eyesight could take him, but gone were his companions, gone were the Keepers, gone were the sun and the wind, the mountainous chill and the radiant heat. There was nothing around him, and yet, there was everything around him. A mist enveloped him, massaging his smooth red-brown skin, tickling his neck where his dark braid met the nape, like the morning haze covering a verdant moor. Nothing could quite prepare him for his first arrival in the Otherworld.

Flexing his fingers through the loose grips of the mists, Brin felt peace and comfort, a tranquil feeling of permanent calm. If he could stay here forever, he would. The stresses of the days and weeks leading to this moment could be a fleeting memory.

Today was his moment. But he was scared, nonetheless.

Breathing deep, Brin took a cautious step forward, heading forth into the shimmering monochromatic shades of white before him. Even as his feet touched solid ground, he felt as though he was floating, gliding to where he needed to be. Though no one told him where it *was* that he needed to be. He was under the assumption that it would be clear, but he was beginning to wonder whether he should have inquired about that a bit further.

Hollow echoes vibrated through the glistening landscape as he took one step forward, two steps, three. Panning the endless horizon offered him no inkling one way or the other. Every direction he turned revealed only the identical expanse of peaks and valleys, absent of life beyond himself. *Have I failed?* he wondered to himself. *Is this just like it was for...?*

YOU HAVE NOT FAILED, BRINNOLHAT, SON OF FANNALHEN AND DENNALHIR.

That feeling of calm immediately left Brin's skin. The voice startled him to attention, sending him in a frantic span of double-takes and shaken regards. "Who...who is that?" he asked. "Who's there?"

The air before him began to ripple, tricks of light taking the shape of something corporeal, something *real*. He wasn't alone anymore. The mists gathered and receded in pulsating rhythms, the ripple seeming to draw the essence of the mists into a physical embodiment. Gradually, the shape became more defined. Talons formed first, long and frightening, capable of tearing a man to shreds without a thought. A distinctive oblong shape grew atop the talons, eminent wings expanding from its sides. Eyes and a beak then became apparent, forming a discernible face as luminous feathers began to coat the body.

As the construction of the form completed, Brin dropped to his knees, bowing in reverence to it. The image before him was still nothing more than a construct of light and mist, but there was no mistaking who was before him. "Almighty Owl," he said, softly yet boldly.

The Owl, one of the triumvirate of Animal Deities along with the Bear and the Wolf, stretched its wings long and proud. Its form descended to the ground, towering over Brin as the god it was. It arced its head back and forth, curious at the young man. Brin remained with his head down, his hands shaking from nerves, some of the mountainous cold returning to send chills running along his spine. Something about coming face to face with a god will do that to a young man.

Young Brinnolhat, the Owl spoke in a voice commanding yet calm, authoritative yet wise. *For what purpose have you come to this domain?*

Brin raised his head cautiously, trying his utmost not to betray any inclinations of cowardice through his expression. Given the pit forming deep in his stomach and the nerves nearly bringing tears to his eyes, it was not a particularly easy task. "I—" He stopped, his voice already cracking. Shaking his head to regain some modicum of composure, he clenched his teeth and started anew. "I have come to complete my Trial," he said with more confidence.

The Owl nodded its head, regarding the young man with interest. It spoke no words, instead only staring deep into Brin's eyes. For his part, Brin did not break eye contact, unsure if this was merely a means for a god to stare into his soul or something to that effect. If *that* was part of the Trial, it was something for which Brin would have greatly preferred a forewarning. Eye contact with his Tribe made him nervous enough as it was. Never mind having to maintain such with a deity.

As the silence extended for an uncomfortable length of time—whether it was but a second or an hour, Brin had no idea anymore—the Owl spread its wings broadly, feathers falling off its form in luminous trickles before returning to mist. A rumble vibrated in its throat, not quite a hooting—

Would a god even hoot? Brin thought.

—but far from a human noise, as well. At last, the Owl relaxed its form, seeming to sigh and breathe deeply. IT HAS BEEN EIGHTEEN YEARS SINCE YOU WERE BORN UNDER MY SIGN, it said. MY SIGN, THE SIGN OF THE OWL, THE MARK OF WISDOM. EIGHTEEN YEARS IT HAS BEEN SINCE THE STARS PROCLAIMED THAT YOU WOULD BELONG TO ME. THIS IS YOUR CHARGE. YOURS IS NOT THE WAY OF THE SPEAR, NOR THE WAY OF THE PACK. YOURS IS THE WAY OF THE MIND. IT IS TO ME YOU WERE BORN, AND IT WILL BE TO ME THAT YOU SHALL PASS ALONG TO THE NEXT LIFE. ARE YOU READY, BRINNOLHAT, SON OF FANNALHEN AND DENNALHIR? It paused, once again staring deep into Brin's eyes, so intently that Brin was confident it could read each and every thought running through his head. ARE YOU READY TO UNDERTAKE THE TRIAL?

With a deep breath, Brin nodded. Adrenaline began to course through his veins, the nerves starting to recede out with the flow of the mists. A cautious gulp traveling down his throat, Brin managed to rise to his feet, flex his shoulders and fingers, and finally breathed out, his eyes locking with those of the Owl. "I'm ready," he said, confidence at last within his grasp. "Let's begin."

Trilling from its throat, the Owl turned side-face to Brin, its gaze panning to the vast and absent emptiness beyond. YOURS IS A TRIAL OF MENTAL ACUITY, YOUNG BRINNOLHAT. A TEST OF YOUR CAPACITY TO CREATE SOLUTIONS USING ONLY YOUR MIND. IT IS YOUR GREATEST WEAPON, YOUR MOST REVERED ALLY. REMEMBER THAT, AND YOU WILL SUCCEED. DO NOT...AND YOU WILL FAIL. REMEMBER, BRINNOLHAT. REMEMBER.

The final words echoing through his ears, Brin closed his eyes once again. When once more he opened them, he no longer could see the world before him. He wasn't blind, necessarily. His body before him was still clear as day. But gone were the Owl and the mists which comprised it. Gone were the beauteous ranges of lifeless mountains, their haunting silence having drifted into nothingness along with them. Gone were the sensations of peace and calm, the dearth of emotions, the absence of everything. Now, there was an absence of absence itself.

Grinding his teeth, Brin tried to move forward. But despite his best efforts, his body would not permit him. He was still as an idol, sculpted out of immaterial clay and stone. He wanted to panic, but even that appeared to have been disallowed. All that was not frozen in place were his eyes and his wits.

His wits...his mind. *Of course*, he thought. *I am armed with only my mind. My most revered ally. But what do I do with it?*

His lungs drew in a breath, but the air began to constrict in his chest. He had a time limit, apparently. Whatever puzzle he needed to solve had to be solved before he lost himself to asphyxiation. But could it even be? What was he meant to do in a world of nothingness, where everything had disappeared before him?

My mind...my greatest ally. But what does that have to do with anything? What am I meant to figure out? Someone, tell me. Please!

The silence was deafening, an echo of all that never was and could never be. His mind called out, for it was all it could do, and the absence of everything roared in its stark quiet. His immobile form continued to restrict, the fire in his lungs growing in intensity in response. He wanted to scream, but he did not know how. He wanted to cry, but his body had forgotten how to generate tears. And he wanted to breathe, but there was a lapse in everything in his mind, a complete gap in his memory.

REMEMBER, BRINNOLHAT. REMEMBER...

The Owl's final words continued to echo in his head. It was *all* he could remember. *What am I supposed to remember? What* good *will it even do? Someone, answer me!* His mind began to flicker, on and off, the echo of the Owl's voice cutting in and out in intermittent bursts. A fog was clouding his head, a dense mist overcoming all of his extremities. The inferno raged in his lungs. He was out of time. Where once he felt nothing, now he was beginning to feel everything. Pain, anguish, anger. It was consuming him. All because he couldn't remember how to breathe. *Come on...you...idiot...Br...Breathe...Re—mem—ber...Breathe...Breathe!*

Suddenly, the mist dissipated, his eyes widening, a vast universe of possibilities exploding in his mind. He remembered how to breathe. His lungs at last filled with air again, the fire quelling. In ragged, tattered wheezes, tears began to leak from his eyes, all the heat traveling through his face as oxygen was restored to his brain. Never had Brin felt so relieved, but there was a solemn anger to his expression all the same as desperate hacks tore at his throat. *Did...did the Owl do this to me? Did it try to kill me? ...No. That's impossible. This is...it's part of the Trial. Remember...what else can I remember?*

The memory of his body surged through him. The feeling of his toes against soft ground, the sensation of warmth and cold on his skin, the thrill of the chase, running through the open fields of the Stone Territory with his sisters. It was all coming back to him.

REMEMBER, BRINNOLHAT. REMEMBER.

With a steady motion, his legs began to function properly once again. Then his arms. His toes and fingers, wiggling in and out of place. His head and neck, turning to survey the open and empty landscape. With an abundance of caution, he took a step forward. Then another. And another. And soon enough, he was running, feeling the thrill of everything and the sensation of nothing once again, all at once. A confident smile creased his lips, followed by an exuberant burst of laughter. *What else?* he thought. *What else can I remember?*

The landscape. That empty, haunting, ethereal landscape in which he awoke. There was something so vibrant yet dull in that view. The absence of color, yet the promise of it to come. The endless expanse of nature, unburdened and unperturbed by the simultaneous purity and impurity of life. He wanted to envision it all. He *could* envision it all. As Brin closed his eyes, the stark image of a mountaintop birthed itself from the ground. As the groundless ground shook in silence, the solitary mountaintop was joined by a brother, a friend, a companion. More and more joined in cooperation with one another, filling that vast expanse that once gripped Brin's eye.

But there were more than just mountains. He pictured valleys and rivers, naked trees and hollow crevasses, cavernous chasms and dense clouds. Like a painting come to life, every detail of his memory took shape. In his mind's eye, his heart of hearts, he envisioned a luminous landscape, an infinite reach, and when he opened his eyes again, it was there. Everything as he remembered it. As a smile crept in once more, those enveloping mists, the herald of daybreak amidst a verdant moor, slithered again beneath his feet, crawling beneath him, interplaying with the flashes of light which he himself created. He remembered.

He *remembered*.

BRINNOLHAT, echoed the voice of the Owl. YOU HAVE SUCCEEDED.

There were no other congratulatory or revelatory words, no sensation of victory. No image of a returning god. Just an expanse of mist covering him, intent on returning him to the place he belonged.

Brin opened his eyes, and once again they were closed.

He returned to where he was, basking in the radiance of the sun as the chills of the mountains prickled his skin. The sensation of mist was gone, replaced only with the commanding finger still affixed to his forehead.

Focusing his vision, a figure came more clearly into view before him. Ko Zaran, one of the wisest of the Keepers, the Tribe that ruled over the vast northern mountain ranges called the Heart of the Land. The old man had a stern yet welcoming expression upon his face, a lifetime of wear and tear settling into the valleys comprising his skin. In traditional Keeper fashion, he wore heavy robes carved from the pelts of the mysterious snow leopards that dwelt deep within the mountains. His long white locks of hair flowed freely in the brisk winds, untied and unstyled as was the norm for this Tribe.

As Ko Zaran removed his hand from Brin's forehead, he could still feel the remnants of the path traced into his skin. Two circles, one encircling the other, a punctuated dot in the middle of it all. The mark which sent him to that different plane of existence. The mark which presented him his Trial. The further Ko Zaran's hand drifted away from Brin, the wider the smile adorning the elder's face stretched. He was satisfied. He was pleased.

"Young Brinnolhat," spoke the man. "You wandered into the depths of our domain, our mountains, the Heart of the Land. Since time immemorial, we Keepers have acted as scions for our revered gods, the bridge between planes. It has always been through us that young people of the Tribes have come to pass through to adulthood. Today, you presented yourself as a child. Now, rise, as a man." He extended a firm hand outward, steady and assured despite his years.

Brin did as he was bid, allowing the Keeper to pull him to his feet.

Ko Zaran placed his hand atop Brin's shoulders, squeezing them tightly, the smile upon his face still just as broad as ever. "Today, in completing your Trial, you have been granted a special gift. You are now a member of our order, the order of Owlsigns. By the grace of the reverent Owl, we hold the depths of wisdom of the Tribes. We are the history, the language, the knowledge. In completing your Trial, you have been bestowed the Boon of Memory. Bear it well, for you are the depository of our histories. Yours is a new chapter in the lineage of our Tribes, of our Land."

Backing away, Ko Zaran extended his arms, another Keeper appearing behind him, holding an undecorated pendant in his hand. The elder Keeper grabbed it and held it out to Brin ceremoniously. "Thank you, Ko Endra," he said to the second Keeper, his steward. "Brinnolhat, it is with this pendant that you shall be at one with your Memory. When you return to your village, the ceremony shall begin in truth. But, for now, please accept this as recognition of your accomplishment."

Graciously, Brin accepted the pendant, that nervous smile finally eroding completely, his heart filling with pride.

Ko Zaran gripped his shoulders once again and turned the boy around, turned the *man* around, to face the companions and figures behind him.

Brin recognized a few of the miscellaneous Keepers from different orders who had come to watch—Ne Shanne, a huntress of the Wolfsigns, and An Rhan, a warrior of the Bearsigns. And behind them, his family, overflowing with pride. His parents, beaming and strong. His sister, Tez, her expression a well of emotion. And…where was…?

"All before us, behold under the sight of our reverent Owl!" called Ko Zaran, his voice echoing over the valleys of the Heart. "Today, we welcome another of our flock into the realm of adulthood. May I present Brinnolhat, son of Fannalhen and Dennalhir, an Owlsign of the Stone Tribe!"

As applause erupted, Brin grew slightly overwhelmed again. He was unused to such adulation and praise. The ceremony over at last, he was rushed by his family, his father, Fannalhen, gripping him tightly within burly tree trunks of arms. Even amidst this cold air, his skin had somehow managed to glisten with nervous sweat. Red paint was beginning to smear off his father's face, the red-brown skin tone gradually being revealed underneath.

As Fannalhen released him, Brin was then met in short order by his mother and sister, who hugged him simultaneously for all he was worth, the red markings upon their faces beginning to streak as well. The air constricted in his lungs once more from the intensity and strength of their embraces. He was fearful that his Trial had started anew.

Once again released, Fannalhen placed a firm hand on Brin's shoulders, a wide row of shining though crooked teeth gleaming in the radiant sunlight. "I am *so* proud of you, son," he said. "It seemed you had struggled with the Trial initially, but I knew you would recover. My wise Owl!"

Though immensely appreciative of his father's words, Brin still found himself peering around the shoulders of his mother and sister.

"What is it, Brin?" his mother asked.

Brin furrowed his brow, narrowing his gaze, trying all he could to see if anyone was standing beyond them. "Um, where…" he began. "Where is…?"

Quickly, Dennalhir turned her head, met with the same confusion as her young son. "What in…" she muttered. "Where is Sen? Tez, where did your sister go?"

Tez's gaze told a tale of more significant frustration. With a roll of the eyes, she muttered, "Oh, you've got to be kidding."

And slowly, that once exuberant and joyful expression upon Brin's face turned to one of dejection and disappointment.

Raucous laughter and the clash of glassware on wooden tables punctuated the tavern's atmosphere. In the stiff, dense air of the mountain pub, conversations overlapped, creating an everflowing din of noise. Orders for refills of corn beer sang in consistent droves, the bartender moving in a whirlwind of activity, his hands never ceasing, but his face never exuding a modicum of stress. This was his business, and business at this tavern was always booming.

One particular table requested round after round with no end in sight. Three people sat in a triangular fashion, three large mugs in front of each of them, all empty as though they were never filled, the last remnants of foam glistening against the interior of the mugs all that remained of a delicious brew.

Sen sat with an air of satisfaction upon her face, hardly feeling a bit of the alcohol coursing through her. Her head was mildly in a fog, but that was quite alright. Nothing she couldn't handle.

"So you're telling me," she said to the man in front of her, his heavy robes opened more garrulously than normal to account for the warmth of the tavern air. "You're telling me, every *day*, you're here? Forget your hunting trips, forget your…I don't know, your food hunting? And you just stay here all day?" She may have been a bit woozier than she thought initially. Words weren't coming to her as easily as they usually did. "Who pissed in *your* breakfast to get you so bitter?" A teasing smile creased her lips, a wide row of teeth showing all the emotion that her unfocused gaze could not.

"Who said I was bitter?" the man said. Turning to the bartender, he held up his empty mug after knocking it on the table a handful of times for the sake of attention. "Hey, Seln! Another o' these! Whaddya think I'm paying you for?"

"Arsah, you've not paid me in five years!" Seln, the bartender, said in response. Both were very young in appearance, probably no more than mid- to late-twenties. "I already lose half my stock every night because Nara never gets drunk!"

The woman across the table, who had introduced herself as Nara, raised her glass to that. Her expression was as steadfast and assured as it had been upon first arriving at the tavern. There was no wavering in her gait, no lack of focus in her gaze. Just a confident smile and a clear desire for more drink. "But just think of all the exposure you get here, Seln!" she called. "'Home to the Woman of the Indestructible Liver!' Come watch the freak at work! Hah!"

Seln muttered something, but it couldn't be heard over the laughter at Nara's sales pitch.

Sen found it genuinely remarkable seeing someone pound down so much alcohol without even a waver. "Seeing how much you put down like that," she said, hiccupping, "I gotta say, you're my hero now. But why are you so bitter?" Her eyes stayed glued to Nara.

"I'm not the one who's bitter," Nara said. "That was *him* you were talking to."

Sen pointed and laughed, adjusting herself in her seat with great exaggeration, positioning herself awkwardly as she stared back at Arsah. "So why are you so bitter?" she repeated.

"I'm not bitter. I just don't much like doing things," muttered Arsah. "And Ne Shanne's such a pain in my ass. 'You're skinning that leopard wrong, Ne Arsah. Don't sneak up on me, Ne Arsah. You can't use a bow like that, Ne Arsah. You can't go to that tavern anymore, Ne Arsah.' What a pain."

"Wow," Sen said, elbows propped up on the table, her chin cupped in her hands. "The life of a Wolfsign. So mysterious, so adventurous."

"And so useful being so Stealthy, so wonderful being a Sneak. I can stow away behind Seln and steal all the beer I want without him noticing!"

"It doesn't work when you announce it, you idiot!" Seln called from behind the bar.

Sen laughed again, snorting a bit too prominently than she intended. She pointed a finger back at Nara. "And you...why are you—" Hiccup. "Why are you my hero like that? How do—How do you do that?" She leaned forward, strands of hair growing more and more undone from her braid as her head bobbed back and forth.

Nara chuckled. "Bearsign. Using Restoration. Suppose its intent was more for battle wounds, but being a Healer does clear out all that alcohol, so I can continue to bankrupt Seln. Beats getting gored by some wild beast out there."

"I hate you all," muttered Seln.

"But why are *you*, Seln?" Sen promptly asked.

"What?" he questioned, matter-of-factly (and somewhat bitterly).

"You, here. Why is that?"

Seln shrugged. "Opened a tavern because this spot is good for business. Owlsign with a Language Boon—what better way to practice and communicate with all the Tribes when they come up this way than by being a Linguist?" He sighed and muttered under his breath, "Language hardly matters for shit with these drunks, though."

"And what about you, girl?" asked Nara. "Not much reason for someone of the Stone Tribe to be up here by herself. What's your name?"

"Oh, right. I'm—" Another hiccup. And another, followed by a sheepish smile. "I'm Sen. Stone Tribeswoman extraordinaire, at your service." Hiccup.

"And why're you here, then," Arsah muttered and mumbled, "Miss Extraordinaire?"

"My brother. He's got his, uh, thing," Sen said, stuttering to find the appropriate words. She pointed her thumb nondescriptly over her shoulder, believing herself to be pointing at the door but, in truth, just directing it at someone's bald head. "You know, the thing out there."

"His...Trial?" Nara said, raising her eyebrow.

"Yeah, that's the bastard!" Sen said with a smile. "That's why. He just turned eighteen, so he's gotta be a man now."

"Well, congratulations in order for him then," Arsah said, raising his still-empty glass. First to Sen, then back to Seln. He really wanted that glass refilled.

"Congratulations?" Sen questioned.

"Well, you're celebrating his success here, no?" Nara asked, raising an eyebrow.

"Uhh...?" Sen trailed off, refocusing herself. She tried to remember. *Brin had the...the thing...and then I was here ... and...*

"Well, did he complete his Trial, right?"

"I...don't know." More and more, she wished that her mug was not empty.

"You...don't know."

"Was it hard to tell," Arsah started, "or did you just leave?"

"I..." Sen suddenly felt a deep shame settling in. She held the mug up to Seln, trying to grab his attention. The bartender wasn't looking at anywhere in particular, but it was clear he was trying to avoid their table. "Another round, Seln." He waved his hand dismissively but grabbed three clean mugs regardless.

"'Nother thing I noticed," Arsah continued. "Don't normally see Stone folk up this way with no face markings. You know, the face paint. Why don't you have yours on?"

"Don't worry about that," Sen dismissed. Her composure still loose and flighty, she began to scour the tables near her, looking for something. "Now, where'd those cards go? Loser pays for the beers."

"Just *somebody* pay for them," Seln muttered from across the way.

Nara raised her hand, holding a deck. "I've been holding them literally since we finished the last game ten minutes ago." She placed them down on the table, silently regarding Sen, clearly far from blind to the Stone woman's suddenly irked demeanor and appearance. "Sore subject?"

Immediately, Sen grabbed the pile of cards from the middle of the table and began dealing them out, the entire deck split evenly between the three of them, far from obliged to address Nara's question. That should have given her all the answer she needed. "Okay, the name of the game is..." She trailed off, her mind blanking on the name of the game that they had played three times in the past forty minutes. "Well, you know what it is. First to get all the cards gets all the cards." Hiccup.

Sen blindly drew the first card from her pile, a six on its face. Arsah and Nara were hesitant at first, but when Seln plopped a trio of filled beer mugs, any apprehension went out the window and was instead replaced with an enthusiasm to make someone else pay for all of the day's imbibements.

Arsah drew next, placing a five down. Nara's four was placed down next. Sen smirked, looking down at the mystery card next to be played from her pile. As an excitable tinge ran up her veins, her thumb and forefinger played along the edge of the card, revealing a three. Annoyed grunts escaped Nara and Arsah's lips while Sen could only smile. She took the four cards in the middle and placed them at the bottom of her pile. "Another good start for me, then."

On the game went, much in the same fashion.

With greater regularity than Arsah and Nara, she managed to capture runs of four, matching sets, an unprecedented run of face cards.

Astonishment and frustration in equal parts ran up her opponents' faces. They could only look at each other, seemingly perplexed at how such skill and cunning could be exhibited in a simple game of chance.

Sen relished in the astonishment. She liked this game. It was easy, especially for her. It had been a while since she lost, and she wasn't about to lose now when four rounds of drinks were on the line.

Arsah and Nara were down to their last cards. Relinquishing his final card, Arsah placed a nine. Next in line, Nara, with two cards remaining, played a three.

Arcing her head, intent on ending the game here and now, Sen haplessly drew a five. Not enough to knock Arsah out just yet.

Drawing her final card, Nara breathed deep and frowned as she discovered that she was holding a seven.

Sen smiled, the familiar tinge in her veins, and drew a nine. Just as quickly as she placed it down, her hand violently slapped the pile, beating out the slightest of twitches on Arsah's end.

Game, match, and tab.

Cockily slipping the final cards to the bottom of her pile, Sen grinned widely, having regained some of her composure. "Well, looks like I'm not paying. Arsah ran out first, so maybe it's time to whittle down that five-year tab." Arsah groaned, a dejected expression glued to his face. *Maybe he won't pay. But I guess that's nothing new.*

"How...?" Nara muttered. "You won four games with ease. It's a game of luck!"

Arsah pushed his frustrated gaze toward Nara, shaking his head. "Did you forget to shuffle from last time? Or is this deck just rigged?"

Sen chuckled, shuffling the cards back and forth in her hand. "What can I say? Luck's on my side, and my wallet is all the fuller for it."

She wanted nothing more than to revel in her victory, start another game, watch the hope disappear from confident faces. If there was anything that Sen had learned from the gambling crowd from her time in taverns, it was that the promise of "one more time" was enough to keep them going.

But the desire was short-lived as natural light came beaming into the tavern, the front door hurling itself wide open.

Sen turned, her expression turning sour as an imposing figure stood in the doorway. The man stood red-faced, and not just from the paint that covered it. The fumes of anger and disappointment colored him in equal parts. Sen averted her eyes as they locked with that of the man, and for his part, the man could only shake his head.

"Chief Fannalhen," said Seln from behind the bar. "Welcome to—"

"Sennalhat," said Fannalhen, ignoring the bartender entirely. "We're leaving."

Dejectedly, Sen began to gather herself, drawing a deep breath before pushing herself off the table to her feet. "Thanks for the game and drink," she muttered to Arsah and Nara.

When she extended her hand to them, the two Keepers looked cautiously at one another.

"The Stone chief's daughter..." whispered Arsah. "And no face paint...Isn't she..."

Nara frowned, backing away from Sen's hand. "I think she is," she whispered back to Arsah. "She's *that* one..."

Sen retracted her hand, sighing deeply as the once-raucous bar began to stare her down in fearful silence. Even up here in the Heart, they had heard of her. Word travels far when you're the daughter of a Tribal Chief. She wanted to smile upon one of the patrons' faces, just to indicate she wasn't some sort of monster. But every face she met only turned away in aversion.

Even Seln bore her no mind, less than he had already.

"You should leave," he said. There wasn't even annoyance remaining on his face. His expression didn't particularly approach *concerned*, either. Just another face in a sea of them that suddenly wanted nothing to do with her.

Solemnly, Sen trudged through the throng of once-eager tavern patrons, her steps echoing along the stone floor, the only face willing to stare upon her that of an angry and disappointed father. Some expressions were justified, and her father's truly was, but for what it was worth, Sen would have much preferred remaining with the cast of folks who did not want her there.

Sen and Fannalhen walked along the brisk mountain path, her father remaining in angry silence. The headwinds running through the Heart had caught Sen by shock, but they had knocked some sense back into her drunken head. Nevertheless, she was still operating in a bit of a fog, her vision not yet fully restored, her balance not perfect. All of which was a poor combination for the purpose of walking along an uneven footpath.

The view was always breathtaking, though. She had been up this way twice, before—once eight years ago, and once on that day four years ago—and the view on the return journey was always worth the trip. From this height, one could see a significant portion of the Land, from the northern moors to the Big Lake, all the way up through the pastel red and orange leaves of the Forest. The view ended at the southern edge of the Forest, but past there was, by all accounts, not a place worth venturing anymore. Not for the past fifteen years, though Sen was far too young to remember those days after the fact.

For all the beauty of the world before her, though, it did little to remedy the situation she now found herself in, stuck in a solitary conversation comprised of the absence of words.

She couldn't abide by that. Mustering up what diction she could, she cleared her throat to grab her father's attention. "So, where are…"

"Your mother and siblings went on ahead," Fannalhen said. He was typically a very gentle and soft-spoken man, thoughtful in his words and humble in his tone. But when the need arose, he could become stern and disciplined. In recent years, that manner was often taken up with Sen. "I sent them along when I went to find you. It wasn't particularly difficult to figure out where you went."

Sen hissed in a nervous breath of air, her teeth clenching. *I made a mistake,* she thought. *I own up to it. But I just…I really needed…* What words could even suffice as justification? Nothing was coming to mind. All that came to her was a wave of nausea that she could not be entirely sure was from the alcohol or from the pit forming in her stomach. Up in this thin mountain air, it was likely some combination of the two.

"You have nothing to say, then." Fannalhen wasn't even looking at her, his cold, stern eyes remaining on the road ahead.

Sen wanted desperately to see just what fire was within his gaze. If there was anger deep-set, remorse, sadness, anguish. Something. But perhaps she had done enough that there was no right for her to know exactly what was running through her father's head.

She shook her head. "I just…I needed…" Sen hadn't intended her thoughts to be the words that would actually escape her lips, but it just happened to be that way. The wind bore down on her, sending chills along her exposed arms. Even nature was working against her, intent on sending her home with the mountain sickness.

An exasperated and angry sigh escaped her father's throat. "You needed what? A drink? At that very moment?"

There was no denying it at that point. "I suppose so, yes."

"Of all times for you to feel the need to put yourself into a stupor, it had to be today of all days? Then of all times?"

Closing her eyes, Sen searched within herself to find suitable words that could serve as an explanation. But she found none, and the temporary impairment of her vision only muddled her line of sight when she opened her eyes back up. Her balance wavered again, her head growing more muddled. "I just couldn't—"

"Couldn't control yourself, yes. I gathered that much." Fannalhen still had yet to break his stride. Were he a man of lesser environmental awareness, he likely would have no means of discerning what was running through his daughter's mind. But he knew. He always knew. "But you could not work up even the slightest of control for today? For your brother's big day? The most important moment of his life thus far?"

"Brin..." Sen muttered. *How could I do this to Brin...?*

"Needless to say, Brin was distraught at your absence. You should have seen him as he re-emerged. I had never seen so happy an expression on his face. How proud he was that he achieved what he did. It's not always been easy for him."

"Because of me," Sen said to herself. Her father did not seem to hear her.

"But how quickly it changed when he realized that you weren't even there for him. No less than a minute after he passed into adulthood, he was wondering where his sister had gone. What had been so important that she had to run off like that. Evidently, it was that she needed to drink, instead."

"You didn't seem to stop me." Sen had intended that only to be to herself, but it got her father's attention. He stopped at last, turning to face her, the fumes of anger once again settling into his face. At last, she had her answer at what was visible in his eyes. It was rage. There was no doubt about it. *Oh no.*

"*You* are blaming *us* for your absence?" His hands and body language accentuated each syllable. "Perhaps we were so intent on hoping the best for Brin that we didn't *deign* to think that you would run off during the most important moment of your brother's life!"

"No, I—""When did you decide to turn tail and run? When was it all just *too much* for you that you could not stand to be here? Can't even be bothered to watch even a second of your brother's—"

"I was there at the start!" Sen yelled, her voice echoing over the valleys. Her fingers curled and uncurled into nervous fists, her body shaking in equal parts from the mountain chill and the nerves coursing through her. "Do you think I don't feel anything about this? Do you *really* think that I don't recognize how much this day meant to Brin and how much of a mess I've made?" The wave of nausea was traveling up again, the pit moving up her throat, an embarrassing display of gas just barely able to be pushed back down. "But when he went under, when Zaran sent him along—"

"*Ko* Zaran," Fannalhen corrected her, though she could care less about Keeper honorifics at the moment.

"—I panicked. All I could think was...was..."

"What?" her father said. "*What* was so tormenting that—"

"What if he failed?!" Sen spat the words as though they were barbs on her tongue. "What if he failed and...he was like me?"

Fannalhen sighed, his strong hands resting on his hips. "You had too little faith in your brother. Clearly, he didn't fail, and clearly, he's not like you, and—"

"Thank you for wording it as *that*, Father," Sen said spitefully. "Great to know that you see him as something entirely different from me."

"You know that's not what I meant, Sennalhat."

"Isn't it? You saw how they treated me in that tavern once they learned who I was. Once they learned *what* I was. You know how many people in the village treat me as such. All because of how I was born. Why should I suffer for that? Why did this system of the Trial reject me like it did? I grew up among the Stone Tribe just the same, but suddenly, I'm different. I'm *worse*. All the same, I'm just a pariah among our people."

"You are *not* a—"

"Oh, don't even deny it. Brin suffered for it all his life, too. Because of me. This was his big day. And here I thought I'd stand not to ruin it merely with my presence. Apparently, I did so with my absence." Sen was breathing more heavily now, the thin air starting to get to her. Nausea once again began traveling up from her stomach, her head growing more and more dizzy and lightheaded.

Fannalhen approached her, placing a firm hand on her shoulder. The anger seemed to have quelled somewhat—it was still visible, of course, but to a lesser degree—and had instead been joined with shades of empathy and earnestness. "I have told you many times, Sen. Those who would think of you so, they are *wrong*. You are my *daughter*. A daughter I love and cherish just as equally as all my children. And no matter what, you will always belong in our Tribe."

"Luck of the draw, being a Chief's daughter," she muttered. "I'd have been thrown to the wilds otherwise."

"Any parent who would discard their child in such a way has no right to call themselves a parent. Now come, we must be getting back to the village before—"

She finally succumbed to the nausea as an eruption of vomit escaped her mouth in projectile chunks. It met the rocky mountain path in a disgusting splash, half-digested bits of bar food interspersed in the mess.

"—before the mountain sickness sets in," Fannalhen finished.

Sen held up her hand as the wave finally passed. "Might be more the alcohol," she groaned.

"...How many did you drink?"

"Uh, four?" *I hope it was only that much.*

"In forty minutes?"

"Guess so."

"Well, we'll work on that, too. Now let's return home."

MEMORY

BIRTH

The wind roared in the nighttime air, the howl of a wolf echoing from deep within the mountains. High in the night sky, clouds began to break apart, revealing a moon that should not be, a moon that could not shine down upon the people below.

The village was hauntingly silent, such that not even a ghost could break the quiet. Fannalhen passed by many guarded huts and makeshift homes, where the anxiety of a people beneath a covered moon was palpable and dense. He noticed many peering out from their doors, hesitantly looking up to the sky, as though they were all fearful of what may rain down upon them should they dare to stare for too long.

But Fannalhen was brave enough to face it. As he patrolled the Stone village, spear readily in hand, dark locks of hair tied back in a braid, he cautiously assured his people that all would be well. There was a confidence to his stride, a bravery to stand tall and firm against whatever the elements may present to him. Ever since the Boon of Courage was given to him after completion of his Trial—earning him the title of Bravesoul—it seemed he was destined to take up the mantle of Chief. When his father passed away, a sudden sickness taking him, Fannalhen succeeded the title to no objection. Not many people could argue against his aptitude for leading a people through adversity. It *was* him who had led a defense against a pack of disoriented snow leopards who had traveled too far south, after all.

But tonight, he knew his leadership would be tested. The people were frightened.

Spear at the ready, an anxious young woman approached him. "Chief! Oh, Chief!" she cried. "The moon! It's...it's ..."

Assuredly, Fannelhen took the woman's hand, clasping it tightly. "It will all be okay. Nothing will happen to you or your family. Please head inside."

The woman did as she was bid, ushering her two young children back into the hut. It was evident the kids had no inkling as to what was going on outside, but they flashed a smile to Fannalhen just the same. The children always seemed to love him. Maybe it was because, despite him being what they may assume to be a mean adult, he still had a four-year-old daughter who he allowed to play with them. He gave the kids a wink, nudging with his head to instruct them to head back inside.

The story remained the same for much of the village. A concerned Tribesperson saw Fannalhen performing his nightly patrol despite the occurrence in the night sky, ran out to seek help, only to be urged to stay in their homes and wait it out. It would pass shortly. "The safest thing that you can do is stay close to your loved ones. *You* are the one who can best keep them safe." More or less, that is what Fannalhen sought to assure his people. Each one who asked, that was the advice he could give. As someone who had never seen something like this occur, he hardly knew what other advice he could possibly give.

As the village, at last, resigned itself to a stern silence, each person having been assured in one way or another that they would be safe, Fannalhen returned to his hut, the Chief's hut, where he had grown up under his father's watchful eye. Never would he have thought that he would preside over his people during an occasion such as this. In times like this, he wished his father were still around.

Standing outside the hut was a good friend, Tawandhar. They had known each other since they were boys, Fannalhen never allowing his elevated status within the Tribe to get in the way of forming a lifelong bond. He was an Owlsign, as noted by the yellow paint adorning his face, and imbued with enhanced Knowledge. Beneath Tawandhar's markings, however, was an expression of apprehension. His fingers rummaged through his palms, nails cutting nervous swaths in the pits of his hands. He paced in place, back and forth, back and forth, kicking rocks a few inches at a time.

"Tawandhar," Fannalhen called out, ensuring he remained as calm as possible.

Some degree of relief seemed to stretch across Tawandhar's face at his friend's return. He met the Chief in stride, putting an arm across his shoulder, ushering him back into the hut. It was a much more elaborate and extravagant hut compared to that of everyone else in the village. It wasn't large by any means, but it still housed three separate rooms: a central meeting room, where Fannalhen would often meet with his council as well as any members of the Tribe who may have a grievance and suggestion to raise; and two separate rooms which functioned as bedrooms, one for him and his wife, Dennalhir, and one for his young daughter, Tez. Well, Tez, and soon to be...

"How is she, Tawandhar?" Fannalhen asked, the warmth of the fire at the room's center welcoming him with some manner of radiance.

Tawandhar breathed out slowly, some nerves and beads of sweat still visible upon his face. His fingers had begun to dig slightly into Fannalhen's shoulder, not to consciously bleed him, but rather for Tawandhar to destress himself. "I do not think we can delay any longer," he said, shaking his head. "The baby is coming."

A chill ran up Fannalhen's spine, the words not being what he had wanted to hear. "Are you certain, Tawa? Is there nothing more that we can do?"

"Denna is in enough pain as it is. We are not a Tribe of medicine. That baby is coming when it wants to come. From then on...well, we will figure it out."

Fannalhen's shoulders tensed, his friend, at last, deciding to remove him from his clawlike nails. "And, what of..."

With some attempt at assurance, Tawa managed a scoff and a confident smile. "The result? My friend, the last Eclipse was over four hundred years ago. I would hazard to say we are a much more educated people now. Whatever that baby winds up being, it will be nothing like what the legends say."

"And what *do* the legends say, again, Tawa? Something inhuman, killing people with just a thought? What does your Knowledge tell you?"

"People will believe what they want to believe, but it does not mean that they are correct."

"I hope you're right."

"When am I not?" Tawandhar flashed a smile, before adopting once more a stern disposition. "Truthfully, though, given the lack of tomes surviving on the subject, it is difficult to convince certain people otherwise. It struck me as odd that the Learneds before me did not log the previous Eclipse in greater detail. Perhaps they did, but there is strangely a gap on the subject amongst our Tribe. One would assume the Keepers would have a more complete record, but each of my fellow Learneds I've broached on the subject who has ventured north suggested that they are at a loss for relevant information, as well. And if the Keepers, the greatest holders of our people's lore, for one reason or another chose not to keep a substantial record of the last Eclipse, then—"

"Are we really going to have *this* conversation, Tawa? I could go on, but we don't have the time."

Heavy, strained breathing began to echo from the rear room. Flashing a parting glance at Tawa, he began to make his way through the source of the noise. To his wife. To his Denna. As the embers crackled from the middle of the room, Tawandhar gave the Chief a reassuring pat on the back, bidding the best of luck. Yet, despite his assurances that all would be okay, Fannalhen felt those same anxieties. No one else was expecting a child at this very moment. Who could possibly know how *he* was feeling just now?

"Daddy?" a soft voice whispered from across the room.

Fannalhen's head whipped to the left, his eyes meeting those of an innocent young girl, her dark locks of hair still finding their way down to the nape of her neck. Her wide, curious eyes looked upon Fannalhen with wonder and happiness, her gentle smile able to lift the chief's spirits with but a single glance.

Fannalhen smiled in response. "Hello, Tez," he said. "What are you doing up? You should be in bed."

Little Tez walked over, carefully staying clear of the fire. "I couldn't sleep," she said. "Mommy sounds like she's hurting."

He shook his head, doing his best to reassure Tez of a situation she surely had no understanding of. "It's all okay, Tez. Mommy is being brave. Can you be brave for me, too?"

His daughter nodded while also attempting to crane her head past Fannalhen's legs. It was apparent that she wanted to inspect his and Denna's bedroom, the source of the noise. When she realized she could not, she frowned and averted her gaze to the front door instead, a concerned pout wrinkling her face. "People are scared."

"What do you mean?"

"I could hear the people outside tonight. They sounded scared."

"Are *you* scared, Tez?"

Tez smiled and shook her head. "No. You protect me, and you protect Mommy, and I know you will protect us all the time."

Such an insightful girl, Fannalhen thought. *We're lucky to have you, Tez.* Embracing her warmly and tightly, the anxiety and fear seemed to melt away. She always had a way with words, even at four years old. She always seemed to know just what to say. "I'll always protect you, child," he said. "Tonight, tomorrow, forever." When he released her from the hug, there was a much more assured and satisfied expression on her face. He hoped that just her father's words were all the validation she would need. "Now, run back to bed. It's late. Everything will be fine in the morning."

Without a word, Tez hummed and skipped back to her room, her wild hair bouncing with every step. Fannalhen watched from the periphery of the room as she settled into her bed, getting cozy and comfortable with some of her stuffed toys, situating herself underneath a charm meant to ward off nightmares.

"She is a strong girl." Fannalhen had forgotten that Tawandhar was still there, so his sudden approach and proclamation had startled him somewhat. "I can only hope my boy ends up like her." Tawandhar had a healthy son born just a year prior, though at the cost of his wife's life. He treasured that boy more than anything in the world. If anyone would know of the anxieties of a wife in labor, it was him. And yet, somehow, it was clear that he was remaining calm and collected through this night. If he could, then so could Fannalhen.

"Narvarho is a treasure, Tawa," the chief said, patting his friend's shoulder. "I can't begin to describe how lucky I am to have Tez, and how lucky any parent would be to have someone like her, but our children are our own unique treasures." With a more confident smile, he turned his head to the next room, Denna's pained breaths still echoing in its depths. "And it's about time I met my next treasure."

With Tawa in tow, Fannalhen entered his bedroom to see Dennalhir laid upon the ground, legs propped up underneath a blanket. Her hair was wild and undone, her face unadorned with the customary red markings of the Bear. She gripped the sides of the blanket tightly as though to find some outlet to ease the pain. In her mouth was a leather strip, her teeth clenched down upon it. Her eyes met his, and though in her gaze was an explosion of pure, pain-riddled fury, there was still a calming and accepting demeanor deep within.

Through the worst of all pain, Fannalhen found comfort and relaxation in the sight and embrace of his wife, and he was grateful that she felt much the same about him.

Popping out from underneath the blanket was a young woman acting as a manner of midwife, with what limited resources for such a position they had in this village.

"Koelhe," Fannalhen said with surprise, drawing the woman's attention. "Why are you here? Don't you have a newborn to tend to?"

Koelhe had just given birth a month prior, another healthy and happy boy. Every time Fannalhen had seen her since, the babe was at her breast. It was odd not seeing that. "You're making a mistake, delivering now," she warned. "I said the Eclipse was coming. You didn't listen."

"The baby comes when it wants to come, Koelhe. Surely, your Foresight would have told you that, too."

The woman sneered and went back underneath the blanket, ready to get that baby free. Koelhe was a Futureseer, which enabled her to see glimpses of events yet to come. It was she who warned of the coming Eclipse, but neglected to mention if anything of note was to happen during it. It seemed the mention of an Eclipse was enough to send her into a panic, as with many others.

Fannalhen shook his head and then knelt beside his wife, stroking her sweat-soaked hair. Her forehead glistened, the union of it with Fannalhen's lips a very damp affair. "How are you doing, my love?" he asked. He gathered from her appearance the answer, but it still felt right to ask.

She spat out the leather strip, her breath becoming more audible and emotive. Through those rhythmic strains, she managed to look up at her husband and say, "I'm—scared."

He stroked her hair more confidently and assuredly, cradling her head softly. "It's okay. Everything will be okay." He didn't quite believe it himself, but one of them had to appear strong. One of them had to be brave.

From underneath the blanket, Koelhe called out, "Just a little more, Denna! Put that strip back in your mouth unless you want to rouse half the village."

Denna did as she was told, clamping down upon the leather, her eyes not breaking from Fannalhen's glare. She gripped her husband's hand tightly, *too* tightly. It felt like every bone in his fingers was about to snap in half. Her breath became quicker, angrier, more rabid, as Koelhe ushered out further words of encouragement and praise. Frothing spittle began to foam out from the corners of her mouth as her face grew redder and redder, the leather strip muffling what would indeed have been intense screams otherwise. Her eyes began to bulge and close in dramatic intervals, her whole body contorting and twitching from the pain. The feeling in Fannalhen's fingers was gone, the tips a shade of deep purple. Denna's grip became one coil tighter, and he could hear and feel a crack in at least one finger. And then...

A soft cry. Almost more a squeak initially, something pure and innocent. A smile stretched across Denna's lips as she relaxed her head against her pillow, spitting the leather strip back out onto her chest, her breath slowly but surely settling, her grip mercifully loosening from her husband's fingers. Fannalhen at first looked down at his hand, relieved that his digits were not mangled. And then he turned and saw...

Her.

Koelhe was cleaning her off and wrapping her up, but there she was. As she handed the baby off to the happy parents, she managed a smile, though a cautious and concerned one, and said, "Congratulations. You have a baby girl."

Fannalhen held his arms out. When the baby nestled into the cradle of his arms, he knew. There was nothing to fear. How could a being so pure and innocent be something to be afraid of? She wasn't a monster. She was just a perfect, wonderful baby girl.

Tawandhar ran outside for a quick moment, only to immediately return to the room, a cautious smile upon his face. "It is still going on. The Eclipse."

Husband and wife, mother and father looked at each other and smiled, shaking their heads in clear mutual confidence. "It doesn't matter," Dennalhir said. "Look at her, Tawa. She is just...she is hope, and life, and wonder. There is nothing to fear."

Koelhe nodded but was less convinced. "That's well and good for you all," she said. "But many may not feel the same."

"What do you mean?" Fannalhen asked.

"I mean, we all know the tales of the Moon Who Does Not Look. People will not just overlook that if they were to know that she was..."

The Chief frowned. There was truth to Koelhe's words, paranoid though they may have been. He knew in his heart that this child was not anything to fear, but perhaps it is only a parent who can see the raw purity in their child. Others may have elected *not* to see that. Perhaps it was for the best. "A vow of silence, then."

"Silence?" Tawa asked.

The new parents nodded to one another, a silent agreement of a mental pact. "We have the benefit of the customary seven days of solitude," Fannalhen assured. "None in this room can divulge what has happened tonight. We will say nothing to anyone, including to this child, save that she was brought into this world *after* the Eclipse, not during. She should not live with the shame of something beyond her control."

"You know, eventually," Koelhe said, "she's going to find out. She's not born under a Sign. She will not be welcomed when she comes of age."

"As long as I am Chief, she *will* be welcomed," Fannalhen said sternly. "She is my daughter, my love, my light. Whatever happens from here on, it will not change that. Do I have your word, all of you?"

Silently, the group of four nodded to one another. A solemn promise, an anxious pact, for the benefit of a special child. Not a cursed child, not a monstrous child. A *special* child. A unique treasure.

"What will she be called, then?" asked Tawa.

Dennalhir smiled to herself, arcing her head toward her husband and the sweet and beautiful baby girl. Fannalhen could see that her heart was filled with love and light, that it was swelling with overwhelming pride. "Sennalhat. She will be called Sennalhat."

Sennalhat. In their language, it meant "Child of Light." A fitting name for a light piercing a dark moon.

CHAPTER TWO

CELEBRATIONS

To call it a "hero's welcome" perhaps would have been overselling it a bit. But that was Sen's perception of the reception Brin received when he returned home.

She and her father had eventually reunited with her mother and siblings along the path returning to the village of the Stone Tribe, but it was not necessarily a joyous reunion. Instead, those last few hours traversing the winding mountain trails of the Heart were sung with an awkward silence, a solemn acknowledgment of mistakes made and words unsaid.

But when at last they had returned to the village, there was the celebration that Sen, deep down, knew her little brother deserved.

When the descending trail leveled off and steady ground was once again beneath her feet, Sen took comfort in the familiarity of the land before her. Her village, the hub of the Stone Tribe and perhaps the most important of the northern territories, sprawled out in a large expanse, small homes and huts of stone and straw lining her view in strict organization. Perhaps it was not doing the village service enough to merely call it a "village." It was much more than that. It was a cultural nexus, an enormous settlement once expanding the entire southern ridge of the Heart. In recent years, that claim of territory had been reduced, but the fact remained that the Stone Tribe essentially had acted as the *de facto* "gatekeepers" to the Heart, almost as though they were second-in-command to the Keepers. Over generations, the Tribe had proudly watched countless youths come of age—or fail to—as they either confidently or nervously requested passage through the Stone lands.

And just the same, the Tribe would eagerly await that return journey, those unspoken indications of a job well done or a failure to complete a task. In essence, while the Keepers effectively ruled the Heart of the Land, the Stone could, in turn, be labeled the Heart of the Tribes.

Bearing this in mind, it was never a surprise to Sen that countless Tribespeople waited eagerly for Brin's return. Not just because he left the village a boy with the intention of becoming a man. But also because he was the Chief's son, his only son.

Perhaps it was because Tez's celebration was so long ago—eight years ago, in fact—and that she did not remember it all that well. Perhaps, also, it was because there was no cause for celebration when she had returned from the Heart four years ago. But when she saw the countless number of Tribespeople huddled up, faces ripe with elation, the rhythmic thumping of spear butts on the ground announcing their arrival, Sen's eyes widened.

There was no verbal proclamation needed. They knew. They could tell by Brin's body language, the smile widening upon his face as everyone he knew, could possibly know, or never heard of, had gathered to welcome him into the throngs of adulthood. He had done it. He was a man now.

You deserve this, Brin, Sen thought. *You've earned this.*

Brin looked ready to burst with excitement as the mountain trail at last led into the village. For all Sen knew, he was priming himself to nearly run out of his shoes before their father stopped him with a commanding grip of his shoulder. Despite that, it was clear Brin wanted to be part of this upcoming throng.

Celebratory chants grew louder and louder, surely enough to rouse the entire island to attention. The ground appeared apt to sunder and shatter from the sheer mass of thumping and stomping, such that Sen feared it might trigger a rockslide. *At least I wouldn't be at fault for that one,* she thought.

Amidst the swelling din of anticipation, Fannalhen led the family to the Chief's hut, indicating soft words to someone nearby that Sen could not hear. The attendee complied, nodding his head, and ran into the hut, returning a few moments later holding a ceremonial bowl. Sen knew what was in that bowl. Something that was never meant for her.

As the Tribe began to slowly encroach upon the family, tightly forming a circle, rhythmic undulations still calling to the heavens, Brin took his place at the center, seeming to take in all the faces gathering around him, the whites of smiling teeth glimmering amidst the orange hue of the setting sun. Fannalhen was not far behind him, receiving the ceremonial bowl and jostling it slightly before filing in behind his son. The crowd tightened the circle, inching closer and closer to the scene, all eager to see what was to happen.

Sen was caught in the middle of the crowd, somewhere five or six people deep in the throng, but that was where she was more comfortable. She did not want to draw the attention away from Brin just with her presence. She scanned the crowd, finding her mother and Tez on the other end, standing proudly in the front row. *This is your moment, Brin. I'm still here. But don't let me distract from it.*

The Tribes' welcoming call reached an uproarious zenith, near enough a song reaching its final crescendo, the sudden cessation upon the raising of Fannalhen's hand causing a resounding echo to bounce on one end through the mountains and on the other through the vast moors. "Today, we are in observance, and in celebration!" called her father, his face glowing with exuberance. His eyes even seemed to be glistening. "Today, in the sight of our Great Animal Deities—the Bear, the Wolf, the Owl—a proud member of our Stone Tribe braved the winding paths of the Heart in order to seek his passage into adulthood. Today, a proud member of our Stone Tribe sought to prove his worthiness to the blessings of the Owl, blessings of wisdom and understanding. Today, a proud member of our Stone Tribe undertook the Trial, approaching it with bravery and tact. And today, a proud member of our Stone Tribe, once just a boy, has now become a man!"

Howls of celebration erupted over the village, a sundering quake running beneath the ground as spears met the earth with wild elation in percussive rhythm. The raw emotion of the act swelled within Sen, chills traveling along her spine as she, too, wished she had something to rupture the earth with. She settled instead for stomping up and down. Taking in the scene, her father seemed intent on making eye contact with every single person present before continuing. For a solitary second, he paused on Sen, his proud smile inching ever wider, giving an appreciative nod to her as she remained for the ceremony. It filled Sen's heart a little more but simultaneously caused it to sink. *Perhaps he does not think much of me at all right now. But I could not bear to miss this.*

The noise subsided once more at the raising of the Chief's hand. Taking two big steps forward, the ceremonial bowl still in hand, Fannalhen placed a hand on Brin's shoulder. "Today, I take even greater pride in knowing that the man you see before you is my son. Today, I present to you Brinnolhat, son of Fannalhen and Dennalhir, a member of the order of Owlsigns, a *true* member of the Stone Tribe!"

On cue, Brin raised high the pendant he received after his Trial, the receipt of which Sen never saw. She was sure it was a lovely scene. But her father's words, while on the one hand filling her with excitement, equally filled her with sadness in the other. *A "true" member of the Tribe. Something I'll never be.* But it was difficult to seclude herself with those defeating thoughts when surrounded by the people who shared a mutual excitement for the sight of that pendant, that ornament emblematic of one who has successfully passed into adulthood.

Brin turned in place in a full circle, letting the cord waver in the air beneath this hand as he held it high for all to see. The chants grew louder as he did so, his name being called out to the skies with percussive intonation.

Placing the bowl down, Fannalhen pulled a small knife from his side, offering it to Brin by the handle. It wasn't a knife meant for battle by any means—rather, it was crafted for the explicit purpose of engraving and carving. Namely, for the Boon with which Brin was now imbued to be permanently written into his pendant. "And now, Brin," Fannalhen said, "if you would do the honors. Do you remember the mark which Ko Zaran placed upon you?"

"Y-yes," Brin said, his voice shaking. For all his confidence and elation at the crowd waiting to greet him, there was still some of that soft-spoken and nervous boy remaining. That was still Sen's little brother in there. "I do. I remember."

Taking the engraving knife, Brin shut himself off from the crowd, suddenly with the realization that what were surely a couple thousand people who all had their eyes on him, watching his every move. His hands were visibly shaking from the nerves, unable to hold either the pendant or the knife steady.

Come on, Brin. You can do this.

Almost as though he was reassured by Sen's thoughts, Brin steadied his hands and quickly but carefully carved his mark into the pendant. Two circles, one on the perimeter of the other, a marked dot in the middle of it all. The rune of Memory. His rune.

The rune a Tribesperson carved into their pendant, and, for that matter, the Boon they were due to receive upon completion of a Trial, was dependent upon which Sign they were born under, and to which Animal Deity that Sign corresponded.

Those born as Bearsigns were granted Boons enhancing their physicality, manifesting as Strength, Endurance, Restoration, Courage, or instilling Fear.

Conversely, Wolfsigns were natural hunters, and as such, their Boons augmented their abilities to the point that some possessed potent senses of Scent, Sound, or Movement. Others became remarkably adept at Stealth. And a select few shared a collective Packmind.

But Owlsigns were the masters of the mind. They were not warriors or hunters. Rather, they were the scholars, the record keepers, the planners. They were the masters of Knowledge, Illusion, Language, Foresight…and Memory.

Returning his father's knife, Brin cupped the pendant and breathed in deep, the reality of the ceremony at last sinking in. Taking the ornament by the cord, the threads of it seeming to take life on their own, Brin slipped his head through, the pendant now safely hanging from his neck. The rune of Memory had a momentary glow, a flash of soft light as its power met with Brin. Wincing briefly, Brin's entire body appeared to twitch.

Not painfully or dangerously by any means. Sen was familiar with the moment from seeing enough ceremonial passages: that twitch was the moment at which the pendant and its wearer were linked. They were no longer person and ornament separately. They were one single unit.

Brin was no longer just a member of the Stone Tribe. He was now an embodiment of Memory.

As he settled back into place, breathing out deeply as the twitching stopped, another eruptive cheer passed through the crowd. Sen could near enough feel her eardrums begin to rupture. It was getting a bit excessive at this point. Sen was eager enough to leave just to get away from the ringing in her ears. She almost did but then remembered the final part of the ceremony.

The bowl. *Gods, I forgot about that*, Sen thought. There were many moments of this ceremony that still caused her heart to sink despite the importance of it all to her brother. It was hard enough not getting to revel in all this herself four years ago. But seeing the excitement held for Brin that was never given to her hurt immensely, selfish a thought as it was. *This is Brin's day, but I still can only think of myself. I just...I just...*

Fannalhen retrieved the ceremonial bowl once again, jostling it and placing his first three fingers inside.

A pit began to form in Sen's stomach, her fingers twitching, her mind racing, a cold sweat running down her back. The chill of the northern wind ran up against her, almost whispering temptations of all and nothing into her ear. Temptations sounded rather good right now.

"And now!" her father called out into the crowd, his finger still dunked into the bowl. "As is the custom in our Tribe. From today, your first day anew, until your final day upon this plane, you, Brinnolhat, shall bear the mark of the Stone Tribe." He raised his hand from the bowl, the three fingers now dripping with yellow paint. "In sight of all, you will wear the color yellow upon your face, a mark of your devotion to the Owl, and a mark of your full initiation into the Tribe. Your face shall never again be naked of it, an everlasting symbol of your commitment to our ways. Please kneel."

Brin did as he was bid, holding his face up proudly to his father.

Fannalhen smiled, stroking a swath of yellow paint across Brin's forehead. Rhythmically, the Chief went from bowl to forehead, bowl to brow, bowl to cheek.

But Sen couldn't stand to watch it anymore. When it came time for the fourth pass of paint, she pushed her way out through the crowd, a sea of faces covered in shades of red and blue and yellow looking back at her, at her naked face, adorned with nothing but the red-brown skin she was born with.

A final cheer and chant erupted by the time she was far away from the crowd.

With one final pass of his fingers, Brin's face was coated in the yellow mark of an Owlsign of the Stone Tribe.

Fannalhen placed the bowl down, yellow residue still affixed to his fingers. There was a hushed silence as he had finished applying the paint, an eager anticipation for the presentation. He remembered that moment for himself all those years ago when *his* father was the one who applied the red paint to his face. He had given the mark to countless initiates over his years as Chief of the Stone Tribe, including to his own daughter, Tez. But there was something much more sacred, more empowering, about a father sharing this moment with his son.

Brin opened his eyes as Fannalhen completed the final pass of paint. Meeting his father's gaze with his own, he smiled broadly, Fannalhen returning it in kind.

"I'm proud of you, son," he said to Brin, choking down emotion as the words passed his tongue.

Brin, for his part, did not appear capable of producing any words at all and instead embraced his father in a warm, tight hug.

Fannalhen wrapped his arms around Brin, squeezing him for all he was worth, paying little heed to the still-damp paint staining his shirt. Perhaps Brin was more cognizant of that, immediately pulling his face back, grimacing at the yellow mark the shape of his face pressed into his father's shoulder. The paint was smudged on Brin's face, portions of his natural skin already exposed. A deep chuckle rumbled in Fannalhen's throat. "We'll work on that, son."

Helping Brin to his feet, Fannalhen raised their arms up together, bellowing a wordless celebratory shout, something akin to a war cry, or maybe his best interpretation of the roar of the Bear. Whatever it was, words were not needed. The large throngs of Stone Tribespeople answered the call, bellowing in equal measure, celebrating the accomplishment of another proud young man who had successfully passed into adulthood. The tired earth roared in protest as spear butts again met the ground in percussive unity.

Fannalhen scanned and surveyed the crowd, all still lined in a circle, respectfully allowing a father and son to share their moment together. It was a beautiful moment, of course. Goosebumps traveled along his arms, that wave of emotion still threatening to escape through his eyes. Though he was a father, he was still a Chief.

His arm wrapped tightly around Brin's shoulder, Fannalhen turned to his right, seeing Dennalhir and Tez, their eyes red and glistening, the onset of emotion too much for *them* to resist, at least. *I'll let the emotion get to me later. Outside of the public eye*, he thought. Truthfully, he was a very emotional man, but something about being in a position of power instilled in him a belief that he should hide that so as to not prove it exploitable. Perhaps a more dated attitude, which he was willing to admit, but he made sure not to bottle it all up just the same.

Within the gathered throng, Fannalhen saw old friends, friendly acquaintances, and new faces all joined together as one. The crowd was singing its celebratory chant, customary for recognizing the completion of the Trial. Meeting each one of their faces, Fannalhen allowed himself to smile and join in on the chant, the words speaking of strength and cunning, wisdom and light, triumph and adversity. The words slipped from his lips initially, but eventually, he could not keep himself from leading the charge. Nudging Brin by the shoulder, his voice was joined by that of his exuberant young son, a wonderful rendition of the chant ringing out into the sky.

Eager to remember every face who had gathered to watch his son's moment of triumph, Fannalhen made certain to match gazes with everyone he could, regardless of it being a gargantuan task. Try as he did, when he completed a pass through the perimeter of onlookers, he immediately recognized that something was amiss. He had remembered Sen being on the opposite end of her mother and sister, deep within that throng of people. Scanning that one section where Sen once was, parsing through the same group of people over and over, the words gradually started to run away from Fannalhen. At first, he thought that perhaps Sen was merely lost in the crowd, pushed and jostled about by the celebrating crowd. *No. Sen is far too strong-willed to let* that *happen. For better or worse.* She wasn't lost amidst the crowd. She just wasn't *in* the crowd anymore. She left. Again.

"Unbelievable," he muttered to himself.

"Father?" Brin asked. "What's wrong?"

Redirecting his gaze, averting it from the source of his disappointment, Fannalhen put a smile back on his face for Brin, gripping him tightly once again. "Ah, no, it's nothing," he said. He raised his arms once again, beckoning the congratulatory song to end. In a slow decrescendo, the voices fell to a murmur, the trembling of the earth softening to a delicate vibration. "Today is cause for great celebration. Please, come and greet Brinnolhat and offer him your kind words!"

In droves, eager villagers approached Brin, much to his unprepared shock. Giving him a subtle nudge, Fannalhen forced his son to mingle with the people, a people he may prove to serve as Chief one day. For the current Chief, though, his focus was elsewhere. To wherever Sen ran off. Despite accepting congratulatory handshakes from numerous of the villagers present, Fannalhen could not fully reciprocate their wild emotive expressions. He just had to make his way through this massive crowd, drag Sen out of wherever she decided to hide herself away now, and then—

"Fanna!" A voice stopped him dead in his tracks. Over the dense sound in the air, it was hard to make out the voice, but as it turned out, the voice came from directly behind him. A firm hand gripped his shoulder. "Fanna," the voice said again.

The Chief turned around, his sour mood allowed a spark of levity, if only for a moment. "Ah, Tawa. Good to see you."

Tawandhar was beaming with excitement beneath his yellow-marked face. His braid had come mostly undone from all the motion in the crowd, though granted, he was never particularly good at tying his own braid. His wife had been more an expert on that than he, gods rest her soul. All the same, he exhibited nearly equal exuberance for Brin as Fannalhen himself had. Tawa was effectively family, anyway; he was like an uncle to Tez, Sen, and Brin. "Where are you off to?" he asked.

Fannalhen was inclined to turn his head back in the direction he was headed, but perhaps that could be something for another time. "Oh, ah, nowhere."

"Is something the matter?"

Instinctively, Fannalhen shook his head, but his eyes spoke otherwise. "No, it's…well, yes, but it can wait."

Tawa was silent a moment, the excitement in his face slightly lessening as though he knew what the issue was. In all likelihood, he did. But just the same, it appeared he had news beyond wanting to express words of congratulations.

"Did you need something?"

"Apart from sharing this moment with someone who is as a brother to me?" The words appeared genuine, initially indicating that that was all it was, and though his smile suggested the same, his eyes spoke otherwise. "Well, yes. A visitor arrived for you in your absence."

"A visitor?" Fannalhen questioned, raising an eyebrow. "Someone other than the couple thousand people gathered here?"

Tawandhar nodded. "He has been waiting in your hut for some time. I do not think he realized the occasion of the day."

"Evidently. Fine then, let's go."

Obliging, Tawandhar led the Chief to his hut, passing a minimal amount of people standing in the path—the crowd of people had yet to have gathered that far into the circle—who offered passing congratulatory wishes to Fannalhen and his family. Pulling the entrance to the hut back, Tawandhar ushered his friend inside, an unexpected sight sitting within, gathered around the fire. The figure was a rather strong man, his dark locks of hair tied atop his head in two vertical buns. Painted vertically across his eyes were two red lines. A tree trunk of an arm escaped from one armless sleeve of a hide garb, veiny and sinuous from a lifetime of wielding a spear.

"I see the Stone Tribe still knows how to throw a party," said the man.

Fannalhen allowed a grin, despite it being more an effort than he wished. "I wasn't aware that I'd be welcoming the Sun Tribe here today, Chief Han'e."

He walked over to the man, offering a hand of peaceful exchange, which was graciously accepted.

Rising to his feet, Han'e smiled as well. "Not the entire Tribe. Just two of us." Nudging his head to the side, toward a periphery Fannalhen had not seen upon entry, a second figure came into view.

Dressed in the same Sun style, the man was much slenderer than the Sun Chief, a bow draped along his shoulder, an impatient scowl affixed to his face.

"I believe introductions are in order. Chief Fannalhen, this is Tol'e, one of our adept Wolfsigns. I thought it best not to travel alone."

Fannalhen nodded his head in greeting, which Tol'e did not reciprocate, electing instead to frown in the shadows of the corner.

"I apologize for dropping in unannounced," Han'e said, sitting back down beside the fire. "My congratulations to you and your family. You must be very proud of your son."

Taking a seat beside the Sun chief, Fannalhen nodded in response. "Yes, very much so. It's been a memorable day for us all."

"I can imagine. Especially after your *middle* child, yes?"

Fannalhen's false grin dissipated, grateful that the act needed not the upkeep any longer. *Watch your tongue*, he thought.

Han'e did not exhibit any malice in the words. More just an acknowledgment of a fact, but it was rather poor form to open with such a snide remark. Regardless, the Sun chief slurped at a small cup of tea, a local variant that he had grown more and more accustomed to over the years. "Forgive me for making myself at home. I thought it would be ruder of me to sit in on a Stone celebration for—*mmmm*, I'm sorry, but allow me to express how delectable this tea is. Your...servant?...out there knows how to brew—but where was I? Ah yes, I was unaware entirely of your son's attempt at the Trial today. Had I known, I would not have barged in like so and interrupted a special day. But your people really *do* go all out with these celebrations. My people hardly have the wherewithal to do so after—"

Fannalhen raised his hand, requesting Han'e to stop talking, which he mercifully did. "That's...yes, thank you, Han'e. Very kind words of you. I apologize for being blunt, but there are a great many things I wished to do this evening, and so I must ask—"

"Why I'm here," Han'e interrupted. "Of course, of course." He cleared his throat, placing the empty cup of tea on the ground. "I think you might know."

Of course. Why else would the Chief of the Sun come here?

"I believe I've given my answer several times before."

"Yes, of course, but that doesn't mean that your mind cannot change over time."

The Sun Chief shifted in place, regret and hope sharing equal possession of the glint in his eye. "I do not mean to impose upon your hospitality after you so graciously allowed my people to settle in the Stone territory."

"There is no imposition at all, Han'e. But you must understand that—"

"No, please, Fannalhen. *You* must understand. *Your* Tribe is not the one that was suddenly left without a home. When the Invaders came onto our shores fifteen years ago upon their giant canoes, we welcomed them with the hospitality that you have since shown us. We fed and lodged them, as custom required us to do. They showed us nothing but gratitude for our hospitality, and then they slaughtered us and took our lands anyway.

"And then when they headed south and took everything away from the Arrow and Haunted Tribes, we couldn't go there. We had to go through the Forest, but you know how territorial the Wood Tribe is. They saw us for thieves on their land, and then *they* slaughtered us. If not for you and your hospitality, we would have had nowhere to go at all."

"Yes, Han'e. I know of what has happened to you and your people, and I offer great remorse for your plight, but I—"

"It is more than just a *plight*, Fannalhen. We are not a people sustained for this sort of life in the north. We made our living on the open waters, a seafaring life. Where the cliffs break the seas here, we have no means for our livelihood. Our numbers are few, our blood among the few cutting a stain from both ends of the Forest. It is only a matter of time before we find ourselves extinct. Unless we are able to take back our home from the Invaders."

Fannalhen frowned. He had heard this request several times now over the years, and it was getting harder and harder to continue saying no. "Han'e, your people only number no more than five hundred these days. With what force could you possibly hope to take back your lands? I understand the desire to return home, but you also treat this land as inhospitable. We have lived here for centuries upon centuries, and we have always managed. It is not impossible to adapt and *live* here."

Han'e only shook his head. "You do not understand. We number very few, yes. But your numbers are great. How many people live among the Stone Tribe? Four thousand? Five? We have so few allies remaining, but what we do have comprises the most bodies the Land has to offer. Just think: all of the free Tribes are here in the north. Granted, the Keepers will never leave the Heart, but the Lake Tribe remains unperturbed. You've allowed what remains of the Arrow Tribe to roam in your lands to the west. Between our four Tribes, that may be seven or eight thousand warriors ready to fight and reclaim the whole of the Land from the Invaders." His fists were clenched, his teeth gritted, his expression speaking of someone trying his damndest to rouse some modicum of support for his plan.

But it wasn't going to work. "I'm sorry, Han'e. From an organizational standpoint, it would be hard enough to unite the Tribes even in the best of circumstances. I have not seen these Invaders or how they fight, but if they were able to best the Sun Tribe, as well as the Arrow Tribe in an open field, then we may be outmatched even if we did unite everyone. They have remained to the south, barred by the Forest for fifteen years now. And if it's been that long, I would be a betting man to say that they plan on staying there. I know it's hard to accept, but your best course of action would be to continue to *rebuild, here*, in the north. There is nothing here barring your Tribe from starting a new—"

"Coward."

Fannalhen stopped. At first, he thought the words escaped Han'e's lips, but both turned their gaze to Tol'e, who still was remaining in the shadows. "Excuse me?" Fannalhen said.

"You heard me," Tol'e said. "Coward." Arms crossed over his body, he took a handful of large steps forward, joining the two at the fire but choosing not to sit. "You would rather live and accept a foreigner stealing your land than die to take it back. What kind of Chief are you?"

Fannalhen rose to his feet. "I am a Chief who cares for his people. A Chief who knows when it is best to fight and when it is best to sit and wait. We would be powerless against the Invaders. That is my final say on the matter."

"Then tell me," Tol'e continued. "How long do you think it will be until the Invaders see the opportunity to push forward? It is only a matter of time, and you are a fool to think otherwise." He did not wait for an answer, instead turning on his heel and leaving the hut, not waiting for Han'e to follow.

Clearing his throat, Han'e rose to his feet as well. Caught between wishing to remain cordial to a gracious host and agreeing with the unrestricted words of a man who merely wanted his homeland back, he shared only another half-smile. "I will remain here for the next few days if you change your mind, Chief Fannalhen. Tol'e's words are harsh, but he speaks from a place we all feel currently. I do hope you reconsider." Bowing his head respectfully, Han'e followed after Tol'e into the throng of people still celebrating a wondrous day.

The mood of the day aside, Fannalhen was not feeling particularly celebratory anymore.

Familiar haunts and warm alcohol were just what Sen needed.

Whenever times had grown a bit too challenging the past few years, Sen always found comfort in the village tavern, a building that strangely managed to be larger than her family's hut. It was a large gathering hall and much more comforting than the cramped tavern she retreated to in the mountains during Brin's Trial. The air was thick with commotion and revelry. Many had retreated as a means to toast to Brin's accomplishments. If anyone asked, she was there to do so as well.

She was sat secluded at a corner table per usual. Even if none were aware of who she was exactly, just one quick look at her would tell the story well enough. She was fine with it, though. She had a beer in one hand while shuffling a deck of cards in the other. While the late morning's session still played a hazy image in her mind, she was recovered well enough to begin once again.

As Sen surveyed the tavern, she watched happy villagers toasting drinks to one another, laughing raucously, and shouting out words of encouragement in Brin's name. Or, at least, they tried to. Invariably, the jovial proclamations were bellowed out for people by the name of Bran, Bront, Brew, and strangely Fishy, but at least a few people got the name right.

"Here's to you, Brin," Sen said to herself, raising a glass to no one in particular. "One down the hatch for you." Silently, Sen chugged down the pint, the warmth of the alcohol filling her with some of the good feelings that she needed. The more she drank, though, the greater her frustration grew with the gathered patrons. *They celebrate him today, but it'll probably just go back to as it was tomorrow. How many of the people here made Brin's life a living hell just because he was a scrawny, weak kid who just happened to be related to me?* Shaking her head, she knocked her head back, letting the remaining contents of the mug slip down her throat. Despite her best efforts to keep her gas down, she inadvertently let out a small belch. A couple nearby patrons cheered as a result. Good for them.

"Sen?" a voice called out. "Sen, is that you?"

Sen looked up from her empty glass, peering around a couple taller folks before she finally saw the source of the voice. Familiar haunts and warm alcohol weren't *all* that Sen needed to feel a bit better. She smiled as a chill ran up her spine. "Hi, Narva," she said.

Sitting in the seat across from her, Narva—people never seemed to like calling him Narvarho—smiled in short order. The two of them had grown up together, their fathers growing up together themselves. Narva was a year older than her, and she was always a bit flummoxed by how handsome he had grown up to be. Underneath that blue face paint were deep-set eyes of shimmering amber-brown, powerful cheekbones, very kind and soft(-looking) lips, a warm smile to piece it all together. He was Sen's closest friend. And probably her only one.

"What are you doing here?" she asked him. "I thought you'd be out *there* somewhere, celebrating with all of them."

He chuckled sheepishly. "I mean, I think that should be said more of you, Sen."

"I *was* out there. Now I'm celebrating *here*." She raised her empty glass to him, proof of how much she had "celebrated" already. "And I'm probably about to celebrate some more if you'd care to join me."

"Heh, sure," Narva agreed, signaling the bartender for two celebrations.

"I'd have thought you'd be off with Tawa somewhere, honestly," Sen said.

He shook his head slightly, brushing the thought away with his hand. "Nah, I've not seen my dad much today. Someone from the Sun Tribe came in to see *your* dad while you all were away and, well, you know how that whole situation goes."

"Hooray, guess it's time we should be *urgently* preparing for battle because *the Invaders are gonna come*." They both chuckled at the thought. They had been hearing that warning for years now, and lo and behold, their day of reckoning had not yet arrived.

Narva shifted in his seat, clearly trying to find some level of comfort on the hard wooden bench. Never an easy task. "So, how was it up there?" he asked.

Sen nervously shrugged. "You know how it goes. Brin did his thing. Then we, uh. We came back."

"Hmph. 'Did his thing?'"

"You know. His thing. His...his Trial. He did it."

Thankfully, the two fresh pints arrived at the table, the bartender smiling to Narva while paying Sen little to no heed at all. Quickly, Sen grabbed her mug, downing half of it in one gulp. Setting it down, she placed her empty hand on the table, still flicking a card in and out of place with her other. There was a silence amidst the noise, an absence of words as Sen and Narva sat awkwardly in place, Narva taking more conservative sips of his drink. There was a concerned look on his face.

"Hey," he said. "You okay?"

Raising her eyebrows, Sen offered a tentative nod. "Huh? Yeah, yeah. I'm fine."

Immediately, Narva reached out and softly grabbed her fingers, holding them cautiously and tenderly. Sen's heart fluttered for a moment before she slightly pulled back.

"Sen?" he insisted. "You know you can talk to me."

She *could* talk to him. She shared a lot more with him than she'd care to admit. With a deep sigh, Sen closed her eyes, gathering her thoughts. "I'm happy for Brin. Really, *really* happy for him. But I really let him down today."

"Oh, I'm sure you—"

"I wasn't even *there* for his Trial, Narva," she spat. The admission was poison on her tongue, and she hated herself for it. "I couldn't stand to watch, so I just went and drank instead."

"Oh, Sen…" Narva put his forefinger and thumb to the bridge of his nose.

"And then, when we came back," Sen continued, "I thought I could handle the ceremony. I really thought I could. But then the face paint came out and…I just…" She closed her eyes, trying to push back tears, pulling her empty hand back to her face and caressing the naked skin there. "After everything he's gone through because of me, to see him so readily welcomed by everyone, it's great. It's really great. But here *I* am, four years past that, the main reason this tavern stays afloat and offering little else. I love my brother, but I'm jealous of him just the same. He now gets a life that I'll never get to have. He's part of the Tribe, and I'm not."

"Sen, no," Narva asserted. "You are *absolutely* part of the Tribe. You—"

"I'm never going to have a face paint, Narva. Not like you or Brin or my sister. I wasn't even given a chance for it. The Keepers, they took one look at me, and they just *knew*. And I couldn't pass a Trial because of it, because I didn't get a proper one. And the only reason I still even have a home is that my father is the Chief. If it were up to Koelhe or someone else, I probably would have been chucked were no one could find me, and—"

"Koehle's a bitch, you know that."

Though tears were forming in the pit of her eyes, Sen couldn't help but chuckle at that. "…Narva, I…"

"You're still here because those of us who aren't complete idiots want you here," Narva asserted, his expression intense but genuine. "It has nothing to do with who your father is. *You*, Sennalhat, always will be part of this Tribe. Forget the Keepers, forget custom, forget Koelhe. You were born here, we grew up together, we have been friends from the start, and I—*ahem*—I care about you. None of that changes, and none of that *will* change."

What was that pause for? Sen wondered. "Narva, I...I ca—" She cleared her throat as well, struggling to find the words. "I appreciate what you're saying. But it's easy for you to say it from *your* perspective. You haven't lived through what I've lived through. You've not heard what I've heard. You just...you can't *possibly* understand."

He was silent for a moment. But then he smiled again. "But I'm willing to try."

Tears were starting to stream down her cheeks, but she smiled as well, shaking her head at him. "You idiot," she chuckled to herself. Wiping the moisture away from her cheeks, she looked at the deck of cards that she had been fiddling with for the past while. "Discuss it over a game?"

Narva laughed. "Come on, Sen. You always win."

"I'll let you win this time."

"I doubt it. Not in your nature. Luck is always on your side."

"You don't know the half of it." She raised her glass, somehow still filled with drink, and clinked the side of his. "Over a drink or three then."

"Only *three*?" he said with a smirk.

"Yeah, I'm trying to sober up."

CHAPTER THREE

Impostor

There's something that's particularly euphoric about the comfort of a pillow after an evening of drinking. All the world's pleasures would crash down in a heap, the soft plush of a headrest becoming akin to the purest of clouds. As the exhaustion piles in denser packs, the draw of a wonderful bed becomes the greatest desire there is.

What's less desirable, however, is getting jabbed repeatedly with the butt end of a spear shaft the next morning until you're finally driven awake.

That was Sen's reality. It may as well have been knocking against her skull. Hammers were pounding in her head, a thousand throbbing sensations erupting in radiant sunbursts to the beat of an angry drum. Never mind the thousand jabs constantly throbbing into her side. She tried to focus her gaze, the world still an indecipherable blur. Blindly, she fumbled her arms to either side of her, trying to feel if anyone was...*there*. No sign of that. She was in her own bed.

There was a horrid taste on her tongue, the lingering feeling of loose vomit. An indication of a fun evening, at the least. Her legs were heavy, her arms useless, her head a painful fog, and everything else just a persistent ache and discomfort.

A far cry from the union of body and pillow from the night previous.

It didn't help that *someone* continued to jab her with the end of a spear. As much as Sen wanted to tell them off, all she could utter was a weak, drawn-out groan. Were it anyone else, most would consider that to be the sign of a person under illness. Most in the know were familiar with Sen's…proclivities, so this sight was a fairly common occurrence.

It didn't make it any easier for Sen to recover each morning, though.

"Get up," spoke a stern feminine voice, familiar yet distant.

Whoever it was, their voice was a faraway echo, the sound rattling in Sen's ears. Even the slightest whimper was torturous enough to hear. *And someone wants to have a* conversation *with me right now?* she thought. *How inconsiderate.*

Sen tried to push herself up to a seated position, all her strength—meager as it was—going into the effort. Tremors quaked through her limbs, her whole body convulsing at the indignity of having to get out of bed. The feeling of nausea roared in her stomach, an unspoken mockery at her thinking that she had hurled up whatever was still in there.

Slowly, her vision came into focus, the natural light pouring into her room nearly blinding her all the while. The amorphous blob standing before her began taking the form of an actual person, not just a disembodied voice. Even as she had (somehow) sat up, whoever it was kept jabbing her with the butt end of the spear. Eventually, it was just a numb discomfort.

Shaking her head to knock herself back into place—and then immediately regretting the motion as her skull screamed at her—Sen opened her eyes and saw a red-painted face staring back at her, those piercing dark eyes sending knives right through her. Their hair was still undone, the dark locks flowing freely down their shoulders and back. The expression on their face was equal parts amused and annoyed. Well, in truth, far more leaning toward the side of annoyed, but there was at least *some* amusement in there.

"Well, good morning," Tez said at last, still jabbing along at her sister. "Sleep well?"

"A funny thing about that," Sen said haltingly, drawing short breaths at the continued impacts of the spear. "Most people don't tend to sleep well when they're being jabbed over and over."

Tez shrugged. "Good thing you're not most people. I've been at this for about twenty minutes now."

"Well, aren't you a sweet, merciful—will you *stop* that?!"

Sweet, merciful Tez, at last, stopped tenderizing her catch, and Sen collapsed back on the pillow, the impact not as wondrous as it had been the night before.

"Are you satisfied now?" Sen asked. "Now I'm awake, and there are forty bruises on my side."

"I don't know. I could start working on the other side if you'd turn over," Tez quipped. Kindly, though, she sat down beside her younger sister, legs crossed over one another, the spear resting on the ground parallel to them. "Seems the day session didn't stop you from having a late night."

Sen massaged the bridge of her nose, a futile attempt to caress some of the immense pressure away. Ultimately, the attempt was unsuccessful. She could barely muster the effort to sit back up, never mind just turning her head to face her sister. "What can I say? I'm a woman of many talents."

"Hmm, clearly. Con a few more unsuspecting folks out of some money to pay for the evening's entertainment?"

"Hey, for *your* information, I had a *lovely* evening." Sen paused and smiled, her eyes traveling inward and outward for a brief moment. "I think. I don't really remember."

"Must have been a great card night then," Tez deadpanned.

"It would have been had Narva actually wanted to play cards."

"Oh, *now* I see why it was a great night."

Though Sen still panned her gaze to the ceiling, she could *feel* the humorous grin Tez was giving her. Turning her head took a great deal of effort, but she managed to look her sister square in the eyes, at least. "And what is *that* supposed to mean?"

"Oh, a night of drinks with Narva. Sounds like a dream come true for you."

"It is *not* like that. He's my friend, my closest friend." *My only friend.* "If it were a dream come true, I'd remember it. Or would I? How do dreams work again?"

"Oh, stop deflecting, dear sister," Tez said, her eyes rich with enjoyment. "No one said you couldn't have a boyfriend."

"Oh, for the love of..." *I am far too hungover for this.* "He is *not* my—"

"Hey, hey, nothing for it. You don't have to get defensive about it. We all grew up together, and·I've seen how you look at him."

Sen shook her head in place, wanting desperately to just project herself elsewhere. *Damned, stupid body. You function fine* with *alcohol.* "Yep, we grew up together. He's a friend, more like a brother."

"Really," Tez said with amusement, trying hard to stifle a chuckle. "Remind me the last time you looked at Brin like that."

"Don't even—"

"Narva looks at you the same way, you know."

"I swear, I'm gonna kill you."

"Great! That leads into why I'm here!" Tez's smile was far too jubilant to instill confidence. Sen felt another wave of shivers and nausea that had little to do with the hangover. She grunted as the shaft of the spear collapsed upon her stomach. "Get up. It's time to train."

Sen groaned loudly. "You gotta be kidding," she muttered. "Pretty sure this village is filled with a thousand of your fellow Bearsigns. Can't you just train with one of them?"

"More than a thousand, but beside the point," Tez quipped. "None of them happen to be a certain sister with whom I need to have a chat."

"Ugh, I'm too hungover for this," Sen said aloud this time.

"Great, won't be much of a challenge for me, then. On your feet."

That caused Sen to only groan even louder. Her body was heavy, unresponsive, useless. Such as she would try to lead her sister to believe, to little avail. Tez merely stared at her with the same unamused expression, watching as the performance was hammed up further and further to the point of disbelief.

Eventually, Sen managed to return to her feet, a miracle in and of itself. She hadn't completely recovered her sense of balance or equilibrium, the world wavering in great humor around her. She remained in the same mussed clothing in which she slept, the effort of throwing on new garb feeling too much a hassle that would require far too many moving parts to adequately accomplish. As she struggled to rediscover where exactly she was even standing as she got ready, Tez calmly braided her hair, fastening it at the nape of her neck in standard Stone fashion. Sen, for her part, at least still had her braid intact from the previous evening, although her hair remained wild and untamed besides.

Realizing that her appearance wasn't going to get better any time soon, Sen sighed, her eyes still heavy and unfocused, her stomach still nauseous and angry, her legs still unsteady and weak. Just another morning in her life. Outstretching her arms by her side, Sen feigned an uneven smile to her sister, long since ready in the time it took Sen just to stand up and not fall down, and said, "Well, do I look ready to get my ass handed to me?"

Tez rolled her eyes. "When don't you? Let's go."

The outdoors was poison as she stepped outside. Some people would cherish the warmth the sunlight brought against the chills traveling down from the mountains. Not Sen. At least, not at this moment. The light was blinding, the fresh air almost miasmic. She wished she were back writhing in her own filth and vomit, a stench that, while objectively pretty terrible, was immensely preferable to the crisp air and clean atmosphere that she was now subjecting herself to. Everything was awful—the air, the smell, the sense of existence. In times like these, Sen often told herself she would never drink again. Sobered Sen often questioned the judgment of Hungover Sen.

For her part, Tez was chipper and amicable to all those she passed by, a godsdamned ray of sunshine on this terrible morning. By contrast, Sen looked like the greatest harbinger of misery, the bags under her eyes fit to carry all the world's sorrow, her eyes still cracked red, her mouth wide open with exhaustion as she dragged her feet through the beaten dirt path, shoes kicking up dust in heaps. Many passersby shot passing glances at her with an indication that she was such a harbinger, but that was nothing new, frankly.

Bearing the stain of embarrassment for long enough, Tez and Sen, at last, reached the training ground, mercifully empty at the moment. There wasn't anything particularly fancy about it, really. Propped up were a couple rows of straw-and-hay dummies, punctured deep with a variety of holes and slashes from where they met the sharp end of a spear. A few open ranges stood adjacent to them, apt for wider melees without fear of an errant strike injuring a standee or attendant. Beyond these arenas stood a shooting range, further dummies set up at a far distance, meant to train Wolfsigns in the way of the bow.

This was never a place for Sen. This was an avenue to train the warriors and hunters of tomorrow. She was neither of those. Growing up, she had been led to believe that her future would be crafted in this arena. She spent long enough hours like these with Tez to instill that belief.

The sisters silently walked to one of the sparring circles, all semblance of joviality leaving Tez once she was out of earshot of passersby. They lined up across from one another, just far enough where their spear tips could not touch each other. Tez adopted a warrior's stance, body standing side-face, feet planted wide, knees slightly bent, the spear held at an upward angle, the tip drawing a line toward Sen's face.

Sen, however, couldn't particularly muster any of these things. Her stance was much more rogue, sloppy. She attempted to hold her spear parallel to the ground, but her sapped strength only allowed her to hold it at a downward angle. There was no effort into her stance, her body language indicating just how much of an obligation it was for her to be there at that moment.

Clearly accepting this as Sen's signal of readiness, Tez charged forward, Sen unable to will her body to react in any way, shape, or form. Tez batted her sister's spear tip down into the ground, just about burying it in the earth, spun on the periphery of her guard, and *thwacked* Sen in the side of the head with the butt end. With all the throbbing going on in Sen's head, she barely registered that something external had made an addition.

Although she barely felt the strike, the momentum still sent her hurtling to the ground in a heap, the dirt so muddy and soft and *comfortable*. She rolled onto her back, an extended groan escaping her lips. The sun continued to beat down on her, its rays flaring her vision. Half her face was battered with specks of mud, the taste of it at least diluting the lingering flavors of last night's vomit.

"You used to put up more of a fight," Tez said, holding her spear in a non-combative position. Frankly, she didn't even appear to have much of a desire at all to continue sparring. Instead, she shifted her weight, planting the spear in the ground, and leaned against it casually.

"You used to not pick on me when I was in *grave* misery," Sen quipped, still comfortable on the ground, spread-eagled.

Tez chuckled. "I'd disagree on that. Those were my favorite times to pick on you. You were just better with a spear back then."

"Good to know, sis. Good to know." *Haven't had much of a reason to pick up a spear in the past four years, either way.*

"Hmph," Tez grunted. Then she knelt, offering Sen her hand. "That's all. Get up."

Sen lifted her head, raising an eyebrow. "That's *all*?" she asked. "Wow, I thought after you were given Endurance, you'd last a bit longer." Graciously, she took Tez's hand, allowing herself to be lifted to her weak feet.

And then Tez drove a fist right into her nauseous gut, nearly sending all the residual vomit up her entire tract.

"Didn't come here to train," Tez said through gritted teeth. "Came here to *talk*."

Sen's head was spinning, her stomach roaring. The blow had knocked all the wind out of her, and she needed to prop herself up on Tez's shoulder for support. Her eyes watered as breath was momentarily scarce. What a great morning. "Well, that was a good conversation starter," she squeaked out, the words strained as they escaped her mouth.

"What better way to grab your attention?" Tez said.

"You can start with *not* cracking my skull."

"No, see, I *needed* that. That felt *good*." The smile on Tez's face was downright sadistic, a side that Sen had never seen before. "That was for yesterday."

"What do you—"

"Don't even start, Sen," Tez growled. "Don't think you can skirt your way around this."

"Tez, I—"

"Shut your damn mouth and listen. We're all pissed at you right now. Biggest day in Brin's life, and you dip away to get drunk not *once*, but *twice*. You—"

"Tez, I know," Sen interrupted. "I already got this lecture from Father yesterday, and—"

"And it didn't change anything. I don't think you understand just how *mortifying* this was for all of us. Bemoan your circumstances all you want, but it gives you *no* right to piss on our little brother's day. Or did you even care?"

"Of *course*, I cared, Tez!" She straightened herself up, the strain still visible upon her face, but a resolute fury and compassion welling in her eyes.

"Yeah, you definitely cared a *lot*, I see." All semblance of sisterly affection in Tez's words and expression went out the door. "So much that you were trying to find Brin's love in a pint glass, huh?"

"What the hell are you—"

"This is a family thing, too, you know. Through the good times and bad, through successes and failures, we stand together as a *family*. Do you remember us all just dipping away for a pint when *you* came back from the Heart?"

"I only remember *myself* doing that," Sen muttered in self-admission.

"But *we* didn't. *We* stood with you. Despite all outside demands to the contrary, we stood with you. We didn't leave you to the wayside. You have *no* excuse for doing so to Brin."

"Tez, I'm sorry. I—"

"Don't apologize to *me*," Tez growled. "It's *Brin* you need to apologize to. Did you even say a *word* to him yesterday? He's beyond just disappointed or upset. He's *ashamed*. He thinks you want nothing to do with him. He can't even fathom what would cause his sister to just avoid him altogether."

Sen closed her eyes, the words cutting deep. She drew a long, shaky breath, trying hard to keep the emotion down. "Seeing him succeed where I wasn't able to, it...it's been hard for me. I've always been—"

"Save it," Tez said, raising her hand to Sen's face. "You don't need to say this to *me*. You need to say it to Brin."

Sen took a breath, anticipating needing to say more, but relented and just nodded her head. "Yeah," she said solemnly. "You're right."

"I remember when he was your greatest treasure," Tez said. "When you would go to the ends of the earth to protect him. I know he misses those days."

"Yeah," Sen muttered. "I miss them, too."

"Then why are you lamenting to me? Go to him. He's probably back at home by now."

There was no argument on Sen's part. Leaving her spear buried in the earth, she wordlessly patted her sister on the shoulder and took a few dizzy, unsteady steps forward before nearly collapsing in on herself. With little to no help from Tez, she corrected her path and headed back toward the village proper.

As Sen stumbled through the village, less to do with the hangover and more to do with the throbbing in her head from Tez's strike, she rehearsed what she would say to her brother. Taking it slow, she thought on whether her words should be eloquent, reverent, straightforward. If she should get on her knees and plead. Whether a simple "I'm sorry" would be sufficient. Ultimately, there likely weren't a plethora of words that could indicate the remorse she felt, not enough to adequately express the inhumanity at missing such an occasion. *Hi, little brother. Sorry I missed the biggest day of your life and the biggest day you'll ever have. Don't worry, I'll try to catch the next one when we get a chance to redo our lives. I'll make it up to you then.* She sighed.

Bright sides. There had to be bright sides. For one, maybe it would spell a new beginning for Brin, a wealth of shining opportunities. He'd get to be one of the most important scholars in the Tribe, being the Chief's son. Another point, the entire village showed up to celebrate his passage and success. Not only that, but Sen's own absence had shown just how much Brin meant to the whole family, so that was some point of solace. And, on top of it all, that wave of nausea was finally beginning to pass. The day was surely going to turn around.

"Oh, *hello* there, Sen," called a familiar, sneering voice. The nausea was back.

Sen stood in place, rolling her eyes as far back into her head as she could muster, and then turned around. Greeting her was the ever-punchable face of Fannadhan. To think that he was named in honor of her father sickened her. The "-dhan" suffix, in their language, indicated the person being close kin to an elder, typically if a father figure was absent. So, literally, his name meant "kin of Fannalhen." *My ass,* Sen thought. *He's no kin of mine or my father's.*

A sea of freckles still shone through Fannahan's red Bearsign face-paint, his wide, gap-toothed smile apt to drive her into a fury all on their own. His blue eyes were piercing and sharp like ice, which matched his cold, cold heart. The only thing about his face that ever gave Sen joy was his crooked, misshapen nose. He carried himself with a swagger and confidence that he never earned, carrying a spear that he was probably terrible with, bearing large arms that he only had because someone somewhere thought it'd be a laugh to imbue him with Strength as his Boon, despite one of his arms being in worse shape than the other.

By the gods, his very presence was insufferable.

"Fann," Sen deadpanned. "You look chipper. Fight any children today?"

He laughed, a haughty, embellished chuckle every bit as pompous as him. "Oh, Sen. Ever the barbed tongue. Here I was just wishing to offer my congratulations to your brother. Surely, I'm allowed that much."

"Yeah, not even. We both know you don't mean it."

Fann continued to smile, one arm behind his back, the other propping his spear up on the ground. "No," he said plainly. "I don't."

"Well, now that we've exchanged pleasantries, I'll be on my way," Sen said, waving over her shoulder. "Hope you have a *shitty* day."

"You know, I was truthfully quite impressed that your brother managed to complete his Trial," called Fann, stopping Sen in her tracks. "After all, he was always a bit...*weak*, wouldn't you say?"

Sen refused to turn around, refused to give him the satisfaction of seeing her stewing with anger. But at the same time, she couldn't will herself to walk away. Heat rose through her body, a much-welcomed change of pace from the nausea rising. Who'd have thought that this asshole was a tremendous hangover cure?

"He did have quite a hard time growing up, didn't he?" Fann continued. "Having to right the wrongs of a certain *middle* child, no? Always living in the shadow of one so...*scandalous*. It's a shame he was never the fighter his elder sister was. Perhaps he wouldn't have had to have someone else fight his battles for him all his life."

A grimace and a twitch ticked at Sen's mouth. *Don't do it, Sen*, she thought. *He's just trying to goad you as always. Don't say a thing, you idiot. Don't say—*"I'd say he's done quite well for himself," Sen said, interrupting her own thoughts. "At least he never grew up with a mother who'd offer him a nice suckle any time he did something only a *good boy* would do."

She could *feel* the color drain from Fann's face just from the subtle shift in his body language from behind. She could hear the deep, flustered breath going in and out of his nose, the rustling of dirt underneath his feet as he shifted in place, the light tap of the spear butt on the ground as he contemplated whether to draw it on the Chief's daughter in broad daylight. Instead, he slowly took a couple of paces forward, the scowl on his face radiating heat and anger toward her. "You really are a bitch, you know that?" he finally said, removing himself from all shades of pompousness from before.

"Why, thank you," Sen retorted. "Your mother was my role model, after all."

Fann took another step closer.

A handful of onlookers had stopped to watch, cautious mutterings ruminating on either side.

Sen eyed both sides, aware that anything that she did here would probably bite her hard. Luck wasn't always on her side, it seemed. On any given day, she would love to sock Fann right in his dumb face.

"My mother...is..."

"The literal worst," Sen quipped. "Now, why don't you go run off and go kick some puppies or whatever it is you do in the morning."

Fann was quiet. Almost too quiet. He always had *something* to say, always had to get the last word in. But instead, he was just standing there, stewing, waiting, considering. The intrigued whispers of the gathering villagers were growing in volume, openly pondering what Fann was going to do, what Sen was going to do, whether they needed to call for someone to stop matters. And despite the loud whispers, everything was quiet. In that moment, there was only Fann and Sen. The wind howled from the mountains, the calling of the valley birds echoing from the hills.

Fann's feet dug into the dirt below, a signature twitch indicating that he was about to do something. He growled deep under his breath, a ferocity underpinning whatever it was he was going to do. He drew a deep breath and then exhaled.

Softly, he said only, "Damned Curseborn." And then he backed away.

Narrowing her gaze forward, Sen silently nodded to herself, that rising heat both quelling and remaining in equal measures. Had there not been at least twenty people gathering, caught in the middle of their morning activities, she may not have let it slide. She may have turned around and socked Fann right in his gap-toothed, shit-eating grin. Maybe just make that gap in his teeth a few teeth wider. But she had more important things to worry about. She had a brother to apologize to. She'd embarrassed herself enough already in the past day. No need to make the situation any worse.

She walked forward, leaving behind Fann's confident snickers. Over her shoulder, she shouted out a collected, "Don't forget to ask for your reward for being a *good boy*," placing extra emphasis on those final words.

Fann's snickering ceased, his expression surely changing to one filled with flared nostrils, a face red not with paint but with fury, teeth grinding, the whole works. Sen didn't bother to look. That was usually how she won their arguments when she wasn't kicking his ass.

Brin was sat by the fire in the center room of the hut, not doing anything in particular. He was just...staring straight ahead. Into the fire? Sen thought it peculiar. She objectively didn't know much about the practices of the Owlsigns. After all, her parents and Tez were all Bearsigns. Scholarly works weren't always a point of focus in this family. At points while growing up, Brin didn't fit in as well as he could have just because of that fact, because he was always more bookish and learned than the rest of them. It was an endearing change of pace, to say the least.

As Sen approached, she decided to flank her brother to the side, gaining an up-top view of what he was doing. He wasn't staring into the flames or anything like that. He was just entranced by his pendant, inscribed with the mark of Memory. His eyes weren't necessarily blank, but they were at the very least unfocused. An unsure expression stretched across his face. Not one of disappointment or sadness, but of concentration and curiosity. That *was* like him.

"It's beautiful craftsmanship," Sen said of the pendant, somewhat startling Brin out of his trance. "And beautiful carving."

Brin looked up, offering an unsettled half-smile at his sister. "Yeah, I guess it is," he said softly.

Sen gave an unsure smile of her own before digging her hands nervously in her pockets. How would she even start this? Well, one step at a time, anyway. Withdrawing a hand from a pocket and gesturing to the ground, she asked, "May...May I sit?"

Brin, looking at Sen only with a sideways glance, nodded.

She brought herself to ground level, seated with legs crossed over one another, the embers of the fire crackling in front of her, shards of wood breaking off in hot splinters.

Brin continued to draw a look at Sen only in half-measures, his hands twitching at his lap. He was picking at his nails, as he was wont to do in times of nervousness and anxiety. Sen wanted to tell him to stop but relented that now may not be the best time to tell him what to do and what not to do. Still, her silent gaze seemed to request it enough because he stopped once he caught wind of the direction of her eyes. Finally turning his head to a further degree, he looked Sen up and down and plainly said, "You look terrible."

Blankly, Sen reached up, remembering the specks of mud and dirt still adorning the right half of her face. She couldn't begin to imagine how much of a disaster the rest of her looked by this point, given how disastrous she felt just when she woke up. Still, she managed a sheepish laugh. "Yeah, see, I'm trying this new morning routine where Tez shoves my face in the mud. I'm hoping it does wonders."

"Sure," Brin said, unamused. "Didn't do much for the bags under your eyes. Or the smell."

"It's...a work in progress," Sen said haltingly. "I hear that the Sun Tribe used to do something like it years ago before they...well, before. Apparently, it did wonders for their skin when they were beaten down by the hot, salty air."

"That's cool, I guess," Brin deadpanned. "The air is neither of those things up here."

"True, but you see, the thing is—" Sen stopped herself. *What are you doing, you idiot?* she thought. *Are you really going to mess this up, too?* "Obviously, I'm not here to talk about skincare routines, Brin. I'm here to apologize."

Brin stared at her for a long while, his expression betraying nothing. "Okay," he said, shrugging nonchalantly. He turned his head back toward the fire, returning to fiddling about with his pendant.

"No, Brin, really. I—"

"I believe you, Sen."

"No, Brin, you're not understanding—"

"I think I understand plenty, Sen."

He turned his head toward her, still expressionless except for his eyes, which spoke in deep hues of disappointment and anger.

"I don't know *what* it is, but clearly there's something about the drink that's much more appealing to you than—"

"Will you just let me say my piece, Brin?" Sen interjected.

"Do you even know what you're apologizing for?"

Sen stared at him with wide eyes. "Do I even—of *course*, I do! What kind of question is that?"

Brin shrugged. "Probably a pretty valid one. You didn't say a word on the way back from the Heart yesterday, and it took the better part of an hour for Tez to rouse you awake this morning. I couldn't even stick around to see that."

"An hour? Huh, she said it was twenty minutes." Brin continued to stare at her with wild, untamed, angry eyes. She had never seen such fury in his face before. "You don't think much of me at all, do you?"

Seemingly caught off-guard, a sliver of emotion returned to Brin's face, that unnatural stone face chipping away ever so slightly. "What do you—"

"Do you *really* think that I'd have no idea of what I'm talking about? That I'd have no remorse or regret for any of this? Brin, I—"

Brin interrupted not with words but with a long, exasperated sigh. He looked down at the ground, scratching at his eyebrow, chips of paint coming loose against his fingernail. Shaking his head, he blinked twice in rapid succession and looked at Sen again; the anger in his eyes was replaced with a more natural and familiar expression, one of sadness and fear. "Sometimes, Sen...sometimes I don't even know who you are anymore. I look at you, and I want to see my sister, but for years now, it's just this...shell of a person. I'm not even looking at the same person at all. The old you wouldn't have...I don't know...been like this. The old you was just always at my side, never leaving me alone, always sticking up for me, even though it was...*heh*, even though, sometimes, it was a bit overbearing. But *now*...now, I see someone who's just...just, *so* far gone, and I don't know how to react or what I'm supposed to say. Are you going to take it poorly? Are you going to forget what I say by the next morning? The longer this goes on, the more I...I..." He stopped for a long moment, sighing deeply, emotion beginning to well in the pits of his eyes. "The more I want my sister back. But...at the same time, the longer it goes on, the further *you* are from who my sister was. I just don't know if there's any going back, but...but...but—"

Sen lurched forth and gripped Brin tightly, feeling his breath heave in and out as wet streams flowed along his cheek and up against hers. She'd heard plenty of admonishments from loved ones to watch her drinking or had seen looks of disappointment or disgust directed her way. But no one had spoken such words of brutal honesty. Everyone wanted to shame her for the actions she had taken but never seemed to want to open her eyes to the person she became. Maybe that was enough. She couldn't say for sure. But all she knew at that moment was that holding her brother tight was what she *needed*. Perhaps what they both needed.

She pulled herself away from Brin, holding him by the shoulders at arm's length, making sure he knew that the tears flowing from her eyes were real, too.

They sat there in a long silence, her arms shaking against her brother, her fingers tensing in and out.

"Brin," Sen said. "Please believe me when I tell how just how sorry I am. Not just for yesterday. But for *all* of this. I'm...you're right. It started small. It started with me maybe just needing one drink when it all began. Then it escalated, and it got worse and worse, and then the reality of accepting just who I am and *what* I am...I can't say that's a justification at all. But dealing with that pain, coming to that realization, coming to terms with the fact that *everything* that was said about me growing up was true...it became impossible for me to do that without some 'help.' I just found the wrong kind of help.

"And it's cost me a lot. I don't have many people left in my corner. I'm sorry that that corner doesn't include you anymore. But believe me—*please* believe me—when I say that I am truly, earnestly sorry for yesterday especially. I couldn't be there for you on your big day. Or, at least, that's what I told myself. After everything that's happened to me since *that* day, I just—"

Brin cut her off by holding her tightly, and Sen lost control of herself, the tears erupting in rivers down her cheeks. "I know, Sen. I know. You...I can't even imagine what it was like. But the truth is...the truth is I'm still scared."

"Scared?" Sen said, still choking up but able to muster a small chuckle. "What do you have to be scared of?"

"I...I don't know what I'm supposed to do, now," Brin admitted. "Where do I go from here? I'm an adult now, but...what does that even mean? What am I supposed to do?"

Sen pushed Brin off of her, looking at him intently, her eyes puffy and red from the tears, much like his. Despite herself, she couldn't help but laugh. "Oh, Brin," she said. "I don't think I'm the right authority on what best to do next. But what I *do* know is how proud I am of you. I know you'll figure it out."

"Looks like we both have some things to figure out," Brin said, forcing a smile to his lips.

"We're charting a boat together in the same waters," Sen replied. "How about we work together to navigate?"

Brin hesitated, an entirely valid and understandable pause at that. But, despite his apprehension and due concern, he nodded. "Yeah. Yeah, let's do that."

"I love you, little brother."

Sen pulled Brin back in closely, embracing him with a strength that had eluded her for much of the morning. She didn't know how to address Brin's concerns. About himself, about her, about what was to come. But, if anything, she remembered the person she was years ago. If anything, maybe to go forward, she'd need to go backwards. But that was too much to think about at the moment. For now, she was perfectly content as she was, holding Brin tightly for the first time in forever. And she wept.

The village was calm under the shine of the moon. The world had settled to sleep, families faintly wishing their children sweet dreams, animals bellowing their final calls of the day for the depths of nature to hear. It was these moments—these simple, pristine moments—that Dennalhir treasured most.

It was her night to perform the nightly patrol of the village. She and Fannalhen would alternate nights. Normally, it was strictly the Chief's job to do so, but Denna was quite insistent that she take a role in it too, given she oversaw the Tribe in just as much detail and authority as her husband. It was nice to enjoy the fresh air, too. So many hours of the days were spent indoors, attending to various Tribal council meetings or offerings of concerns or grievances that these momentary pleasures were something to look forward to.

There was much to be happy about in this village. There was a sense of euphoria lingering in the air after Brin's passage into adulthood. So many people remained in the grandest of moods, floating by on a dream and a wisp, the future bright in their eyes. Maybe the same could be said of Denna's family as well. Earlier in the day, she had walked in on Sen and Brin in a warm embrace, silent yet loving. A sight she hadn't seen in, well, years. It was immensely heartwarming. She only hoped that it was a sign of good things to come for Sen. It was so hard as a parent seeing her as she was for so long.

Even the wind was quiet as Denna wrapped up her rounds. Nature itself seemed to be bidding the world good night. With a smile and a nod, she couldn't help but offer the same wishes to nature.

Her eyes intent upon her hut, Dennalhir walked without a care across the village square, thankful for another day of peace.

Until that peace was interrupted by a sudden rustling.

Denna stood to attention, her spear drawn, her ears sorting out the source of the noise. Out from the darkness, two forms came shuffling into the village: a woman, perhaps about ten years younger than she, and a boy collapsed at her side, a boy not much younger than Brin. As Denna examined them more closely from afar, her eyes widened. There was something *wrong* with these two. They looked almost *feral*. Their clothes were ragged and torn, bearing an appearance almost akin to hand-me-downs that had never been washed. Their hair was wild and knotted, frizzled and filthy. Never mind their articles of clothing. It looked as though they themselves had never been washed. There was a fearful look in the woman's eyes, an expression of pure helplessness, an emotion almost untamed. Her eyes shimmered in the moonlight, liquid reflections bouncing off her brightly colored irises.

In a heavily accented voice, the woman weakly whispered, "Please help." And then she collapsed.

MEMORY

LANDSLIDE

THE YEAR 1544 ANNO SALVATORIS
3 YEARS AFTER THE INVASION

"Come on, guys! Keep up!"

Sen's voice echoed through the valleys as her retinue of unwilling participants kept a close distance to her. For all their talk about wanting to try this course out, they were undoubtedly dragging their feet about it.

"Slow down, Sen," said a gap-toothed boy, his face adorned with a sea of freckles. He was heaving with heavy breath, sweat pouring down his face. Despite the ridge being broad enough for twenty people, he was hamming up the whole "lack of balance" routine quite a bit. "We're gonna fall if you keep going like this!"

Sen looked back at her friends, a wide smile on her face, chuckling to herself at the false bravado they had shown not half an hour ago. "Come on, Fann. Don't be a baby," she said. Peering over Fann's shoulder, Sen caught a glance at a more confident, assured expression. Which she knew was actually hiding some genuine fear. All the more amusing, really. "Narva, what about you? Are you wanting to duck out, too?"

An exasperated sigh escaped Narva's throat. More and more, it just looked like he was annoyed at how slowly Fann was moving through the pass. As he gave the other boy a gentle nudge to the side so he could pass, Fann embellished a falling motion, waving his arms erratically, sputtering this or that about how he almost fell down the mountain. Narva rolled his eyes but patted his friend on the shoulder just the same. The gentle mountain breeze tugged at Narva's braid, whipping it forward and back against his shoulder. There was a degree of majesty to it, far more than Fann's frizzed and wild braid that barely held in place.

"You know, Sen," Narva called out, "When you said we were gonna do an obstacle course, I thought you meant down in the training yard. Not up here in the *mountains*." The final word echoed throughout the Heart, insistent on informing the Keepers, wherever they are, that these were *indeed* mountains.

Sen dismissed the concern with a flick of the wrist and a grin, returning her hands proudly to her hips. "Right, because running in circles on flat ground is *so* fun," she said. "You have to be creative sometimes, guys. You have to think outside the box. One of these days, we're all going to be exploring the Land. It'll pay to adapt to more fun scenarios!"

Fann bent over, his hands on his knees, trying hard to force a smile. "You call this a *fun* scenario? I'm exhausted!"

"Hey, it's not fun with that attitude!" Sen called out. "Be more adventurous, Fann! You never join us stuff like this. Enjoy it!"

"We're not all lucky like you, Sen." Fann chuckled to himself, good humor returning to his face. "Who's gonna say 'no' to the Chief's daughter? I mean, my mother would kill me if she knew I was out here without an adult!"

"She'd probably kill you even if you *were* with an adult," Narva quipped. Laughing, he kindly slapped Fann on the back, pulling him close jovially. Sen shook her head, the smile still stretching across her lips, proud to have these two idiots as friends. "Really, though, Sen. You're definitely lucky that your folks let you do this stuff all the time."

"Yeah, they were always stricter with Tez than with me, for whatever reason," Sen said. "Guess that's just how it goes. That's okay, though. It gives me more reason to see all this." She gestured her arms back the way they came, the Stone Territory sprawling out as far as their eyes could see. The morning mists spread over the moors leading to the Forest, spelling almost a haunted atmosphere before entering those dangerous woods. "Maybe one of these days, we'll go out there, see what's in the Forest!"

Fann broke away from Narva's friendly grip, his body tensing as he shook his head and raised his hands slightly. "I don't know, Sen," he said haltingly. "I was told the Wood Tribe aren't good people."

"Oh, please, Fann," Sen scoffed. "I'm sure they're fine. Did your mother tell you that, too?"

"I mean, yeah, but—"

"Fann's paranoid mother aside," Narva interjected, "I think I agree. Do you remember when Chief Han'e came to the village with his people? I heard my father saying the Wood Tribe wouldn't let them stay in the Forest, so they killed a lot of them."

"Come on, that can't be true," Sen said, brushing away the thought. "Han'e's people lost their home, right? Why would the Wood Tribe do that to them?"

"I don't know. I got bored and stopped listening after a while," Narva chuckled.

"Point is," Fann said. "Maybe we wait on the Forest for a while. Let's just...do whatever this is, I guess." Sen pointed an approving finger, her white teeth glimmering mightily in the morning sun. "See, *that's* the attitude that you were missing before!" She adopted an expression of pure satisfaction, despite Fann's half-hearted assurances. It was more than enough for her. "Okay, we're not too far now."

The ridge path still maintained its width, though the traversal was far less a straight shot. Some minor climbing was involved, hardly a challenge for a grown adult, but for a couple ten- and eleven-year-olds, it was as close to mountain climbing as they had ever experienced. The wind began to pick up slightly from the altitude, the temperature falling in a precipitous drop. Fann and Narva began huddling together to share some warmth, their short-sleeved shirts doing little to protect from the at-times biting winds. Sen, for her part, was kept warm by the promise of a fun challenge, a thrill, and an experience shared with friends.

"I've been scouting around here for a few weeks now," Sen called over her shoulder, unaware whether her friends were really listening. "Trying to find the perfect balance of thrill, challenge, and fun. There's a lot of really wide chasms here, a lot of natural footholds, some big jumps. But I think I got the geography just right with this one."

She turned around, watching as Fann and Narva's eyes widened at the sight before them. A wide-open clearing, peppered with sheer drops, platform-like rock formations, a gap passable only along an extremely narrow footpath half a foot wide. Fann's jaw dropped as he looked between it and Sen, back and forth, back and forth. Struggling to find the words, he merely stuck out his hand, gesturing to the sight. "So…what is this, Sen?"

"I told you!" Sen exclaimed. "An obstacle course!"

"Sen…honestly, this looks dangerous," warned Narva. "I think Fann is right to be a bit cautious."

"You guys worry too much," Sen replied. "Just take a look at the depths of the drops. They're not any more than a couple feet deep. It's not gonna hurt any of us. Do you really think I'd take you guys somewhere that I think you'd get hurt at?"

"Well, you wouldn't take *me* any place like that, anyway," Narva quipped. "Him, I don't know. He gets hurt pretty easy."

"What, I do not!" cried Fann. "That only happened once…okay, twice."

Sen smiled. "Well, I made sure this was something that even *you* could do, Fann. Come on, guys! We're gonna face scarier stuff than this when we're older! Until then, we should find fun ways to train like this! My father tells me I'm gonna be a Wolfsign just like Narva, so we're gonna need to run across things like this, and Fann, you'll be a better warrior for it if you're good on your feet!"

The two boys cautiously stepped forward, peering their heads over the ridge. Their nerves appeared to be quelled somewhat once they got a closer look at Sen's course. Accepting expressions stretched across both of their faces as though they both came to the realization that perhaps Sen *was* telling the truth here. With that assurance, their posture became less rigid, more relaxed, joviality returning to their faces. Silently, they exchanged curious looks to one another, a wordless conversation about surely detailing how much fun it could be, how much trouble they'd be in if they got caught, whether Sen was crazy. The usual conversations they had as a group, really.

Narva scoffed and smugly grinned. "Okay, okay. You win, Sen. Let's try it out."

Sen raised her arms in triumph, pumping them up and down as though it was her greatest victory. "Look, I'll even go first so you can see there's nothing to worry about. I ran this a couple times already, anyway."

"Of course, you did," muttered Fann. "Some of us are kept indoors. Others get to run around in the mountains."

"You don't have to mask your jealousy, Fann." Sen smirked. "I know my life is much more fun than yours."

Before he could make some snide remark, Sen took off, running toward the edge of the ridge with a confident stride. In one quick motion, she jumped over the first chasm, hardly a dangerous jump by any means, and landed on the first rocky platform. Maintaining her balance on one foot, she shifted her weight in midair to her other foot, landing cleanly on the next platform.

Finding her center of gravity, Sen launched herself forward with speed, so self-assured that she would find her footing on the next platform without worrying where her feet would end up. Across the disconnected eleven platforms she crossed, the cheers and whoops of her friends from behind but fleeting glances of sound in the wind.

Upon reaching the final rock formation, one slanted at a slight angle, Sen stopped herself, careful not to let her momentum carry her too far forward. The next and final part of the course was the narrow ridge. The slant of the rock formation faced her toward the adjacent rock wall, putting her in a good position. If she wanted to sidle across the ridge, she would have to make the jump, position her feet *just* right, and hope her center of gravity didn't lurch her backwards into the shallow depths below. The first couple of times she tried this course, that was her strategy, one that had (mostly) worked for her.

But that wasn't what she wanted to do here. To be frank, she wanted to show off a bit for her friends. She wanted to try something new. Pointing herself at an angle to the rock wall rather than directly facing it, Sen jumped as far as she could toward the ridge, her front foot just barely catching the edge. Before her rear foot could land on the ridge, though, she planted it along the wall, *pushed* herself forward, lurching in the air with added momentum, and landed on the flat surface ahead with a roll and a flair.

From across the course, she could hear Narva and Fann hooting and hollering in celebration and awe. "That was *so cool!*" Fann shouted as he jumped up and down with excitement. "I've never seen *anyone* do that!"

Even though the course took little time at all for Sen to complete, she still found herself out of breath. She planted her hands on her knees, satisfied with her run through, basking in the glory that her friends had so readily bestowed upon her. The wind itself seemed to cheer her on, refreshing her with a cooling breeze that cleared all the sweat away from her. She let out an audible exclamation as the adrenaline wore off a tad, some aches and sores settling into her legs.

But just the same, she wanted to feel the same rush from watching her friends try to run this course, too. That was the whole reason she brought them here. She wasn't going to show off for them, only to call it a day and go back home. There was *glory* to be won here, and they all had to share in it. "So, is one of you gonna go next, or no?" she called out over the ridge.

"Fine, fine," Narva said, readying himself into a starting position. Before Sen could give a command to go, he took off, following much the same route that she had. There was a certain athleticism and grace to Narva's movements that always astounded Sen. Everything was so smooth, so effortless. One foot went in front of the other, his traversal across the disconnected rock formations bearing an image of flying and gliding. He was a hunter on the prowl, his quarry somewhere on the other end of the course. Even when he made it to the narrow ridge, he didn't hesitate. He didn't size up his path like Sen did. He just...did it. And just as Sen pushed herself off the rock wall to reach the other side, Narva did the same. But rather than plant one foot on the ridge and one on the wall, he planted *both* on the wall, gaining greater distance on the volley off, flourishing it further with a gracious midair spin. He even landed perfectly on his feet.

"*Heh*, show-off," Sen muttered. "Trying to show me up at my own game?"

"I mean, I *do* train at this stuff more than you do, Sen," Narva said with a smirk.

"Excuse *you*, when do you come up here to do fun stuff like this?"

"Wouldn't *you* like to know?"

"Oh, I *would*. I very much would. Now, how about you—"

"Shut up, both of you!" called Fann. "Watch me do it now!"

Fann was…less graceful about it, to put it kindly. His movements were far more hesitant, a methodical thought put into every single motion of his body. From the first jump across the initial chasm, it was clear that this was not something he was accustomed to or comfortable with. So nervous was he about the three-foot drop beneath the rock formations that he took slow steps onto each one, planting both feet on a particular pass before moving on to the next. And when he made it to the narrow ridge, there was no airborne flair, no gravitational trickery. Just a young boy cautiously and slowly planting as much of his feet onto the ridge as he could before *slowly* sidling along its length. It wasn't pretty, and it wasn't flashy. But he did it.

Sen clapped for him just the same. "Hey, you did great, Fann," she said.

The freckled boy forced a smile onto his face, rolling his eyes in the process. "Yeah, yeah, I'm sure you're super impressed."

"No, really, I mean it," Sen retorted. "This isn't something you normally do, but you still got it right on your first try! Be happy with that."

His smile was more genuine after that. "Thanks, Sen," he said. "I guess you're right. Maybe I should have gone first and just let you guys upstage me after that. I wonder if that'd have been better."

Narva brought his hand down on Fann's shoulder in a long, exaggerated motion before squeezing his friend tightly. "I mean, hey. Couldn't have been worse."

"Oh, you're gonna get it later, Narva," Fann said, laughing. "Just you wait."

"Oh, I look forward to it," Narva said. "You'll have to beat me back to the village first, though!" Narva immediately took off, jumping toward the rock wall and pushing himself toward the slanted rock, landing cleanly without breaking his stride. Swinging himself back around, he planted on the platform formations and strode along in a cockier jog than before, almost mocking his friends with a no-look wave in so doing. In what seemed like a moment, he was already on the other side of the course.

"How's it feel that he's better at your course than you are?" Fann said with a smirk.

"Ah, beat him up for me later," Sen chuckled. "That'll let him know how I feel."

"Done and done. Guess we should cross back over. I'm, uh…I'm just gonna walk along the lower ridge there. Think I had enough excitement on the first go."

"Heh, suit yourself, Fann."

With almost a shade of dejection, Fann climbed down to the lower section. Narva's laughter echoed from the other side of the ridge. He shouted mockeries that Sen couldn't quite hear over the wind, but she was certain that they were very clever, very witty, and very Narva. For her part, she readied herself to just run the course over Fann's head, adding her own humorous insult to injury to the situation. But just as she was about to take her first step forward, her eye was drawn to a section above her course, a wider chasm on the upper level, the drop leading right back down to their current level. *Show me up on my own course, will you, Narva? Well, I got something here that even you can't do!*

Without warning, Sen followed an adjacent path to the upper level, climbing the last bit to reach the top. The view was incredible, but her choice immediately drew Narva's attention.

"*Sen!*" he called out over the wind. "*What are you doing?!*"

"Hey, just watch! It's gonna be great!" Sen answered, a huge smirk on her face. The chasm was much wider than she had anticipated from up above, but she could make that jump. She could do it in her sleep. There was nothing to worry about.

"*Sen, that might not be a good idea!*" Fann called from below, still slowly making his way through the lower level of the course.

Sen couldn't really see where his voice was coming from, his form lost amongst the rock formations jutting out from the earth.

"*Yeah, it looks pretty dangerous!*" Narva added. "*You really shouldn't!*"

"What, worried I'll show *you* up now?" Sen yelled. "It'll be fine! Just watch!"

Planting her feet and taking off, Sen felt the push of the wind carrying her forward, lifting her, encouraging her momentum. As she took off into the air, she felt the will of nature itself gliding her along that airy nothingness, the worried calls of her friends from down below acting as a heedless backdrop to her effort. She wasn't concerned, though. She had it. She was going to make it.

And when she landed, that sense of triumph filled her with elation. She had never made a jump that wide. She did it. She had shown up the person who showed her up.

But that moment of triumph was just that, a moment. A fleeting, cautionary moment. When the ground beneath her began to crack and quake, Sen's body froze. Narva shouted indecipherable somethings to her, but in that next fleeting moment, the lines of communication between her mind and her body were severed. She flailed in place, her balance knocked out of sorts. And then the ground beneath her gave way, sinking and sliding down the slope that led into her obstacle course as a brief grunt pierced her ears from below.

At the last moment, Sen reached up, finding a grip to pull herself up. But, just as that motion lifted her upward, the swing of her legs sent the shattered earth outward. The more she pulled herself up, the more the earth crumbled, and in the ensuing quake, the entire ridge began to sever, crumble, and fall. There wasn't much time. Scrambling back to her feet, clumsy and frantic, Sen ran as fast as she could before jumping down to the lower level, nearly landing on Narva, missing his outstretched arms entirely. She landed with none of the grace and acumen with which she had a short time ago. There was no time for flair. She was just happy to be back to safety.

The earth continued to shift and slide down the path, surging through the lower level of the course. And down the face of the mountain. Wordlessly, Sen and Narva rushed to the edge of the ridge, watching stones fall apart on impact with other stones, a rush of powerful earth surging downhill. Toward the village. Sen put her hands on her head, her teeth gritting, a deep pit forming in her stomach. She bit down on her thumb as she, helplessly, watched as her village, *their* village, lay directly in the path of destruction.

Tears of fear streamed down her face as she gripped tightly to Narva, unable to look. Villagers the size of ants, drawn to the eruptive sound, cleared their homes in a panic, all in a rush to safety. She could barely watch. The tears kept flowing. She was about to watch her village get flattened, and it was all her fault. She couldn't watch. She couldn't—

They missed. The stones missed. Sen and Narva stood with mouth agape as, miraculously, the rockslide just passed through the village, coursing through the village square, but it didn't appear that any of the huts were hit, and, more importantly, no one appeared to be hurt. Instead, a herd of people seemed to gather around where the stones stopped. Even at this height, Sen could see their gazes averting to the mountains. Towards the kids enjoying a good time gone horribly wrong.

At last, Sen let out a breath. She barely registered that her breath had caught in her throat for the past while. Her body still shaking, she slowly let go of Narva, and slowly, they allowed themselves to laugh. And cry.

"By the gods," Sen muttered. "That was close."

"Too close," Narva agreed, his own breath ragged and nervous.

They were silent for a while, unable to move from their spot, unsure of how they would address what happened up here. But then, a different thought hit them.

"Wait," Sen said. "...Where's Fann?"

"...*Gods*," Narva muttered to himself, running off into the lower section of the course.

They found Fann lying on the ground, his arm twisted in the wrong direction entirely, his face cut up, his clothing torn. He was right in the path of the storm of stones. Tears were flowing from his eyes, pained tears, angry tears. Writhing on the ground equal parts in agony and fury, he tried to divert his attention away from the ugly sight of his arm, seemingly shattered from the impact. Through incomprehensible mutterings, he began to froth at the mouth, rageful spittle pooling at the corners of his lips. Sen didn't have any words, nor did Narva. They just helped their friend to his feet and slowly and carefully trekked down the mountain path.

An hour passed by the time they returned to the village. At the sight of the rockslide stood Sen's parents and Tez, along with Narva's father, Tawa, and...Fann's mother, Koelhe.

Immediately, Koelhe ran to her son, showering him with words of worry and affection, kissing him atop his forehead in a way only a mother can. "Oh, my son, my sweet, sweet son," she whimpered, holding him tightly, careful of his clearly broken arm. "What happened to you?"

Tears were still flowing from Fann's eyes—only agonic tears now—but he could scarcely find any words to say. "I...we...I don't—"

Koelhe shushed him, burrowing his face into her bosom, holding him tighter and tighter to the point it looked like she may smother the boy. But then her face, that wild, untamed face, glared toward Sen, all shreds of motherly love gone from her eyes and instead replaced with fiery, unbridled fury.

If Sen didn't know any better, she'd have thought Koelhe had gone feral. She certainly bore more the appearance of a wild animal than a woman of the Stone Tribe. But whatever the case may have been, Sen was frozen in place again. Those fierce eyes had her locked where she was.

"You..." Koelhe growled. "It was *your* fault!"

"It was...it was an accident!" Sen tried to explain, her words not finding their way to her tongue.

"Look what you did to my boy, you monster! I knew you'd do something like this one day. You damned Curseborn! Stay away from my son!" Without any further protest, she dragged Fann away, the boy's whimpers disappearing along with the voice of the wind.

At Koelhe's leaving, Sen and Narva's parents jumped in and held their children, expressing far more concern for their children's safety than anger, though not exclusively so.

"We'll talk about this later, both of you," Fannalhen commanded. "You both have some explaining to do."

Sen and Narva nodded in unison, just grateful that no one in the village was seriously hurt.

But something far greater was now eating at Sen. Something she didn't expect. "Father?" she said to Fannalhen, the Chief partway to returning to the hut.

"Hmm? What is it, Sen?"

Sen blinked, a frown parsing her lips. "What did she mean...? She said, 'Curseborn.'"

The Stone Chief shook his head, frowning in return. "It's...it's nothing."

"What do you mean?" She turned her head to Dennalhir. "Mother? What does it mean?"

Her mother, warm and comforting, knelt beside her, a firm hand upon her shoulder. "Sen, my sweet. It's nothing at all. I promise you. Koelhe was just scared and angry, and she didn't know what she was saying. We're all just grateful that you three are okay."

Tears streamed down from Sen's face again, and all she could muster was an apology consisting of broken words. Dennalhir gripped her daughter tightly, Sen returning the favor. Though she was grateful that everyone was okay, she could not help but wonder what combination of fear and anger would lead to labeling someone as a "Curseborn." And still, she wondered what that even meant.

CHAPTER FOUR

HAUNTED, HUNTED

THE YEAR 1556 ANNO SALVATORIS
15 YEARS AFTER THE INVASION

For the first night in quite some time, Sen had retreated to bed without the aid of a drink. It was difficult, immensely so, the urge to wander down to the tavern all too seductive. But as she lay in bed, her eyes drawn across the room to Brin, already sleeping peacefully, she realized that it would be worth it. Straining and sweating in her sheets profusely, she had to take this step. This all-too-important first step.

The sight of her siblings resting with total contentment was enough to drive her to try. So, she closed her eyes, tightly, painfully. Then she breathed, slowly and methodically. The first breath came with a shudder, a quiver. The second was more subdued. By the tenth, she was feeling some degree of centered calm. By the twentieth, her head was relaxed and comfortable upon her pillow.

I can do this, Sen thought. *Just one breath at a time, and—*

A commotion from the other room roused her to focus.

"Oh, dammit," she muttered aloud, much louder than she had intended.

The noise was growing in volume, a multitude of voices collectively chiming in a cacophony bordering on panic and anxiety.

Sen arced her head out from the side of her bed, seeing only a flowing mass of bodies gathering in the common area, their faces obscured by the gathering darkness of the nighttime air.

Tez was next to rise from her bed, her dark hair a scramble of wavy, un-braided locks, her face naked of the red Bearsign paint, as was allowed when one was to sleep. The paint had typically masked the small scar adorning the left side of her chin, the result of a misaimed spear tip during a training exercise. With her face bare, it was clear as day (or night, as it were), though by no means embarrassing. A warrior was meant to have scars, and there was no shame in exhibiting them.

"What's going on?" Tez said sleepily. Her voice was groggy with a shade of irritation. She had been fast asleep for near on an hour at this point, and whenever she was roused from sleep too early, it was not always a pretty sight. At the least, she kept the bestial rage at bay for now.

Sen shrugged at her question. She could still barely make out who was out in the common area, the acoustics lending only so far as to make her parents' voices distinguishable. Everyone else was just a muddled mess. It sounded like a different language entirely, quite frankly. Sen could feel her fingers twitching anxiously, her body heating up voraciously. "Apparently, it's a great night for a party," she muttered. "Not like any of us need to sleep."

Even in the darkness, Sen's sweat glistened and shone. Tez appeared drawn to her tense body language. "Are you holding up okay?" she asked.

"I'm just fuckin' great, sis," Sen growled. "Not a care in the world right now."

"You look about as great as Mother did when she was birthing Brin," Tez smirked.

"Oh, how great for me. I appreciate being compared to Mother's eternal radiance." The commotion continued to irritate her, every spoken word in-stilling a desire to punch new holes in the walls. Her section of the room had been suspiciously less homey after the previous blemishes she created—for various reasons—were patched up. Brin had his spirit ward, and Tez had an ornamental half-spear. Why couldn't Sen just have a bunch of holes?

The sisters diverted their attention to their brother, still sleeping as though he were a baby. Not a care in the world, an, at times, mighty snore shaking the foundations of his bed.

"I'm always impressed at how he can sleep through anything," Tez remarked. "Remember when he slept through that time the Arrow Tribe marched through the streets? They were practically right outside this wall."

Sen forced a smile. "How could I forget? All that hooting and hollering they always do, it's amazing they get the jump on anyone when they're practically announcing their arrival."

Tez chuckled and then arced her own neck out into the common area. "Much more subdued than whatever's going on out there, though."

Wiping the profusive sweat from her brow and instinctively running her damp fingers through her hair, Sen grunted in agreement. "Maybe we should see what's going on. If nothing else, to tell them all to shut up already." Quickly, she rose out of bed, discarding her sleeping robe and exchanging it for a tunic and trouser combo that wasn't speckled with mud.

The speed at which she moved seemed to surprise Tez, as her sister had barely made it to the edge of her own bed by the time Sen was fully dressed. She looked a mess otherwise, bearing the appearance of one who had come down with the mountain sickness in earnest. *If only that were the case.* "Guess I'll see you out there," she said to Tez as she walked by, sparing a parting glance at the still-clonked-out Brin.

As she emerged from her room and into the common area, the loud din quelled to a murmur, all eyes diverted to her as her father knelt to light the center fire. There were far more people here than Sen realized. Naturally, her parents were there, her mother the only one still adorning her Bearsign paint. Immediately next to them stood Tawa and, surprisingly, Narva.

What are they *doing here?*

Both looked tired and frazzled, as though they, too, were pulled out from bed against their will.

If something's important, it makes sense for Tawa to be here. But why's Narva here, too? Continuing her ocular sweep, Sen eyed Koelhe. Wonderful, horrible Koelhe. Even though she was Fannalhen and Dennalhir's junior by a few years, she looked like she was at least fifteen or twenty years older. Grey hair, wrinkles, old and batty eyes. *Hatred's a hell of a drug.*

The few others present were more of a surprise.

As the flames crackled and illuminated the room with better clarity, she could make out the long and plain face of Rantalha, one of the Tribe's Wolfsigns, an expert prowler and hunter thanks to his muted footsteps granted by his Stealth Boon. His expression was permanently straight and stoic, borne of little humor. Frankly, he always frightened Sen as a child. But, more surprising that Rantalha's presence was that of Sharrabha, another accomplished Wolfsign, her posture proud and assured, her hair wild and free.

I thought she'd still be out hunting in the Heart somewhere. I never see her around these days.

The Sun Tribe chief Han'e was present, too, for some reason. Sen remembered Narva telling her that he had arrived while Brin was undergoing his Trial, but she was unaware that he remained in the village. And rounding out the menagerie was the permanent sullen frown of Grafhar. He was a bit of a sad sight of a man. His mouth always seemed stuck in a mode of anger, his brow never finding a means to raise upward. Despite his relatively young age, the top of his head was covered only by tiny strands of hair, the resultant attempt at a Stone braid a laughably bad sight. Draped along his neck, over his shirt rather than under, was the rune depicting Language. Generations ago, the Owlsigns imbued with Language were integral as interpreters for intertribal dialogue. Nowadays, the Tribes largely shared a common tongue, so Grafhar's talents were, to be blunt, wasted. It didn't help matters that he was a mute, too. Nature had a twisted sense of humor, sometimes.

All present stopped everything they were doing to stare at Sen, some with more jovial expressions, others with glares of pure hatred. *All in a night's work, really.*

"Sen?" Dennalhir called out. "What are you doing up?"

Sen raised her eyebrows and scanned the room, trying desperately not to let sarcasm overcome her face and words. Not an easy task. "Well, I *was* about to drift off to a wonderfully peaceful sleep, but then Grafhar started making a ruckus over here." The mute stared at her angrily, as was his default. His hollow eyes screamed all the obscenities in the world at her. That was a reward for Sen in and of itself.

"Are you okay, Sennalhat?" asked Tawa. "You look like a fever has taken you."

Apparently, her sickly appearance was readily apparent. "Yeah, Tawa, you can call it the mountain sickness if you'd like."

Koelhe muttered something under her breath. Not loud enough for Sen to hear, but with enough of a sneer and pompous body language for Sen to want to push her straight into the fire. From the look of it, her father was entertaining the thought as well. *It's great that he and I share the same intense hatred for this woman*, she thought.

Fannalhen stepped forward, near enough to reach out for Sen's shoulder. "You don't need to be here, Sen," he said. "You can go back to bed if you wish."

As if on cue, Tez appeared behind Sen, much more put together than she could possibly be. Both at the moment and just in general. "Father, if you saw how much of a struggle it was for her to *almost* fall asleep," Tez said, "you'd know she's not getting back to that point any time soon."

The Chief moved a little closer, a much more private distance. "Are you okay?" he asked softly. "Do you need some air?"

Sweat was pouring from Sen in buckets. Fresh air did sound great, but curiosity was even greater. "Why's Grafhar here?" she said, evading the question entirely. "Did we all forget how to read?"

Fannalhen smirked, actually amused at one of Sen's quips for once. He was silent a moment, regarding her, thinking of an adequate response, when at last he chuckled and said, "Maybe Koelhe, but she's a lost cause at this point anyway."

Sen and Tez both snickered, jokes at Koelhe's expense being a family tradition. But that still didn't explain why she, and everyone else for that matter, was here. "Are you gonna tell me what's going on here?" Sen asked. "Seems a bit impromptu for a late-night card game."

Firmly, her father patted her shoulder, his mammoth hands strong enough to crush every bone in there if he really wanted to. She was happy to be on his good side today. "Stay over here," he said. "It's a bit of a council matter, so if anything happens...I'd prefer you safe if you're intent on staying."

Sen shrugged. "I'm intent on the thought that I'm not getting to sleep any time soon, so whatever."

Again, Fannalhen smirked before turning to walk toward the throng of advisers. On wordless command, they parted, Sharrabha joining Dennalhir, Tawa, and Narva on one side, with Koehle, Han'e, and Rantalha moving to the other. Grafhar fell into step behind Fannalhen, a quill and parchment at the ready.

Okay, really. Why is Grafhar even here? Sen thought. But then she saw past her father's burly form, and her eyes caught view of a truly sad and frightening sight. Two people, a middle-aged woman and a young boy about the same age as Brin, cowered against the wall, their eyes illuminating with fear. They huddled up to each other, less for warmth and more for safety in numbers. They looked terrible, even by Sen's own standards. Their faces were hidden under dirt and muck, scars fresh and old visible upon their exposed faces and arms. Their clothing had been reduced to rags, such to the point that they would be better served by wearing feed bags or some such. Those would at least give them some warmth as opposed to whatever it was they were wearing now. Their skin was a darker shade of red-brown than Sen had ever seen before, even darker than the Sun Tribe, so they had to be from further south than that.

The Stone Chief knelt beside them, slowly extending a gentle hand toward them as though he was offering food to a frightened, stray dog. Sen frowned at the sight. It was horrible. What could have happened to these people? "It's okay," Fannalhen said softly. "You're safe now. Do you understand? You're safe now."

The unknown woman backed away as far as she could, but then started rambling, speaking in a tongue that was essentially gibberish to Sen's ears. But the gibberish was thoughtful, meaningful. And then she realized. *She doesn't know our Words.* The Words. The common tongue of all the Tribes, developed over generations. If this woman was so far removed that she never learned the Words...

Then that would explain why Grafhar was here. To interpret and translate. *And here I thought we were just giving him something to do.*

"All of you, give them some space!" Fannalhen commanded, to which everyone obliged.

The gathering dispersed to the other end of the room, save for Grafhar, who remained at the Chief's side. They all formed a throng near Sen, Narva giving a slight nod and smile as he filed in next to her. Sen forced a half-smile in recognition before returning her attention to the conversation in front of her.

His hand still outstretched toward the strangers, Fannalhen spoke slowly and cautiously, wanting not to frighten them. "You do not know our Words, and that is fine," he said, enunciating each syllable while gesturing each word with a hand motion. He looked to Grafhar, then back to them. "This is Grafhar. He will let us talk to each other."

On cue, Grafhar approached them slowly, hesitantly reaching a hand out. Despite initial aversion, the woman, still cradling the boy in her arms, allowed Grafhar to place his hand on her forehead, breathing deep as a slight illumination glittered from his chest.

"The absorption of Language," Narva whispered to Sen. "Never thought we'd have a need to see it again."

"Never thought someone wouldn't know our Words by now," Sen answered. It was a very gentle process. Linguists, as they were called, could extract foreign tongues with but a single touch, which was handy way back when. In an instant, they could speak and write anything. Or, just write, in some people's cases.

His job complete, Grafhar backed away, quill and paper at the ready. He nodded for the Stone chief to proceed.

Fannalhen turned his attention to the newcomers, speaking in a more natural tone as Grafhar quickly transcribed. "He will translate for us. Please know that you are safe here. But please, tell us who you are."

Grafhar showed them the note, and the woman quickly shook her head before panicking in her native tongue. Grafhar translated, showing the Chief her answer. *"No. We are not safe."*

"What do you mean? Please, tell us. Who are you? Why have you come here?"

The woman sighed and hesitated a moment, but the boy nudged her to answer. There was no way around it. *"I am Shara, and he is Ran. We are in hiding. From the thieves of our Land."*

"From the Invaders?" Han'e called out. Sen turned and noticed his calm demeanor had shifted to something more furious.

"Man of the Sun," Shara said through Grafhar, recognizing Han'e by his traditional Sun fashion. *"We are kin, to an extent. We, too, lost our lands to who you call the Invaders. But you still have claim to your own lives. My people, our people, we do not."*

The realization seemed to have struck Fannalhen immediately. "You're of the Haunted Tribe."

Shara forced a smirk at the label. *"We are what you call the Haunted, yes. Far from our true name, but if that is what you wish to call us, then by all means."*

"I was unaware your people still lived," Fannalhen admitted. "When your Tribe did not come north, I feared for the worst."

"The worst did come for us, Chief Fannalhen." Her face was grim, a mixture of anguish and sorrow. Her eyes pierced through the low light, nearly shining in the encroaching dark. *"We did not lose our lives, but we lost our people."*

"I...do not understand."

"The Invaders, the men and women who came by the large canoes and wielding their Deatharms, they did not merely settle upon our territory. They built upon it a great City, with tall huts made of cold grey stone, some with smoke escaping from the tops. They have built it far and wide, taking our lands and also the Arrow Tribe's lands to let it cover to the ocean. But they did not build it on their own. In fact, they did not build it at all. We built it."

"You built it?" Fannalhen asked, his eyes narrowing. "Why would you build this...City for the Invaders?"

Shara scowled, the words offending her. *"We did not build it for them by choice! We were forced to! We are their slaves!"*

Collectively, the room gasped at the admission. "Slaves?" Fannalhen questioned. "I had no idea that the Invaders would..." He trailed off.

"Would you have rather the knowledge that our people were merely killed than taken into slavery?" Shara bit back. *"Because we were killed, too. Those who*

refused faced the wrath of the Invaders' Deatharms. Eventually, we learned not to refuse. But we are a people almost gone. We number less than one hundred."

Fannalhen was silent, unsure of how even to address that. Sen was speechless, too. She had heard stories of the Haunted Tribe, the mysterious people of the south, but they were a people reclusive even before the Invasion, a mystery wrapped in an enigma.

"A City of Invaders, built on the backs of a hundred slaves…it's absolutely reprehensible."

"Far more than one hundred, Chief Fannalhen," Shara corrected. *"We are not the only slaves there."*

"Pardon me?"

"Those who escaped death, but not the Invaders themselves, they have found themselves in the grips of servitude, too. People from all Tribes."

"But the Invaders have not made their way to the north. How could they have anyone from the northern Tribes?"

"When you discard those who are deemed unworthy of the Tribe, where are they to end up? Those unfortunate few who fail their Trials, banished with nowhere to go. Years ago, they lived nowhere. Now, those spaces of nowhere are under Invader rule. Stolen and conquered without mercy with the wrath of their Deatharms."

Outcasts and castaways, coupled with those (un)fortunate enough to survive their lands being taken…the very thought chilled Sen to her core. Her father was no exception. "These…'Deatharms' that you keep speaking of," Fannalhen said at last. "What are they?"

Shara frowned and shook her head, her expression marked in equal parts by fear and anger. *"Weapons of horror. Weapons of fear. Weapons of death. They scream into the air as they attack, a thunderclap atop a thunderclap. And before you can do anything, you are dead. To challenge them would be a mistake."*

"But even in the face of certain death, you made your way here. Why, and how?"

"We had help and were given an option. Stay and die, or run and live. Given the chance, what would you do? It has been fifteen years since I have known freedom, but Ran has never known it. He was only a baby when the Invaders came. Should he not be allowed the chance to pass into adulthood as a free man? When given the

chance, would you not run as far away as possible? We have not rested for days. We have been afraid to close our eyes. Why is the 'why' such a concern?"

Fannalhen bit his lip and nodded, stroking the whiskers along his chin. He was deep in consideration, his brow furrowed, his eyes narrowed, slowly and cautiously regarding these two runaways. "I suppose the 'why' matters little," he said, "but what of the 'how?' You said that you had 'help,' but who helped you?"

Shara paused. The growing look of concern and heavy thought on her face did little to assuage any feelings of confidence in Sen. *"I do not know who it was. All I know is they freed me and Ran, and we did not give it a second thought."*

"So, you mean to say," Fannalhen said, eyes wider with confusion, "that an unknown person, out of the goodness of their heart, walked into a slave camp and freed you and your son, and only you two?"

"Ran is not my son. I have known him for all his life, yes, but we bear no relation."

"Then this person freed two people just *at random?*" There was a rise in the tone of his voice, something bordering the line of shock and anger. Fannalhen's mouth was agape, his brow raised. The admission left him stunned. Sen had a hard time believing it, too.

When Shara read Grafhar's translation, she had no answer. It was clear that she had not thought on it for a moment. *Were I in her position, I might do the same,* Sen thought. *Why would I question it? What other option is there when you're offered your freedom?*

"What are we to do?" the Chief muttered to himself. "Did you think that you may have wandered into a trap? Did you think you may have suckered *us* into a trap?"

"A trap?" Shara posited. Vigorously, perhaps hopelessly, she shook her head, denying so adamantly that it was beyond the realm of possibility. *"It couldn't be. It was not."*

The young boy Ran cleared his throat, nudging Shara with his elbow. Grafhar stood at the ready. *"But, the lost. They warned me. They said they could..."*

"No," Shara reiterated. *"It is impossible. Impossible."*

"Hold on here," Fannalhen interrupted. "The lost 'warned' you? What do you mean by..." Then it hit him, and he silently vocalized an *ahh* to himself. "The lost. Right. Haunted beliefs. Say that's all true. Say you *were* followed.

Your coming here has put our Tribe in the face of danger." The sternness in his face froze Shara and Ran both. They gripped each other tightly, fearful of punishment in the midst of a lifetime filled with nothing but false retribution. They had known the face of anger and danger, but surely it was not in any way comparable to that of Sen's father. Either way, Fannalhen let out a long and exasperated exhalation, closing his eyes and flexing his fingers in and out. He turned to his gathered council, a conceding uncertainty illuminating his face. "We need to discuss this, a long discussion. Grafhar, take the two of them to a guest house, give them a bed for the evening. We'll figure out what's to be done with them by the morning." Grafhar nodded, gesturing to Shara and Ran to leave with him, to which they softly obliged, too nervous to spare a second glance for the Stone chief. "Sen, Tez, Narva, I apologize for asking this at such a late hour, but we need to discuss this as a council. Would the three of you mind stepping out for a while?"

Sen wanted nothing more than to sweat herself out into a comforting sleep, but there was no talking herself into that scenario at the moment. "Yeah, fine, okay," she said. "Come find us when you're done." She walked softly through the room, Tez and Narva in tow, trying not to make eye contact with some of the less friendly types in the room.

The nighttime breeze was quite refreshing after being holed up in her own sweat for however long that was. She was still immensely discomforted, but at least she could suffer in the fresh air for a bit. "So, where to?" she asked her companions.

"You sure you're okay?" Narva asked her. "Whatever you have, it doesn't look like any mountain sickness I've seen."

"She's detoxing," Tez said, hand affixed to her hip. "Let's try to get her through this night and see what tomorrow will bring."

Narva grunted, nodding his head blankly. "Hmph, well, I was going to suggest a round at the tavern, but that might not be for the best then. What about a round of cards, instead? I'll even let you beat me, Sen." He smiled broadly, that dumb, endearing, handsome smile of his.

A game or two would certainly help keep her mind free and occupied. "I don't think you've ever *let* me beat you, but sure. We'll have to go by the tavern but let's just stay outside it. Tez, are you coming?"

"No, that's alright. I'll leave you two alone," Tez said, discretely winking to her sister, much to Sen's chagrin. "I'll go help Grafhar, wherever he drifted off to with the runaways."

They all nodded to each other, headed off to their separate tasks, looking forward to this strange night coming to a close.

Fannalhen was silent, his hand absently stroking his chin, trying to make sense of what just transpired. As he scanned the room, his eyes passing from his wife to his closest companions to his lesser-known associates, their expressions all spoke the same. An unspoken chorus agreeing that they would not know what to agree upon.

"Slaves from the Haunted Tribe," Dennalhir said softly, shaking her head. "And who knows what havoc they have in tow? As much as I cannot fathom what they have gone through just to get here…"

"The issue now is, what are the consequences?" Fannalhen said.

"Did I not warn that it was inevitable, Fannalhen?" Han'e said, little humor in his voice. "Whether it is one person or fifty, the Invaders are relentless. It is only a matter of time before they are at your doors, demanding that these two be returned."

Fannalhen looked to the ground with dejection, his thoughts muddled and foggy. He had endured much in his years as Chief, but to harbor runaways from a brutal invading force? How was one to assess the right thing to do? "What would you have me do, Han'e? Return to sender and call it a day?"

Han'e crossed his arms, a deep frown on his face. "Do you value your people as a whole more than the lives of a select few?"

"What kind of a question is that?" Fannalhen began to pace, his hand rummaging through his thick locks. "We are speaking of one person whose life was irreparably destroyed and another who's never known a true life. And when they are presented with an opportunity to start anew—"

"They put *us* in danger, is what they have done," Koelhe interrupted. "I don't know if you've noticed, but the Haunted tend to have valuable reconnaissance below the dirt. If you—"

"Tell me, Koelhe," Fannalhen said, returning the interruption. "Have you ever seen *anything* to prove a person is able to commune with the dead?"

"Have you seen anything to *disprove* it?" She raised her brow, her expression serious and foreboding.

Fannalhen sighed, knowing that she had a valid point.

"Whether it's true or not, that boy implied that *something* is coming. We don't know what, but it's coming. And I'd *much* rather send these two back from where they came if it meant our village and our people are left untouched." Koelhe folded her arms and grunted.

"We are *not* entertaining the idea of trading life for life," Denna asserted. "How would we be any better if we saw these two lives and sold them away for our own comfort and well-being? We'd be no better than slave traders ourselves!"

"If you'd rather your own people die in their place, be my guest," Han'e muttered. "But if you are taking no issue with the Invaders rummaging through your village, I'd suggest you come prepared. Unless the lives of a few matter more than the lives of the many."

"I never said they mattered more," Fannalhen asserted, his tone flustered. "But we'd be condemning those two likely to something worse than just servitude if we sent them back. If these 'Deatharms' are real, then..."

"They're real," Han'e confirmed, "and they're terrifying. If you don't hand those two back, you're likely to face an entire horde of them just for standing in the way."

A throat cleared from off to the side, Sharrabha stepping forward with a confident stride, falling in line next to Narva. "That's *if* these Invaders are even on their way here. We don't know that for certain."

"So, you would neglect to prepare because they might *not* come," chimed Rantalha, his stoic voice reflecting his ever-present monotonous expression. "What a bold strategy."

Sharrabha outstretched her hands, gesturing to punctuate each syllable escaping her lips. "All I'm saying is, we may be panicking over nothing. The Invaders have stayed to the south of the Forest for fifteen years. Why would that change now?"

"Pretty sure they've not had a slave escape this far north, so there's a first time for everything," Han'e said, rolling his eyes. He turned his gaze back toward Fannalhen. "But, it's *your* call at the end of the day, Chief."

Fannalhen sighed, burrowing his face in his hands, fingers stretching at the skin. "Let's entertain the idea that a force *does* come from the south. A large force. We number in the thousands in this village alone. Surely, we can overrun whatever they throw at us."

Han'e shook his head. "You've not seen the damage they can do with just a *small* force. They're efficient and merciless. It would be foolish to underestimate someone you have never once encountered."

The Chief nodded, conceding the point. "Yes, that's valid. So, then, we would need allies. Say we are successful in uniting the northern Tribes. Han'e, could we count on the Sun Tribe's assistance?"

The Sun chief paused, scratching at his chin, silently considering the question. A bit too silent for a bit too long.

"Han'e?"

"For one so hesitant to heed my Tribe's call these last few years, you certainly are expectant of us to help you in an instant."

Dennalhir jumped forward to challenge the man on his words, but Fannalhen outstretched his arm, barring her from taking another step. *His words are harsh, but true.* "So, we cannot count on the Sun Tribe. There are others in the north."

From the corner of his eye, Fannalhen could see Tawa pacing in place, scratching the back of his head nervously. "Are you certain of that, Fanna?" he asked.

"Why would I not be?"

"Well, consider what remains up here. South of the Heart, discounting the Sun, we have the Arrow, Lake, and Wood Tribes. The Arrow Tribe, while still the finest archers in the Land, have become far too scattered and diasporic. It did not help matters that the Invaders stole away their horses, which stripped them of their mobility on a battlefield. The Lake Tribe is still recovering from their Long War, and that ended a century and a half ago. You would think that they have resolved their differences by now, but still, they cannot help but fight amongst each other for one reason or another. And as for the Wood Tribe—"

"I'd sooner stand with the Invaders than with the Wood Tribe," Han'e said grimly.

Tawandhar frowned and grimaced at that. "Surely, you don't mean—"

"Shut it, Tawa," Koelhe snapped, that all-too-familiar sneer and snarl affixed to her mouth. "*We're* not the ones who met death while trying to escape from death. We all know the Wood Tribe is beyond territorial. Basically fanatical about the Forest. We'd have better luck trying to ride the Bear into battle. They're not worth the effort."

"Fine, then," Fannalhen said. "What about the Keepers? Sharrabha, in your travels up there, have you had any indication that they might—"

"I'm going to stop you right there, Chief," the huntress said, "and just say no. The Keepers are just as territorial about the Heart as the Wood are with the Forest. They're just...not as militant about it. Unless we want to bring the fight into the Heart, they're not helping."

Dennalhir looked at her husband cautiously, a frown creasing her lips. Resignation and defeat shone in her eyes, a solemn acceptance glittering within. Fannalhen returned his face to the palms of his hands, burrowing himself deep into hiding, frustration mounting at each refusal and dismissal. "So, we're without a paddle," he admitted.

Sarcastically, Koelhe clapped, a sadistic smile on her face. "Well done, Chief. A very productive battle tactic. I'll add it to your list of sterling achievements."

The Stone Chief growled, the rumble in his throat quaking amidst an otherwise quiet delegation. "So, what are our options if there *isn't* a force coming?"

Nobody seemed to want to entertain that thought. It felt like a foregone conclusion to the contrary. "Send them one direction or another," Rantalha said plainly. "Anywhere's better than here."

Shaking his head, Fannalhen was at a loss for what to do. It felt wrong to trade two lives for the good of the Tribe. It felt worse knowing that the Stone Tribe would be alone in this fight. When his eyes met with Denna's, her solemn expression spoke of the same emptiness.

"If we were to disguise as well as hide them, though..." the Chief muttered to no one in particular.

"Fanna..." Tawa said, cocking his head. "You are not suggesting...."

"Not suggesting, no. Just pondering. If an Illusionist would be so kind as to..."

"My friend, you know that is taboo." Tawa's expression was stern. "Though Illusion could potentially resolve our dilemma, you know as well as I that giving one's own pendant to another is an affront to—"

"I know, Tawa. I know." Fannalhen raised his hand in silent command. "I'm just...weighing all of our options. And that may as well be the end of the list." He sighed.

Han'e grunted, a thought clearly bothering him. "Something still doesn't add up, though. How did two weakened, disheveled runaways manage to make it out of a slave camp flanked by however many heavily armed guards? I can't be the only one who finds that suspicious."

"It doesn't sit right with me, either," Fannalhen admitted. "Whatever happened...I don't like it."

They all sat in revered silence until, one by one, the gathering dispersed, returning to their respective homes or guest housing.

Fannalhen remained in the common room, alone to his thoughts as the fire crackled to nothing. When the embers finally quelled, he sat solemnly in the darkness, focusing not on Dennalhir as she silently retreated to bed, but on Brin, content and happy in his own bed.

Two lives, for the good of the Tribe, he thought. *What am I to do?*

He never thought the smell of pine and maple could grow so nauseating. When he reached the clearing and emerged into the open air, nothing but wide-open moors before him, he couldn't help but breathe it all in, relishing the difference.

His men filed in behind him, all of them in the customary blues of his personal guard. He looked forward to changing out of his blues once he returned to the south. The skirmishes in that forest left him too many speckles of red on his sleeves than was truly befitting a man of his stature. It was all part of the job, though. He rubbed his hands together, trying to file away the stains of red embedded into his skin before he pushed back strands of his shaggy auburn hair. Standing in satisfaction, he rested a hand on the base of his flintlock pistol, fastened in a holster along the side of his upper thigh.

One of his men approached him at the side, a larger flintlock rifle resting on his shoulder. "Ah, General, sir," he said. "We can handle the rest from here if you choose. There is no need to trouble yourself further."

"Ah, not a bother, Captain," the general said, his thin lips flush with a smile. "I've not had a good hunt like this in years."

His eyes bright, he turned his gaze back toward the northern horizon. The mountains loomed far in the distance.

CHAPTER FIVE

STRANGERS

For all the anxiety of what had just happened in the family hut, there was a strange peacefulness to the nighttime air. On a typical evening, this would have been pleasant. It would have meant the night winding down, a handful of tavern patrons bidding a pleasant stumble back home as they left the establishment, Sen not normally long or far behind them. The only persistent sound in the air was the rhythmic chirping of grasshoppers. It was past hours at the tavern, not that that ever meant anything, but even inside was home to a stillness, a collective sleep. There were people inside, to be fair, but with far less rowdiness than was ever typical.

It was eerie. For one evening, everything was turned on its head. The Haunted returning, slave camps to the south, an Invader march. It was a bad day for Sen to quit drinking.

She and Narva sat outside the tavern, the musky aromas of beer and vomit ever so enticing. More than anything, it was a test. If she could sit this close outside, willing herself to remain outdoors, well, it was a step in the right direction.

Having Narva in front of her was a help. Not necessarily a *big* help. But *a* help. Any time she craned her head toward the doors, her curiosity piqued by a sudden noise or a spark of laughter, Narva would clear his throat. Heartily and obnoxiously. He'd have that look in his eyes, that expression that screamed, *Don't even think about it*, but Sen could only interpret it as a challenge, a distraction in and of itself. It was worth it just to see that he, well...

Anyway.

As the distant din of nearby frivolity went on in the tavern, Sen and Narva remained outside, sat at a table that Narva had borrowed from the establishment along with a deck of cards. It was a rarity for him to so willingly subject himself to such punishment, but clearly, he was willing to be a glutton for it tonight. Sen appreciated it.

She stared at him from across the table, her thumb eagerly shifting her top card back and forth, back and forth. She smirked as she spied beads of sweat trickled down his forehead, matching hers, drop for drop. Casually, Narva bit his lip, grimacing as he looked at his meager pile, a paltry sum of cards remaining. The center pile was, impressively, growing larger and larger. Sen felt the tinge, the chill running up her arm, tingling up her veins and up through her fingertips. Victory was within her grasp. Narrowing her eyes at Narva's pile, she spied two, three cards remaining, half his deck parsed through the pile in the middle of the table.

There was an eight at the bottom of that pile. She couldn't forget it. A distinguishable eight, the top-left corner ripped and torn, the center stained with what she hoped was jam, giving it the distinction of a false ninth character unfitting with the rest. She had just played a four, a harmless, useless four, and with an unrelenting eagerness, Narva slammed down his card, revealing a...two. Still nothing of worth there.

Sen smiled, her thumb twitching outward, nearly flicking a seven at the middle deck, Narva's frustration growing into an even more discernible grimace.

His teeth were quite near to a snarl, his breath so close to a growl, his voice approaching an under-breath curse. Hopefully and hopelessly, he flipped his next card, the twitch chilling up Sen's arm, and there was just a useless nine. Narva's fists clenched as he looked at his single remaining card.

Sen relished in his frustration and anger, softly giggling as he rolled his eyes and looked up to the stars above, questioning how in the world he could be so…unfortunate. It wasn't for Sen to know, either way—when it came to fortune, *this* was her game.

As she flipped over a five, she slightly pulled her hand back, Narva immediately ready to slam his hand down with the card underneath. Regardless of the result, he seemed intent on slapping that deck with the hopes that something, *anything*, under his hand would allow him to claim the deck.

Sen was ready for that move, and as she saw the split moment when Narva's hand was separate from the card, she slapped her hand in between, resting it firmly atop the large pile, Narva's firm grip resting atop hers.

Their hands stayed there a moment, Sen drawing pleasure from the unknown beneath her hand, Narva merely exhibiting shock at the speed at which his opponent managed to get her hand in. Sen felt another shiver up her arm, though not the one typical of when she played cards.

"You know," she said, teasingly, "if you wanted to hold my hand, all you had to do was ask."

Narva grunted, not quite amused, but a smirk still slyly creasing his lips. "Pretty confident play there, Sen. You know, if you're wrong, I get the pile, and we play on."

"What a great risk, and what a great reward. I'm anxious to find out."

"Then, go ahead. Let's find out."

Sen chuckled, glancing down at her hand, still covered by Narva's. "Well, you may have to, you know, let go of my hand. I'm a bit pinned otherwise."

"May just as well," Narva quipped. "Your hand's a bit sweaty, anyway."

"Welcome to my evening." Her breath caught as Narva lifted his hand away. Just as slowly, she raised hers from the pile, the subtle quiver in her veins drifting away as her fingers dragged along the stray card atop, her smile widening as she looked down at the sight, her eyes glowing as they met Narva's stunned but expected expression. The expectation that somehow, some way, that final card atop the pile was going to be the eight which sandwiched all the cards together, the eight that would give Sen the pile and the game, the eight that would crush the victorious dreams that Narva never had a chance of having.

Sen chuckled as she pulled the cards closer, calmly merging them with the collection she already had, and placed them at the center of the table, her eyes not once breaking from those of the man across from her.

"So," she said. "Do you wanna—"

"No, Sen," Narva interrupted, raising his hands to punctuate. "I think getting trounced three times in a row is enough for me." He shook his head, his expression somehow simultaneously speaking astonishment, annoyance, and disbelief. "How you do this every time is beyond me."

Sen shrugged, her body language filled with satisfaction. "Luck, I suppose. Luck and practice."

"I'd assume more the former than the latter when it comes to a game of chance."

"I'm just very good at chance, apparently." She shimmied in place, Narva's disappointment all the reward she needed right now. All the *distraction* she needed right now. "You know, if there ever gets to be a competitive circuit for this, I'll split the reward with you." Unwittingly, she winked as she said it, immediately straightening herself out on instinct and pretending she didn't just do that.

"If they don't figure out how you're counting cards or whatever it is you do," he answered with a laugh, paying no heed to the wink. "No one goes undefeated like you with a game like this."

"No one, 'cept me," Sen said. "Maybe I'll meet my match one day. Maybe."

"That's a very strict 'maybe.'" Narva looked off to the side, drawing his eyes back toward the village center, in the direction of the prior congregation. "Do you think they're still going at it over there?"

Sen shrugged. "Who knows? What a strange night."

"You're telling me," Narva scoffed, a frown adorning his face. "Frankly, I didn't even know the Haunted still existed."

"No arguments here," Sen agreed. "Honestly, I never knew much of them even before...all of this happened."

"I mean, I learned a bit from listening to my father speak about them in passing."

"That Knowledge of his comes in handy, I'm sure," Sen said softly.

"I suppose, though I'm not exactly sure how much our Tribe's Learneds know of them, anyway, him included." He sighed sharply. "Ah, well. Either way, the Haunted...they're *weird*, to say the least."

Sen leaned forward, curious at the description. "How do you mean?"

Narva grimaced, furrowing his brow in consternation. His eyes drifted aimlessly from one nondescript point to another, as though trying to grasp some loose thought that wasn't quite coming to him. "Well, think on this first: do we even know the Tribe's *actual* name?"

There was a momentary pause in Sen's motion, an intention to say something, but the words froze in her mouth, impeded by a lapse in her knowledge. But was it even a regrettable lapse? Narva's point was valid. Did *anyone* know it?

Across the table, Narva took her silence as answer enough and nodded. "See? I mean, *I* don't know it. My father doesn't seem to, either. That Tribe has been so secluded for generations that it's a wonder we even know they exist in the first place."

"I heard they don't even undergo the Trial," Sen admitted. "But I think that's about the extent of my knowledge."

"I don't even think *that's* true," Narva said. "But who am I to say? I feel like I wouldn't recognize a single one of them even if they punched me in the face."

"Yeah, you've always been bad about recognizing when someone's about to punch your teeth out." Sen smiled.

With an exasperated sigh, Narva chuckled to himself and flashed a grin. "Well, maybe if *someone* didn't sneak up on me all the time, I'd be more cognizant of it."

"Aren't you supposed to be able to *hear* when something's coming up behind you? Wasn't that *your* special prize from the Trial?"

Narva threw his arms up in defeat. "Always poking at someone's blind side. How you wound me." He clutched a hand to his chest in exaggerated mockery, so overcome and overwhelmed and overacted.

As much as Sen wanted to add some fuel to this fire, she diverted her attention back to the topic at hand. "But back to their Trials..." she said. "I think we would know if they were coming through here, no? Our village is the only possible point of entry into the Heart. Going any other path would be more trouble than it's worth."

"But does that not sound like a Tribe content with evading view?"

"Well, I guess, but…" Something still ate at Sen. Something so intrinsic to the mystery of the Haunted Tribe. "Why go through the effort of hiding at all? Are they hiding something from us? I mean, other than themselves? We probably could have helped them when things went south down south!"

Narva sighed, burying his chin in his palms, silently considering the point. There was a scholarly pensiveness to his expression, something far more expected of his father than he. He was always a considerate, elaborative type, but not typically within the realm of cultural thought processes, so it was odd for Sen to see. These were strange times indeed.

"Have you ever heard of exactly *why* we've all called them the 'Haunted?'" he asked.

Sen shook her head. "It's just…something I've always called them without much thought otherwise. Like they're a myth or something."

"*Heh*, well. Something else I've heard sounds more the stuff of myth than anything else I've ever seen."

"Really," Sen pondered, intrigued. "Go on, then."

"Keep in mind that this is just rumor and word of mouth, and nothing that any of us have surely been able to confirm, but…" He paused, visibly formulating his thoughts so as to not make them sound ridiculous. "Apparently, they can commune with their dead."

Sen blinked a few times, trying to discern whether Narva was joking. Across the table, his face remained completely deadpan. Nothing to suggest any semblance of a joke. "They commune. With their dead." Even as she repeated it, it didn't sound any less absurd. "How would they even—"

"Hey, I'm not here to explain it," Narva interrupted. "This is just what I've heard. The name we've given them is so intrinsic to what they really are: haunted by their dead. I don't know just how much of a two-way path it is, but at the very least, the dead speak to them. What they say, I have no idea. But if them losing their entire culture to the Invaders is any indication, I doubt it's anything of use."

"Narva!" She chucked a card at him with the intent of hitting him in the arm, but it got caught in an updraft and curved away, back to the table, nearly returning to the same spot.

"I don't say that as an insult," Narva said, his eyes widening, hands open before him. "My point was just that the dead don't seem to give them any sort of warning about things. Maybe they literally *are* just haunting them. Think about it. If there was some dead voice whispering in my ear all the time, I'd stow myself away, too."

The wind picked up along the side of Sen's head as she frowned, eyes not breaking from Narva's serious tone. "I don't know if that's quite how I'd put it. What if they can...I don't know, *control* who it is they're speaking to? If there're people waiting for them in the Otherworld, but it'd be a long time before they meet again...I don't know, call me crazy, but that doesn't sound like a bad thing."

Leaning back in his seat, Narva silently considered the point, but the dead-pan frown did not leave his lips. "It just seems a bit...how do I phrase this? If that's the case, they're robbing themselves the opportunity to properly grieve and move on."

"What if you could do it, though?" Sen asked pointedly. "What if you had the chance to speak to your mother?"

Narva was silent, a bit stunned, frankly. He bit his lower lip, shifting uncomfortably in place in his chair. The flash of a thousand and one words that he could possibly say radiated in his eyes, expressions of sadness and grief and anger and longing. But all that could escape his lips was, "But what could I say to someone I never even met?"

"Narva..."

"Not that I'm angry, by any means. Just, I don't know who she is or what she looked like. And I don't think that I missed out on having a mother, thanks to how close our families have been and how *your* mother has always treated me as one of her own. But, really, what would I even say?" He stammered, the intended words coming out as nothing more than inane syllables that just stuck together, bereft of any true meaning.

"I'm sorry," Sen said, reaching her hand out over the table. She noted some hesitation in Narva's eye, but eventually, he placed his hand in hers, warm and firm. "Here we were talking about the wild mysteries of our Land, and then I *had* to bring the mood down. Ah, classic me."

Behind a flash of white teeth rumbled a deep chuckle, assured and friendly. Narva looked at Sen with kind eyes glimmering in the moonlight. "Hey, I'm fine with that," he said. "That's the Sen I've always known."

Instinctively, Sen blushed, her cheeks flushing with a warmth not lost on her friend. His smile grew wider, a bit too jovial a reaction. She wanted to slap him right then and there, but she was content with letting him wordlessly mock her.

"And you know something else," Narva continued, intent on returning to the previous point. "If I recall correctly, I think they used to wear death masks, the Haunted. Some sort of unity between them and those who came before them. So, maybe you're right. Or maybe they're still just a spooked bunch of folks and they scared themselves into forced solitude. Either or." He laughed.

Sen rolled her eyes but could not help but laugh, too. Even in the face of an anxious unknown, there was a serenity to the moment, a calmness whispering in her ear to cherish it. The sweats continued as she sat outside the tavern, but she was wholly and completely entranced and taken in the moment, in the laughter, the silent wind carrying their voices along into the openness ahead. She wasn't thinking of the frivolity of what was beyond that door next to her, its accompaniment with the inviting and fleeting aroma an ever-present invitation. She wasn't thinking of the difficulty of falling asleep just a short time before. She wasn't thinking of the pervasive failures which always seemed ready to rear their ugly heads. All that was on her mind was *this* moment, this shared moment between two friends. Just...two friends.

As their voices quelled, she looked down at the table and noticed Narva's hand remaining in hers. A couple rapid blinks of the eyes confirmed that it wasn't an illusion, and she was quite content with that. She looked up at him, a sly smile still affixed to his face. She couldn't help but continue to smile, herself. "Hey, thanks for tonight," she said quickly, before any prevailing thoughts prevented her otherwise. "I...I needed this."

Playfully, Narva shrugged in response, but he wasn't so dense that he couldn't hear the intent of the words. "Of course, anything for…" He trailed off, *his* mind apparently working quicker than his words. "Yeah, anything."

An immense warmth filled Sen's chest, a near fluttering. She could feel her hand twitching underneath Narva's, but gratefully, he didn't take that as a hint to pull back. Her sweats grew more intense, but they weren't due to a want for alcohol this time. "Hey, um," she stammered. "I, uh…I l—" She trailed off, her attention caught elsewhere.

"You…what?" Narva asked, his curiosity piqued.

Sen's curiosity, however, was still drawn off to the distance, beyond where Narva sat.

"Sen?"

Sen narrowed her eyes, trying to make sense of the dark shapes entering from the nighttime shadows. Nudging her head to direct Narva's attention that way, she could see three distinguished forms approaching, unfamiliar, walking in an unusual triangular formation. Additional shades took shape beyond the three, one skulking along to Sen's right, deeper into the heart of the village, another to the left, past the tavern and into the outskirts.

In the dim light, she could barely make out the complexions of the approaching trio, but the glimmer of nearby torchlights gave the impression that these men were of much paler complexion than she, not quite a white tone, but far from the red-brown of her own skin. They walked along with an assured stride, the rear two holding long pole-like instruments, lacking a uniformity in their width along the length of the tools. They weren't using them as walking assistance but rather resting them atop their shoulders.

At the front stood a man brimming with confidence, judging entirely from his stride. As he drew closer, Sen noticed the complexities of his attire, crafted from more intricate cloths than she had ever seen, colored in a deep blue she did not know was possible in such clothing. Defined details of his face came into better focus, a plain face bearing incomplete whiskers, a fascinating contrast given that he appeared to be somewhere in his thirties, judging from the onset of early wrinkles settling into his forehead and cheeks. His eyes pierced through the nighttime air, an illusory dagger jabbing into Sen's soul. Tufts of wavy auburn hair flowed down his head, tucked behind his interestingly small ears. He didn't bear one of those long poles like the other two did, but Sen did notice something much smaller strapped to the outside of his left thigh, where she had often seen Wolfsigns like Narva place hunting knives.

Though she lost sight of the man who prowled into the village center, Sen paid particular attention to the other investigative man, him being close enough to survey in greater detail. He maintained much the same posture as the triangle formation directly in front of her, but he held his pole-instrument in two hands, like every bit the weapon she assumed it to be. He stalked slowly and methodically, hushed whispers of passersby and onlookers fading as hut doors slammed in an audibly rhythmic sequence, often punctuated by frightened gasps or indistinguishable curses.

They were strange, these mystery men. Unknown to these parts yet carrying themselves with an overconfident bravado like they owned the place. Sen couldn't help but show her displeasure. But at the same time, her heart pounded, her hands growing clammy.

And when she made eye contact with the lead man, she froze entirely in place. He stopped in his tracks when he noticed Sen's gaze, apparently accepting it as an invitation to approach closer. Shakily, Sen withdrew her hand from Narva's, and her companion rose to his feet, immediately meeting sharp chagrin from the lead man's lackeys, and shuffled behind Sen. Mustering up what courage she could, Sen inhaled and steadied her eyes, balling her fists as her nails dug into her palms. She gritted her teeth and calmly maintained the mutual glare, though nervous sweat trickled down her forehead.

"Sen..." Narva whispered, almost as a question. There wasn't any doubt in her mind what he intended by the unspoken words.

"Yeah," she muttered. "It has to be."

The leader stopped within an arm's reach of the table, hands folded at his waist. He stared slightly over his shoulder, said something incomprehensible to his underling. Voicing no objection, the assistant—servant, lackey, underling, Sen didn't quite know what to call him—calmly walked toward the tavern, weapon still at rest on his shoulder, and pushed the door open. All vibrant commentary within the tavern suddenly ceased, the interior atmosphere suddenly becoming still as death, hardly a whisper daring to be uttered. The man slowly closed the door, nodding to the leader in so doing. Heat ran the length of Sen's body, her heart continuing to pound, and the new arrival calmly took his seat across from her, his remaining lackey standing pat at his rear.

They sat in silence, each slowly regarding the other, waiting for whoever would break rank first and utter the first word. Sure enough, it was the leader of the front who spoke first, nodding his head to Sen and Narva both and saying something in a tongue neither of them understood. Sen and Narva looked at each other, unsure of how even to respond. Recognizing this, the man may have repeated himself, or perhaps he said something else entirely and was speaking a bit quicker. It was clear upon his face that he fully knew they had no idea what he was saying, but that didn't stop that grin on his face from digging into them both.

"Hey," Sen said to Narva, not breaking eye contact with the newcomer. "Go into the tavern and see if there's a Linguist in there.

Visibly, Narva balked at the request. "Are you off your nut?" he hissed. "You *do* realize who they are, right? And that one of them is literally *inside* the tavern right now?"

A chill ran up her arm and she nodded. "I know. But unless the runaways neglected to divulge on some aptitude on these folks' parts to remove people's voices, I'd say everyone is okay in there right now. And it doesn't seem like *this* guy is itching to talk to anyone else at the moment." Narva did not seem in any greater rush to comply, until Sen turned to him and looked up, nerves wild in her eyes, and quietly muttered, "Please."

Narva sighed, shaking his head before finally and sullenly departing into the tavern, the silence so deafening that she feared his entry would send the place into a frenzy. But instead, he was just another silent and fearful face in the crowd, his voice the only one singing out amidst the chorus of nothing.

Those silent moments stretched on and on as Sen awaited Narva's return, a stillness only exacerbated by the ever-present cold stare of the man seated across from her. His eyes were so sharp, so haunting, the blues of his irises freezing her in place as though she dove into a pool of ice. The grin still affixed to his lips, he nudged his head down toward the table, to the deck of cards waiting to be dealt. He said nothing, made no other motion, intent on sitting quietly with hands folded until Sen made the first move.

Initially, Sen shook her head, perhaps more vigorously than she intended. Not accepting the rejection, the man nodded once again to the cards, his expression more serious this time. *Gods*, Sen lamented. *I'd never thought I'd not want to con someone in this game.* Seeing no alternative, she pensively picked up the deck, calmly shuffling, trying with great effort to not yield anything in her expression, despite the runs of sweat continuing to drip down her face. *I can just tell him I'm detoxing.*

Mercifully, Narva returned a few minutes later with a reluctant Linguist.

Well, given everything, I'd imagine she was more reluctant to stay in there, Sen thought. She could smell that the woman had had at least two drinks already. One more of those, and she wouldn't be any use for whatever *this* was about to be.

Narva, having accomplished his task, filed in behind Sen once again, his eyes not breaking from his counterpart behind the seated leader.

Sen looked over her shoulder and said to Narva, "What's going on in there?"

Exasperated, her friend sighed and threw his hands up. "...Nothing," he said, forlorn. "He's just...standing in there. Watching. No one's saying a word."

Nodding, Sen redirected her attention to the Linguist. "And her?"

"What about her? I just grabbed the first Linguist I could find. I wasn't about to stick around there any longer than I needed to."

Fair, Sen thought. Whoever the Linguist was, it was lost on her. Given how large the Tribe was, it wasn't exactly surprising that she didn't recognize the woman. There was a nervous air about her, a shifting expression traveling from the stranger to Sen, an unspoken desire to understand what even was going on. It was much the same as was displayed on Narva's face, though more overt. The woman looked on Sen with disdain, though that wasn't anything new. Sen didn't need her for pleasantries; she just needed to know what this man was trying to say to her.

"So, what do you need me for?" the woman said, slightly slurring her words.

"What else would I need you for?" Sen answered sharply, furrowing an eyebrow at her. "To figure out what the hell he's saying so we can figure out why the hell he's got men patrolling the village."

Her eyes widened. "There are *others* who are—"

Sen raised a hand, silencing her. "Yeah, I don't like it either. We don't have much a choice here."

The Linguist sneered. "And why should I help *you*?"

There was no way for Sen to roll her eyes further into her skull. Nudging her head to the stranger, she said simply, "*He's* not giving me any other option. Let's call it easier to just get this over with now."

The woman had no clever retort; she just stood with hands on hips, visibly eager to be done with this and get back to her drink.

Grabbing the stranger's attention, Sen made a series of hand motions. First, pointing a finger back and forth between him and the Linguist, then taking the ball of her thumb and pressing it to her own forehead, and then removing it to give a thumbs-up signal.

The man accepted the explanation, nodding to the Linguist, who still gritted her teeth at Sen.

Begrudgingly, she walked up to the stranger and pressed her thumb to his forehead, breathing in deeply as a faint glow emanated from her Language pendant.

The stranger's man instinctively moved to action, but the seated man was quick to call him off with a wave.

The wind intensified as the Linguist did her work, becoming less a whisper and far more a howl, a wolf in the night. Sen didn't fear wolves; she'd been surrounded by them her whole life. But the howling did little to instill confidence.

The Linguist pulled back, calming herself with another deep breath. The stranger kept his sly smile, an intrigued and perplexed expression settling into his brow. He looked upon the woman with morbid curiosity as though she was some oddity that was meant to be studied. Like an animal.

Sen cleared her throat, averting the Linguist's nervous eyes back toward her. "Ask him who he is, why he's here." *I know the answer to both*, Sen thought to herself, *but how else am I going to start this?*

Regarding Sen with piercing anger, the Linguist sighed and spoke flaw-lessly in the stranger's tongue, paying little heed to the stranger's rising, surprised eyebrows. Surprised as the stranger seemed, however, there was an inequal burst of amusement, a soft chuckle rumbling in his throat. He said something in response to the Linguist, which the woman took with a discomforted grimace.

"What did he say?" Sen asked.

The woman looked at her, her brow furrowed. "I don't know what you're playing at, but it needs to stop."

"He said *that*?"

"No, that's what *I'm* saying to *you*. I hope you know you're playing with fire here."

Sen tossed her arms in a shrug, shaking her head with confusion. "Much less playing with the fire and more that it happened to sit in my lap and is in no rush to be extinguished. Now, what did he say?"

The woman paused, closing her eyes for a second longer than a standard blink. *"So quick to business. And here I thought we had agreed to a round of cards."*

Rustling from behind announced Narva's approach. "Sen, don't tell me you're trying to fleece one of the *Invaders*," he whispered sharply.

"Believe me," Sen muttered, the deck of cards held tightly in her hand. "There's no one else I'd rather *not* play a round with. I'm more frightened of what will happen should I not play." Before entertaining any objections, she started to instruct the Linguist to describe the rules as she did, but almost as quickly as she began, the stranger raised his hand to silence them both.

"I've learned, already. Don't trouble yourselves."

How fortunate for you, then, Sen wanted to say. In a flash, she dealt out the deck, splitting it evenly between the two of them. In silence, she and the stranger flipped their cards with rhythmic efficiency, the rush and chill so familiar to Sen coursing through her arms with each play. Disproportionate-ly, the stacks made their way to Sen, a methodical efficiency that was second nature to her. The stranger showed no signs of panic or frustration. He just allowed the game to progress as it was, Sen's triumph a foregone conclusion right from the outset.

With a handful of cards remaining in the middle of the table, and the stranger down to his final card, the man made his final play, a face card, to which Sen responded with a face card of her own, seizing the pile and the game. She held her position, frozen in sudden silence, awaiting some sort of retribution for winning a game that was, for her, always winnable.

But where many had shown disdain and anger at being trounced in such a manner, on a game based entirely on chance, the stranger merely kept his smile, a patient disposition washing over him as he eyed Sen with cold regard. The wolven wind continued to howl, immaterial tendrils of gusts entering and dissipating from view as Sen watched the man, waiting for him to say *something* next.

Glass shattered, and a woman screamed in the tavern, and then a hush fell once more.

Immediately, Sen jumped to her feet, pushing off the table, but a clicking noise held her in place.

The Linguist and Narva sucked in their breath as Sen slowly turned back toward the stranger, who now held the weapon previously strapped to his outer thigh, pointed right at her. He shook his head, grunting with disapproval, and motioned for her to return to her seat.

Sen complied, but not before hearing an echoing whimper ruminating from the tavern. She planted her hands squarely on the table, fingers digging up splinters of wood, and she *waited*.

Silent moments became silent minutes until finally, the stranger, through the Linguist, said, *"Are we going to have a rematch, or not?"* He arced an eyebrow, his weapon still pointed at Sen.

Gripping nervously at the split wood until the bark shards started to pierce her fingers, Sen gritted her teeth, wanting little more to do with a game with this man. But she needed to entertain him, nonetheless. "Safe to say you're not from 'round here," she said, "and I doubt you traveled all this way just to play cards."

The stranger's smile returned. *"Your doubts have merit,"* he said, slowly withdrawing his weapon from the table and placing it back along his thigh.

"Who are you?" Sen asked bluntly.

"A stranger," he answered. *"A stranger in a stranger land."*

Blood marked the table as Sen pulled her hands back, pulling the splinters out from her fingertips. She eyed the cards as he did, his cold glare motioning her to deal out a new hand. She flicked out cards to herself and the stranger one by one, paying little care to the ones which landed past the edge of the table and into the man's lap. "That doesn't quite answer my question."

As he collected the stray cards adorning his lap and the dirt below, the stranger flashed a hint of satisfaction in his grin, a strange array of joviality and calmness that was unsettling. He seemed a bit *too* eager to be picking up his own cards, *too* intrigued to be speaking to a random passerby in the dead of night. And it was all the more uncomfortable when he situated himself back at playing position, his hand resting atop his pile of retrieved cards, standoffish in his body language but welcoming in his facial mannerisms.

"I'm still not hearing an answer," Sen muttered, much more sharply than she intended to someone who had just pointed a weapon at her.

"Who I am matters little to you, I'm afraid," the stranger said. *"However, what I seek, that is of greater import."*

"And we've established that it's not a card game, and yet here we are." Reluctantly, Sen flipped her first card, the damaged eight that she had played on Narva previously.

The stranger made his play, a matching card, allowing him to take the minimal pile.

Given the circumstances, she couldn't be too stingy on the generosity. "Unless you're just looking for directions, in which case, you're probably a bit too far from home for me to help out."

Methodically, the two opponents played card after card, Sen gradually sweeping more and more of the pile towards herself, the rush enough for her to lose herself in the moment. The more she claimed for herself, the more aggressive she became, running combos and setting up bold gambits that caught her foe entirely off-guard. Some would call this game one of chance, but to Sen, there was so much more strategy involved than that. Luck was naturally there, too, but she'd gamed enough people to devise an absolutely deconstructive plan for each game.

The stranger, for his part, was entirely unfazed by the looming defeat. In fact, he appeared to accept it. It was...unsettling. *"I wouldn't say that I am the one who is lost, I must admit,"* he said after a period of focused silence. *"Rather, I'm trying to find a companion of mine who is lost."*

The back of her throat scratched, but Sen continued to focus on the cards. "How concerning," she said. "I hope your...companion is okay."

"Two companions, truthfully." He awaited Sen's next move, watching her place a face card. Eagerly, he flipped over his subsequent card, revealing another face. He looked across the table, only for that jovial façade to break as Sen played another face.

The chill ran along Sen's arm, and when the stranger flipped over his next card, it was a useless three, allowing Sen to take the pile for herself.

He grunted something to himself, probably a curse. The Linguist didn't translate it. *"I must say, I fear for the safety of my companions. We were separated some time ago. I am...hopeful that I'll find them again soon."*

Wanting nothing more than this game to be over, Sen grunted an acknowledgment and then played a final combo to claim the last pile, the stranger's cards gone in the blink of an eye. "Well, I hope you'll get to see them again," she said, masking her meaning to the contrary.

"I'd have to say I'm close, if you can believe it. There can't be too many places for them to run off to."

"When you word it like that, it sounds as though they're hiding from you."

"Well, that would be preposterous," the stranger said. *"They've nothing to fear from me."*

Sen forced a smile, wanting not to draw his ire. But still, the words slipped out. "If you've come this far, whoever you're looking for might not wanna be found."

The stranger was quiet, coldly regarding Sen. She anticipated he was awaiting another hand to be dealt, but as she dispersed the cards, the man watched them fly off the table, paying little regard to them as they lay on the ground. He stared at Sen, the smile fading away, revealing a man who no longer feigned interest in a card game. He leaned forward, elbows resting upon the table, his fingers linking together to form a bridge for his chin to rest upon. *"Let's say that you're right,"* he said. *"Would you happen to have seen any* lost *people traveling through your lands lately?"*

Narrowing her eyes, Sen maintained a straight expression, wanting not to give away anything. "Lot of people come through this way. It's not for me to say who was lost and who knew where they were going."

"How curious. Permit me to rephrase. Would you say that any of them looked as though they were...running from something?"

"You mean like a wild animal?" Sen asked, much to Narva's audible groan from behind. "I mean, that happens every now and again."

"Oh, I assure you. They're far wilder of animals than any other creature wandering these wastes."

These wastes? Sen repeated to herself. *Animals? This piece of...*

Another crash sounded from the tavern, and another.

Sen nearly flew out from her chair, but Narva held her back, another round of clicks echoing in her ears. She turned back to the stranger, anger intermingling with fear, as he held the weapon out, as did his rear guard. At some point, one of the patrolmen returned; he merely rested his pole weapon on the ground, staring at the scene with amusement.

"I will ask it plainly," the stranger called through the Linguist, drawing Sen's attention from the continuing ruckus in the tavern. *"Are there two escapees hiding in your village right now?"* There were no more games in his speech, no more beating around the bush. Simultaneously, he maintained the appearance of one both angry and serene, ferocious yet docile.

Sen growled. She could have just said *no*, but instead, she decided to say, "What do they have to escape from? I thought you were looking for your companions."

The man shifted in his seat, the grin returning to his face. He eyed his men, asking softly a question to his returning underling at a volume no one else could hear. The man whispered something in response, to which the stranger offered no visible reaction. He turned to his other man, nudging his head toward the tavern.

The second man walked toward the establishment, pushing the door open with the same unsettling calmness as the other, and finally, the ruckus ceased, punctuated by a final shattering of glass. The two men exited the tavern, rejoining the stranger and the other, as Sen nervously stared at them alongside Narva and the Linguist.

Nodding to each of his men, the stranger bent to the ground and drew a card, the damaged and marked eight that Sen had played a few times previously. Rather than return it to the deck, the stranger stood and took it with him, depositing it to the pocket of his trousers. *"The subtlest of blemishes reveals the greater whole,"* he muttered through the Linguist, to Sen's confusion. He stared at each of them for an uncomfortable moment, fixating slightly on the Linguist, and muttered something beneath his breath. *"Perhaps I have acted too harshly. I must thank you for your hospitality."* With a nod of the head, he turned around, directing his men alongside, the glint of the moonlight bouncing off the shining surface of the tool at his thigh.

Sen watched in silence as the stranger led his small retinue away, back into the darkness, back into nothingness.

As they faded from sight, Sen ran to the doorway of the tavern, the floor littered with shards of glass, and one woman nursing a cracked nose, but beyond that, no harm done. The patrons and bartender looked at her with shock and fear, emotions she was far too stunned herself to experience. Turning back toward Narva and the Linguist, she tried to form words but was entirely bereft of them.

"What..." Narva muttered. "What do we do?"

Furiously, Sen shook her head. "Nothing. It's done. They've left. It's over."

"It's *done*?" Narva pointed out exasperatedly. "You can't possibly expect to believe that that's it."

"It has to be." There was subtle desperation in her voice. *I took care of it. I talked them down, and they left. I handled it...right?* "We can't get hung up on this."

"...What?" Narva looked to the Linguist, who couldn't even bear to look at Sen. Instead, she just walked away, bypassing the tavern and strolling along the dark path leading home. For his part, Narva stepped closer to Sen, grabbing her by the shoulders. "You do realize who those people were, right?"

"I think we *all* do, now."

"Sen, those...*things* they carried," he growled. "I'm pretty sure those are the 'Deatharms' that they were talking about. I...I..."

Sen patted the nervous hand on her shoulder, but immediately Narva pulled back. "They left, Narva. They could have done more, but they didn't. It's...it's over."

Burying his face in his hands, Narva paced back and forth, breathing deep as he looked skyward. "For all our sakes, I hope you're right. But...but this isn't just something we can sweep under the rug. Your father *needs* to know."

Rattled was her breath as she nodded in agreement. It would be stupid of her not to say anything. They stood in silence, staring at one another, trying to find the words necessary for the situation but finding nothing. So, they turned, walking toward their respective homes, away from everything that just transpired.

Sen wallowed in the uneasiness as she slowly traipsed home. A pit formed in her stomach, everything inside threatening to lurch forth onto the ground. She continued to sweat, but as she wiped away the beads from her forehead, she reminded herself, *They left. I took care of it. We don't need to worry anymore.*

But something irked at her still. Turning back toward the pub, she recalled the stranger and his retinue departing the scene. "Weren't there *five* of them...?" she wondered aloud. Awaiting something in the night to come out, she braced herself, but finding nothing amidst the darkness, she shook her head and resumed her return home.

The family hut was starkly quiet, the anxiety of the evening apparently long since quelled. As she wandered through the center room, she rehearsed in her head just what to say to her father. *Sorry, I think the Invaders may have been here and I talked to one of them. But hey! Don't worry! They left!* Something told her that her father may not have been inclined not to worry.

Peering into her parents' bedroom, she saw her mother and father lying peacefully in bed, both of them snoring away. She couldn't bear to wake them up for this. *It can wait*, she thought. *There's nothing to worry about.*

Against the peaceful silence, Sen solemnly and nervously traversed the dark hut and settled into her bed, her siblings deep in sleep as well. She stood quietly, looking to the window, and then back to her bed. *I took care of it. It's over.*

It's over.

CHAPTER SIX

Thunderclap

The Year 1556 Anno Salvatoris
15 Years After the Invasion

Sleep was not going to come easy tonight.

Sen sat at the edge of her bed, staring into the vast nothingness that lay at her feet. Tez had returned and scurried off to bed before Sen had made her way back to the hut, and Brin was still fast asleep, having slept through the entire ordeal in the other room. But Sen? There was too much keeping her up.

It wasn't even the detoxing anymore. Those sweats disappeared some time before. Now they were entirely driven by nerves, an anxiety of the unknown, of what would befall their Tribe in the days to come.

She stared at Brin's sleeping form, a powerful snore erupting from that small frame. *What chance do I even have of being a role model, little brother? I can't take one step forward without taking five back.* She buried her face in her hands in a feeble attempt to mask herself and her tears from the world. If there was one thing that she was accustomed to, it was burying her shame. Usually, that was done with alcohol, but even she could realize how little that would help at this moment.

It was quiet. Outside the hut, the village slept, many unaware of what had transpired outside the tavern not too long ago. Sen had faced none from her father's council on the return home, suggesting that their discussion did not last anywhere near as long as she thought it would have. Her parents were fast asleep, the worries of the sudden appearance of two Haunted runaways apparently doing little to hinder their sleep patterns.

Facing her siblings was one matter. How would Sen begin to even explain what had gone on with that Invader tonight? *I'm on the slimmest of strings with them both. If this blows up in my face, if it blows up on us all, I'm done. I've had enough screw-ups already, but this would be the worst of them all.* Listlessly, her gaze craned to the common room, the remaining embers of the center fire crackling away to sleep. *Even the flames are managing to rest.*

She threw herself backwards, firmly and squarely onto the bed, her eyes peeled to the ceiling, the straw and stone patterns entrancing her, swirling and mixing into intricate shapes that meant nothing to anyone, but they were worth deciphering either way. It was something to do, something to occupy her mind. That was something she desperately needed right now.

That smug bastard's face kept cycling through her memory otherwise. His sickening grin, overconfident demeanor, hateful words hidden beneath a falsely kind face. All of it made her nauseous. He reminded her so much of Fann, but at least Fann was overt in his intentions, saying exactly what he meant, even if his intentions were always dumb as shit. But *this* man, this stranger, this Invader...he was a different breed entirely. *There have always been people who pissed me off, who fought with me just for the sake of it...but he's the first person who's legitimately frightened me.*

Sen readjusted herself, throwing her legs onto the bed, resting her head firmly on her pillow. Tomorrow was going to be a new day. She had to remind herself that. Tomorrow was going to come. Everything would be fine in the morning. She wanted to believe that. She *had* to believe that. When she closed her eyes, the weight of everything came crashing down on her, all the exhaustion and stress and fear and tears. Everything was heavy, and it was all lying on top of her. But for all the fears of what the next day would bring, the sight of Brin at peace put her at ease. Sweet, innocent, kind Brin. The heaviness didn't seem so bad in that moment, and when all the weight was bearing down on her eyes instead, she allowed herself to drift to sleep. A much-needed sleep. A well-deserved sleep.

Which was interrupted by a bang, a crash, and a thunderclap.

Sen shot out from bed, the world a shade darker—it had to have been a couple hours since she drifted off. Whatever that noise was, she wasn't the only one who it roused back to the world of the living.

Though Sen was practically flying out of her bed already, Tez was more cautious and slower to get up, a groggy crankiness visible in her face. "Ugh, isn't it enough to only get woken up once in the night?" she grumbled.

Leaning against the doorframe, still dressed in her dirty casualwear from the past day's activities, Sen dipped her head, stray hairs flowing down her face. She trembled and whimpered, afraid of what the next step was bound to bring.

"Sen?" Tez questioned. "What is it?"

The residual sound of that bang was still carrying through the air, quite possibly the longest and loudest sound Sen had ever heard. She couldn't turn to face her sister, opting instead to eye her from her periphery while shaking her head. "Nothing good," she muttered.

From behind, there was a rustling of sheets. "Tez, I said it was nothing good," Sen repeated. "You should—"

"Sen?" The voice wasn't that of Tez. Sen turned to see Brin at last roused from his sleep. At least there was *something* that could wake him up from a deep sleep. "What was that sound?"

Sen shook her head again, stunned to silence. "Just stay here, Brin," she commanded.

Brin started to lift himself out of his bed, one leg already on the ground. "But, I—"

"*Stay here*," she repeated. Thankfully, her little brother obeyed, slipping his legs back beneath his sheets. Sen closed her eyes, fearful tears welling as she turned herself back around. Tez's presence was looming to her side, a calm hand making its way to her shoulder. "Where are they, Tez?"

"Who?" Tez asked. She had wrapped herself in her sleeping robe, drawstring pulled tight to prevent the front from flying open.

"The escapees. They're not safe."

"You don't mean that's—"

"Where *are* they, Tez?"

"Northern part of the village, close to the mountain path, but, what are you—"

"We have to get them, now." Sen was primed to shoot forward, but Tez immediately held tightly to her sister.

"Have you lost your mind?" Tez hissed. "Come, we'll go together." She turned to grab the ornamental half-spear from the wall above her bed, tucking it under her arm. "Let's move."

With no further objections, Sen and Tez made for the exit, the background noise of their parents rousing from their bed echoing through the empty hut against puzzled objections as they heard their daughters' departure. Into the chilled night air they ran, the biting wind a sharp contrast to the distilled warmth of the hut's interior. There was no time to think about anything else; as soon as they were in the clear, they had to break for that safe house.

But there was no time to react when they were immediately met by an unknown force. A chorus of clicks sounded in unison, and out from the murky darkness stepped a line of men holding those long pole-weapons. Those..."Deatharms." Sen froze in place, gripping Tez's hand firmly as she took in the sight. There were more of these men than she realized there would be. She was mistaken in thinking that there were only five in total. They had to number at least ten that she could see, plus who knows how many more lurking in the shadows, and all of them were pointing Deatharms directly at her.

And out from that throng, that imposing lineup of mystery men, came the stranger from before, dragging behind him a familiar sight, a struggling woman, the Linguist from earlier in the night. As she was thrown to the ground before them, Sen quickly realized the injuries sustained to the woman's face: her nose was bloodied, bruises forming in the bags under her eyes, her lower lip cut, a far cry from the woman who had begrudgingly translated for her just hours prior.

At that moment, Sen's parents burst out from the hut, unadorned and wearing naught but their sleep robes, themselves clearly shocked at the sudden sight of men holding Deatharms against them.

As curious onlookers began to filter out from their homes, forming a tight circle around the scene, Fannalhen pushed in front of his daughters, kneeling before the battered Linguist. "What is the meaning of this?!" he bellowed. "Who are you people?"

The Linguist coughed out ragged breaths, looking up helplessly at Fannalhen. "Please...forgive me, Chief," she whispered.

Fannalhen lifted her chin up by the strength of his hand, shaking his head calmly and serenely. "You've done nothing wrong, Dantalhat," he assured. "You have nothing to apologize for."

"They...they made me..." Dantalhat, the Linguist, muttered. "They made me lead them to you. I..." She broke down in tears, frightened and apologetic. Sen didn't want to think of what they did to her as a means of coercion.

"It's okay, child," Fannalhen said softly. "I am Chief. These are my duties." He stood up, tall and proud, not a shred of fear in that strong face. He puffed his chin out, his stance wide and assured as he stared down the men before him. "I am Fannalhen, Chief of the Stone Tribe!" he called out to the Invaders. "For what purpose have you come? For what *reason* have you viciously assaulted one of our own? For what aim have you seen fit to trespass upon our territory and threaten us?"

The stranger bore down on him with his harsh gaze, that sickening smile returning in force. His eyes flashed toward the whimpering form of Dantalhat on the ground as he stood silent and waiting. The way that smile stretched across his lips, it was disturbing.

The Linguist was refusing to turn her head toward him, and the longer she bided, the deeper the chuckle that rumbled in the back of the stranger's throat.

From behind her father, Sen growled. *He's* enjoying *this show, the sick bastard*, she thought.

The man folded his hands at his waist, maintaining a healthy distance between himself and Fannalhen.

Sen had seen her father charge at men for far less, but this was not a normal situation. It was clear that he knew that. His posture seemed to scream for the opportunity to deck the bastard right in his smug face, but his legs did not cooperate with that desire. Hard as it was, it was for the best. The men behind the stranger were still as statues, barely moving even to breathe, and the looming threat of their Deatharms made them all the more frightening.

Clearing his throat, the stranger continued to stare at Dantalhat, ravishing her whimpering form in the dirt. When she didn't turn to face him, he cleared his throat even louder. Still receiving no response, he turned back to of one his men and nodded.

On cue, one man stood forward, pointed his Deatharm to the sky, and in a loud crash, the air erupted with another thunderclap, smoke billowing out from the end of the weapon.

Dantalhat screamed, burying her face in the dirt.

The gathered crowd stood to motion, ready to rush at these Invaders, but at the first sign of motion, the soldiers fanned out, adopting a new formation, Deatharms pointing into the crowd, stopping them dead in their tracks.

Sen desperately wanted to rush forward, but her mother's grip on her arm prevented her from doing so. Cursing softly under her breath, she threw her head to the side, spitting on the ground in disgust. Fannalhen tensed his shoulders in front of her, growling deeply at the sight of his people being held hostage in such a manner.

As the echoes of the Deatharms faded into the air, the stranger stepped forward and yelled something at Dantalhat in his native tongue. It was loud and harsh, undertones of fury peppering each sound and syllable escaping his lips.

The Linguist rose to her knees, tears streaming down her cheeks, and turned back to face the man. With notable reluctance, she answered in the tongue, what Sen could only assume was a translation that she had been so unwilling to be part of. *What have I done to this woman?* she thought. *How could I do this to her?*

The stranger's eyes flared at Fannalhen. That piercing gaze that so threatened to stare them all dead. There was an eruptive fire in those eyes, a blaze which so dearly wished to engulf everything in sight. But when the Stone Chief refused to back down at the sight, continuing to meet the man's fury with that of his own, the stranger laughed heartily and deeply. Frighteningly so. And when words escaped those lips, suddenly calm and measured, that all-too-familiar biting wind sent shivers up Sen's spine.

Dantalhat was still hesitant to translate, wanting no part of this exchange, but when the stranger's glare pierced her once more, she saw she had no choice. With wide, battered, and terrified eyes, she looked at Fannalhen and, with a nervous stutter, repeated, *"I will be blunt and brief. You have something which belongs to me. Actually, two things which belong to me. I'll have them back now."*

"You have some gall and nerve to enter our village with such claims!" bellowed Fannalhen, waving his arm out to the side. "We do not know of what you speak, but I am willing to wager that you have no proof!"

"Spare me your theatrics and unwarranted pride, Chief," the stranger said through Dantalhat. *"Two of my people! My people! They lay within your keep, and I want them back!"*

"First, you say we have your things, but now that we have your people! One is not the same as the other!"

"They are exactly the same, and you creatures hardly have the right to argue otherwise! I've been kind enough this evening, asking so politely to have my property returned to me, but my kindness has its limits!"

Fannalhen jerked a hand toward Dantalhat's trembling form, still fearfully sobbing between forced interpretations. "Do you call *this* being kind?! Look at her! You'd stoop so low as to call her and us 'creatures' when that's all that you've proven *yourselves* to be?!"

The stranger shook his head with amusement. *"No, that is proof of my loss of patience. I did have a most pleasant exchange earlier this evening, however, with that fierce young lady behind you. You've the same disgusting resemblance. Your daughter, I presume?"*

Sen couldn't bear to look at her father right now. She couldn't handle whatever expression of disappointment he was about to flash at her. Feeling Tez's grip loosen and her mother's removal of her own hand from her, both sucking in dismayed gasps of air, Sen just glared ahead, smoke and steam nearly billowing out from her nostrils in anger. She wasn't even aware of whether or not her father actually turned to look at her. It was beyond her realm of caring at the moment. All she wanted was to see this bastard beneath the dirt.

But it was all the more surprising and comforting when her father answered, "Whatever my daughter said to you, I'm sure it was more than warranted, bastard." Sen smiled.

With a scoff, the stranger put a hand to his chest, feigning incomprehensible offense. *"Hmph, how mighty you all think of yourselves. 'Bastard,' 'animal,' 'creature,' all words with which you've aimed to wound me, as though you see me as your lesser. But I'll allow you this knowledge:"* He took two steps forward, hands still folded at his waist. *"In the Savior's eyes, you're nothing. Nothing until I grant you something. If anything, you should be grateful that I've given those things a purpose, a purpose to which they so desperately need to return. And so, I will say but once more: return them to me."*

Fannalhen took two steps forward of his own, a mountain towering over an anthill. "And *I* will say *this* only once. Our people are not your property. We do not belong to you, and you do not own us. Leave our Land at once."

The stranger smiled with amusement. That fire appeared to quell in his eyes, replaced instead by what resembled a modicum of respect for the Stone Chief. But in that same flash, his brow furrowed, his eyes narrowed, and he grunted with exaggerated disgust. *"Hmph. A shame, really."* In a swift motion, his hand dipped down to his thigh, brandishing the small Deatharm which lay strapped to the outside. As he turned it upward, a flash of light and a puff of smoke simultaneously erupted.

Sen barely heard the thunderclap as her father was knocked backwards, blood spurting out from his right shoulder. The blow sent Fannalhen to a knee, clutching the wound.

Fearful screams burst out in the crowd as Sen rushed first to her father and then set her eyes on the stranger, only for a firm grip to hold her back from behind. Sen could barely muster any words to match her anger, and Fannalhen could only froth with rage as he sucked in the pain.

Relishing in the sight of the village Chief on his knee, the stranger turned his back to them, fishing something out of his pocket and placing it inside the small Deatharm. He turned back around, extending the weapon back toward Fannalhen, holding it out with outstretched arm, turned sideface to his target. *"I must warn you that my next shot will not miss,"* he said. *"Return them to me, now."*

"No!" a voice cried out from behind, meek yet ferocious.

Sen jerked her head backward, breaking free of what was apparently the huntress Sharrabha's grip of all people (when she arrived, Sen had no idea), and locked eyes with Brin.

Her brother still had his Tribal paint adorning his face, none of it coming off in the course of his sleep. He stood defiant and angry, pushing past his siblings and mother, and standing between the path of the stranger's weapon and the target of his father's chest, arms outstretched at his side. "Leave our village, now!"

"Brin, what the *fuck* are you doing?!" Sen hissed at him. "Get back here!"

Much of the gathered crowd was wondering the same, to see timid Brin standing so mercilessly and confidently, a far cry from the boy they had all come to know over the years. Sen felt helpless as the line of rear Deatharms had diverted much of their attention to the action before them, their aim matching that of their leader. Sen wanted nothing more than to burst forward, grab her brother, and get out of there, but the threat of whatever was lodged in her father's shoulder was enough of a deterrent to stop her, beyond the ironclad grip of Sharrabha holding her in place.

"Son, what do you think you're doing?" Fannalhen growled through pained breaths. "Please, get back in the hut."

"No, Father," Brin said, not even turning to face him. "I'm standing up for our village and our people! We all have to right now!" He just about snarled at the stranger, his outstretched hands turning into angry fists. "And we won't allow people like *you* to order us around!"

Murmurs of agreement resonating in the crowd, tentative initially but growing in immediate volume. Many had begun to stomp their feet on the ground, a rhythmic expression of solidarity and tenacity.

The stranger, for his part, appeared impressed and lowered his Deatharm, though he did not go so far as to return it to his thigh holster. He smiled and looked upon Brin with silent regard, saying softly, *"You're a brave one, aren't you, boy?"* After a momentary silence, he craned his head over his shoulder and called out something resembling a command to a handful of his men.

In response, two men stepped forward, one walking toward Brin, another toward the crowd to Sen's left.

Fannalhen turned to Dantalhat, furious spittle spraying from his mouth as one of the men drew closer. "What did he say? Gods, woman, *what did he say?!*"

The Linguist tremored in place, a violent wind carrying through the pathways of the village center.

The stranger displayed a menacing grin stretching from ear to ear, the Deatharm still ready in his hand. His body language was all bravado and self-assurance, not a hint of doubt or questioning visible in his motions. He obviously took great pleasure in watching Dantalhat fumble over her words, in seeing his man approach with violent intent, in witnessing Fannalhen groveling angrily on his knees.

And the greatest of all came as he finally heard the Linguist interpret his words as, *"Take the boy and whoever else. I guess it doesn't matter* who *we come back with, does it?"*

Anger and fear seething through her body, Sen tried to leap forward, breaking free of Sharrabha's grip but finding herself hurled instead into the tight clutches of her sister. Deatharms pointed precisely in her direction as Tez tried to save her from an imminent onslaught, and Sen could only watch in horror as that brief moment of Brin's defiance dissolved into the timid fear that she was so accustomed to seeing from him.

Brin shriveled at the soldier's approach, trying so hard to back away and into the safe arms of his father, but just as Fannalhen reached out, grimacing from the open wound in his shoulder still flowing crimson streams, a fierce hand took Brin by the arm, pulling the boy away with great force.

Sen fought hard against Tez's grip, trying desperately and futilely to release herself and charge after her brother. *"Brin! No! Briiiin!"* she shrieked, her voice reaching inhuman pitches.

Brin tried to fight the man off, pulling against the current and attempting with what strength he had to drag himself back to safety. He called out for his parents and Sen and Tez, frightened tears billowing down his cheeks, exerting every ounce of willpower he had to give himself even the slightest sliver of hope.

The stranger watched with great satisfaction written all over his face at the sight.

Somewhere in the distance, another member of the Stone Tribe was being dragged off, but this sight, *this* horrid, disgusting sight, it put the worst smile on his face. Holding the family in place with an aim of his Deatharm, he flipped the weapon around, holding it by the long shaft, and smacked Brin on the side of the head with it, knocking him out cold.

The boy rested limply against his captor, an ideal time to rush him in the momentary distraction had there not been four people lining up their shots in that direction.

The crowd was in a tremendous furor, the loudest Sen had ever heard the village. Angry cries for vengeance and retribution were drowned out by the desperate few holding people back, fearful of the retaliation facing them should they make any sudden movements.

Slowly, the soldiers began to filter back into the darkness; the two holding the new captives went first, Brin's unconscious form disappearing into the hopeless void.

Sen screamed with rage, clawing at her sister's arms to chase after him, damning the danger. *Godsdamn it! Tez, you fucking idiot! Let me go, let me fucking go!*

The more Sen struggled, the greater the pleasure it seemed the stranger took. His smile was voracious and indulgent, unfeeling and remorseless. The more his men filtered out into the night, the greater the expression grew. He laughed to himself, a self-satisfied aura of accomplishment settling deep. He turned to walk away himself, his work done for all he cared. But something stopped him. He craned his head back toward Fannalhen, who was still clutching at his shoulder, his head lowered in shame.

"Ah, Chief?"

Everyone looked at the stranger with shock as he spoke in their tongue.

"I have learn *some* your words. Your...*ugly* words. And, what did I say?" He looked down at his Deatharm, that smirk returning, the smirk spelling something vicious. "Ah, yes. Next shot won't miss."

The thunderclap was louder than anything Sen had ever heard. The flash of light startled her so much that she did not immediately recognize the spurt of blood bursting from her father's chest.

Fannalhen lurched backwards, the full force of the blow knocking him off his feet and onto his back. There was stillness in the air, nothing beyond the lingering echoes ascending to the stars.

Sen could feel the grip around her loosen, the tension surrounding her turning to nothing. She was free to charge at the bastard, but her legs didn't work. Slowly and fearfully, she turned her head, her whole body shaking. She couldn't hear anything. She could only see her mother and sister cradling her father, her mother yelling for something, or someone. Tez was pressing her hands hard to her father's chest, rivers of red streaming through the gaps in her fingers. When she turned her head to lock eyes with Sen, she shouted something, but Sen couldn't hear it. She saw her sister's lips moving, her eyes puffing and reddening, but nothing besides.

All strength in her legs left her. She certainly didn't feel the ground as she met it. She didn't see the stranger depart into the night under the cover of the chaos he had sown. She didn't hear the gathered Tribespeople explode into a riotous panic at the sight of their Chief struck down. She didn't hear Tez's pleas for her to sit with them for one final moment, the last moment her father would ever endure on this plane of existence.

And, above all else, she didn't hear her mother's anguished, inhuman wail as Fannalhen, great Chief of the Stone Tribe, drew his final breath.

INTERLUDE

TOMORROW, AND TOMORROW, AND TOMORROW

The lecture hall had long since emptied by the time Aritz felt it was time to leave. He stood at the front of the room, arm propped against the presenter's podium, hand stroking the ungroomed whiskers adorning his cheeks. Within those empty seats, the Founder envisioned a crowd of his followers, his proud subjects, all eager and holding on to every word which dropped from his lips. He had a desire to speak in dense volumes, the cavernous depths of the empty hall repeating his words in a perfect echo like all good subjects should. Words of gratitude and reverence, appreciation and admiration, all exuding pomp and sycophancy across their hapless, cookie-cutter faces.

That was what he wanted to envision. That was what he was used to. *That is what I have worked toward all these years, a respect I've so desired and so deserved,* he thought.

But a mind does not always do what a mind should. For as much satisfaction was in his heart at the sheer excitement paid by those who would do so much to kneel at his feet, there was still discontent settling into Aritz's chest. Stretching out into the sea of nothing before him, where the same faces of eager students of proud Ferrandan heritage once sat, a new wave washed ashore. Suddenly, those seeds of assimilation were plucked from the earth, instead replaced by mighty and full-grown oaks of defiance. Where once sat a host of accepting and loyal students now sat a virulent and combative crowd comprised of one face. One angry, disavowed face.

Her face.

That deepening scowl, those fiery eyes, wild and untamed, a noble savage in her own right. *Or, no more "noble" than I remember them*, he thought. Her words played on a loop inside his head, those biting and accusatory words.

A people and culture do not cease to exist simply because your eyes have shut.

Fiery words, discordant words. "Untrue words," Aritz muttered to himself.

He backed away from the podium, leaning his tired body against the chalkboard at the front of the room. Traces of white dust were surely staining the hues of his royal adornments, but it was no bother. By the end of the evening, many would see it as a design choice, and by week's end, many more would be clamoring for the materials to turn it into a clothing line. He was the trendsetter of trendsetters, and he could likely stroll down these streets in naught but his underclothes with shite dripping down his leg, and it would be seen as the new summer style. No, he cared little for all that.

Exhaustion was settling into his old bones. These sea voyages were getting more and more taxing as the years went on. Age and a family were often a well enough excuse not to travel for so long at sea anymore. Granted, there were plenty of perks to being seen as a god amongst mortals, a figure larger than myth, a creation myth in and of itself. This tiny nation was his to do with what he wanted. He relished and ravished that. *I am a myth made real, of course*, he thought.

But little things, little arguments with nobodies like this girl, all reminded him that, at times, Aritz a Mata, Founder of Ferranda and a Lord of the Acrarian Kingdom, was, at the heart of it all, naught but a man. And a man is not immune to his faults, nor impervious to his mistakes. Be that as it may, one thing was clear in Aritz's mind.

"It was no mistake," he muttered. "That culture ceases to exist because I deemed it necessary. My eyes remain open so all others can stay shut."

Despite such assurances, those wild eyes remained unpleased, unsatisfied. In a collective snarl, the audience shook its head, a thousand words of defiance shouting out in silence one more time. Aritz looked upon the imaginary crowd with contempt, so emblematic and companionable with the foe he had so heartily squashed all those years ago. A foe occupying lands that were meant for him and him alone.

But as those faces faded back to nothing, restoring the lecture hall to its once empty state, Aritz was still pleased. He knew he would think on this moment for only an hour more, and then he would never think on it ever again. At the least, it would pop back into his mind only when he was forced to return to this land.

He dusted the chalk dust off from his backside, suddenly deciding that it was not a trend he truly wanted to start. With a deep breath, he ascended the stairs, proffering one final glance at that seat of contention before, at last, departing through the wide-open doorway.

When he turned the corner, the plump Scholar Hernan was waiting with an eager smile, hands folded at his waist. "Savior's breath," Aritz said, startled at the sight.

Hernan had restored that air of superiority that once filled him upon Aritz's arrival in the city, some manner and degree of undue confidence filling his form. Even despite that, he was still dripping with sweat, his face a glistening river of bodily secretion. His silken robes clung to his robust stomach, stains pouring through in dark puddles underlining the crevasses of his chest.

"The act of standing for so long taking a toll on you, Master?" Aritz opined sarcastically.

The thinly veiled jab did little to deter Hernan's obsequious smile. His jowls jiggled and wavered in place as he cleared his throat, a soft cough pooling into a red and damp fist. "Why, my Lord, it would have been rude of me not to await you and escort you back to your manor."

"I'd have not held it against you, were you to be rude for a change," Aritz muttered, passing the Scholar by.

Hernan had to turn and shuffle quickly to keep up, his breath heaving and wheezing to maintain the Founder's pace. "I must offer one thousand apologies and one, my Lord," he panted. "For that nasty business in the lecture."

Aritz shrugged. "There has been nastier business within this city. There *was* a people's war fought here, remember."

"Why, yes, of course, of course. But to call question to your...*magnanimity* and...your...your honor and integrity, it is just...just..."

"As banal and superfluous as your egregious platitudes, Scholar."

Hernan adjusted his collar, shifting the descending V-line of his robes upward to counter the pace at which it dropped. "Ah...yes, quite." He cleared his throat weakly, evidently a point of habit when he felt compelled to offer some piece of grand wisdom, but given how out of breath he already was, it came across instead as a murine squeak. "You must know that is not the standard to which we hold our students at this University! We as a body hold you in the highest esteem and the grandest regard!"

"And the boldest reverence, too, I hope?" Aritz didn't bother turning his gaze toward the Scholar, focusing his line of sight directly ahead through the long corridors of the University, his forceful footsteps echoing through the cleared hallways.

"Yes, of course, of course! Only the boldest, my Lord!"

The Founder rolled his eyes, trying his mightiest to hide his disgust while also tempted to proffer the deepest scowl to drive the pest away. *This man cannot earnestly be the Master Scholar, can he?* The corridor seemed longer upon exit than it did on entry. The light at the end of the tunnel loomed further and further away, and the longer the Scholar remained by his side, the greater he felt the need to reach that light.

"Rest assured, my Lord," Hernan continued. "As soon as we find that miscreant child, she will be punished thusly and righteously!"

"As soon as you find her?" Aritz questioned, raising an eyebrow at the wording of the assertion. "Is there not a register of every student at this University? I believe that was my stipulation upon its establishment."

"And we have followed that stipulation accordingly, I assure you!" The Scholar actually seemed offended at the reminder. That sycophantic grin vanished for the briefest of moments, flashes of disbelief and anger visible in that portly expression. "Per our admission guidelines, each student has provided their familial lines and backgrounds and their ports of origin, on top of the rigorous interview process through which they must undergo! We have followed your instructions to the letter!"

"...But?"

Hernan sighed, subtle defeat audible in the tone. "But…I've no idea who this student is."

"Then surely you must not have met her?"

"That class has been unchanged for the length of the semester, over two months past now. I assure you—I have never seen that student before today."

At that, Aritz finally averted his gaze toward Hernan. "Are you sure none of your peers are familiar with that girl? Or have you grown senile and paranoid with your age?"

"Senile?!" Hernan scoffed. "My Lord, you are fifteen years my senior!"

"And you would call *me* senile in such a manner, then?"

"N-n-no, I would never!"

Ah, there's the blathering idiot once more, Aritz thought. *How I missed him.*

"I speak only as a means of caution! We care for your safety and your legacy, and it would behoove us all if you—"

"I think I've faced greater challenges than a dissenting twenty-year-old girl," Aritz interrupted. "I believe I'll be fine."

"But, my Lord! At the least, permit me to escort you back to your manor. Your safety is tantamount and paramount!"

"This must be the most dangerous University student ever to have existed if my fate is in *your* pudgy little hands, Scholar." The Founder centered his gaze back on the path ahead, that light finally growing closer and closer.

Curious gazes popped out of occupied lecture halls as the discussion echoed through the corridor. Eager whispers ruminated from the engaged students, all trying to sneak a peek at the rumored arrival of their great Lord. Seeing a legend in the flesh for even the briefest of moments was the highlight of their lives.

Dull and thankless though they are, Aritz pondered.

"But, my—"

"I assure *you*, Master Herban," Aritz asserted, stopping dead in his tracks. The need and desire to leave this man's presence were growing more and more outweighed by the need and desire to shut him up. "I have faced greater dangers whilst relieving myself in the privy than *you* will ever endure in your meager existence. While you sat to grow fat off the riches and wealth of our nation, I was sowing the seeds upon which you've grown fat. While you asserted your own importance learning of the achievements of greater men, I was the man upon whom those achievements were written. It is not I for whom fear tolls; it is fear for whom *I* toll. Do you understand?"

Hernan stuttered and stammered, his face pouring sweat in torrents. He stroked his thick, meaty fingers through his glistening strands of scattered hair, the waterfall of sweat dammed and diverted into a separate stream. "M-m-my Lord, I—"

"*Do you* understand?" Aritz repeated.

Nervously and vigorously, Hernan nodded, the drops of sweat splashing every which way. He was too rattled to turn loose any further pompous adulations.

Aritz grinned, his brow deeply furrowed, his glare deep-set with malice. "Good," he whispered, drawing just as much fear out of the Scholar with a single word as he had with his entire commanding rebuke. "I will return to my manor, and I will away on the morrow. I anticipate this being my final journey to Ferranda."

There was shock and despair flooding Hernan's eyes and something else flooding his trousers. "B-but? My Lord? Do you abandon us?"

"Abandon? Hardly." Confidently, Aritz brushed the notion aside with his hand. "The fact of the matter is I am aged, and I've a family. I would rather spend my waning years in warmth and comfort, surrounded by luxury and companionship, than I would in sycophantic squalor, surrounded by men of false ambition and low cunning." He stood tall over the Scholar, the man nearly crumbling in fear as rivers welled in his eyes, the salt of his tears intermingling with the salt of his sweat. "And I anticipate this being our final interaction. Instruct the future of our nation well, on this day, and tomorrow, and tomorrow, and tomorrow. All the more reason for me not to have to return here."

Wanting not for a response either riddled with meaningless platitudes or cursed with nervous station, Aritz turned on his heel and at last approached the light leading out into the city. He could have sworn the final sounds he heard of the University was the soft weeping of a weak man. *Aw, I must have broken the poor bastard*, he thought. *What a shame.*

Strolling through the streets of Ferrand City held little of the same appreciation and regard as it had on the way to the University. Aritz was tired, irritated, and above all else, was merely looking forward to going home.

Citizens and passersby may as well have gawked and swooned at the sight of him sternly walking the lonely roads, the precipices of industry an auditory backdrop to their excitement. Two decades ago, that would have meant something to him. Nowadays, it was just noise. Noise interrupting his ideal soundless world. He had no need for reminders of his importance to this nation. When he looked out into the throng of people eager to make even the briefest of acquaintances, he didn't see the civilized, developed world he so ardently crafted in his own image. He saw a gaggle of apes, hooting and hollering for station far above what they were capable or deserving of. He saw a people in desperation for the chance to be equals when they did not know how they could achieve such a goal.

There was no mistaking that his was the face of a nation. The statue adorning the University's courtyard was merely one example of this. As he continued by his lonesome along the cobbled walkways, his gaze spanning from the southern coast peeking out from behind the realms of industry to the grand forest standing tall along the northern horizon. Banners flew proudly, some bearing his house's personal coat of arms, others a stylistic rendering of his facial contours. Storefronts bore his name, at least three competing breadmakers battling for the name of "Founder's Bakery." At least eight regional dishes were named in his honor, some variant of "Aritz" or "Mata" included in the name, all screamed into the faces of passersby by street hawkers hoping to peddle enough food to afford to live another week. Even the priory bore more of his likeness than that of the Savior. His image was carved into the vast majority of the stained-glass windows, a reminder unto all of just how important Aritz was to their way of life.

That was not necessarily by their will in the early years.

A tired smile creased Aritz's lips as he, at last, returned to the manor, a palace all unto itself. It was the very emblem of extravagance, a diamond standing tall atop a pile of dung. The premises of the manor had expanded over the years, stretching further and further outward and overtaking more and more of what was already a relatively small city. A stone walkway led to the manor doors, elaborate and intricate shrubberies flanking him on either side along the path. Through the wide slats of the front gate, a crowd of gawkers watched intently as his backside drifted further and further from their view, a final tease of heavenly royalty disappearing from sight.

Amidst the rabid calls and desperate pleas beckoning him from further and further away, Aritz exchanged an exhausted nod with his doorman, a capable-looking lad who wanted nothing beyond an exchange of pleasantries before opening the door. *Thank the Savior*, he thought. The manor's interior blocked out the raucous volume, acting as both a sanctuary and fortress in keeping the undesirables away. As the years went on, the definition of "undesirables" had become broader and broader.

Heavy footsteps echoed atop painted marble flooring as Aritz ascended the regal stairway to his chambers. Serving and cleaning staff stopped what they were doing, some nearly dropping pails filled with water just to bow in reverence. *What a lonely existence*, he pondered. *Surrounded by dozens too fearful to speak.* When he refused to look down upon his staff, opting instead to wave his hand off to the side in a dismissive manner, a hushed murmur rumbled from one side of the room, deep-set with worry and panic. Aritz could not hear distinctly what they were saying, but all signs pointed towards it being fraught with fear of reprisal. Just as soon as he flashed a stoic glance down at them did they scatter like rats. As they did so, he turned his attention back to his ascension, grinning to himself all the while.

An unfazed doorman stood outside his chamber, his expression dignified and calm. Aritz respected that. It was refreshing to see someone not blubbering or fawning over him. "Good afternoon," he said, no hint of disdain in his voice whatsoever.

The doorman nodded. "Good afternoon, my Lord."

"Only one of you today? I believe normally there are to be two."

"There's another," the doorman agreed. "He just had to, well, 'relieve' himself for a moment."

Aritz shrugged. "Can't fault a man for that. I'd be remiss to deny one his bodily needs."

"Some needs are more...an urge, if I may be frank."

"Ah." Aritz turned and peered over the parapet, down toward the throng of staff hard at work below. "To be young with the manor to yourself and your parents are not home. I remember those days."

The doorman was noncommittal, sternness and stoicism remaining in his chiseled jawline and piercing blue eyes, a flintlock pistol resting along his outer thigh. His deep olive skin had benefited from the summer's sun.

Aritz found it strange that he desired to carry on a conversation with the man, one-sided though it may be. *Perhaps* this *is what it's like for those with whom I've no desire to speak. What a wonder to experience it for myself.* "I'm impressed at the diligence to which you all keep my manor. Each time I return to Ferranda, my home only grows in extravagance."

"I'd not know of the specifics, my Lord," the doorman shrugged. "I only guard the doors."

"Hmm, yes, quite so. Well, you've done a marvelous job of it."

"Thank you, my Lord."

"I wonder, is there some convening of council to determine the expansion of my estate? I recall my property being only half the size when last I was here five years ago."

The man retained his deadpan and disinterested expression, offering only a shrug and a twitch of the lip. "If there's a council, I'm not part of it, my Lord."

Aritz smiled one of genuine pleasure as opposed to the mocking pedantry he was so accustomed to. "I'm sure you must be curious of the thought process, sir."

"I'm just a doorman, my Lord. I only guard the doors."

The bluntness of the man's words thoroughly amused Aritz. "What's your name, son?" he asked.

The doorman was silent for a moment, staring off into nothing. But eventually, he blinked, returning to reality, and nodded to the Founder. "I am called Nic, my Lord."

"Nic," Aritz repeated with a smile. "You need not guard my door this day. I will make do on my own."

The first modicum of emotion, at last, broke through the man's stern expression, if only for a moment. "My Lord," he said, emotionless returning. "I must advise against that."

"Your concern for my safety is endearing, Nic," Aritz said. "But I am departing on the morrow, and I do not envision any difficulties this evening."

"On the morrow, you say?" Nic asked, his interest slightly piqued. "Gone as soon as you've arrived."

"Just so. Do look after the place in my absence. I envision this my final evening in Ferranda."

Truthfully, Aritz expected some manner of groveling or sniveling at the admission, but Nic kept his stone face, not breaking his façade for even a moment's breath. He grunted in acknowledgment and nodded, accepting the news with the complete opposite reaction of that blubbering mass of blubber called the Master Scholar. "You will be missed, my Lord," Nic assured. And that was that.

Aritz grinned and firmly patted the man's shoulder, reaffirming, "I will be okay for an evening. Take a page from your partner's book and indulge those...urges. The door will still be here on the morrow."

Nic said nothing more. He just nodded and walked away, his heavy footsteps thumping down the marble stairway. *What a fascinating individual,* Aritz thought. *If only I had met him sooner.*

Retreating to his chambers was a tremendous reward for the time he had to spend mingling among the commonfolk. The world out there, it was privy only to the history of which they were taught, the history as dictated by a noble victor. But inside Aritz's chamber, inside this vast expanse of memories, this *was* the history.

From end to end, each item and material represented a trophy, each trophy a memory. His bed was immediately enticing as the afternoon sun reached its peak, but first, he needed a reminder of ages past before he was to leave this realm behind forever. Intently, he focused on an elaborate shelf, each unit housing something unique and special. An enchanting breeze rolled in from an opened window, the curtains drifting along playfully against a shadowed corner, a blind spot where the light from the sun drew did not reach. The breeze felt delightful, invigorating, as he propped his hands atop the bottom shelf.

Photographs in black and white stood in golden frames, crafted from ore deriving of the Northern Mountains. It was a new art, this idea of photography, one that Aritz was initially dismissive of when first introduced to it, but he warmed up to the idea rather quickly. The capture of a memory, and a manner of which he did not cry foul towards, was immediately appealing to him. Some three decades after he was introduced to the concept and he was still unclear on how the process even worked, it being brought to the island by an eager bright mind from back in Acraria.

He smiled as he examined the individual photographs. One depicted Ferrand City in its infancy, housing a mere quarter of the homes and industry to which it was home today. The smile widened at the memory of one of his greatest hunting trips, an enormous felled beast strung out behind him, the wagon in which it was returned to the city nearly collapsing under its weight. To this day, Aritz still could scarcely believe that he defeated the beast, but the knowledge made him feel no less a god compared to those around him. Faces long since gone, faces of only fleeting acquaintance, lifelong companions and bitter rivals. All of them a story to tell, all of them a tale to remember.

All the more reason Aritz held on to that final picture at the end. Himself with a fierce female companion, fury and cunning in her eyes. A woman he trusted, and a woman who betrayed him. He shook his head, hers the only bitter memory he had of those years.

Trophies littered the upper shelves, each a victory and a conquest in the telling. He took great pride first in that half-spear he won off of a foe, besting them in swift and brutal combat. Ornate and beautiful ores lined the top shelf, each an initial excavation of those early years scouring the Mountains for materials. He still had no idea of the purpose of the mask he found once; he'd never seen any wearing them as he recalled, but it was an interesting find in a tucked-away settlement, nonetheless. So many treasures, so many stories. But none the greater than his favorite...

"Huh," Aritz grunted aloud. Perplexed, his eyes stared down at an empty stand, once displaying an ornate flintlock pistol. A priceless treasure, one with which he crushed a rebellion. Trophies were trophies, but *this* was sentiment. "Could have sworn it was here earlier," he muttered. "Now, where could it have...."

With confusion, his eyes scoured the floor, thinking initially that some loose rattling elsewhere may have knocked it loose from the stand. There was nothing beneath the shelving unit, nothing underneath the war table. *Surely, it couldn't have sprouted legs and walked off on its own accord. How odd.*

Aritz was ready to call for a doorman that he had already dismissed when the fluttering breeze called attention to another matter out of place. Crinkling in his ear came the sound of a paper nearly aloft in an updraft, its flowing folds calling to him from the direction of his desk. Scrunching his brow, he cautiously approached the desk, his fingers carefully drifting along the strong wood. Flicking away some odd necklace that was acting as a paperweight, his eyes focused on a handwritten letter, no pomp surrounding it. Just a basic note scribed on basic parchment. *Perhaps it was unwise to dismiss that lad*, he thought.

As he slowly picked up the letter to read, the wind intensified, a howling sea breeze roaring at his back, each item in his chamber seeming to prance and scream along with the wind. He focused his eyes and read on.

It is convenient what one would be led to believe, is it not? Memory is truly a fickle thing. Perhaps in your years, you truly have forgotten. Perhaps you merely choose not to remember. A shame either way. Others have not the capacity to remember because they have not been granted the proper events with which to remember. That is a shame, too. Indeed, it would be shameful were all to know upon what their nation was built, to what their heritage amounts. To see that whom they revere as a god is naught but a man, or perhaps a lesser being than even that. A monster. A demon. A disease. Perhaps the final label is most applicable. A disease which felled a land. You may think yourself of a higher power, but there are still those who know the truth. There are those who remember. We remember the worst of it all. We remember the Harvest. Do you? Perhaps that which has been left for you will help you remember. Memory need not be a fickle thing.

He dropped the letter to the ground, stunned to such a degree that the thousand questions that should have ruminated in his mind failed to do so. Questions that should have included the subject of how someone even managed to enter his chambers unimpeded and a host of other questions deriving from that. His gaze averted to the door, so near yet so far.

Words are merely words, empty threats to one such as I. Something so unsubstantiated and baseless has no power over me. Whoever left this letter, they have nothing.

But still. The Harvest. *A term I haven't heard in a long time.* Something spread so deeply through the black market of thought, something so ridiculous that people wanted to believe it simply for the absurdity of it.

A letter meant nothing to him. But those final words hung in his mind. Something that had been left for him…What was it? Hands on hips, he scanned his desk, spotting nothing out of the ordinary initially. Just a mess of scattered papers that had been blown about by the wind, writing implements stored in various fashions…but what about that paperweight? He reached for it, grabbing it by a long chain that hung slack from its body. He picked it up, holding it at eye level, and as he drew in its shape, a simple circular body of simpler stone, figures more ornate and intricate began to jump out at him. As he inspected the markings, his eyes widened in recognition as he realized just what it was he was holding. A pendant. A relic from an age long gone.

And these markings, he wondered. *So familiar.* A rune he became more and more acquainted with as the years of establishment went on. A circle entrapping another circle, the center of the piece marked by a punctuating dot.

Memory. How fickle, indeed.

CHAPTER SEVEN

The Mourning After

The Year 1556 Anno Salvatoris
15 Years After the Invasion

She should have felt something beyond a purgatorial nothingness. Every bone and muscle should have ached, first from the strain of being held as though she was feral and ambling to kill, and then from the shredding of every fiber of her being upon the sight of a river of red. But no longer.

There should have been sound. Not the void of heavy air bearing down upon her nor the vacuum of noise surrounding her. Such a short time ago, every whimper and shout, every breath ragged and full, they rang so clearly in her ears. But no longer.

There should have been a lingering acridity on her tongue, the residue of her stomach's contents deposited onto the ground before her. So desperately had she wanted to vacate her soul from her body, carry herself along on with the wind, to fly away, far away. But instead, her stomach had other ideas. Maybe that was all her soul was at the end of the day, bile and vomit upon bloodstained dirt. The intermingling of her soul and the earth below should still have danced on her tongue. But no longer.

There should have been the residual stench of burning finding its way into her nostrils. That horrid, devilish plume dancing through the air in retched victory, taunting her with a vengeful smile as it threw forth an instrument of death. The advent of burning flesh should still have screamed through her. But no longer.

There should have been the image of a happy family, a loving husband and wife, parents who gave everything and more to three happy children. A party of five basking together as an orange sun glowed to the west, illuminating the mountain peaks in gold as it whispered its daily goodbye. Proud parents resting gently against children of strength ursine, cunning lupine, and wisdom strigine. But it was a vision of impossibilities, a dream that forever lingered. But no longer.

The only vision that held truth was that of a fallen warrior, a grieving widow, and a mourning daughter, a picture holding no place for children of error or weakness.

Sen wanted so desperately for that vision to be false. Time had slowed. Her mother's head craned skyward in an elongated fashion, the muscles in her neck flexing and straining as she bellowed to the heavens, a roar befitting a bear. Tez was shaking their father's motionless body back and forth, doing her utmost to will life back into it as red eruptions burst from his chest in intermittent spurts. Beyond what was right in front of her, the entire Tribe could have been rioting, crying, or standing still.

Sen couldn't see anything past that bloody sight.

She reached out helplessly, her body failing her as tears blindly streamed down her face. The world began to make sound again in muted volumes, the white noise clouding Sen's ears quickly evaporating. She became more aware of Tez's erratic pleas, words formed indistinctly into an indecipherable tongue. Her mother had used up every ounce of strength in her voice as her bestial roar faded into a shocked whimper. And as time restored to its natural state, Sen was suddenly cognizant of her own actions and reactions, finally hearing for the first time the grinding of her teeth, the pained attempts at sobbed breath, the near-rabid frothing at her mouth as she pushed herself to her knees with all the strength she had.

Tez turned to face her, all color drained from her normally assured and collected expression. Smears of blood were splattered across her face, matching the red puffiness of her eyes. With shaking hands, she reached out to her sister, Sen's fingertips caressing those of Tez as she was slowly pulled forward in a tight grip, her sister throwing her arms around her in a tight embrace. Sen could barely move. Not for the strength at which Tez held her, but for the sight of her father, lifeless and bloodied. She looked down at him for the first time, her heart swelling as her sister's sobs echoed in her ears. Hardly was she aware of her mother kneeling at her father's head, her expression much the same as her own. All else beyond Fannalhen's form was a blur.

Streams of blood had flowed from the corners of his mouth, carving little red paths down his cheeks and onto the dirt below. A crimson puddle pooled and expanded beneath him, the river from his chest still flowing downstream.

When at last Sen broke free of Tez's grasp, she didn't even take a shuffle-step forward. All she remembered was pushing her sister away and collapsing onto her father's stomach, clawing manically at anything for purchase. Perhaps it was the adrenaline, or perhaps it was just a return of strength. But Sen felt a renewed vigor as she gripped the threads of Fannalhen's bloodsoaked robe, pulling it toward her, lifting her father's heavy body up ever so slightly.

His eyes still lay open in shock, his dark brown eyes once a twilit sunset and now a sun gone to rest. Coughed sobs exited Sen's throat as the tears flowed down her cheeks in earnest, her entire body heaving up and down as it mourned along with her. Her voice returned to her in a soft squeak at first, a sequence of sounds resembling those of a mouse. She let him down gently, kicking up loose dirt as she pushed herself forward to hold his head in her hands, fingers running through those thick locks of proud Stone hair. Soft squeaks became dense whimpers, and dense whimpers became full-bodied wails.

"No..." she managed to say at last, the emotion barring the necessary words before they could reach her tongue. "Please, no. Father..." She gripped his head tighter, touching his forehead with her own, skull knocking against skull as the full motion of her cries carried her to and fro. The salt of her tears mixed with the blood spattering her father's cheeks, a sanguine river becoming a crimson ocean. "Daddy, please. I'm sorry. Please, no, no, no, no, *no, no, no!*" Her body turned fetal, head resting against the warm flow of his chest, the side of her face and hair soaking in it. *It's my fault. All of it,* she thought. *This blood is because of me. I may as well soak in it.*

Nuzzling against Fannalhen's breast, Sen's tired eyes closed. Fleeting images passed of a flight atop burly shoulders, a bear teaching its cub to roar, to stand mighty and strong. Chapters of a hero, saving his proverbial damsel from dangers resultant of the damsel. Pictures of an assured and sympathetic hand offering a guiding light in both the lightest and darkest of times. A hand that no longer could stand as that same beacon.

A shudder rippled through Sen's body as she opened her eyes again. From this angle, her father and Brin looked so alike. And at the recognition, a second shuddering wave tore her soul. *Oh, Brin,* she thought. *Godsdamn it all, Brin! Why couldn't I...it's all my fault. Both of you!* In her head, Brin was reaching out to her, calling in a panic for her, specifically. The further she extended her own arm, the further his drifted away. And where his face was at first deep-set with panic and fear, it became more and more accepting the farther away from her he became. Almost as though that's what he wanted. Almost as though that's what she deserved.

Her eyes snapped open, densely aware of her surroundings. A cautious crowd approached, led by the familiar faces of the Tribal council, faces all strewn in shock. "I won't let them see you," Sen muttered to the corpse. "It's not real. None of this is real. I won't let them make it real." Absently, she rested her hand atop her father's abdomen, positioning her head on his chest as though it were a pillow. "Do you remember when you'd let me lay like this? After you'd let me run myself ragged out in the Heart? Back when things were so simple. Before I had to think about anything other than being a child. Please, take me back. I want to go back." She clenched her eyes, the rivers threatening to flow once more. "Please, take me back to when I didn't curse you and Brin to your deaths!"

A presence loomed behind her, though whether it was her mother or Tez, she couldn't be sure. Whoever it was, they placed hands atop both her shoulders, resting their head on Sen's back, wordlessly staying in place, just existing, breathing, supporting. A second set of hands appeared before her, holding tight to her own, and when Sen craned her gaze upwards, she locked eyes with her mother, trying her hardest to force a reassuring smile but failing entirely. Dennalhir lay herself prone, gripping her daughter's hands tightly as she rested atop her fallen husband. In that warm familial embrace,

Sen managed to lose herself, a calming warmth against an impending dark. In that warmth, she could feel a third set of hands holding her tightly. A family come together in parts.

The momentary peace could only last so long, though, as Sen's attention was drawn to a presence emerging from the dark, drawn at last to the commotion. At first, it was a shadowy blur, something incorporeal descending to a physical plane. But as the dim light of nearby torch fire illuminated that dark corner, the shapes became more defined, bearing resemblance closer to a human. One body became two, and as cautious steps carried them forward, the finer details of their faces became clearer. A woman and a boy, complexion darker than Sen's, hair still ragged and clothes still tattered.

The runaways.

Suddenly, those self-defeating feelings of worthlessness inside Sen's heart disappeared. While she bathed and basked in her dead father's blood, there was a greater trouble standing before her. A greater reason. She lifted her head, viscous crimson stuck to her face as though she had devoured her father's heart. The sight of her struck greater fear in the runaways' eyes. *Good,* Sen thought. *You* should *be afraid of me. I am* the Curseborn, after all.

Shrugging herself free of the pairs of arms and hands engulfing her, Sen rose to her feet, and with a ferocity she didn't even know she had, she sprang forth, faster than she had ever run before. Right for the Haunted. The boy barely knew what to do; he settled for huddling behind the woman's legs. Which was a poor place to hide as Sen rushed the woman by the throat up against the outer wall of the nearest hut, nearly dragging the boy along with them.

From the force of the impact, the hut could very well have been brought down. The foundation wavered as the woman was driven nearly through the wall itself, the mixture of straw, wood, and stone unable to withstand the brunt.

Sen snarled as she held her grip tightly around the runaway's throat, the woman's face turning a deep red as she futilely attempted to pry herself loose. At that moment more beast than woman, Sen breathed heavily through her nose, fumes of rage burning the ground beneath her. Cries of protest vaguely rang out from behind, but she didn't care. All that mattered to her was that these two understood what they had done. "*You...*" Sen growled. "It's all *your* fault! If you hadn't come here..." Angry tears mixed with the blood, her grip shaking as the Haunted woman's eyes grew heavy. "It's all because of you! *You* did this! *You* killed my father! *You* kidnapped Brin! It's—all—fucking—*YOU!*" In punctuation for each word, Sen didn't even recognize that she was slamming the woman's head against the wall. Not enough to break or damage, but still enough for the attempts at prying became more frantic from both the woman and the boy.

Sen heard her name being called out from behind but paid it no heed. Even when it drew closer, it mattered little to her. Only when hands stronger than hers pried her loose and turned her around did she recognize her mother's calming presence, her firm hands gripping her shoulders, holding her in place.

"Sen," Dennalhir repeated. Despite the despair in her eyes, there also was a solemn stoicism, an assertive command needless of words that only a mother could master.

Her body not in control of itself, Sen crumbled to the ground, no longer drawing her awareness to the frightened duo behind her. She curled into a ball, every inch of her shaking. Her eyes remained drawn to the dirt, unable to lock eyes with her mother.

"Sen," Dennalhir said again. "Look at me."

Assertedly, Sen shook her head. "No. I can't."

Pushing her daughter's chin up with the lift of a finger, Dennalhir offered a slight, reassuring smile. Her eyes were dim in the pale darkness, but Sen could still see the earnestness dwelling within them. "You *can* look at me," her mother affirmed. "Look at me, not at them."

"M...Mother..." Sen blubbered, averting all manner of eye contact entirely. She wanted to turn away, face no one, but her mother would not allow it.

"This is not *their* fault," Dennalhir continued, gesturing her head to the two runaways. "We cannot put the blame on them. I want you to know that, and I want you to understand that."

Sen shuddered and managed a nod, whimpering soft curses to herself as emotion continued to well in her chest. "But—but...them coming here—"

"Has nothing to do with what has happened tonight." From the look on her face, it didn't appear that Dennalhir believed that herself. There was a tentativeness, a hesitation in her words. Anger and vengeance roared in her eyes, too, but the subtle twinge of her face...maybe she just didn't know *what* to believe.

"But if they hadn't come here, then...then... then...!"

Their foreheads met, a conciliatory gesture, Dennalhir running her firm and warm fingers through Sen's hair. "Listen to me, Sennalhat," she asserted. "Yes, maybe their coming here brought the Invaders here. But that does *not* mean that it is their fault. They are not the ones responsible for the position they're in."

Sen breathed deeply. *If it's not* their *fault*, she thought, *then we all know whose it truly is.* She shuddered again, fingernails soaked with blood and mud as they dug into the palms of her hands. So heavy were her eyes that she could not draw them up to meet her mother's when she started to say, "You're right. It's not their fault. We all know it's—"

"*Not you.*"

Confused, Sen looked up, the stoicism and assuredness still ripe in her mother's eyes. Her head was being held in place, no escape one direction or the other as her soul was thoroughly examined by that piercing gaze.

"We know who is at fault. We know who to blame. And the only ones responsible for the situation those two escaped from..." She drew deeply as she prepared to say the next few words. "For your father and brother...It's those Invaders. The only ones deserving of your anger...are them."

Sen traced her mother's eyes for any shade of untruth, doubt, foreboding. But she found none. There was only honesty and earnestness in those pools, and for a brief moment, she allowed the weight of those burdens of blame to be lifted and retreated to the images of that small bear cub carried atop shoulders of brawn.

She barely remembered weeping like a baby in her mother's arms.

The shadow of the Heart loomed over the Stone village in the morning after. At the base of the mountain range, it appeared that the entire Tribe had gathered.

The mountains standing tall like a watchful protector, Sen knelt and placed the first in a set of stones atop the cairn acting as her father's grave. It was as custom dictated. One born of the Stone Tribe was born of stone itself, and when one passed, they were returned to the stone. Some Tribal folklore claimed that the Heart itself was comprised of generations upon generations upon generations of cairns and that the Keepers were guarding not only the realm to the Animal Deities but also to the souls of the lost.

Sen wasn't so sure about all of that, but, as the youngest family member present, she had the honor of laying the first stone, drawn from the trails of the mountain ranges themselves. Her knees dug into the soft patch of loose dirt under which Fannalhen lay, a sacred plot near the foot of the mountains reserved for the Chiefs who have watched over the Tribe since time immemorial. She ran her fingers across the soil, her skin still dyed with shades of red, letting the patches of earth trickle through the creases. After allowing herself a long moment, sharing a final idea of presence with the first man who cared for her, who accepted her, who loved her, and placed her stone firmly in the dirt where she guessed his heart was resting underneath.

Tez approached from behind, stone in hand, her eyes puffy and hair unkempt. She rested her hand on Sen's shoulder, embracing her tightly when she could not bring herself back to her feet. The two sisters stared listlessly at the blank patch of soil, now bearing two stones. The wind gentled them, a cradle in a treetop swaying calmly and harmoniously. Nature was silent save for bestial echoes from deep within the mountains. It was the mourning after, and nature itself shared in their grief.

Neither could stand on their own and when their mother knelt beside them and placed her stone beside theirs, the three women spoke in silence, words uttered only in the clasp of hands and the flow of tears. There was a patient crowd behind them, sniveling noses and shuddering sobs ringing in unison, all holding stones to lay upon the plot in respect. But if these were to be the final seconds, minutes, or hours that they would spend with Fannalhen, they wanted them to last in perpetuity. Whether it was indeed seconds or hours that passed, none of them could say for certain.

But when at last they rose to their feet, still linked together at the hands, they parted a final tear to the earth, a drop of life from which more could hope to bloom, and stole themselves away to the side, wordlessly nodding to those at the front of the queue to step forward.

One by one, Tribespeople in various states of mourning approached the plot, each stacking their offerings in short order while simultaneously offering words of condolences to the grieving family. After a while, the faces all began to blend underneath paints of red and blue and yellow. But even as the faces Sen *could* differentiate passed, she was hardly in sorts to acknowledge them beyond any shred of appreciation just for showing up. She was grateful to Tawa and Narva for being among the first to queue, but she could manage a smile to neither of them. Rantalha and Sharrabha promised any assistance they could muster as they walked by, but Sen was in no position to accept that. Grafhar exchanged grieving nods, but Sen was in no shape to try and draw words out of him. Koelhe and Fannadhan managed not to look smug for once, but Sen couldn't find it in her heart to tell them to piss off regardless. Even the Sun Chief Han'e offered his respects, but she didn't know what sort of retaliatory battle she'd be drawn into if she humored him with a conversation.

Hours passed, the sun at high noon by the time everyone had a chance to place their offering upon the plot. By procession's end, the pile of stones stood near as tall as Sen. Ensuring that all had their chance to say their peace and make their offerings, Sen, Tez, and Dennalhir retreated for a moment, drawing the final stones from the mountain path, and crowning the top of the cairn, sealing the contents underneath. The custom was completed as it was meant to be, begun and finished by the family. The body of the great Stone Chief Fannalhen rested somewhere beneath this mound of carved earth, returned to the stone from which he was born. Such was the way of things.

The three embraced in a somber circle, words unneeded, tears all that were necessary. They looked at one another, then at the cairn, then back at each other, uncertainty painting their complexions, but a faint trace of hope lingered in Sen's heart amidst the anger and anguish. *One of us is lost*, she thought. *But another can yet still be found.*

The gathering fell to a hushed silence, all attention drawn to the family. Parting words were customary on the part of the grieving parties, though memorials typically numbered in the dozens rather than the hundreds or thousands which had assembled for Fannalhen. It was looking less a eulogy and more a sermon.

Dennalhir broke first from the huddle, wiping persistent tears from her eyes. Sen continued to hold on to Tez, but her gaze was affixed to her mother. *To be able to stand in front of everyone now, like this...I forget sometimes that she was just as strong and brave as he was.*

Clearing her throat amidst the silence, her mother looked first to the cairn, then to the skies, then to the crowd. She spoke in soft tones, audible only to those first couple dense rows, but she was confident her words would make it through the throngs. "My husband...your Chief...I can't even begin to describe to you what this loss feels like," she began. "He was a man destined from the moment of birth to undertake his role, and he performed it with bravery, with honor, with respect, and with dignity. His was a tenure that saw the drastic change of who we are as a collective people and how we dignify ourselves when faced with the adversity of our fellows. He was a man who always saw the value in raising a hand of peace more than a hand of war, and yet he fought as a bear when the need arose." She paused to take a breath.

Sen parsed through the first few rows of people, seeing familiar faces against unfamiliar, a dry eye a scarcity in the crowd.

"Most, if not all, of you have known Fannalhen for the great Chief he was. Not so many were fortunate to know him for the great man he was. The great husband he was. The great father he was, as my daughters will surely attest." She turned to face Sen and Tez, eyes rife with emotion, lip quivering, the shells of burden encompassing her as Sen quickly realized how hard her next words were about to be. "As would my son, if he was with us today."

Diverting the rivers from her eyes, Dennalhir retreated behind the cairn, placing her shaking hands atop it, whispering something soft and heartfelt and indecipherable to the body beneath.

A deep pit formed in Sen's stomach. She had to release Tez from her grasp to take a step back and breathe. There was one other she needed to hold onto, and right now, she couldn't.

Tez stepped forward next, the waterfalls having diverted merely to a soft-flowing stream instead. Sen could not remember ever seeing her sister for anything other than the fierce warrior she was. Sometimes, it was easy to forget that there was a real, feeling person beneath that tough exterior.

"I don't know what I can say to follow up on what my mother has said already," Tez said, her voice shaking at intermittent intervals. She forced a smile and a chuckle, taking her own words in good humor. "What more can I say about the man who helped raise me into the woman I am today? Who helped raise three wildly different children and turn them into three wonderful adults upstanding and upholding our people's way of life?" As though she could feel Sen being taken aback at being included in that grouping, Tez turned and smiled, managing a wink at her younger sister. "He was a chief, a father, a warrior, a confidant, a sage, a mentor, and a friend, all of those just to me. I can't even begin to think what he was to all of you. And...I...it's hard." She averted her gaze, turning her back to the crowd. Burying her face in her hands, Tez's entire body heaved and shuddered as the rivers overflowed through the slits of her fingers. Messily, she wiped them away, her cheeks glistening and damp, and managed to say over her shoulder, "I don't know what any of us are going to do without him." After that, she couldn't summon any further words and sought comfort in her mother's arms.

The crowd awaited Sen's words next, and as she took in the sight, she had to take a handful of steps backward to prepare herself. *For four years, almost all of these people would refuse to give me the time of day,* she thought. *Now, here they are, awaiting my word. Or they're merely feigning interest in what I would say. But they're still not looking at me with hate or disgust just the same...*From the corner of her eye, she could see her mother and sister offer her encouraging smiles, nudging her onward with a tilt of the head. Sen calmed herself and stepped forward, maintaining her gaze on the cairn. Something stopped her as she neared the front of it, some invisible wall impeding the onward march.

Deep within that soil, she could feel her father's presence. She could envision him, but not as the heroic, comforting, commanding, and diligent man she knew he was. All she could see instead was the image of him falling to the earth, like a tree bereft of a steady base, the crimson trail following him down in a crescent arc. The clap of thunder rang in her ears again and again while arbor collapsed to earth again and again. The louder the thunder became, the clearer it grew that the falling body did not bear her father's face. There were stark similarities, but often that can indeed be said of the commonalities between father and son. Each crash of thunder brought with it a distinctly different cry for help, but all sharing the same thread: Brin's voice. The Deatharms roared in her ears one by one, red explosions fouling the air at each interval, Brin's face contorting and decaying with each blow until nothing remained but a battered and tenderized husk. A shell with an enormous shadow looming over it. One so close in appearance to herself.

Sen gasped and backed away, muttering *No* to herself a few times. She blinked a few times, refocusing her gaze on the anxious and eager crowd now turned perplexed and impatient. Tez and Dennalhir immediately realized something was amiss and rushed to her side, holding her hands in place as tremors engulfed her limbs. Sen forced her eyes to stay open for fear of repeating whatever it was she just saw. Her breathing intensified, growing more ragged and unstable, hyperventilating as one final thunderclap rang in her ears. It took all the effort in her body not to scream right then and there. "I-I-I can't," she whispered to herself. "I can't..."

"It's okay, Sen," spoke her mother softly, pressing Sen's head onto her shoulder and running her fingers through her thick hair. "You don't have to say anything. It's okay. Your father knew exactly how you felt about him."

Smothering herself against the warmth of her mother's shirt, Sen tried to hide away from the crowd, the embarrassment...but most importantly, the noise now far away. Distant echoes still hummed in her head, but as long as she maintained eye contact with her mother, those nightmarish images would fade away. Her mother would protect her. She—

"Of course, she can't manage to say anything at all," a voice muttered from within the crowd, spoken softly but still loud enough to hear. "She knows she's to blame, so what's the point in humoring us?"

Sen's nostrils flared at the familiar voice. Her head flung around, her eyes a furious haze of welled tears and rageful smoke.

Koelhe pushed her way to the front of the crowd, apparently deciding to return to her hateful self while still in the midst of a memorial.

"What did you say?" Sen growled.

The wrinkles on Koelhe's face danced with arrogance and antipathy, her grin sinister. "I think any here among us would know first to blame you before anyone else. Your father and brother would still be here if not for you."

"How dare you!" Tez screamed, spinning around with tremendous force, forgetting that she still held Sen at the hand. "You have no right to say that!"

"No?" Koelhe scoffed, apathetically stretching her arms above her head. "Did she not tell you of her little card game with the Invaders?"

"A card game?" Tez responded with amusement and annoyance. "So, Sen played cards and probably won. What's your point? She's done that with just about everyone in the Tribe and beyond."

Everyone except this *bitch*, Sen added in her head. *Still waiting for that day.*

"Don't play dumb. I've heard *all* about how she goaded and mocked the Invaders to their faces and probably cheated them as she always does. Or how she had the audacity to call them filthy animals, foul creatures, insolent inbreds. Or that she challenged them right then and there! Does that not ring any bells at all?"

"No, it doesn't," Sen yelled back. "Because none of it happened, you miserable piece of trash!"

"Then you deny what that poor beaten Linguist sang to us, how the demon spawn of the Stone Tribe brought horrors to our doors and laughed while doing so?"

"I don't know *what* the hell that woman was selling, but I can tell you bought it off her and are trying to sell less for more!"

"So, you still deny it, then?"

"Deny what? Complete lies?" Everything was a watery blur before Sen, her tears engulfing everything. "Are you that hateful that you would even try to pin my father's murder, my brother's capture, on *me*?!"

Another body pushed its way to the forefront, arms crossed beneath another arrogant face. "You *are* Curseborn, after all," Fann said with his ugly, gap-toothed smile. "Ill fates would follow you around no matter what you do."

"Hold your tongue," Dennalhir growled, pushing her away past her daughters, "before I rip it out myself."

"Are we speaking too much in the way of truth, Dennalhir?" Fann asked spitefully. "Or must I pay a price if I say what you are too far gone to hear?"

"You'll pay a price if you continue to mock me and my family's name, you and your mother both!" Sen was still shuddering and wished she could draw some of her mother's Courage. Dennalhir's eyes burst with flame, her pendant glimmering in red beneath her shirt.

"We're so frightened," Koelhe said sarcastically, rolling her eyes. "You don't have your husband to protect you anymore."

"I never needed him to protect me."

"How heartwarming," Fann sneered. "But he got what he deserved, and the same will fall on you soon enough."

Dennalhir took two large steps forward, Tez not far behind.

Sen stayed back, already shaken enough by her vision. *And just when I had knocked loose the self-blame, these assholes shove it right back.* Angry tears flowed down her face as her fists shook in place.

"Do you want to repeat that?" her mother snarled, within spitting distance of the two.

A sinister smile creased Fann's lip. He shrugged, smugness deep-set in his complexion, so irremovable from every pore of him. "It's his own fault. And yours. Letting that disgusting *Curseborn*—" He emphasized the word with disgust. "—stay within our village. She should have been banished a long time ago. If it were anyone other than the Chief's precious daughter, they would have been thrown to the Forest for that Tribe of savages to devour. But she was born into such wealth and privilege that she can spend half her days drunk and the other half insulting our very culture, and it was all enabled by *you* and your *dead husband!* And it's so satisfying to know that after all of that, it was *her* that got him killed. What a delicious bit of—"

That speech had gone on for too long. A merciful duo jumped at Fann and knocked him to the ground. Not content with merely shutting him up, one of the saviors took it upon himself to give him the beating of a lifetime, wailing away at the bastard's face. When Sen cleared her eyes of the tears, she realized it was Narva and Tawa who provided the welcomed interruption, and it was Narva who saw fit to paint Fann's face in shades of black and purple.

"Get off him!" Koelhe screamed. "You savages, get off—"

There was no need for Koelhe's speech either. Dennalhir immediately walked up and punched the hateful woman in the nose, dropping her to the ground in a single heap.

A halted murmur became a chaotic shout amidst the crowd, hundreds trying to push forth to see just what the commotion was, the noble front lines holding those behind them back out of respect. Narva landed a few more punches on Fann's face before Tawa pulled him up and dusted him off, cleaning the blood from his knuckles with a clean cloth. Even after that thrashing, Fann—somehow—had the strength to return to his feet, screaming ferocious nothings at those present in bestial tones, blood pouring from a shattered nose, a handful of tooth chips spurting from his mouth. He was immediately surrounded by Tez, Narva, and Dennalhir, and as much as Sen wanted to join in...

She looked at her father's cairn, solemn and silent, dignified and honorable. *This isn't what he would want. As much as he hated them, and rightly so...he wouldn't want this. And especially not here.*

It wasn't in her to join the ranks. She pushed past the commotion, paying little heed to the voiced objections from her sister, burrowing deep into the crowd. Away from those bastards. Away from a necessary fight. Away from her family and close relations.

And away from her father. For the last time.

Hours had passed before Sen had received any further company. She had retreated to the family hut. Calling it anything other than the Chief's hut was strange to her, but, well, there was no longer a Chief. At least, at the moment, there was not. It stood to reason that her mother would take up the reins at least in the interim, but it was typically a role that would pass to the son. But in the absence of Brin? Well...that's where it would get tricky.

Sen sat at the edge of her bed, face buried in her hands. For hours, she did nothing but stare at Brin's empty bed, examining every inch of it. The crumpled sheets that he had abandoned the night previous, the bodily indent that had grown in the mattress over eighteen years of sleeping in the same position, the potent aroma that smelled so distinctly of him. *You should still be here, Brin,* she thought. *This isn't fair.*

That vision continued to play over and over in her head. Volley after volley of death fell into his chest, his face growing more and more accepting of his fate. But she couldn't shake what was the most disturbing part. Herself as a shadow looming over it all. Why was she there? Was she pulling the trigger? Was she always a part of him by virtue of being his shadow? Was this her curse, just to be a shadow offering only death? She wondered if she was her father's own dark shadow. Whether curse or coincidence, she felt a chill at the similar manners of death.

She clenched her eyes as the thunderclaps continued to scream in her mind. Each clap brought deeper tears to her eyes, each impact taking a little bit more out of herself. Each repetition of Brin's growing apathy at meeting his end tearing more and more from her heart.

"*Gods,*" she gasped, the act of breathing painful. She ran her face through her hands, the pits of her eyes stretching against the friction with her fingers. "What am I gonna do? How can I...damn it."

Her head dipped, the floor enough of an entrancing sight and distraction that she barely noticed she finally had company again.

"Hey," Tez's voice said. "You missed out on a hell of a fight."

Sen looked up and saw Tez casually leaning against the doorframe. There were cuts and blemishes on her sister's face and arms, but nothing too serious. It was never anything too serious with Tez. She *hmphed* and shrugged. "Do you really think Father would have wanted us to fight like that at his godsdamned memorial?"

"I don't think you realize how willing he was to come to blows with others when it came to you."

That didn't exactly cheer Sen up. "Glad to know I was the one thing that drove him to violence without fail."

"That's not what I meant. He would never hesitate to come to your defense whenever someone would say…well, you know." Tez pushed herself off the frame and walked over to the bed, sitting herself down beside her sister. "I hope you know all of us—myself, Mother, even Narva and Tawa—we all feel the same. You saw it out there. For all the Koelhes and Fanns in this village, there are twice as many who would stand up to fight for you. I hope you know that and understand that."

Sen sighed deeply and loudly. "It sounds more like pity to me to need so many to come to my aid. Like I can't exist in this Tribe without a certain amount of validation from elsewhere."

"Sen, you know that's not—"

"What's even going to happen to me now that Father's gone?" Sen looked fiercely at her sister, her eyes heavy and puffy and red from anger and grief. "As much of a dick he is, Fann's right. I had the fortune of being the daughter of a Chief whose say was the final. If I was born any lesser, I'd probably have been thrown into a river right from birth."

"You don't know that, Sen. Plenty of—"

"You don't know *that*, Tez! Before I was born, when was the last Eclipse? Four hundred years ago? Are there any multi-centenarians around for you to ask what it was like for them?"

Tez was silent, her eyes pensive and considering. She folded her hands in front of her, her thumbs twiddling back and forth in quiet thought. "You know that Mother's not going to let anything happen to you. Nothing will change."

"Forgive me if I'm not exactly brimming with confidence," Sen frowned. "Where is she, anyway?"

Shrugging, Tez couldn't help but chuckle to herself. "Ah, cleanup, I guess you could say. We did make a bit of a mess out there." When Sen didn't reciprocate the laughter, Tez reached out, grabbing her sister's hand firmly. "Then she called an impromptu council. I believe they chose Tawa and Narva's hut out of respect for everything going on."

"A council? For what?"

"Tribal affairs still go on. Nothing out of the ordinary, I'd assume." She forced Sen to look at her, unwilling though she was. "Hey. Everything is going to be fine."

Sen forced a short smile but then returned her gaze to Brin's empty bed. There was something so hypnotic and enticing about that bundle of stuffing and feathers. She had watched her little brother grow from a timid boy to a less-timid man, but an intelligent and curious one all the while. For him not to be there anymore, it was...unthinkable.

The two sisters sat in silent regard of one another for a few minutes, accompanied only by each other's presence. A draft of wind drifted in through the significant dent Sen had forced into the outer walls the night previous when she nearly threw Shara into next week. The chill prickled Sen's skin as she scrunched her shoulders together for warmth. The ward hanging above Brin's pillow danced in place, no longer finding its intended use in deterring nightmares. If it wasn't stopping Sen's vision, then maybe it didn't work well at all.

"You're going to go after him, aren't you?"

The suddenness of the question surprised Sen, her eyes widening with shock and her breath catching in her chest as she turned to face her sister. There was no humor in her face, no apprehension in her eyes, no ticks or twitches to indicate doubt. She just continued to stare dead ahead, entranced by the empty bed by which Sen herself had been so entranced.

Tez shrugged and chuckled softly to herself. "Since I came back, you've done nothing but stare at his bed. If I didn't know you any better...I'd say you were considering doing something rash."

In a quick manner so as to not draw forth the visions, Sen closed her eyes and managed a smile. She hadn't intended to be so transparent, but the last few days had not exactly left her at her best. Memories of Brin, so carefree and happy, tried their hardest to come back to the forefront of her mind, fleeting only in short bursts.

"There are some days that I think they all have a point," Sen admitted. "That perhaps I *should* have been cast away a long time ago."

Her sister's head snapped toward her so quickly she thought it might fly off her neck. "I told you, Sen. That will never happen—"

"But the thing is, maybe they're right. Maybe I *was* left with a curse. Or maybe I wasn't. I don't know. I could be cursed, or I could just be recklessly impulsive. Or it could just be both, and they dangerously coexist. But let's say that I *am* cursed. That doesn't mean that I can't make things right. It doesn't mean I can't do anything good for this Tribe. Whether they'll accept what I do or not, it doesn't matter. I need to do what *I* think will make things right. And that starts with Brin."

"You're serious, then. You've thought this through."

"What I've thought is that I'm leaving by day's end. And I'm not coming back until I've brought our little brother back home where he belongs." She rose to her feet, pulling her hand away from Tez's, and chanced a final look at Brin's bed before she made for the door.

"Where are you off to now, though?" Tez asked.

"Well, I need to know where it is I'm going. Heard there're a couple people in town who might know."

CHAPTER EIGHT

CHRYSALIS

THE YEAR 1556 ANNO SALVATORIS
15 YEARS AFTER THE INVASION

The safehouse was a particularly unassuming hut. Calling it a safehouse at all had always struck Sen as odd. There had never been a time before now when she saw a need to label it as such, but times were changing, and they were strange times indeed.

Made of the same composition of stone and straw as was typical of Stone Tribe architecture, it sat in the shadow of the Heart, the mountains' looming stature bearing the appearance of a fortress ready to rain down fury against those who would cause harm.

The mountain breeze flushed against Sen's face, her braid freely flowing with its gusts. Her skin prickled as the bite sent a chill through her. As she walked along the beaten path leading to the hut, she folded her arms, rubbing them vigorously for some added warmth. She couldn't help but wonder how these refugee southerners were coping with the drastic change in weather. She had never been down south, or even to the northern ridge of the Forest for that matter, but all she knew for sure was that it was much more comfortable than being beneath a mountain range.

Of course, much more was on her mind than how these two were coping with the weather. *Are they enjoying their freedom? Are they enjoying more what it cost us to give it to them?* She had to bite her tongue before she was even within spitting distance of the hut. There was one thing she needed: information.

And she wasn't going to get it by nearly throwing that woman through a wall again. *Probably. I didn't get too far with it the last time.*

The village was tremendously quiet for a Tribe that had just watched a memorial turn to a brawl. As Sen looked over her shoulder, eyes narrowing as the mountain breeze blew into them, she could not hear a soul stirring. It was as though the entire village had either disappeared or collectively decided to take a nap. She had hoped to hear even one echo of a toast to a fallen hero, but there wasn't even that. Be it mourning for a Chief or shame for what a memorial became, this degree of silence was unsettling. But it just made for all the more confidence that no one would find it odd that Sen was walking out this way, out to have another conversation with someone that she had nearly throttled to death the night previous.

She should have felt nervous or apprehensive, but she was perfectly fine. When Sen approached the door to the hut-turned-sudden-safehouse, she didn't feel much at all. The time for sorrow, mourning, and anger had passed on this day. All that cared to flow through her body now was a drive to find and return her brother to where he belonged. And it was here that she would find her answers.

With a light rap of her knuckles, Sen tapped the door to the hut but waited only for the sound of internal movement before she opened it. The speed at which she threw the door ajar clearly startled the two Haunted refugees. They didn't appear to recognize the person who burst into the home initially. They held each other tightly, concern and fear strewn across their faces, the boy burying his face into the woman's chest. It was only when their line of sight became clear, realizing just who it was who stood beneath the threshold, that the woman backed away more carefully, her free hand reaching behind, feeling for how much purchase she had remaining before she'd be bereft of places to run. As Sen examined her more closely, she didn't realize just what a number she had done to her the night before. A prominent bruise was visible upon the woman's throat, a discoloration of grey and blue that still managed to shine through against her darker skin. Her arm was stiff and rigid, surely from the brunt of the impact with the outer wall she was nearly thrown through. There was even some dried blood on her arm and neck. It was apparent that no one had offered fresh and clean water with which she could tidy herself.

"Didn't realize just how strong I was," Sen quipped, realizing quickly that it was not the time to joke while this refugee was cowering just at the sight of her.

Sen held up her hands in a gesture that tried to say, *I'm not going to hurt you, even though we're a day removed from when I nearly choked you to death*, but for one reason or another, it was not a particularly convincing display.

Both of the Haunted continued to back away, the woman more afeared than the boy.

"I only want information," Sen assured, approaching them cautiously as she would a deer. "Just tell me what I want to know, and I'll be out of your hair."

The two runaways stared at her blankly, fear and distrust visible in their eyes but in a manner that was intermingled with confusion.

Sen continued to take slow steps forward. "Hey, it's okay. I'm sorry for what happened last night, truly. I know it might be a bit hard to trust me right now, but I'm not here to hurt you."

Still, they remained silent, save for confused and concerned grunts.

"Your names were Shara and...and Ran, right?" She tried to express a warm smile, though it felt forced. She could only wonder how forced it actually *looked*. "My name is Sen, okay? You can call me Sen." With a nod, she outstretched her hand, offering peace with the same hand that nearly dealt death the night before. She cared little for the irony. "It's okay. I'm not here to hurt you."

Shara opened her mouth to say something but then closed it and shook her head, continuing to hold the young Ran up against her. She shrugged as words failed to escape her lips.

And that's when it hit Sen. "Ah, *gods*," she cursed. "I forgot you don't know our Words." She grunted to herself, grimacing with the act, the friendliness she had once exhibited now home to visible frustration. Shara continued to look at Sen with consternation, but the Stone woman cared little. "I *knew* there was something I was forgetting. No Linguist worth their salt is going to pal around with me anytime soon. Shit, what the hell am I going to do? How am I even…" Her self-mutterings devolved into something less resemblant of words and more so of inane tongues and babblings akin to a language a child would create for themselves. She paced around the room, back and forth, fists clenching and arms throwing, frustrated with herself.

"I…uh…I?"

The voice startled her. Sen peered back to her side, seeing Ran wide-eyed and curious, pushing himself out of Shara's grip.

"I…uh? I know Words of some," Ran said haltingly, his grasp of the tongue evidently loose at best.

Excitedly, Sen jumped forward, the frustration on her face turning so quickly to elation that it was enough to draw concern from the two Haunted. She just about sprinted towards them, sliding on the ground as she skidded to a halt. Dust and dirt kicked up in her wake, a sudden windstorm following her with every quick step.

Shara looked ready to jump through the wall and just do the job for Sen, but Ran stood firm, even though he looked ready to cry.

"You can understand me?" she said, her voice rising in tone.

Ran stuttered while attempting to find the words to say, so he settled instead for nodding assuredly.

Sen smiled, trying to put both of them at ease with little success. Neither appeared particularly trusting of her intentions. *Which is fair,* she thought. Still, she had some degree of care for their well-being now that she was gone from the heat of the moment. Her eyes drew toward Shara, nearly at the far wall as she hesitantly took more and more steps backward. "How is she doing?" Sen asked Ran, not breaking eye contact with the fearful woman.

Ran looked at his companion, tilting his head one way and another, trying to gauge her current demeanor beyond what Sen could discern for herself. "She is fear," he managed to say.

"Fear?" Sen asked.

"She fear of you," he clarified. "We *both* fear of you."

"Well, that goes without saying."

"She almost was lost one."

"Lost one?"

"Dead," Ran said, meeting eyes with Sen. "She almost dead from you."

Sen stared at Shara, who was raising her uninjured arm to her throat, massaging the tender area with her fingers. Noticeably, she winced and grimaced at her own touch, a raspy and heavy wheeze rumbling from deep within her windpipe. Her eyes watered from the discomfort, strain visible on her face just from the act of breathing.

Lowering her head, Sen averted her gaze to the ground, shameful of what happened to Shara by her own hand. "You have my deepest apologies," she said. "My father and brother were taken from us so quickly, and I...I wrongfully placed the blame on both of you. I know nothing will take back what I did in my blind anger, but I hope you can accept my apology."

Ran stared at her blankly, perhaps not fully following her train of thought. He silently blinked before at last saying, "Your father. Your father Chief?"

Sen furrowed her brow, a slight frown creasing her lips, and she nodded. "Uh, yes. There was more I was addressing there, but...yes. Fannalhen is—well, *was* my father."

"Chief good man. Let us stay here. Sorry for dead."

"Ah, yes, I appreciate the sentiment, but I am also just trying to—"

"Why you here?" Ran asked bluntly. "Why you come?"

Taken aback by the sudden question, Sen cleared her throat and nodded her head. She could already tell that the boy was finished with the conversation and wanted little else to do with her. *He's just like Brin.* She traced a directionless line in the ground with her fingers, biting her lower lip as frustration settled into her chest. "It was not just my father who was taken from us. My younger brother was captured by the Invaders, too." *In lieu of both of you*, she wanted to add but thought against it.

"Yes," Ran said. "Why talk to us?"

"Because I need information."

The boy paused, narrowing his gaze at Sen. "In...for...?" He was puzzled by the unfamiliar word.

"I need to know what you know. About where Brin—about where my *brother*—is being taken to. Where you and Shara escaped from."

"Where we...?"

"The slave camp Shara mentioned last night, yes." Sen's expression grew grim, her eyes hiding in the shadows cast where the day's light did not reach.

"If my brother is being taken there, I need to know everything I can about it. Please."

Ran appeared hesitant. The memory of the place clearly weighed hard on him. At the mere recollection, his hands started shaking, his expression growing more pallid. He gritted his teeth and flexed his shoulders, the words heavy enough on his tongue but the experience of it clearly massive within his mind. He shook his head and closed his eyes, managing to squeak out, "Bad place."

Sen carefully approached, kneeling as Ran squatted to the ground, arms wrapped around his legs. "Please. Everything and anything that you can tell me. I'm going to bring my brother back, but I need to know what I'm dealing with here."

The boy looked up, no longer scared but instead confused. "How you bring him back?" he asked. "How you do this?"

"I'll come up with a plan. I have to. I don't have a choice."

"If you go," Ran warned, "you not go back here."

"I'll take my chances. Now, please. Just tell me." Without realizing, Sen had placed a comforting hand on Ran's shoulder. Her only indication that she had done so was Shara's immediate reaction to rush forward and defend the boy, but she quickly relented.

With a deep sigh, Ran looked up at Sen and nodded. "The thieves of Land came. I small boy then. They take our Land, our Tribe Land. Many are lost. Big huts build on our Land."

"The Invaders, they put their slaves in big huts?" Sen asked.

Ran shook his head. "No. Big huts are for them. For thieves. They live in them. Big huts cover all the land along water. They take Arrow Land, too. Many huts, big huts. They live in them. Yes?"

Sen leaned forward, concentrating intently on Ran's loose grasp of the language. "The Invaders have built a large settlement...a big village for themselves?"

The boy nodded and continued. "No Tribes walk in big village. Thieves call village 'City.' They walk in City, Tribe do not. Big big hut in middle of City where thief Chief live. Tribe live close to big big hut."

A big big hut. That would give Sen a landmark to look out for. "Can you describe this hut? So I know what to look for? If the camp is nearby, then knowing what it looks like will help."

Ran frowned and concentrated but came up empty on the words necessary for proper description. He sat himself down, his legs growing tired from the prolonged crouch, and breathed deeply. "Big. Big big. Like mountain. Biggest in City, bigger than you know."

"Easy enough to find then," Sen said confidently. "And the slave camp? What can you tell me about that?"

"Bad place. You can't go."

"I can and I will. Please."

A wave of frustration and concern overcame the boy as though he wanted so desperately to dissuade Sen of the notion but knew not the words to say so except in his own tongue. Reluctant, he relented. "Tribe kept in chain. Chained at feet. We not walk anywhere. We fed bad food. Only no chain when thieves make Tribe work. We build big huts. When Tribe lost, thieves not care. Many Tribe in chain."

"And my brother will be kept there?"

"You not go there," Ran asserted. "Thieves watch camp, watch Tribe. They have Deatharms. They kill if you go there."

Sen was unconcerned. "I'll find a way. I know where to go and what I'm looking for. The rest, I'll work out as I go along."

Flustered, the boy stuttered and stammered over words in his own tongue interspersed with those of the common Tribal tongue, incredulous at Sen's blind confidence. He raised his hands up in confusion, his brow furrowing.

When Sen realized that he wasn't going to form the necessary words easily, she gripped his shoulder more firmly and forced a smile. "I understand your concern, but there's no talking me out of it. I'm doing this. And one way or another, I'm coming back." She rose to her feet, meeting the equally incredulous and fearful eyes of the Haunted runaways, and nodded to them both. Standing tall over them both, she felt akin to the mountains which stood tall over the safehouse, but she was no one's mountain. She knew that and accepted that. *Sometimes, though,* she thought, *an anthill could substitute for a mountain.*

She made for the door but arced her head over her shoulder once more. "I wish I could offer you both something in return," she said softly. "In return for your help. But I have nothing to offer but my apologies once again. For what they're worth." She opened the door and walked along the silent path back home.

▼

The good thing about deciding to live sufficiently was that she did not have much to pack up for her journey south.

Throwing together a travel pack, Sen only packed up a couple changes of clothing and not much else. She had no weapon to pack for she was not granted one, no pendant to stow away for she did not earn one. Much of her life was jammed into this hide pack, and part of the remainder was being forced to travel south. Soon enough, she'd ensure that he'd be coming back north.

She passed a final glance at her bed with the patchwork covering the holes in the wall, and then to Brin's bed, still indented with his small form. She nodded to herself with self-assurance, intent on returning soon. Not just intent. *Guaranteeing* that she would return soon. As she threw the strap of her travel back diagonally along her shoulder, Sen took a deep breath and whispered, "Okay. Let's do this."

When she turned around, she did not expect her mother to be standing beneath the threshold.

"Going somewhere?" Dennalhir asked sternly.

Countless times over the years, Sen had been quite poor at sneaking out of, or into, the hut, unaware of the levels of noise she would create. There were several occasions where she thought she was acting sly and sneaking out of the hut without alarm, most typically to see the few friends she had growing up, a number that became in shorter and shorter supply as the years went on. Half the time, she'd be stopped by one of her parents on the way out. The other half of the time, she'd be cornered on her way back in. In those moments, she'd try to weasel her way out of trouble, attempting to come up with a believable story on the spot and typically failing miserably. When that pit in her stomach formed, there was no telling what nonsensical tale would come to her in a panic.

But not this time, she resolved. There was no pit, no panic, and no reason to lie. She knew what she was doing. She didn't care who knew what she was doing. And there was no talking her way out of it. "I'm going to get Brin back," Sen said confidently.

Dennalhir raised her eyebrows, her arms crossed. A slight twinge of concern flashed across her lips, but her no-nonsense expression was much more dominant. "And if I was not here to stop you, you would be fine with following Brin to your own death?"

Sen frowned. "You don't think I can get him back, then, huh?"

"It's not a matter of whether I *think* you can get him back," Dennalhir said. "It's whether you *should*. And on your own at that."

"So, your solution is just to leave it alone and let Brin die down there?" Sen opined incredulously. "You'd rather he toil and rot away than have someone bring him back?"

"That's not what I'm saying at all!" The concern flashed more prominently this time, steam nearly pouring out from her nose. "But if you go down there, there's no guarantee that you're making it back up. I've already lost your father and one child in the past day, and I'm not losing another!"

"You're not going to lose me, Mother, and you're not losing Brin, either. I'm getting him back!"

"Those Invaders have who-knows-how-many Deatharms at their disposal, an army that held back an entire Tribe with a clap of thunder, and you think that you alone can do this? How can you be so sure that you won't be lost yourself?"

Cold sweats began to pool along Sen's spine, the chills prickling the skin of her forearms. "Because I know what I can do, myself, and I know I'll be successful," she said with less assurance.

"But how do you *know*?" Dennalhir repeated, placing more biting emphasis on her words.

"Because I don't have a choice!" Sen admitted, throwing her arms in the air. Her lip quivered as she turned her head up and around the room, trying not to let her mother see the frustrated and angry tears welling in her eyes. "Because it's me who has to make this right. No one else. Me."

Dennalhir dipped and shook her head, massaging her fingers along the bridge of her nose. "Sen, what are you talking about? This is not a burden that you need to bear on your own."

Sitting back down on the edge of her bed, Sen stared ahead at Brin's bedding, wishing so desperately that his lazy bones were back in that pile of feathers already, a book strewn across his chest, streams of drool flowing down from the corners of his mouth. *His pillow still has some of the residue from his face paint,* she thought. *He was so excited to wear it that he never wanted to take it off.* The idea of failure was not one she considered lightly, nor was it one that she wanted to consider at all.

"Koelhe and Fann spoke truly, you know," Sen muttered.

"I doubt it," Denna said plainly. "They rarely do."

Sen shook her head. "I was wrapped into that dumb card game with that Invader—the one who killed Father. I didn't have a choice, and maybe for the brief moment that I lost myself in the game, I somehow made things worse. And me being the stupid person I am, I assumed that somehow, *I,* of all people, convinced them to up and leave without any further questions. I could have said something before...everything. But I didn't. And now Father is dead for it, and I...I..." She trailed off, burying her face in her shaking hands.

Her mother was quiet for a few seconds but then joined Sen on the bed. Resting a warm hand on Sen's knee, Dennalhir shook her head, clearly doing her best to reassure her daughter. "I've told you, Sen," she said. "I've told you several times already. This was *not* your fault, and it never will be. The likes of Koelhe and Fann and all of their ilk, they have too much blind hatred in their hearts to ever be able to see a clear and full picture. This...situation. What happened with your father and brother...it would have happened regardless. The moment those two runaways wound up in our village was the moment we consigned ourselves to the consequences. We all knew that. We all anticipated that. We just didn't think the consequences would arrive so soon."

Despite the words, Sen continued to frown, her hands folded in on one another, her thumbs twitching against each other. "Blind hatred or not, there are still going to be those who will blame me for their arrival just on the basis that I'm still alive and still in this village."

"Sen, there is no reason for—"

"Yes, there's no reason for me to blame myself and none for those who would wish to blame me, either, yet the blame is still placed!" Her eyes were wide with emotion, her deep pools of brown shimmering with flickers of red fury and passion. "You don't understand, Mother. Really, you don't. You and Father gave me a life that any child would be deserving of, and I have always counted myself lucky for that. But because of my birth, because of the *curse* that I've been so unluckily stuck with...you can't deny that I am the root of the blame just based off of that. Any stroke of misfortune upon this Tribe, upon this village, it's never the fault of anyone but the Curseborn."

She had expected the words to ring hollow to a parent's devotion to their child, but Dennalhir sat there quietly listening, nodding in acknowledgment, regret and sadness visible on her face. "You know your father and I had done our best to do right by you. We tried to hide that from everyone as much as we could because we wanted to ensure that they saw you for the kind and warm person that we know you are, rather than the cursed child that they want you to be."

"Then Koelhe ruined those plans, huh?" Sen forced a chuckle and grin, the thought of that hateful woman sending shudders through her spine.

Nodding, Dennalhir scoffed and grinned. "I must admit, it was rather satisfying to knock her flat off her feet. I've wanted to do that for over twenty years now."

Finding herself unable to smile at that, Sen let it happen before allowing her prior emotions to return. "But, see, ever since then, I've been seen as something less than human. A pariah of some sort. When you're a child, the words don't mean much to you, but as you grow older and words and demeanors start to add up together, it becomes painfully more obvious that you're seen as something different. That's how it was for me. And as much as you and Father tried to pretend to the contrary, I knew it was true. I knew you were just trying to protect me. But when the truth was finally confirmed, and I knew that I was just living a lie, it almost felt a justification of everything that the criers of 'Curseborn' had said of me.

"And that's no fault of yours. But any time I act in even the slightest of error, it's an affirmation of what they want to be true about me. I'm tired of being looked at like a pariah, but there's never been anything I could do about it. And it was easier to just get lost in a stupor instead of facing those issues head-on. It never felt like I could do anything to rid myself of the label. But now, I have that opportunity. It'd only be a sliver of a good thing in the eyes of the village in the grand scheme of things, but if it helps at all, I must take that chance. If there's one good thing I can ever do with my life for the good of the village, it would be to find Brin and bring him home. That's why I have to do this, and that's why I cannot fail."

They were both silent for some time. When Sen looked at her mother, she could see in her eyes that she recognized it was pointless trying to talk her out of it. Gripping her daughter's knee more firmly, Dennalhir sighed, the maintaining of eye contact growing more difficult for her. "I'd be lying if I said that this does not frighten me, Sen."

"I know."

"But I learned long ago that sometimes, I just need to let these scenes play out as you wish them. I know I can't stop you. I can only ask that you come home to me safe. I want my babies home, all of them."

"And you'll have them all home before you know it, Mother." Sen tried to reassure her with a smile to little avail.

Dennalhir released Sen's leg and rose to her feet. She walked out of the door before standing back under the threshold, uncertainty flashing in her eyes. "But when you come back with Brin," she began, "what comes next? What do you think will happen in this village?"

Leaning forward on the edge of her bed, Sen thought on the question for a moment before eventually frowning and shrugging. "I suppose that's something we'll figure out when it happens."

Seemingly satisfied with the answer, Dennalhir nodded and walked off into the other room. For her part, Sen sighed deeply and chanced a final glance at Brin's empty bed before rising to her feet once more, adjusting the travel pack on her shoulder, and exiting the hut. No need to sneak off with a believable story this time.

She left the village limits without pomp or attention. There was no need to announce that she was going to set off on a quest that most, if not all, would decry as a suicide mission.

Sen didn't care. She didn't need their approval. She just needed to bring Brin back. Whatever happened after that, would happen.

The village limits passed by in her periphery as the verdant moors outstretched before her. The tall and bountiful leaves of the Forest peered out from the southern horizon, a few hours march from where she was standing now. Refusing to turn around, she focused on those imposing trees, where deep within lay the combative Wood Tribe. She was unsure whether she'd rather face a horde of them or a horde of Invaders. Soon enough, that answer would become clear to her.

Taking those first few steps outside the village was the hardest part, but the rolling grassy dunes became a welcoming comfort the further she stepped out. She looked forward to returning by week's end with Brin in tow, those soft moors beckoning them to their return home.

The mountain breeze called to her one last time, the chill of fresh air against cold stone prickling her skin once again. Futilely, it bid her to return home, to forsake this fool's errand, to come up with a plan. But that wasn't the way Sen operated. She improvised, she went with the flow, and right now, that wind was blowing to the south. She'd follow that all the way to the City. With any luck, a northerly wind would draw her back home, where she'd once again be greeted warmly by her mother and Tez and—

"Leaving without saying goodbye?" called a familiar voice.

Peering her head in one direction and then the next, Sen caught sight of a welcomed face leaning against a nearby tree. How she didn't notice him earlier was beyond her. Underneath that blue paint was his typical casual and collected expression, his kind smile beckoning her closer. "What are you doing out here, Narva?" Sen asked.

He approached her warmly, hands stuck in his pockets as he huddled his body together against the mountain chill. "Is this my punishment for starting a brawl at the memorial this morning? You're taking off without a word?" He chuckled at the thought and swayed his body back and forth to keep it moving.

Sen smiled. "As much as I do enjoy seeing someone other than myself kicking the shit out of Fann…"

"Your father's memorial was not the right place for it. You're right. I'm sorry."

"No, no, it's okay. I did appreciate it. Didn't really know that your father had such a wicked right hook."

"Well, he *did* grow up with *your* dad," he said with a laugh. "Couldn't have him winning *all* of the friendly spars."

"He couldn't have it, but it *did* usually end up that way."

"Can't fault the man for trying."

"Heh, I suppose not."

They stood in the chill beneath the shadows cast by the tree, skin continuing to prickle in the cold. Exchanging warm smiles with one another did little to raise their body temperatures.

"So, you're going this endeavor alone?" Narva finally asked.

"What are you—"

"Tez told me," he interrupted with a smile. "Don't worry, I'm not going to talk you out of it. I'm just surprised that you're not taking her or your mother along with you."

Sen shook her head. "I can't ask that of them. Absent Brin sliding into the role as Chief, there needs to be a collective leadership effort. My mother and sister need to stay here. So, then it falls to me to do this."

"It falls to you, sure. But that doesn't mean you have to go it alone. If you want me to come along with you, I'm more than willing to—"

"Narva." Sen silenced him by firmly grasping his hands, holding them up to face level, near enough to her that she could kiss them. Despite the temptation, she did not do so. "Please. I can't put you in danger like that."

Raising an eyebrow at that, Narva scoffed. "It's for that same reason that I can't let you do this alone. Never mind whatever waits for you down where the Invaders have holed up. The *Forest* is going to be dangerous enough on its own."

"No, Narva. Please. This is something I have to do alone."

He smiled and shook his head. "Whatever your rationale for that line of thinking may be, it's still going to get you killed. And I'm not gonna let that happen. I won't be able to handle another death like that, not to another person I care about. And, besides…" He pried his hands loose from Sen and turned back toward the tree. After taking a lap around the base of the arbor, he suddenly had a travel pack along with a bow and quiver in his hands. "You don't really have a say in the matter. Brin and I don't share the same blood, but he's family to me as well. I'm coming with you whether you want me to or not."

Sen shook her head and chuckled to herself. "You idiot. You really don't know what you're getting into, do you?"

"If it's something involving you, I'm sure it'll be something interesting."

Heeding no more arguments, Sen and Narva departed. The village disappeared from sight until the only thing beckoning them from home was the looming peaks of the Heart of the Land. They set their eyes southward, to the Forest and whatever dangers lurked within. And whatever dangers awaited, they would be nothing compared to the drive to find Brin and bring him home.

Memory

Retaliation

It was a beautiful day to do absolutely nothing at all.

The village square was alive with hustle and bustle, Bearsigns and Wolf-signs from all over the Stone Tribe rushing to their destinations. Idle conversations of passersby bore the fruit of little nuggets of information, minute snippets of anecdotes leaving an open-ended story.

On a bright and sunny day like this, Sen loved nothing more than to lay about in the square, doing little else but probably get in people's ways. They never threw a fuss about it, though. She was the Chief's daughter, after all. As long as she wasn't getting into trouble, they couldn't be any less fussed about what she was up to.

Today, Sen was happy to have Brin join her during her afternoon leisure time. She always tried to get him out of the hut every now and again. He was a bit too much a pasty recluse for her liking, and it wasn't just herself who thought that. Their parents equally shared joy in watching the two of them go about their days together. Whenever Brin could be convinced to separate himself from a book. Granted, he still wasn't apart from his reading materials at the moment, but at least he was outside.

They squatted beside the central flame, Brin being a bit too entranced in whatever he was reading.

Sen leaned over Brin's shoulder, forcing a smile onto his face as she tried to decipher the hand. "What's going on in this story?" she asked, squinting her eyes at the pages, unable to make sense of it all.

Brin held up a finger, always his indication that he was in the middle of a fascinating sentence, and closed the book with a marker jutting out. "It's a bit of a scary one," he said. "Uncle Tawa gave it to me a few days ago. It's about a giant floating head that flies around and eats people." His eyes widened and his eyebrows rose up and down, a sinister giddiness that always unsettled Sen whenever he got too engrossed in his scary stories.

"A giant head?" Sen laughed. "What, did Tawa decide to write something about Father's big head flying around?"

"Honestly? I thought the same at first," Brin chuckled in response. "But it's a really old story that's been passed along the Tribes for a long time."

"Really," Sen pondered. "I've never heard of it."

Brin shrugged. "Not exactly a fun bedtime story for Mother to tell us. Unless cannibalism puts you at ease."

"Nothing like a nice meal," she quipped. "All that meat and protein is good for you." Instinctively, she pounced on her brother, pretending to gnaw at his thin arms. Brin squirmed and giggled, gently knocking her away with his book. "But, really. What's it about?"

"I wasn't kidding," Brin deadpanned. "It's literally about a giant floating head that eats people."

"But, I mean, why? Don't all these tales have some origin or reason, other than scaring us kids?"

"Maybe they scare *you*, but not me."

"Brin, you were scared by your dinner last night."

"...The elk was still moving."

"You had the rump."

"Okay!" He threw his hands up, a bemused smile stretching across his face. "But *stories* don't scare me. They just teach lessons. They're meant to be scary because they're meant to teach."

"So, then what's the big old lesson being taught here?"

Eagerly, Brin opened the book back up, pointing out different passages he had made note of. "The legend goes that it started with a bad winter leading to a big famine because all the animals went somewhere else. It was bad enough that whole families were starting to die off. Because the hunting ground was so stagnant, a lot of the younger people wanted to migrate elsewhere, make a new home someplace else with better hunting spaces. But the village elder was against it and said that, as a people, they had to brave the famine and not run away from it. But the younger people didn't listen, and they killed the elder instead, chopped off his head, and threw it and his body into a lake. But then, when they were making ready to migrate, the elder's head rose from the lake, now with wings and taller than a normal man's body. And he ate all of them."

Sen's jaw dropped, stunned into momentary silence. "But what happened to the giant head? Where did it go?"

Brin closed the book and examined its binding. He quickly flipped through the pages and shrugged his shoulders, putting the book on the ground. "It's kind of unclear."

"Unclear?" Sen questioned. "You'd think that someone would have caught sight of it eventually and figured it out."

"It's a *story*, Sen," Brin chuckled. "It's not real."

"But still. What happened? Why is it unclear?"

"Well, I still have a bit to go, but from what I've read, it apparently went and ate neighboring people for no real reason."

"Gah!" Sen started. "Then what lesson is being taught here?!"

Again, Brin shrugged. "I don't know. Listen to your elders? Don't go against your leaders and then kill them or else bad stuff will happen to you? Seems a bit cut and dry."

Shaking her head, Sen regarded her brother with amusement and astonishment. "You're a bit too clever for a ten-year-old."

"You might catch up if you picked up a book every now and again," Brin quipped.

She waved his hand at him, brushing off the remark with a smirk. "It's not as easy for me as it is for you. In the time it takes me to read a page, it almost seems like you've read the entire book. It's like the words are backwards sometimes."

"You just need to practice at it more," he said with a smile. "Maybe soon enough, you'll be able to read *five* pages by the time I finish the book."

"Oh, you little jerk," Sen laughed. In a motion just as quick as his barbed tongue, she punched his shoulder, maybe a bit too forcefully. The blow nearly knocked him off balance. "For all those heavy books you carry, you'd think you'd have more than twigs for bones."

"I blame it on being sick."

"After a few years, that excuse doesn't work as well, you know."

"It doesn't hurt to try, though." Brin massaged the ache away from his shoulder, grimacing slightly as he peered his skin for any signs of immediate bruising. "And what's *your* excuse? How've you been getting out of all that training with Tez?"

Sen shrugged. "She just cleared her Trial. She's too busy now."

"Is that what *she* says, or what *you* say?" He flashed a knowing grin towards his sister, a gentle prodding at an assumed truth.

"Let's just say two things can be true and call it a day." She leaned herself back, supporting her top weight with her elbows as they dug slightly into the soft dirt. "It's only for a little while, I'm sure. I'll enjoy the downtime until Tez starts prodding me awake with her spear butt again. Only when that happens, I'm making sure she wakes *you* up, too."

"Aw, what did *I* do?"

"Nothing. That's the point, dummy." She stuck her tongue out and rasped spittle toward him, little sprinklings of rain in intermittent bursts. "Eventually, you'll need to be strong enough to at least *pick up* and *hold* a spear. Not all the world exists in books, you know."

"The more interesting parts of the world do."

"Brin."

"I know, I know." He forced a smile, sneering at her with his eyes, annoyed that his big sister was telling him to do things. "Fighting just has never been something I wanted to do."

The thought amused Sen. Not necessarily that of Brin finding a thrill in the fight (though it was a rather fascinating mental image), but of battle being borne of desire and enjoyment rather than necessity. "No one sane ever enjoys fighting," she said. "We do it because we have to."

"So Tez doesn't like fighting?"

"Are you kidding? Just because she's good at it, it doesn't mean she enjoys it." She stopped a moment, staring into the middle distance between Brin and the center flame, and relented a half-frown and a shrug of the shoulders. "Well, maybe she enjoys picking on me a bit. But she doesn't enjoy it because she's looking to pick a fight. She only does so because she's a big sister who likes to be a pain in the ass sometimes."

"Only for you," Brin smiled. "Never for me."

"Don't worry, I'll make sure that changes." She leaned closer, a sinister and wicked smile parting her lips. Embellishing a devious laugh, she made sure to stare deep into his eyes and pierce his soul with her gaze, to rip apart those futile notions that only *she* would ever be the victim of Tez's cruelty bestowed upon her by virtue of Tez being the oldest. "We'll make a warrior of you yet. Or at the very least a strawman capable of sticking a spear out."

Perhaps there were some hard truths in Sen's playful ribbing. The earnest smile dissipated from Brin's face at the exchange, his expression turning more pallid and wistful.

"Hey, it was only a joke, little brother," Sen assured.

"No, I know," he said. "But you're right, too. I guess I got too used to being the weak one of the family that I—"

"That's not your fault, Brin. It's not like you can control when you get sick. Those shakes you used to get all the time were scary."

He nodded. "But it doesn't mean I can't do better."

"No one's asking you to be on the frontlines," Sen smiled. "Just that you feel competent and confident enough to defend us if the need ever arises."

"And do *you* feel that competent and confident?"

She couldn't help but snort at that. The idea gave her a rather amused grin. "Confidence? Sure, I'm always *brimming* with it. Competence? Well, let's just hope the need never actually arises and we should be in good shape."

Brin's smile returned. *Deprecating humor has always found a way to his heart, for whatever reason,* Sen thought. Maybe it was a relief to hear others bring themselves down after how difficult his own childhood was from a health standpoint. Or maybe he just liked hearing his sister say she had a strawman's competence with a spear. *Either or.*

He looked back down to his book, his marker sticking out from the back end of the pages. "Do you want to hear how the story ends? We don't really have to start on the spear *now*, do we?"

Shuddering, Sen was discontent with remembering the floating cannibal head after she had already successfully forgotten about it. "You know, maybe I *will* go and find Tez. Some training would probably do me some good if that monster finds its way here."

"Don't be a baby."

"I'm not. I'm just being *pragmatic*."

She patted a hand on his shoulder to indicate her farewell and left him to his horrific tales by the fire. Rising to her feet, she pondered what wonders would await her on this lovely and beautiful day. She could go for a walk around the village, maybe sample the mountain paths, find a new tree to claim as her own. The world was hers, a spring of hope at all the possibilities.

When she turned around, that spring of hope became a winter of despair. The smile on her face evaporated into an unamused and melancholic frown as she came face to face with that smug, arrogant grin plastered across Fann's face. He stood far too close for comfort with that ugly, freckled face and gap-toothed smile.

"Aw, what a wholesome scene, a brother and sister spending time together," Fann said with a hint of embellishment.

He had really grown in the last four years, and not in any of the good ways. He'd grown taller but not wider, an awkward stretch of gangly bones and flimsy limbs. His arm was clumsily bent at the elbow, unable to be held out straight; it never fully healed after that day in the Heart. He never forgave Sen for it, and that he was effectively sheltered for it by his mother only exacerbated the matter.

What *had* changed the most about him was that amused grin. When they were younger, there was a cautious innocence to it, something lacking confidence but filled with earnestness. Nowadays, there was just something mean-spirited and two-faced about it, offering friendship with his words but enmity with his lips.

"Still wish you had a little brother or sister to play with, Fann?" Sen asked. "Don't worry, it's only a matter of time before you're surprised with a happy little accident."

"How kind of you to say it would be a happy little one. Never thought you to wish happiness on anyone."

"Surprised you're even aware of what happiness is, with that household you grew up in."

"Oh, I'm plenty aware. Don't you worry about a thing." He pushed past Sen—or attempted to walk through her as his shoulder bore a surprising degree of impact—and settled next to Brin. "And how are *you* doing today, Brin?"

"Fine," Brin deadpanned, not breaking eyes with his book.

"Leave him alone, Fann," Sen warned.

Amused, Fann turned his head to Sen, scoffing at the warning. "What, am I not allowed to have a conversation with your brother?"

"If it were up to me, you'd not be allowed to have a conversation with *anyone*. Figure I'd be doing everyone a kind service."

"I truly admire how pure-hearted you are," he sneered. He turned back to Brin and put a hand on the book, gripping it firmly by the edge, primed and ready to tear it loose from the boy's clutches. "Oh, I've always wanted to read this one. Do you mind if I flip through it for a bit?"

Brin held onto the book more tightly, annoyance and concern stretching across his brow. "I mind quite a bit, actually. Now go away."

Fann put a shocked hand to his chest, feigning offense to the boy's strong words. "Why, I'm shocked at the poor manners you've grown up with. Have you been spending too much time with your sister?" He flashed a sinister glance toward Sen, tutting his tongue and shamefully shaking his head at her. "Maybe she never told you that it's polite to share with others."

Sen took a few steps forward, her fists clenching. "What do you *want*, Fann?" she demanded. "Do you really have nothing better to do?"

"What, can I not stop by on a sunny afternoon stroll and check in on some longtime acquaintances?" Shades of malice flickered in his eyes, a fire threatening to crack the icy blue of his gaze. "Or are you going to drop another boulder on me if I don't leave?"

A quick glance at Fann's mangled arm brought a smile to Sen's face. "Could always make your other arm match, if that's something you're looking into."

"Oh, no, you don't have to trouble yourself with the symmetry. I'm perfectly fine with the distinctiveness." Though he didn't break eye contact with Sen, his grip grew tighter and tighter on Brin's book. "Now, Brin, what was I saying about manners and sharing? I've been looking for a good new book to read. Why won't you share yours with me?"

Frustration was welling in Brin's face as he grew less focused on the words within and more concentrated on keeping hold of his book. Weakly, he grunted and struggled as Fann sadistically pulled and pushed the book back and forth. The soft rasp of torn pages scratched across the plane as the binding grew more and more undone by Fann's efforts.

Furious at the sight, Sen rushed forward and pushed Fann to the ground, breaking his hold on Brin's book. "That's enough!" she yelled. "What the hell is wrong with you?"

Passersby stopped in their tracks as the action ramped up, many having peered in as a curiosity toward the tense discussion.

Sen stood over the freckled jackass and sneered, watching his expression grow in amusement, before she turned and helped Brin back to his feet.

But with her guard down, Fann clearly saw the opportunity and struck from behind, shouldering Sen aground before tearing the book away from Brin and chucking it in the center fire.

As Brin's eyes welled with shocked tears, Fann laughed devilishly, an ugly combination of squeals, brays, and snorts which sounded less that of a human and more of a terminally ill goat. The pages crisped and crackled as black smoke billowed upward, wisps of the burnt contents floating helplessly in the breeze. Brin's initial instinct seemed to be to run into the fire and pull it out with his bare hands, but after a short forward jerk, he instead sank to his knees and softly whimpered, a mournful mewling for his lost story.

And as he sat quietly, staring in shock as the pages crumbled away, Fann saw fit to forcefully kick him in the side with the bottom of his foot, shoving him down to the ground, that inhuman delight still braying as he added an additional couple of stomps on the boy's abdomen. So entranced was he in his enjoyment that he barely had time to notice Sen diving for him and tackling him to the ground.

Sen was surprised at how heavy Fann was in his lanky frame. It was an effort to keep him to the ground. Futilely, Sen tried to pin his shoulders to the ground, but he was far too strong. Instinctively, he attempted to headbutt Sen in the face, but she pulled back, kneeing him in the stomach in return. He grunted, spittle snarling through the gap in his front teeth as he tried to push himself up. In the act of rising, he threw a punch at Sen, but a voice resembling that of Tez screamed inside Sen's head to raise her arm to block. Surprisingly enough, she listened and successfully turned it aside with her forearm.

Keeping her knees planted on Fann's waist, Sen rose her arms to her side, blocking either side of her face. Fann's blows were wild and reckless, greater impact drawing from his intact arm than his damaged one. And cleverly, that's where Sen knew to strike. Timing her blocks perfectly, she turned away a blow from Fann's good arm, only to swing her opposite hand into his bad, slamming it down to the ground in a painful heap. Fann held back a shrill scream, stifling it in his throat. Pained tears pooled in his eyes, the cold ice melting into a vast ocean.

And in that stunned moment, Sen brought her other fist down like a hammer. Right into his ugly face. It crashed into the bridge of his nose, his entire face scrunching into a ball. Rivers streamed from his eyes as she brought her fist down again and again, forcefully grunting behind every blow, eruptions of crimson strands shooting out in bursts as bone and cartilage crunched beneath her fist.

After a fury of blows, which may have lasted seconds or hours, she felt someone weakly trying to pull her off Fann. Somehow, Brin managed to succeed and Sen lay flat on her back, looking up to the sky, watching the clouds roll in to block the sun. Those clouds were looking darker than she remembered them being a short while prior.

With the adrenaline wearing off, Sen pushed herself to her feet, standing high over Fann with Brin at her side. In a daze, Fann rolled onto all fours, spitting blood into the fire. He turned to look at Sen, his nose reduced to nothing, his face a bloody mess. A snarling smile passed his lips, and he chuckled at Sen, saying nothing with his words but saying everything with his eyes. Unsteadily, he rose back to his feet, pushing through the gathered crowd, many of whom were stunned by the brutality, others aghast at Fann's cruelty, others lamenting a conflict between the youths of the Tribe.

Beyond the crowd, Sen could distantly hear a shrill voice calling Fann's name. She gave herself three guesses to whom that voice belonged, and the first two guesses didn't count. Not wanting to stay for the show, Sen grabbed Brin by the shoulder and turned toward the family hut. "Let's get out of here," she said.

They silently passed through the crowd as they watched them in equal silence. After a prolonged period, Brin looked up at Sen and said, "At least we know you're competent, then."

"Tez's bullying was good for something, I guess," Sen quipped.

Brin smiled softly and sighed. "Why did he—"

"Because he's a piece of shit," she interrupted, "and thought who better to pick on than someone who wouldn't fight back. Too bad he forgot he was talking to two people."

"Does this mean I have to start training with you and Tez now?"

Sen considered him quietly for a second but shook her head and smiled. "How about, for now, we see if Tawa has another copy of that book? We need to know how that story ends, after all."

Brin nodded. "Nothing's worse than an unfinished book."

The night loomed as Sen sat in bed across from Brin. A commotion sustained throughout the village for much of the remainder of the day, and though she was curious as to the cause, she thought it best to lay low.

Eventually, her mother returned, her father in tow, both with looks of exasperation on their faces. They peered into Sen and Brin's bedroom and quietly approached. Their gazes were affixed to Sen, and their eyes filled with apprehension and concern.

Sen arced her head toward them, biting her lower lip nervously. "What's wrong?"

"Was it worth it?" her mother asked.

"Can I not defend my little brother whenever a certain shit rears his ugly head?" Sen asked abrasively.

"By all means, you're encouraged to," her father smiled, before his tone became grim once again. "But anything you do to him...just remember that there will be equal retaliation from Koelhe."

"...Why? What did she do?"

CHAPTER NINE

PERSISTENCE

The tree limbs were a beautiful pastel of reds and oranges and yellows. It was more beautiful than any work of art they had ever seen, colors so vibrant and rich against a fading golden horizon. There was often the adage that one needed to stand aback to more deeply appreciate a work of art. But this was not such a case. The Forest was stunning from up close, like something out of the tales of spirits and heroes they were told as children. It was a living painting, a legend made real.

But just the same, a foreboding air danced on the winds as Sen and Narva approached the mouth of the Forest. At times, the greatest beauty could hide the ugliest terror. And with the Forest within a stone's throw, they couldn't help but hesitate their impending steps forward. They stared into the darkness beyond the veil, and the darkness too stared into them, sinister abandon calling back to answer the words of nothings.

Chills rattled through Sen's bones as the Forest growled to her past its beauteous veneer. For his part, Narva wasn't holding up much better. He had drawn the bow off from his shoulder, gripping it tightly in one hand while his other nocked an arrow at the ready. Beads of sweat trickled down his brow as fingers shook along his bowstring. They looked to one another and then back to the looming woods, teeth grinding and shoulders scrunching as they tried to will the nerves away.

"Well," Narva deadpanned. "You ready for the hard part?"

Nervously, Sen managed a sheepish chuckle. "Anything that waits for us in that City will be nothing compared to this, right?"

"You'd think so, but..."

"But?"

Narva paused, his attention seemingly diverted elsewhere, but he refocused quickly. "Maybe it's more equal footing. Maybe not. At least we *know* how the Wood Tribe is."

"And I can't imagine that they're going to be happy about us just waltzing through their territory. At least with the Lake Tribe, you can avoid that giant pond that they like to die in. We can't exactly go *around* the Forest."

"Southerners must have found a way, though, right?" Panning his gaze from one edge of the horizon to the next, Narva scanned thoughtfully for a possible route around the woodland borders. "The Sun, Arrow, and Haunted Tribes had to come north all the time for their Trials. Could they really have not just, I don't know, *swam* around?"

Dismissively, Sen shook her head. "You *do* remember that there aren't any coastlines north of the Forest, right? It's all sheer cliff faces once you catch sight of the ocean. Why do you think the Sun Tribe is so miserable up here?"

Narva shrugged his shoulders. "I can think of a few reasons."

"The point is," she continued, animating her hands to illustrate her point, "the only way north or south is through the Forest. Which means...the next day or so is gonna suck."

They sat and evaluated their options, neither in a rush to venture forth into the breach. The Forest loomed over them, taunting them with whatever lurked within while promising that which waited for them beyond. The only way out was through, and they both knew it.

"I remember my father saying a few times," Narva said, "that the southern Tribes considered passing through the Forest more of a trial than the Trial itself."

"I've heard the same," Sen agreed. "But we don't have much of a choice. The longer we dally here, the more danger we're leaving Brin in. We have to get him back, and we have to get him back yesterday."

Narva nodded. "Him and…well, you *do* remember that we had another person taken from the village as well, right?"

Her eyes widened subtly. She turned her head away from him slightly to hide her astonishment at forgetting that detail. *It's not just Brin,* Sen reminded herself. *And it's not just our Tribe. Remember to keep things in perspective, you idiot. This isn't all about you and what you need to do.* "Yeah, of course," she said aloud. "Of course, I remember. It's just, Brin being taken hit far closer."

"I know, I know. Just making sure you don't lose sight of the bigger picture."

The bigger picture. And what a big picture this is turning out to be.

The wind cried out, beckoning them to enter the Forest. Wood creaked from up high, the tall branches groaning with the same pain and gloom as what surely awaited them inside. Beyond the cracking of timber and the rustling of leaves, nothing resounded from within the depths. Any extraneous noise on their parts would alert the Wood Tribe to their presence. They had to go quickly and quietly, nothing giving them away.

"So, how do we do this?" Sen asked. "If southern Tribes have gone back and forth for generations, there must be an easy way."

"If this were fifteen years ago, maybe," Narva said with doubt. "But I'd imagine the Wood Tribe is a bit testier these days with mass migrations northward through their lands."

"We're also not an entire Tribe attempting to settle on their territory," Sen retorted. She rubbed the skin of her arms, trying to caress away the goosebumps prickling their length. "We're two people, moving fast and quiet, not making a scene, not causing a fuss."

"We're also very clearly not of their Tribe. We're gonna stick out whether we like it or not. I hear they have eyes everywhere in the Forest. Like the trees talk to them."

"They live in the trees, and they have a lot of Packminds," she said dismissively. "Look, are you coming or not? I was content with going this alone, but if you're looking for excuses to turn tail and run, then you're more than welcome to cry wolf and go home."

More tightly did Narva grip his bow's riser, his fingers grooving into the woodwork. He winced and grimaced but relented with a nod. "We're in this together, Sen."

Sen rose back to her feet, offering a hand to help Narva up to his own. Graciously, he accepted the outstretched hand and was pulled up, trails of his natural skin fighting through the blue face paint, his nervous sweat painting all the picture it needed. Her own curiosity bewitching her, Sen stared at the Forest not with fear or foreboding as she had previously, but with discontent and longing.

"You do have to wonder, though," she said. "How *did* the Invaders make it through the Forest with those numbers?"

Audibly, Narva shuddered. "I think I'd rather not know."

She frowned and shrugged her shoulders before running her fingers through her loosening hair. "Only one way to find out. You watch my back, I'll watch yours."

Narva tapped his pendant, a runic light glimmering from underneath his shirt, outlining three curved lines enveloping one another. The mark of Sound. He managed a smile approaching a degree of confidence. "Anything comes up behind us, I'll hear it. Don't worry."

Sen nodded and took that important step forward. "So long as it's not too late by the time you hear it."

The Forest seemed to laugh at them as they entered its depths.

The flames crackled as Dennalhir looked past the embers. Seated at the head of the fire, the light illuminating the interior of her hut, she stared in silent regard at her gathered council. As she felt the immense emptiness of the absent seat to her right, she sighed and examined the varied expressions displayed upon her gathered few.

Tawa, Sharrabha, Rantalha...Koelhe. It was these four who had acted as Fannalhen's dearest advisors for over two decades. At the moment, there were more significant matters of importance than deciding who should stay and who should go. And she had a strong idea of who she wished to go.

So much to consider, so much to do. It was enough for Dennalhir to grow lost in her own thoughts.

"Denna?" a voice called, breaking her from the trance.

She shook herself, blinking thrice to refocus her gaze. Looking up, she saw Tawa peering around the hue of the fire, eyebrows raised, lips slightly frowned, knuckles still scraped and red. Seeing signs of battle on Tawa was unusual and unfamiliar, but given the circumstances? Not at all unwelcomed. "Ah, sorry, Tawa," Dennalhir muttered, rolling her head along her shoulders. Her neck gave a satisfying crack. "What were you saying?"

"I asked what we are to do with the Haunted runaways," Tawa repeated. "We housed them under the pretense of protection, but we no longer...ah." He trailed off, the obviousness of the reasoning enough for any present to pick up on. It appeared he suddenly found himself caught in the same trance as she was moments prior.

"I believe the question is valid, Denna," Rantalha agreed, that perpetual composure in his voice betraying nothing, as usual. "To speak bluntly, the reasoning for their being here is no longer of consequence to us. They arrived here to hide, but no longer is there reason *for* them to hide." He paused, listlessly raising his shoulders above the flames. Even sitting down, he still managed to tower over the flickering embers. "Do we remain obligated to house them, provide for them? Shall we welcome them into our Tribe as one of our own? Or do we spurn them loose, allow them to go wherever they may go?"

Sharrabha turned her head sharply toward Rantalha, brow furrowed and fists clenching. "Do you see human life only as an 'obligation' to keep alive, Rantalha?"

"No, not at all, my friend," he responded. "My question was an earnest one. I cannot be the only one in thinking that we do not owe them anything. But by our own good graces, we can allow them either to remain or depart. Of course, we can leave the final decision to them, but what if one party feels one way, and the other feels the opposite?"

"I understand your point," Sharrabha said, "but if we wished them to leave, where would they go? Their homeland is, of course, out of the question, and they have either no or limited knowledge of the Words. They have few options as it stands already."

"And I do not disagree with that assessment. But we also must consider any cries for...retribution against them. We would be remiss if we did not address potential lingering resentment toward them amongst our Tribe."

"Resentment?" Tawa scoffed incredulously. "It was not the two runaways who killed—" He stopped himself a word too late and sucked in his breath, baring his teeth regretfully. "Apologies, Denna," he said, turning remorsefully to her.

Dennalhir raised a hand to brush off the remark, unaware of her subconscious tremors. "As you were," she said.

"Right," Tawa said hesitantly, regarding his friend carefully.

It was a trait Dennalhir had long admired in him, a collectedness in times of strife, but also a conscious consideration in the moments when he began to lose himself. That he had been able to hold himself together over the past day—for the most part—after his closest friend had been mercilessly killed was nothing short of impressive. *How you manage this, Tawa, is beyond me. But I am relieved to know that someone is able to.*

Tawa refocused his attention back to Rantalha, clearing his throat and rubbing the back of his neck. "Do you truly believe that a substantial number of our Tribe would rather blame two innocents over the bastards who..." He stopped and gulped. "Who *killed* Fannalhen? Who kidnapped Brin and—"

"I am not of that mind, Tawandhar, believe me," Rantalha assured. "But people will believe what they wish to believe, regardless of factual understanding. It is not lost on me that some would see the Haunted arrival in our village as a harbinger of Invader arrival. I am not saying that I agree with it, only that I understand why some may feel such a way."

"And then are we to punish these two," Sharrabha said, "for the misgivings of what would surely be a select few? Because a handful would be under the impression that a foreign bystander is of greater blame than a foreign Invader?"

"These are difficult threads to weave, Sharrabha," Rantalha warned, his arms crossed and face forever stoic. "I don't have the answers. But to continue along that thread, say we are of the opinion to allow them to stay. What happens if a rogue few decide they must take matters into their own hands? What if they see justice as being attainable only through an action that they themselves are willing to take? Mustn't we account for that, as well? And in that scenario, who are we to owe our protection to more: the many or the few? Is our protecting of the few in truth endangering the few? If we spurn the few, are we then infringing upon the values we uphold as the many?"

The gathered sat in thoughtful consideration, intermittent self-mutterings serving to break the pause in communication. Dennalhir looked from face to face, the three debaters wordlessly exchanging considerate expressions to one another. A twitch of the eyebrow, a shrug of the shoulder, a twist of the wrist. Koelhe, for her part, merely hid behind her own face, the light and shadow cast by the flames obscuring whatever was ruminating in her mind.

"Do we have a consensus?" Dennalhir asked her counsel.

Once again, they exchanged glances at one another, but it was imminently clear that there was still much to think on. "This may be a discussion to table for another time, Denna," Tawa admitted. "I would have thought this to be rather cut and dry, but I must admit that Rantalha presents some very valid concerns."

"Yes," Sharrabha added. "Morally, it does sit better with me to allow them to stay, but there have been very legitimate concerns that we must consider beside the fact. In the interim, however, I trust that we have no objections in allowing them to stay until we decide one way or the other?" Rantalha and Tawa nodded while Dennalhir felt a slight upward curse of her lips. Koelhe remained silent.

"There *is* another matter to consider, however," Rantalha added, straightening his already imposing form. The room fell to a deeper hush as his deep voice reverberated through the room. "And that is, frankly, who it will be that succeeds Fannalhen as Chief of our Tribe. As we know, it is custom to pass it along to the firstborn son, but, in Brin's absence, how are we to determine the succession...temporary or otherwise?" An uneasy air fell over the room at his final words, but Rantalha stayed unfazed. "And, as a corollary to that, in absence of a Chief, by what authority do *we* have to determine a matter such as what to do with the runaways?"

Dennalhir pondered this a moment and then looked to Tawa. "Is there any prior precedent for this...situation?"

The rune on Tawa's pendant fluttered beneath his shirt, four diagonal lines converging on a circle, before dimming once again. Tawa appeared to illuminate from the stored Knowledge, but as his eyes opened, no spark of confidence emanated within. "I cannot say that there is," he said. "But I also cannot say that there is not. A fallen Chief with a still-living male successor, though said successor is not present. It presents a different scenario than with the days when a male line ended and chiefdom passed along to a new family."

"So, then, what are you proposing?"

His shrug spoke little of certainty. "It has been rather silly that we have had only male Chiefs to this day. Across all the Tribes, truly. Perhaps only the Wood Tribe places women in higher positions of power. But we? We *are* the largest of the Tribes. Perhaps it falls on us to establish precedent."

"*Heh*, why not?" Sharrabha agreed. "No need to think too hard on this. There are few whom I respect more than you, Denna. You'd make a great Chief."

"I second the notion," Tawa said. "As great an example of Stone values as Fanna was. It is only fitting that you share this distinction with him."

With grace, Denna bowed her head, doing her best to hide a smile. "Is this proposition to your liking, Rantalha?" she asked. "Is it acceptable?"

His face continued to betray nothing. "I will say that it is not traditional, but..." He rolled his shoulders, something bordering on disinterest fluttering in his eyes, breaking through the walls he had long put up. "These are far from traditional times."

"Then if we have no objections, then—"

"Moving so quick that we reject any notion of objection, then?" Koelhe finally spoke, half her face illuminated by the flames, half embodied in shadow. "I'd argue that such a bold decision must be made *unanimously*."

"Oh, come off it, Koelhe," Sharrabha said with rolling eyes. "Would you really say there are others better suited for this than Denna?"

"Oh, I would," she answered. "I really, really *would*. Can we really say that *she* is the model of leadership to which we must uphold ourselves? Is *she* the answer to all of our questions? Is *she* the one fit to lead us out from the dark when she has long invited the dark into our quarters?"

"Here we go again…" Denna heard Tawa mutter under his breath, massaging the bridge of his nose with his thumb and forefinger. He could barely stand to look at Koelhe, let alone address this repeating argument.

"Please do elaborate," Dennalhir commanded, her patience already thin. "Please explain for all of us my grand invitation to all the darkness in the world."

As she leaned forward, the details of Koelhe's face came into greater focus. Her eye was still red and swollen from the blow she had received earlier in the day, marks of dried blood oozing from her cheekbone. Wild strands of her greying hair fell into her eyes, her deep-set wrinkles scowling in greater course than she herself. Her lips smiled, but her eyes did not. "It all began when all the world's darkness came screaming out of your—"

"Vulgar," Rantalha deadpanned. "Compose yourself with dignity. This is still a council meeting."

Koelhe sneered at the interruption, though showed no remorse for her intended remark. "My point remains, how can we call *her* a model of leadership when she allowed her *Curseborn* child to waltz about the village without a care in the world? Any and all misfortune of the last two decades is placed squarely on *her*!" She pointed an accusatory finger at Dennalhir, holding it ferociously atop the flames, paying little mind to the wafting heat caressing her hand.

"Beyond what happened last night, what tragedies have we actually faced as a Tribe since Sen was born, truly?" Sharrabha posited, her delivery barbed and biting.

"I warned them!" Koelhe shrilled. "I warned them both that the Eclipse was coming! They didn't listen, and they ignored all my warnings!"

"That answers nothing. What has actually happened beyond anything that's to do with your son? Yes, she was playing with your boy and Tawa's and they caused a rockslide that broke Fann's arm. Then she broke his nose in defense of her brother. Nothing else ever happened!"

"Lies!" As she grew more animated, Koelhe knocked embers loose from the pyre, swinging them around as though she could bend the blazes to her will. "Lies and falsehoods! The dry seasons, the flood, the Invasion, all of it—"

"Either were natural occurrences that had happened even before Sen was born, or were entirely independent of her birth," Tawa said, rolling his eyes. "Are you truly suggesting that a *seven-year-old girl* was responsible for a group of foreigners stealing our lands?"

Sharrabha shook her head, narrowing her eyes spitefully toward Koelhe. "You've let hate blind you. I hardly know what drives you anymore, but it's nothing for the good of this Tribe."

"Watch your tongue!" Koelhe snarled. "I am *still* a member of this council!"

"Though why, I have no idea," Tawa muttered. "I hardly think that were it Fann in Sen's position, a boy borne under a centuries-old superstition so ludicrously ridiculous that it defies anything our informed scholars teach us, that you would treat him with the same enmity that you show her. He's already the biggest shit in the village, and yet you treat him like the purest gold."

"Vulgar!" Koelhe retorted. "We are still in a council mee—"

"Your son *is* a shit," Rantalha interrupted. "When speaking truths, I hardly consider it a vulgarity."

Much to Dennalhir's surprise, the slimmest of upward creases stretched his lips. A historic occasion—the first time Rantalha had ever exhibited even the slightest of emotions.

"Meanwhile," Tawa continued, "Sen had been nothing but the sweetest child growing up until you decided to make her living hell and turn much of the Tribe against her. And for what reason? Because Fann wound up with a broken arm? Ridiculous."

"It is because *that* is the way of things!" Koelhe growled, spittle dampening a few flickers of flame. She was nearly to her feet, towering over her assembled peers in a show of undue command and defiance. It was poor custom. By tradition, the only one allowed to stand during such gatherings was the Chief. But still, she continued. "Because the Eclipse is a harbinger of death and misfortune! And it was my *duty* to inform as such. But when I informed our *dutiful* leaders, they ignored my warnings!"

"More like, the warnings you claimed to see never came to pass," Dennalhir said, leaning back on her feet. All the power in the room was hers despite Koelhe standing tall above her. From below, she held her calm air despite wanting to symmetrically paint the other half of the woman's face. *I've always known Koelhe to be insufferable, but this? This is something beyond.* "Is that not right? Tell me, Koelhe. You are a Futureseer. You indeed saw the Eclipse coming. But there was much and more that you could have foretold. You could have prepared us for the Invaders marching into our village, killing my husband, and taking my son. You could have prepared the other Tribes in standing up to the Invader assault on our Lands. Three Tribes could still have their homes. But no, you gave up on using your Foresight when it showed none of the death and destruction that you so earnestly believed Sen's birth would bring. Instead, you preferred to *make* such predictions come true by your own hand. And what good has that done for the Tribe, for the village? My daughter has found herself lacking in purpose for four years now, and that was *after* the years of torment by *your* hand. Do you want to speak on the values upheld by our Tribe? Because you are an embodiment of none of them. Now, take your seat."

Sputtering and animating to find the words fitting a retort, Koelhe just waved her arms and scowled, seating herself further away from the gathered assembly. She leaned against the wall of the hut, crossing her arms like a child put in a punishment corner. Her eyes met with no other's.

To break the silence, Sharrabha cleared her throat. "Shifting the topic back to Sen a moment..." she began. "Is she alright? I've, well...the taverns appear quiet, so I'd wager she's not there. Normally I see her wandering about by her lonesome at some hour of the day, but I can't recall I've seen her since the memorial."

Dennalhir and Tawa exchanged a knowing look, humble and apprehensive, but equally proud and hopeful. "She..." Denna paused. She wanted to cry out her name in hopes that she would immediately come running home, but she had accepted that that was not possible. Her daughter's tenacity was a trait she admired but also one that she feared. "She's decided to journey south. To bring Brin back home."

In unison, Sharrabha and Rantalha gasped. To see such momentary shock on Rantalha's face was the next in a series of emotions Denna had never seen on the man's face before.

"Narvarho, too," Tawa added. "He decided to accompany her. I tried to speak against it, but he said, 'Sen is not going to let herself get talked out of this, so neither am I.' As a father, I fear, but...as a kinsman, I hold nothing but pride."

"Ever the romantic, that one," Sharrabha quipped. "Here's to their inevitable success." She raised a hand like she would a cup in toast, though no drinks were present.

"More their inevitable demise," Koelhe muttered in the corner, her grin acting as proof that she cared little who heard. After sitting so absently and silently from the rest, she finally turned her gaze and locked eyes with Denna. Her eyes seethed with malice.

"You would *dare* wish that on my daughter, on my family?" Dennalhir growled.

"It's hardly a wish. Merely an inevitability. She's walking to her own death, and the Tribe will be better off for it." She rose to her feet, though to depart the hut rather than tower over her peers once again.

Dennalhir watched Koelhe take a handful of steps toward the door before she spoke. "Savor these final moments in here, for they will be the last you spend in this hut. You are hereby and in perpetuity banished from this council."

Koelhe stopped and chuckled, not even bothering to turn her head back toward the gathering. She stood where the light of the flame could not reach her, the shadows being all that strove to greet her. "Do you even have the authority to decide such a thing? I didn't think we had yet confirmed you as Chief."

"In absence of a sitting Chief, someone must still make decisions for the good of the Tribe. I will gladly carry that mantle until the time comes."

"What a fascinating precedent," Koelhe said, her tone curious. She remained at the precipice for a handful of uncomfortably silent moments before at last readying herself to leave. "I'll await news of the Curseborn with bated breath. Remember, Fannalhen is no longer around to protect her. I wonder who will in his stead."

The wind howled as Koelhe left, the rest of the council remaining in unease. Dennalhir felt the pit in her stomach grow. She did not want to consider failure as an inevitability. She knew Sen wouldn't live by those odds. She knew Sen wouldn't allow failure.

But that fear was persistent.

Hours had passed, but they could not have been more than halfway through the Forest.

The depths of the woods had been eerily quiet for all the haunting calls that had beckoned them forward. Sen had expected perhaps even a few woodland creatures scampering through the depths the further they ventured in, but there was just...nothing.

Even the wind appeared loath to enter the Forest. And here they were, hours deep into this trek, and no ill to show for it save for a perpetually raised heart rate.

Sen and Narva had not said a word to each other since stepping past the initial tree line. They knew that any extraneous sound could mean the worst for them, so they opted not to risk it. It was best to operate with an overabundance of caution when dealing with the Wood Tribe, or so they assumed. They wouldn't have known—they hadn't seen any of the Tribe since waltzing in.

With that overabundance of caution perhaps came an embellishment of slow movements, an exaggerated sneaking about through eroded leaves and scattered twigs. That may have come to their detriment, as nightfall arrived sooner than they would have liked, and for all the dangers presented to them in the depths of the Forest, wandering about while unable to even see two feet in front of them would have been all the worse.

Silently, they rested up along a tall tree, depositing their travel bags along the north facing so they would remember in which direction to head in the morning.

In the darkness, setting up a makeshift camp was a bit of a kerfuffle. In the absence of moonlight, they stumbled about helplessly and hopelessly, bumping into each other while ensuring not to audibly curse as they lost the items they just placed on the ground. As they reached out to one another to gather purchase of proximity, they were content enough just to kneel down, find soft earth, and lay for the evening. *The sun will rise soon enough*, Sen thought. *And soon enough, we'll be out of this anxious realm.*

Holding onto Narva's arm put her a bit more at ease. In the pitch black, she could not make out any of the details of his face, but she had to guess he was smiling, albeit nervously. She knew she was. She didn't know how much time had passed in the dark, but she didn't want to let go. She wanted to feel that security in the shadows, that sense of belonging in an unsure world. Feeling more secure in remaining upright on her knees, holding Narva at arm's length, Sen was hesitant to fall to the ground and retreat to her dreamscape.

A tingle ran up her arm, that familiar shimmer, and wind passed by her left ear. She heard Narva grunt in pain. "Narva?" she hissed. "What happened? Are you okay?"

He was still holding on to both of Sen's hands, though his grip of her left had loosened. "*Nngh*, yeah," he whispered. "Something grazed me. I—Shit, behind you!"

Immediately, Narva's pendant began to radiate beneath his shirt. Sen quickly rose to her feet and turned, Narva following in short order with his bow at the ready.

"Lower your bow, boy," a voice called from the dark. "I have ten yeomen with their sights on you."

Sen couldn't see him, but she could feel Narva raggedly lower his bow and withdraw his arrow. His bones seemed to rattle in place.

Footsteps approached from up front, and suddenly a torch was lit, an emblem of royalty illuminated in the dark. Though his form was still primarily encased in shadow, Sen could still make out a crown of sticks and twigs sat atop a mane of long, white locks. The man's face and revealed arm were multicolored, painted in shades matching those of the Forest's trees. Sen could not see the tone of his eyes past the shadows, but from the prominence of his brow, she could only surmise there was little hospitality in his glare.

"Who...who are you?" Sen murmured.

The man stood firm where he was, moving only his torch so as to paint the picture of Sen and Narva's expressions in his mind. "I believe that is a question best reserved for you." There was no humor in his voice, but no anger, either. It was unsettlingly calm. "What are two Stone Tribespeople doing in our Forest?"

"Please, we don't want any trouble," Narva stammered. "We just wish to—"

"Your traveling hand speaks otherwise, boy," the man asserted, his voice still unquestioningly firm. "I wasn't lying about my people in the trees. There are seven Packminds and three Listeners. The three can hear you rustling through your quiver, and the seven are passing that along to one another, and to me."

"Narva, don't be an idiot," Sen warned under her breath.

Narva immediately put his arms back at his sides, growing stiff as a board.

"And so, once again, grant us a reason for your being here. Who are you, and why has the Stone Tribe taken shelter in our realm?"

Sen could feel her teeth rattling from the nerves, but she mustered up what courage she could and calmed herself. "We mean no disrespect in our coming here. But I am afraid I have to answer your question with a question of my own." She paused and cleared her throat, keeping an eye on the man for any change in his demeanor. There was none. "Have you seen a band of Invaders pass through here?"

That got the man's attention. He took two steps forward and held the torch up closer, closing the gap between him and Sen. Greater details of his face became clearer to Sen: his weathered and tired eyes, the grooves in his skin where spearheads had cut into flesh, and more importantly, the specks of dried blood splashed along his neck and face. "Who are you to ask of the Invaders?" he asked.

"My name is Sennalhat," Sen said with as much confidence and assurance as she could muster. "I am the daughter of the Stone Chief Fannalhen. With me is my companion, Narvarho." She wasn't sure if Narva made some sort of acknowledging gesture or if he remained rigid as a tree. "The Invaders came to the Stone village, attacked our people...and killed my father. They would have passed through here on their return journey, but with two extra people. Two people they captured from our village. One of them...is my younger brother. We're following their trail so that I can bring my brother back home."

There was soft consideration in the man's weathered eyes. Something bearing resemblance to...remorse? Sadness? "So, not even Chief Fannalhen could..." he muttered to himself.

"Pardon?"

The man shook his head. He turned sideface to them both and nudged his head ahead into the darkness, his unseen band rustling away in the trees above. "I am the Chieftain of the Wood Tribe. Follow me. We've much to discuss and you've much to see. You're in no position to argue otherwise."

There was no disputing that.

CHAPTER TEN

ONE OR MANY

"There's no chance this isn't a trap," Narva whispered to her.

"I wouldn't go *that* far," Sen answered. "Maybe slightly above 'no chance.'"

Bereft of options to the contrary, they continued to follow the dim beacon held by the Chieftain. The old man bore enough confidence that Sen and Narva wouldn't make to run that he didn't even bother to turn face and keep an eye on them. The two Stone travelers did not know him by any means, but if he was in a position of authority among the Wood Tribe, his reputation had to have been borne of the same cloth as his people. Reputation alone was enough to deter Sen and Narva from running off.

That, and the constant threat of the world above. The Forest continued to sleep, the only nocturnal critters to speak of the hunters traversing the trees. Branches creaked and leaves rustled overhead, the yeomen amongst them silent as death. From Sen's judgment, it appeared that even with his sense of hearing augmented by the Wolf, Narva could scarcely hear them. Even in the pitch darkness, Sen could see that his reactions were delayed, ragged, panicked. Far from the assured air he carried with him back home.

The dry torchlight hardly flickered in the Chieftain's hand. As the lone glimmer in a world of darkness, Sen had hoped it would have served as a beacon of hope, of guidance, of light. But as she stared into the shadowy depths, the Forest answered only with this flame staring menacingly into her.

There was a stillness to the fire, a different behavior altogether, something unnatural, something bearing the same ferocity as the man holding it.

She could not take her eye off that malicious glow, though, for fear of losing herself within the Forest's grip. She feared the moment she removed her eyes from its glimmer was the moment she would be lost either to the elements or the people commanding the elements. But just the same, she couldn't help but drift her eyes elsewhere in some feeble attempt to scan a place to hide, a true beacon of light beckoning escape in lieu of undue reckoning. Her feet continued propelling her forward, but her eyes and her heart were running in a different direction entirely.

A sudden wind howled in Sen's ears, catching her completely off-guard. Nearly tripping over her own feet from the startle, she could hear Narva jump out of his shoes—but at *her* movement, not the wind's. *That's odd*, she thought. *I couldn't be the only one startled by that wind.*

Within the dark nothingness between darker outlines of tall trees, arrays of light burst into view in a cascading splatter pattern until nothing remained of the Forest itself. Slowly, she turned to Narva, what little of him she could find, but he carried on his way, unperturbed by the sight. *Can he not see this?* she wondered.

A grey shadow fell into the black, and it was screaming Sen's name. *"Why, Sen? Why?"* it pleaded. *"Why have you done this?"*

Breath catching in her chest, Sen stopped in her tracks, drawn to the discernible shadows. "Narva?" she called out, reaching for her companion but neither hearing nor feeling him. The grey form tried to rise back to its feet, able only to push up to a seated position. Her legs froze and her arms began to shake as a second shadow walked to the first, a darker grey shade distinguishing it from the fallen. A Deatharm took shape within the form of an outstretched arm, that black wind once again howling from behind. The armbearer opened its mouth, and out came only the shrill shriek of death.

"Sen, please!" the wounded shadow cried. *"Stop!"*

The voice. So familiar. No, the voices. Two simultaneous cries, differing in tone. Confidence and timidity, commanding and frightened. One bearing the drive of a leader, the other acting as a shadow of both what was lost and what was to come. Into two the voices seemed to split; into two the shadows became, ever so slightly.

The dark grey shadow screeched once more, and its Deatharm roared in response. A final desperate wail bellowed, and in a resultant splatter of light, the duo of screams became a singular entity. The timid voice separated from the confident, a frail form of light grey scrambling away on its backside, unable to rise to its feet and run. The dark shadow seized the opportunity, engulfing the fearful one in its mist, trapping it, smothering it.

Sen thought she could hear one final call for help, but it was drowned out over the sound of the encroaching black wind. It howled like a rabid wolf, snarling and growling with the ferocity of a starved beast denied its next meal. The light grey shadow screamed at the top of its lungs as it was lifted into the air, the darkness overtaking it. A final shrill shriek filled the air, the sound conjoining with the black wind, and when all was again silent, there was only one shadow. The monstrous, shrill one.

And it locked eyes with Sen. Her legs remained frozen in place, the Forest having withdrawn them back to the earth. In a panic, Sen tried to find the Chieftain's beacon, or Narva, or the hunters from above. But she was alone. Slowly, the shadow crept towards her as she furiously tried to will her feet to motion. An unsteady twitch propelled the shadow forward as it held out its Deatharm. The darkness encroached on Sen, closer and closer, fanning out in all directions until all she could see was a dark grey becoming purely black. As the Deatharm came into close proximity with a following roar, a final shriek split Sen's ears. Gripping her head in her arms in a feeble attempt to shield herself, the shadow's face snarled up against her own.

It was like looking in a mirror.

"No!" Sen yelled. "No, please, no!"

"Sen!" a voice cried. "Sen!"

Sen continued to yell and scream, a force from behind jostling her back to reality. Her heart raced as she opened her eyes, finding the darkness once again but not the imposing dread which accompanied it. The sinister shadow had departed, and the familiar line of labyrinthine trees returned. Nothing remained of the pleading shades, almost as though they were never there.

Blankly, she moved her hands across her body, pressing against her face, shoulders, chest, and legs, feeling no dampness beyond a frightened sweat. Finally, her legs functioned once more and she turned to find Narva, hand still tight upon her shoulder, faint arrays of concern and fear only barely visible upon his face.

Off to the side, the Chieftain stood silently, the torchlight subtly illuminating his face. There was no equivalent concern upon his face; if anything, there was only a sense of annoyance and inconvenience at having to stop.

"Sen!" Narva repeated, holding her shoulder even tighter. "What is it? Are you okay?"

Disoriented, Sen could only shudder in place, nervously looking about her shadowed surroundings. "Narva? Where...where are—"

"We're in the Forest, remember?" he assured. He pointed to the Chieftain, half-reminding, half-accusing. "We were following the Chieftain, yeah? Wherever he's taking us?" He leaned in a bit closer, his mouth right up to her ear, his breath prickling her skin. "We did wonder if this was a trap, yeah? Was that...?"

Her teeth rattled, her skin clammy and cold. "I...I..." She stuttered and stammered, fearful of turning back around. Fearful that the shrieking shadow would overtake her. Or that she would become the shadow. Her own shadow.

Angrily, Narva's head jerked backwards, his hand gripped more tightly around his bow. He took a handful of aggressive steps toward the Chieftain, and even Sen could hear the rustling of trees settling into place.

"What kind of tricks are you trying to pull with us, old man?" Narva demanded.

The Chieftain remained unamused, the torch flame holding still in place, a consistent orange glow illuminating his features. "Am I to blame for your kin's sudden terrors?" he asked. "Is that a fault of mine?"

"Your Forest, your territory! Wherever you're leading us, there's obviously something hidden in those—"

"There are no ghosts in the Forest, if that is what you are implying," the Chieftain said plainly, the flame continuing to hold steady. "We are not the Haunted—we do not claim the dead walk within our realm. Whatever tricks are being played upon her mind is of no will of the Forest, I can assure you. We do not play host to malevolent spirits."

"Then what's wrong with—"

"How should I know? I just met her, and you should know her better than I. Ask her yourself. I have more important matters to attend to, and you have little choice but to follow. Now, come." The Chieftain turned, the wooden crown atop his head swaying as he shifted on his heel. The rustling overhead quieted, faintly becoming little else but soft wind on the horizon. The torchlight grew more distant, but it continued to stare into them both with an all-seeing eye.

Cautiously, Narva approached Sen, still in shock. "Are you okay?" he asked comfortingly, gently placing his hand back on her shoulder. "What happened?"

Vigorously, Sen shook her head, her hands balling into fists, fingernails digging into her palms. The echo of the shriek still rang in her ears, the desperate pleas for her to cease tearing her asunder. The voices of one she would never again see, and one she hoped to see again. The sounds of their voices were dancing away on the wind, far from her grasp, so close within reach, but the encroaching darkness prevented her from holding on to them both. And the shadow delighted in that.

"I can't explain it," Sen said haltingly. "Not right now. I...I need time to think on it."

"Sen?" Narva said with a raised eyebrow. "You know you can count on me to listen and help you make sense of it all."

Deep down, she knew that would comfort her, but now was hardly a time for comfort. She took his hand in her own, thought about kissing his fingers before moving against it, and decided instead to clasp it between her other hand. "I know. Really, I know. I just need time to make sense of it to myself before trying to make sense of it to another." *Where would I even begin to explain it, anyway? I don't even understand what it was I saw.* She drew her eyes past Narva, to the fading torchlight disappearing into the shadows. "And besides, unless you want to get trapped in the dark under threat of death..."

Faintly, Sen could make out Narva's warm smile breaking through the murk of the Forest. "A discussion for the morning, then."

"If we make it that far, sure."

An unfamiliar breeze flew in from behind—far less sinister than the one before—pushing them onward towards the Chieftain, as though the Forest itself was willing them forward. *Whatever is out there, even nature wants us to see it*, Sen thought. *If nature wishes us to bite it, who am I to argue?*

In an ebb and flow, the torchlight continued to beckon them. From so far away, it was easy to forget the intimidating being carrying it. But Sen and Narva quickened their paces, breaking near into a jog, paying little heed to the out-stuck tree roots threatening to remove them from their feet. *Because in a realm under the constant threat of native retaliation, why should the realm itself not get in on the fun?* Sen thought. The flame drew nearer and nearer, almost frozen in place, until it at last hit Sen that the Chieftain had stopped moving. Turning to face the duo, his face revealed feelings of exhaustion and anguish, far from the stoic and angered carvings ingrained upon it previously.

"We're here," he said plainly, his eyes engulfed in the black shadows cast by the torchlight.

Confused, Sen turned in place, examining what little she could see around her, seeing only the faint shapes of trees and precious little else. "Wherever 'here' is, I'll take your word for it," she quipped.

"Uh," the Chieftain grunted before drawing his eyes upward. Shrilly, he whistled, piercing the silence like an arrow. The ground quivered beneath their feet, a woodland threatening to be rent apart by nature. Sen held her arms out for purchase and balance, reaching for Narva's arm but finding it nowhere in the darkness. A feeling of vertigo filled her head and stomach as she felt a sensation of being dragged upward. The ground remained unsteady, unleveled, as though it was floating through the air.

And then Sen noticed the trail of the torch flame trending downward as it whipped into the night air.

Faint glimmers of light came into greater view as she finally realized they were no longer on terra firma. The shaking ceased, and as clarity was restored, she noticed the ropes holding a platform of wood steady, a range of Tribal dwellings adorning the treeline, an unamused and unimpressed Chieftain staring at her panicked face, and Narva on all fours, dry heaving from the upward momentum.

Sen sighed with relief and collected herself, taking a cautious step forward to entrust that the platform would not collapse in on itself with the added motion and weight. "So," she said. "We're here."

The Chieftain cared little to acknowledge her, instead opting to nudge his head toward the treetop village. He seemed intent on exaggerating his motions as much as possible; every step he took swayed the airborne platform.

If I didn't know any better, I could have sworn there was a smirk on his old face.

As he left the platform—ferocious swing-set and all—Sen quickly became privy to the presence behind her. Turning sharply, she locked shadowed eyes with a host of hunters, ten in total. *Clearly the yeomen the Chieftain spoke of,* she considered. *Not an idle threat in the least.* They were imposing, threatening figures, each with an ornate bow of much greater make and quality than anything she had seen up north. Even in the dim light, she could see they were all adorned with markings meant to camouflage them amidst the Forest's foliage, their skin a collage of reds and oranges and yellows. Each was draped in lighter pelts than what she would normally wear—deer, from the look of it—all of which were cut at the sleeves, revealing more substantial musculature than she was accustomed to from Stone Wolfsigns.

When the hunters approached closer, drawing into clearer light, the exposed arms revealed a greater concern. Sen gasped as she took it all in. *Camouflage paint can't hide wounds like this.* Deep gashes peppered arms and faces alike, dried blood and untreated scars a trait shared among the ten present. For all the things she had heard of the Wood Tribe, *this* wasn't one of them. This was different. This was worse.

"What..." she muttered, stunned. "What is this? What happened?"

One of the hunters stepped forth, hand still gripped tightly around his bow before wrapping it back around his shoulder. His face was a mess of scars crisscrossing each other, some old, some fresh. His hair had been woven into thick locks and tied at the back, but some of the locks had come undone and ragged, peppering his nose with each step. "The Chieftain ordered you to follow, did he not?" he said, his voice like gravel when combined with his central accent.

"Well, yes, but..." Steadily, Sen sidestepped toward Narva and helped him to his unsteady feet, his complexion pale beneath the blue face paint. "Why have you brought us here? Why would your Tribe allow outsiders into your village?"

"We do not have the authority to say," said the hunter. "Only our leadership has the right to speak to outsiders in such a way. Now go."

Sen nodded, helping Narva steady himself with one hand on his chest, the other on his back. Narva, for his part, winced as he brought a wrenched hand to his stomach, hunched over as he slowly and carefully trudged across the swaying platform, graciously finding peace atop the fixed wooden platforms bridging the trees. Frankly, Sen was surprised he didn't drop back to his knees and kiss the walkways.

"Come on," she said to him, pushing him in the direction of the Chieftain's distant torch. "You holding up okay?"

Narva chuckled, his eyes still watering from the strain. "You know, I really don't like heights."

The admission was near enough to stop Sen in her tracks. "All those times we spent in the mountains and *now* you don't like heights?"

"Okay, maybe I just don't like climbing trees. Is that some sort of subcategory of a fear of heights?"

She rolled her eyes, gripping his wrist as she quickened her forward pace. She knew better than to attempt a conversation with the Chieftain—*Half because he seems too unpleasant to carry a conversation, and half because he's too unpleasant not to be frightening,* she muttered to herself—but she stayed within a few paces of him, cautiously following in his wake with Narva in tow. For being outsiders in a place that so famously detested outsiders, Sen had expected the people of the Wood Tribe to be out in droves. *I'd prepared myself for these folks to be staring arrows and daggers into us both before placing literal arrows and daggers into us both.* But, eerily, the village was at rest. Beyond the flickering torchlight, there was hardly a peep in the trees. She wanted to say that, as a people accustomed to dwelling high in the trees, they were likely quiet as a means of sustainability. But this? This was something beyond that, beyond a people naturally quiet.

Inside the huts carved as extensions of the mighty oaks, there was little in the way of movement. No suspicious window glances, no children protesting against their scheduled bedtime, no familial arguments or companionable banter, even in hushed tones. There was just silence.

The Chieftain moved forward with a purpose, his path set on a giant tree in the center of the village, the tallest in the Forest as far as Sen could tell. At the heart of the tree was a large opening, a wide depth visible even in this dim light. From deep within came a bright illumination, far more so than she would have expected from a people so concerned with remaining hidden amongst these wooden heights. Strange as it was, the air grew less silent, livelier as they drew closer to the tree, a din quickly becoming a commotion in more anxious and erratic notes.

Sen's heart caught in her chest as she saw the Chieftain's shoulders visibly tense, his pace quickening, his fingers grinding along the shaft of the torch. Such to the point that he was no longer concerned with the outsiders he forced along and more with whatever was transpiring within that tree.

Finding herself in equal curiosity, Sen followed after him, dragging Narva near enough by the heels of his feet. As the tree came into reach, an acrid aroma flooded her nostrils, a miasma so appalling that very nearly did the bile from her stomach erupt upwards. Covering her mouth, her eyes watering, she took a handful of brave steps forward, keeping the Chieftain in her line of sight, and gasped at the horror within.

Lined in rows, a host of warriors and hunters lay prostrate, marks of red seeping through shirts and trousers. Some were motionless, easily identifiable as beyond the realm of the living. Those with blood pouring from their skulls may have been the lucky ones. Those with visible stomach wounds had expressions of shock and horror affixed to their faces; they had to have suffered. Suffer like those who still lived, writhing through pained cries, blindly feeling at the red river pouring from their sides or limbs. Frantically, men and women alike tended to the wounded, offering some sort of liquid medicine likely doing little else but dulling the suffering. One woman in particular stood out to Sen, a more ornate fixture draped along the threads of her hair, woven through in an intricate pattern. She bore no camouflaging paint, allowing her natural skin tone to shine through, but her arms and face were coated in red just the same.

"This is…" Narva started with a gasp, unable to finish the sentence, his hands clasped to his mouth in shock.

"Horrible," Sen finished. Her hands shook, her stomach still threatening to empty. Cautiously, she approached the Chieftain, who had contented himself to stand in the middle of everything, taking everything in, removing the wooden crown from atop his head in stunned silence. She didn't know whether to leave him be or to offer a comforting hand, but somehow, both options seemed incorrect.

"Chieftain!" cried a voice, the voice of the woman with the intricate headpiece. Her hands remained hard at work on the fallen warrior to whom she was tending, but her eyes drew fire from Sen and Narva's presence. "Are you aware that there are outlanders behind you?"

Restoring the crown back to his head, the Chieftain turned, almost forgetful of the company he brought. "They're from the Stone Tribe, Matron," he said. "They were passing through."

"Last I was aware, our lands are far from Stone territory. We do not 'pass through' their lands on a whim."

"It's not on a whim!" Sen exclaimed. "We were—"

"Quiet," the Chieftain commanded. "You are not to speak unless spoken to."

And you do pass through for your Trial, bitch, Sen wanted to say, but thought better of it.

"What of the Elder?" he continued to the woman he called Matron. "Has he been found yet?"

The Matron frowned and pointed her hand a few rows over, signaling an older man sat up, his head lolling forward and back, an elaborate crown atop his head far more regal than the Chieftain's, bearing more a resemblance to elk antlers. Blood was dripping from his shoulder and chest, blood spatter dribbling down his chin. "We were lucky to have found him when we did," the Matron said. "Another hour without treatment and, well. Who knows what would have happened? At his age, it's not even a guarantee he's to make it even with treatment."

"You old fool," the Chieftain bemoaned, his teeth gritting at the Elder. "I told you not to go down there. I told you it was dangerous. 'Elders know best,' my ass."

Eyes still drawn to Sen and Narva, the Matron rose to her feet, having apparently finished with the person she was working on. Whistling to her medical support, she pointed at several untreated Tribespeople still writhing before taking steps toward her visitors. She stood level with the Chieftain, perhaps only an inch shorter than him, her arms and hands lean and bony yet strong beneath all of the spattered blood. She bore a youthful appearance despite exhibiting the air of a woman in her middle years. Looking Sen and Narva up and down, she frowned, narrowing her gaze almost spitefully. "I've still yet to hear an explanation for their being here, Chieftain. You know as well as I that outsiders are forbidden in our midst."

"I've no need for lectures, woman. I'm the damned Chieftain," he growled. He bared his teeth like a wolf preparing to lash out at its prey and turned to Sen. "Girl. Explain to her why you've come. Explain it all."

Without sparing a second, Sen complied. She detailed everything of the past day and a half, starting with the two Haunted runaways who had escaped captivity in the newly established City and sought refuge in the Stone village. And then how the Invaders set foot in the village, demanding their return, only to turn around and be content with killing her father in cold blood while "accepting" her brother as a suitable replacement hostage in addition to one other.

"...And, so I'm going to get him back and bring him home. I had no choice—*we* had no choice—but to come through your territory. Under ordinary circumstances, we would respect your territory and your hold over it, but these are far from ordinary circumstances."

Both the Chieftain and the Matron were quiet. Sen wanted to say that there was some shred of empathy visible in their expressions, or compassion, or remorse. But the same furor with which they greeted Sen and Narva remained, the same anger, the same frustration.

"Then it would appear the fates of our Tribes are intertwined," the Matron muttered.

"What do you mean?" Sen asked.

"Same as happened to you," the Chieftain lamented. "Look around you. Is it not obvious? Are these wounds not unique to those weapons they carry? Just as your Tribe was beset by the Invaders, so were we."

"But, how?" Narva chimed in, incredulous at such an admission. "How does the Wood Tribe fall so easily? Your Tribe is one of the most ferocious and adept in the Land!"

"When we have the element of surprise, yes," the Chieftain admitted. "But have you ever stared down a force of those Invaders with their tools of death when they know exactly where you are? We stood no chance."

"But how did this all happen? How did you lose so handily?"

The Chieftain sighed. "It all makes sense now why a host of them was marching northward. They met us with such a ferocity that I thought unnatural in another man. Marching so intently to retrieve people that they see only as *property*? It is inhumane and barbaric. But such is the foe we are now facing. No longer is this just a matter of our southern brothers and sisters being displaced. The entirety of our Land lies in danger if they now have the confidence to best us and proceed through the Forest.

"When they came from the south, our Packmind scouts immediately alerted one another. There were so few of them against so many of us. It should have been easy. But we were careless. We gave away our positioning too readily. They seem to be trained only in one skill, and that is to kill. Our scouts stood no chance against those tools they used, those 'Deatharms' as you called them. In our hubris and panic, we tried to meet them again in the open field and from above in the trees. But their weapons were too quick, too deadly. They slaughtered us handily, and we retreated to lick our wounds.

"But we did not consider that they would be coming back from the north. And before we could regroup and recover, they slaughtered us once more, and this time even more handily. Our best and brightest went down with but a whimper. We are not a fighting force anymore. We are a Tribe left with little else but healers providing only relief from a pain that will inevitably kill. What can we do in the face of this? We can no longer protect and defend our Forest as we once did. Our way of life is threatened, and now we fear that the sun will set on our Tribe."

The room grew starkly quiet, many present shocked—though agree-ing—with their Chieftain's grim assessment. A deep pit formed in Sen's stomach, a horrid reality of what was happening beyond her own borders. And yet—

"I grieve for your people, Chieftain," she said. "Truly. But nothing I can say will bring your people back. And I still have to move on. I'm just trying to get my brother back."

The Chieftain frowned. "Then I must wonder. What is your brother's life worth against those who died at the hands of the Invaders? Look around you. How many do you estimate lie dead or dying? I do not want to count them all. But is your brother's life worth more than all who lay before you?"

"That's an unfair comparison, Chieftain, and you know it." Her fists balled, her hands shaking. She could feel Narva approach closer, but she preemptive-ly brushed him off. "My brother was not the reason the Invaders slaughtered your people. He was just an innocent bystander who was unfairly taken."

"And yet he still has his life. That's more than can be said for my people." He gritted his teeth, those wolven fangs ready to strike once more. "Tell me, girl, and tell me honestly. Do you earnestly believe that you will return safely? Do you really think that you will emerge from the City with both your brother and your life? And not only that, you will return to your home, your village, your Tribe, and go about as though none of this ever happened? Your goal is filled with folly and false hope. I urge you to give up while you still have your life and go home while you still can. Your brother is gone, but *you* still have the chance to live. Do not waste it."

"No," Sen asserted, her own wolven fangs bared for all to see. "I will not stand down, and I will not allow my brother's life to be forfeited to an army of foreign bastard slavers! I refuse to accept that. Even if I can only save one life, it is better to have saved one life than none."

"And if you not only fail, but die in the trying?"

Sen breathed deep, puffing her chin and chest outward, her nose scrunch-ing and eyes flaring. "Then I will die knowing that I did not give up. I will die knowing I fought to my last, as a proud woman of the Tribes and a proud patron of our Land."

Surprisingly enough, the Chieftain actually grinned at this. By his standards, anyway. It was perhaps a humoring grin, but a grin, nonetheless. He crossed his arms and stroked his chin, pondering the veracity of Sen's words. As he closed his eyes, Sen got the impression that he was remembering all those who were lost in the past day or two, those who fought to their last for pride in their Tribe, for the protection of their Land. When he opened his eyes again, his expression only confirmed that as a single tear dropped from the corner of his eye.

"Your words hold weight, girl," he said. "But we are also faced with a harsh truth."

"And what's that?"

The Matron stepped forth. "The fact of the matter is, the Invaders marched north to retrieve two of their Haunted slaves, but they came back with two Stone Tribespeople instead." Though the words were accusatory, she took no pride in divulging them. There was even a shade of remorse in her tone. "If the indiscriminate slaughter of our people resulted in your brother's capture, then neither I nor the Chieftain can speak to your safety here."

"Word travels fast in a smaller Tribe," the Chieftain added. "And two outlanders in our midst is cause for alarm enough. Even lodged in our protection, I would not deem it wise for either of you to stay once it is known that not only two Stone Tribespeople were here, and not only were two Stone Tribespeople taken as slaves, but also that one happens to be your brother? We are a combative people and a vengeful people. These are not days for cooler heads."

"Then, what do you expect us to do?" Sen asked, her hands outstretched for guidance. Narva filed in next to her, his expression defiant yet respectful.

The Chieftain lit a torch and handed it to Sen, holding tightly to it as Sen held it in kind. "Leave immediately. For your own sake. Whether to the south or the north, you must leave." As Sen gripped the torch more firmly, the old man pulled himself closer, his concerned tone growing grim once more. "But the next time you return to our Forest, I cannot promise that our encounter will be under as welcoming of circumstances. Go, now."

He released the torch and stared at Sen, fire meeting fire, their ferocity matched with one another. Without further questioning, Sen and Narva complied, gripping the torchlight tightly. They followed the path back to the raised platform, too flustered and groggy to speak other than being grateful to have met the Wood Tribe and still have their lives.

The platform lowered, returning them to the earth below, and they ran. Into the darkness. Into the Forest. Into the unknown.

CHAPTER ELEVEN

Consequences

She had hardly ever seen her mother in such unassured distress.

When Tez returned home, Dennalhir was sat by her lonesome, eyes focused on nothing but the flickering flames in front of her. Hers was always an expression of warmth and welcoming in the best of times, sternness and command when warranted. But these were by no means the best of times, and her mother's face shone in dull tones crying solemnity, doubt, and sadness.

Tez, for her part, shared much of the same emotions. It had been a long day, after all. While so often she had decried her sister's tendencies to seek solace and respite in the drink, she couldn't deny its efficacy. A night at the tavern with round after round of toasts to a fallen hero had done her heart good, if only for a little while. Momentary lapses in grief to progress through difficult times. Her head was fuzzy, though not indecipherable, heavy, though not bearing the weight of stone. As she stood in the doorway, eyes unfocused, stomach churning, ears ringing, she found herself met with two realities.

One was the realm of distractions and revelry, the depths of which Sen had grown so accustomed. A world of which Tez had not always known the benefits but had now come to terms with. A world where all the troubles seemed so minute, so insignificant against the company of like-minded individuals, focused on little else but the night ahead, and sucks to whatever else attempted to matter.

The other was the realm within this hut, the stark reminder that the night just spent was truly what mattered little. That this evening was just a distraction that Tez needed, but one that was not sustainable. This was the reality of truths, the rhythms of anguish and anger, the elegy of a person lost, and the mournful aria of those they left behind.

As Tez stood in the doorway, she had to make her decision—which reality was to be the one she chose. While the raucous chorus still singing on the breath of the wind held temptation in her ear, the rich notes of excess still rife in her nostrils, there was a greater pull that forced her to the realm in which she needed to be.

She stepped forward into the hut, approaching the center flame behind which her mother continued to sit in silent consternation, one leg crossed over the other, hands folded in her lap. Dennalhir had untied her braid, allowing her dark locks to flow in waves along her broad shoulders. Glistening sweat peppered her forehead and arms as a result of the heat of the flames. Her eyes stayed glued to the radiant dance of reds and oranges before her, as though the pyre would hold answers to a question she did not know to ask.

Arcing her neck above the peak, Tez looked down to her mother with consideration, thrice blinking to regain some modicum of focus. She steadied herself back on her feet, despite her disheveled clothing and pendant half escaping her shirt offering a clear indicator of how her night had been going.

"Mother?" she asked, clearing her throat to force down a burp. "Are you alright?"

Dennalhir looked up, her concentration broken from the flames. She managed a warm smile, that familiar welcoming beacon of hope, and outstretched an open hand to her side, beckoning her daughter to take her hand and sit. Tez complied with little objection, the idea of getting off her feet an alluring prospect. When she fell to her rump, the weight of a thousand stones lifted from her. This hard, uncomfortable piece of flooring suddenly became the most delightful thing she ever had the pleasure of sitting upon. The flames were wonderful, too. Her blood was kept warm by the drink, such that she had little awareness of just how brisk it was outside.

"My daughter," Dennalhir said, still holding tight to Tez's hand. "Did the evening treat you well?"

Forcing a grin that bordered on overexuberance, Tez leaned back and sighed deeply. "Given everything, maybe letting loose every once in a while isn't so bad a thing." She closed her eyes, and immediately the world spun around her. "Stressing that it's only once in a while, of course."

"Given everything, maybe a little more caution would be preferable." The warmth had departed Dennalhir's voice, something icy and sharp replacing her tones. "You and I are all who remain, now."

The exaggerated grin left her, and she could only find a stark frown as a substitute. Tez scanned her mother's eyes and lips, something so stern and cold gripping them both. Something that approached…fear? Anger? Some combination of the two? "It won't be just us for much longer," she assured. "Sen will be back soon, and Brin with her."

Her mother sat in cold silence, the frigidity of her posture overtaking the warmth of the flames. "Do you believe that? That she will return?"

The bluntness of the question took her off-guard. She bit her lip, unable to meet her mother's eyes. "I would like to think so."

"You knew that she was going to go," Dennalhir said, the words barbed as they left her lips. "Didn't you?"

Tez hesitated. *Knowing and wanting are two separate things entirely*, she thought. "Yes, I knew," she said at last. "I knew there was little hope in convincing her otherwise."

"She did always share that with your father. That stubbornness and drive. There was never any stopping him when he set his mind to something, even if it may not have been in his best interests. It seems only fitting that Sen would be the one to inherit that from him."

"Given everything she's had to face in her life, she'd have been hard-pressed not to wind up as stubborn as she has."

"I can't argue against that," Dennalhir sighed, her breath rich with acceptance and doubt. "But it still doesn't mean that I wish there were times where we *could* convince her otherwise."

"When this became centered on Brin, I think we both knew, didn't we?" Tez closed her eyes again, fighting the rising nausea and impending dizziness. "That there would be nothing stopping her from trying to get him back."

"I just wish that weren't the case." Dennalhir's gaze returned to the flames, hoping to find something in there to soothe her.

"What else was she to do, or any of us to do?" Tez posited. "We can't just let Brin rot down there. We have to do *something*, don't we? But even if Sen sat and thought of the bad that could happen, I doubt she would let it stop her. For better or worse, she knows what's right to do. She's always known. But too many in this village don't see it that way because, well, we all know why."

"That we do."

"And I'd be a fool to say that I'm completely confident that she'll come back. But I would rather be that fool who still believed in her regardless. I *have* to believe it. We both do. And we know for certain that she would set our Land ablaze if it meant getting her little brother back. She's always been protective of him, and she's always stood up for him, regardless of the consequences. All I can do right now is just toast to her health and hope for the best."

A sly smile creased Dennalhir's lips. "And is that what you were doing tonight? Toasting to her health?"

"A few toasts, for a few people," Tez admitted. "A toast to health, a toast to memory, a toast to life, and a toast to those we hope to see again in the Otherworld."

"*Quite* a few toasts, then."

As if in response, Tez's temple began to throb and pulse, radiating discomfort and heat with hammering efficiency. "I think I've preemptively given some future toasts, as well."

With a sigh, Dennalhir reached for the pot heating beside the fire. She picked it up by the handle and lightly shook it, revealing the sound of liquid swishing around in waves. Grabbing two nearby cups, she poured out the contents—a calming, relaxing tea, by the smell of it—and held out one cup to Tez, enough only to fill halfway in both cups. "Then, to Sen's health, and Brin's return."

Gladly, Tez toasted to that, the last toast she would hope to do for quite some time, and downed the liquid, the aroma pleasant as it danced down her throat.

As she placed the cup back on the ground, watching Dennalhir gently sip at the tea, it became clearer to her that something further bothered her mother. Dennalhir remained distracted, her mouth twitching with uncertainty. She tugged at her long locks absently, twirling the end of a strand around two of her fingers as the flames continued to dance in front of her.

"What else?" Tez asked.

"What do you mean?"

"I mean, there's clearly something else on your mind, Mother. You've never been one to grow silent as soon as you divulge what's bothering you. Normally it's a struggle to get you to shut up afterwards." She chuckled for the sake of levity, but it was not reciprocated. "If there's something you need to speak on, then, for now, it's me that you'll work with. Family sticks together, right?"

Dennalhir glanced at Tez in her periphery and relented a subtle smile. She downed the rest of the contents of her cup, nearly slamming it down to the ground upon completion. "I suppose Sen acting as she deems is right regardless of consequences is something that she shares with me."

Craning her head in confusion and interest, Tez raised an eyebrow. "What do you mean?"

After a pause, her mother said, "I expelled Koelhe from the village council."

"Really? Why?"

A scoff was all the response that was needed. "Do you really need to ask?"

That brought a broad smile to Tez's face. "No, I suppose not. But regardless. I think everyone else on the council would agree that it's been a long time coming. Personally, I'm surprised that Father didn't remove her a long time ago."

"Well, that was *his* choice," Dennalhir said with a shrug. "Believe it or not, Koelhe's father was quite amicable and friendly toward your grandfather when he was Chief, and as an act of good faith to keep the familial relations tightly knit, your father appointed her to the council after he became Chief. It was a big deal then, remember. She was the first woman ever to be on the Tribe's council. And for those first few years, she was fine. Paranoid, sure, but fine. It was only when Sen was born that things started to change. It was incremental at first—some snide remarks, general snark where there wasn't previously. But after that rockslide twelve years ago when Fann broke his arm, it all changed for the worse, as I'm sure you remember.

"But your father couldn't bring himself to banish her from the council. Call it wanting dissenting opinions, or call it wanting to keep rivals, antagonists, enemies—whatever you wish to call her—closer to him, he thought it best to keep her on. Even when things progressed to where they are now, he kept her. Despite everything she inflicted upon Sen, every action of Fann's that she conveniently overlooked. Maybe your father was a better person than I. But I could no longer listen to her sully Sen's name, our family's name, wishing ill on our blood. And, so, I saw no other option than to remove her."

"But do you even have that authority?" Tez asked. "I mean, are *you* Chief now? Is it Brin who is meant to be Chief?"

"Until such time that we appoint someone, I took it upon myself to act as Chief," Dennalhir said. "And given we have no idea when…or *if* Brin may return to us, it seemed a decision best saved for sooner rather than later."

Thoughtfully, Tez stroked her chin, covering her mouth in silent consideration. Reality was silent save for the crackling embers and a soft wind politely knocking at the door. "I understand the necessity, but…" She shook her head, grunting with concerned frustration. "I feel as though it sets a dangerous precedent."

"Truthfully? I feel the same. Koelhe appeared cognizant of the precedent as well, and that's what concerns me the most."

"What did she even say to begin with? What was enough to demand she depart so quickly?"

"Among other things? Wishing for Sen's failure, surely wishing not only her death but also Brin's. But also…" She paused and frowned. The flames continued to crackle and spark against the silence.

"…Also?"

As she bit her lip, Dennalhir, for the first time, bore the image of a woman fearful for her life. Tez had always known her mother as strong, fierce, every bit the warrior as her father was. She was a woman who had known fear, having stared it squarely in the eyes, but never succumbed to it, never grew wary of it. But now, for the first time, there was that flicker of hopelessness, that momentary glint of hesitation which was so foreign to her mother, so alien to her face. In waves, the browns in her eyes seemed to quiver as though damming a river threatening to flood. Storms primed to erupt in her face. And as the river began to quell and the storm subsided, Dennalhir worked up the strength necessary to sigh and calm herself, confidence slowly brimming to a return, but anxiety still claiming a home in her expression.

"She warned that your father is no longer here to protect us. And that she wonders whether there would even be another take his place."

The comment knocked Tez back a bit. She pushed herself to a more upright seated position, shaking off the drowsiness and unclarity plaguing her vision. As she stared wide-eyed at her mother, she couldn't help but wonder what the comment could even mean. And yet, all she could hazard to say was, "We're still strong without him. We can always protect ourselves, by ourselves. Why would she—"

Immediately, Dennalhir shook her head. "Stop and think on that a second more, Tez."

At that moment, it hit her. *Oh,* she thought to herself. *Oh, shit.* "You don't mean...a coup?"

Her mother nodded. "If I've set that precedent by acting in such a way, then..."

"No," Tez proclaimed emphatically. "That's ridiculous. On what basis would she even stand to call *herself* the Chief of our Tribe?"

"She's been vocal about the Eclipseborn for over twenty years now," Dennalhir muttered, regret audible in her voice. "And even more so about Sen. That much is evident to anyone."

"But that matters for nothing! It was *yours* and Father's decision to make after Sen was born. You both chose correctly, and there are countless who would agree with that!"

"And there are countless still who would take Koelhe's side on the matter." Grim was her mother's tone, abrasive and cutting. "Do remember that she has swayed a lot of people to her side in the last eight years."

Tez grunted knowingly. "And Sen has only suffered more for it."

"And now I'm sure you understand why I do not take her threat lightly. They're not merely the parting words of a woman filled with little else but hatred in her heart. And they're not hollow words, either. We need to take this seriously."

"Then, what do you suggest?"

Grimacing, Dennalhir only shook her head. "I don't know," she said. "But we need to figure it out soon."

"Hmm," Tez mumbled in acknowledgment. She scrunched her knees upward, resting her arms atop them. Her forehead fell forward, impacting with the bone of her knee with greater force than she intended, pulsating pain radiating through her skull. With a deep breath, she looked back up and said, "Well, who do you know that we can count on through all this?"

"Tawa," her mother said without hesitation, "I think is the most obvious one."

"Plus, any close relations of his who would follow his lead."

"A sizable number, at that. His family has always been an important one in this Tribe. I can only hope Narva would offer the same if he...no, *once* he returns with Sen and Brin." The correction warmed Tez's heart a bit. *A little hopefulness is what we need right now.*

"And what of the rest of the council?" Tez asked.

At that, Dennalhir could not work up a definitive answer. "They're somewhat wild cards, in my eyes," she admitted. "Sharrabha has spent so much time hunting throughout the Heart that I find her more disconnected from the affairs of her own Tribe. She's always seemed a bit more neutral toward the situation with Sen, too. I can't say for certain where her allegiances would lie."

"And Rantalha?" The thought of his stern and unmoving face sent shivers down Tez's spine.

The mention of him put even more consternation upon her mother's face. "That...is a good question. I can never say much for him or what his thoughts are, but..." She buried her face in her hands, a subtle groan echoing deep from the chasm within. "If anything, I know he will think practically. What that will mean, though, I don't know."

Tez couldn't help but grunt with disgust. *So, after generations of our family watching over our Tribe as Chiefs, we can only say with certainty that just one member of our council will stay on our side. Damn it all.* But just as that frustration set in, an idea sparked in her head. "What about the other Tribes?" she proposed with widened eyes. "The Arrow and Sun Tribes especially! You'd think that they would bear some degree of fidelity to our family once they were displaced in the Invasion and Father granted them parts of our own territory. Chief Han'e should still be somewhere in the village, no? And, yes, the Arrow Tribe is somewhat nomadic, but they should still be wandering somewhere in our territory, so it shouldn't be difficult to find them, so..."

She trailed off as she realized the defeat and solemnity in her mother's eyes. Dennalhir only shook her head, wiping the glistening wetness away from her brow. "We can't. It'd be wrong of us to involve other Tribes in what is really an internal affair. I fear it would set just another dangerous precedent that, were we to bring in anyone just for the sake of numbers, anyone could do the same. I have to say no."

"Damn it," Tez muttered. Exhaustion was settling into her. The air grew stuffier and warmer, her arms heavier and denser. Her head remained a fog, perhaps only more so with the added anxiety of everything going on. But for as run-down she felt, she could only imagine how much more so her mother had to have felt. As she closely examined her mother's face, she could see the fluster in her eyes, the wrinkle in her brow, and the twitching of her mouth. Her thumbs twiddled about one another, a nervous tremor gripping her hands fiercely.

The last two days have been horrendous, and here she is, not even granting herself a moment's rest, Tez pondered. *I need to figure out how to help.*

Rising to her feet, Tez struggled to find her balance against that devil called gravity and stumbled over to the door. "I just need some air," she called out over her shoulder. "I'll be back in a bit. Unless you want to join?"

Dennalhir seemed to consider this for a moment but then politely shook her head. "I think we both need the solitary time right now," she said.

The brisk nighttime air was refreshing. A cold mountain breeze prickled her bare arms, the location of her overcoat now suddenly a mystery Tez was set on solving. Thinking first to saunter back to the tavern in hopes of finding it there, she shuffled on through the village square, paying little heed to those around her.

"Such a lovely night, isn't it?" called a familiarly smug voice. Loudly, Tez groaned and turned, finding Fann seated by the square's welcoming pyre. "A little nippy tonight, but it's always wonderful by the fire."

He was always kind of ugly, especially with that misshapen nose of his that never failed to spring some enjoyable mental images in Tez's head, but the added scars and bruises he earned today only added to it. One of his eyes was swollen about halfway shut, a dark shiner forming in the bags beneath. His lips were split in a number of places, his lower lip in particular having ballooned to about twice its normal size. A deep cut ran along the length of his cheek, which Tez was perplexed as to how he gained a gash running that long. But through it all, Fann still managed to smile that broad, shit-eating smile that only ever made Tez want to knock his teeth out. Or, as it were, a couple more than the ones she knocked out earlier in the day.

"You're looking good, Fann," she answered. "Truly a face *only* your mother could love."

"Ah, so catty, as always," he quipped, pushing himself up to his feet with some notable struggle. As he stood, he propped something up in his hand: his spear. In the faint light, Tez could see the slight glimmer of a rune from the tip of the spear. The mark of Strength, which some Strongarms—such as Fann—would elect to imbue into their weapons rather than a pendant or ornament. For his part, Fann actually crafted a pendant as well, though it wasn't as though he was granted any extra Strength. It was more just he was a pedantic sod.

That he was granted Strength after his Trial was always such a mockery in Tez's eyes beside the fact. Perhaps the Bear took pity on him for his busted arm and sought to help compensate. But this was a man who had always lacked the mental fortitude to stand up for anything without the prior approval of his mother. That he should be physically stronger than she based on pity? What a joke, and what a waste.

"It seems your family is dropping off, one by one," he said with snark. He flexed his shoulders, the bones cracking into place. His spearhead continued to glimmer as his good arm tensed and receded. "How unfortunate."

"It seems your family's place on the council has dropped off, one by one," Tez responded. "How unfortunate."

"Oh my, if only you shared your sister's wit. Such a pity that I'll never get to hear her snide remarks again."

"Don't worry, it won't be long before her wit breaks your other arm."

Haughtily, Fann laughed, the act revealing a row of chipped or missing teeth. His gums were still red and raw from the beating he took, and yet here he was, acting as though he could best anyone. "Ah, I'll miss these banal and hollow threats your family offers mine. A shame those threats will be nothing but wind when all is over."

Tez narrowed her eyes, her teeth grinding. "Let's see. Broken arm, broken nose. A face somehow made uglier. But you're right. We're *full* of empty promises and threats."

He took quick limp-steps forward, baring his teeth widely in a snaggle-toothed broken snarl that bore the intent of intimidation, but only looked comical and disgusting. Still, the intent was there. "Just remember this," Fann warned. "Your family has been on the chopping block for years. It's about high time we brandish the axes."

The temptation to throw another punch to his face was high, but instead, Tez settled for hawking back and spitting in his ugly face. He took it without objection as she turned to continue to the tavern, wanting to spare no further words with him.

When she hazarded a final glance behind, he continued to stare her down with a smirk.

CHAPTER TWELVE

CONFESSIONS

THE YEAR 1556 ANNO SALVATORIS
15 YEARS AFTER THE INVASION

It was hard to assess how long they had been running given how dark it remained within the Forest, but if Sen had to guess, she'd have said it was about three days.

At least, that's how it felt. It couldn't have been more than half the night, but every step forward bore the weight of ten whilst lugging three of herself on her back.

She could hardly be certain of how hollow or not the Chieftain's threat and warning was. Being an outsider in the Forest was dangerous enough, but to be linked to some degree of responsibility for the merciless swath cut through the woods by the Invaders? Probably better to walk on the side of caution.

Granted, sprinting through exhaustion with a torch threatening to extinguish further and further into the depths of a starkly dark woodland while keeping a close eye on an equally exhausted companion was far from toeing a careful line, but such was the lot she had cast. Despite the roaring protests from her legs and feet, the further the distance she put between the Wood Tribe village and them, the better.

It'd have been nice of Tez to lend me some Endurance, she told herself in ragged, heavy thoughts. *She'd have left me in the dust hours ago.*

Everything hurt, everything burned, and at this point, a stray arrow to the backside would be a tremendous release and relief. But such a courtesy was not granted to either of them as they continued to traverse stray roots, densely solid trees, stealthy rocks, and each other's stupid and clumsy feet.

For each moment Sen sought to hazard a glance back toward Narva, just to make sure he was still hot on her heels, she found herself running headlong into a tree with enough force to send timbers crashing to the earth. It was enough to swear her off looking back in curiosity and concern, difficult though it was. It was better to keep her head on her shoulders and focused than to find it flat on the ground with a world spinning around it.

Nocturnal creatures roused in curiosity at the sight of two humans fearful in their scurrying, chirping and creaking their objections and confusions. If anything, it was a sign of civilization, or a return to the resemblance thereof. The further they drifted away from the Wood Tribe encampments, the more prominently the outside world showed its face. Here was more reminiscent of a peaceful and nondescript forest as opposed to the fortress-like and impenetrable woodland that lay within the central depths.

At long last, with lungs at fiery capacity, torchlight all but dimmed out, and legs but a useless bodily extension that merely got in the way, Sen and Narva found themselves at the outer ridge of the Forest. Moonlight finally shone overhead, the beacon of a hope long lost and found once again. Even in the midnight darkness, the grass seemed to glow in verdant green, the lunar caress shimmering against the glistening dew gathered amongst the swaying blades.

From the sight of it, Sen collapsed with relief. Only narrowly did she avoid slamming her jaw atop an outlying root, but she didn't care. They had entered the Forest, encountered the Wood Tribe, ran for their lives.

And lived to tell the tale. That was more than enough reason to collapse helplessly in a pile of soft coniferous dirt.

Narva held few objections to that, too. There was at least some attempt at grace and dignity whilst descending to the ground as he propped himself up against a tall tree and slid on down, but at a certain point, the effort wasn't worth it, and his rump landed squarely atop a pile of rocks. A gentle squeak escaped his lips, such to the point that Sen was under the assumption that he may have introduced his fruits to the unforgiving earth. His watering eyes offered nothing to suggest otherwise.

As dirt seeped into the crevices of her shirt and trousers, Sen's gaze remained affixed on the glittering terrain, a sudden wave of warmth splashing her in a manner of tease. Never had she felt such warm air. The Forest truly was a barrier not just separating the north of the Land from the south, but also the cooler climes from the warmer. She could only imagine the difference in broader daylight. For now, though, she could already feel dribbles of sweat forming from more than just the hours she had spent traipsing through the Forest.

Tossing the extinguished torch aside, she turned on her back, all the effort in the world going into the motion, and positioned herself to face Narva. His face was red and puffy, his paint half-removed from the river of sweat that had cascaded down for the past while. Exhaustion was evident in his eyes, his lids threatening to fall and shut. He yawned in a mighty roar, probably the fiercest he had sounded throughout the entire ordeal in the Forest. Sen barely had the strength at all to even match it.

"We did it," she whispered wearily. A part of her—an extremely small part which still held delusions of having some retained energy—wanted to sit up and stare him in the eyes, but the ground was too comfortable. Truly the most relaxing dirt she had ever lay in, and she had had her fair share of collapsing and passing out in a pile of mud. "We made it." If there was anything carrying her voice over, it was the strength of relief.

Narva's head dipped up and down in a quick jerk, his eyes still struggling to stay open. A soft chuckle murmured in his mouth, the slightest of upward curls lifting the corners of his lips upward. "Maybe next time, we *do* try going around. I've always wanted to try rock climbing."

"You may have a point," Sen said, managing a laugh. "At least if we fall, we'll land in the water."

"Fall from high enough, that can still hurt, you know."

"Yes, but at least that freefalling fear only lasts a few seconds, as opposed to hours upon hours."

Weakly, Narva raised an unsteady hand in the image of a toast. "To quick deaths rather than fear of."

"To the hope of getting fifty hours of sleep in the next five." She couldn't even be bothered to replicate the toast.

They lay there in comfortable silence, the dirt encircling Sen like an earthly blanket, nature aiming to grant her the rest and sleep she so earnestly deserved. She knew that the second her eyes were to close was the moment she would embark on the greatest sleep she could ever hope for. The wind whistled in a soft lullaby, the boughs creaking hypnotically overhead. Far off in the night sky, the moon smiled down on her, bathing her in a nocturnal glow. As the sound of her own breath—in and out, in and out—rocked her to the throes of sleep, Sen readied her eyes to close, the lids inching closer and closer to each other, so close to meeting in their nightly embrace, and—

"Sen."

Loudly, Sen groaned and pried her eyes back open. Somehow—and for some reason—Narva was wide awake, his eyes still visibly heavy, but his focus lucid. Massaging the pit of her eyes against the bridge of her nose, Sen pushed herself to a seated position—somehow—and looked upon him with annoyance burning in her gaze. "You're kidding, right?" she asked incredulously. "You were falling asleep just a minute ago."

Shrugging, Narva could only chuckle. "I think I managed five hours of sleep in that minute, so I'm well on pace for fifty in five."

"Of all the times for you to rediscover your wit."

"I'm just that exhausted that it's the only thing coming to me at the moment."

"And you're keeping me awake just to tell me this."

Slowly and softly, Narva's warm smile eroded, replaced instead with something more akin to a frown, a distant vision bygone in his gaze, the streaks of remaining paint creasing against the ridges of his face in subtle consternation. "No," he finally said. "That's not it."

"Then excuse me as I lay my head down," Sen murmured dismissively, waving her hand aside to brush off whatever he deemed was so important. "Don't worry, you still have my—" Broadly, she yawned, finding at last that ferocious strength Narva had exhibited not so long ago. "—my undivided attention."

"What happened, Sen?" he asked abruptly. "Back in the Forest."

"Gonna have to be a bit more specific there, friend. We saw a lot back there."

"I'm not talking about what *we* saw. I mean what *you* saw."

Now, he *did* have Sen's undivided attention. She sat more upright, the palm of her hand digging into the rich soil as her weight bore down more heavily upon it. "What...w-what do you mean?" she pondered hesitantly.

"Don't think I forgot." It was impressive that he was able to manage that degree of snark and sass in his state. "We said we'd talk about it later, no? I'd say it's later enough."

All of the welcoming radiance of the southern warmth left her, and a chill rattled her bones in its place. The faint echo of a shrill shriek rang in her ears, a shadow engulfing her vision for the briefest of moments. She twitched, gripping the earth below more fiercely, fists pulling up entire mounds of dirt. A shudder held her in its grasp, and in an instant, that wave of exhaustion and fortune gave way to the embrace of fear. Vigorously, she shook her head, a solitary tear stealing away down her cheek. "No," she whispered. "Please, no."

Narva twitched in place, unsure whether to approach or maintain his distance. "Hey," he said. "It's okay. It's just me, okay? You can tell me."

But could she? Was this something that she absolutely *needed* to tell him? Was this not a battle she needed to face alone? Much like this entire journey? She had every intention of facing all of this herself, so why would she need to divulge every thought and motion that popped into her head?

But still, it was Narva. Her eyes met his, wholly and solemnly. Even in the pale moonlight, his eyes managed to glimmer, something so ethereal and warm, so inviting and enticing. She couldn't help but be drawn to them, to him, to his warmth and understanding. Something pulled at her, something invisible yet strong enough to put strength to her knees and shuffle herself forward. Toward him. And when she was near enough to touch, she knelt before him, meeting his gaze from his seated position, the wave of emotion coursing through her, choking up through her throat, heat rising in her face, rivers flowing down her face.

And she fell into him, face burrowed into his shoulder, her body convulsing with raw emotion. Her open hand rested upon his broad chest, tears staining through his shirt until, at last, he wrapped his arms about her, spindly yet strong. There was a warmth and familiarity to the embrace, something she couldn't quite recall and yet remembered so fondly and distinctly. One arm remained entangled around her back, the other combing attuned fingers through knots of tangled and loosened hair. He said nothing, the breath from his nostrils warming the nape of her neck as she continued to heave sobs into his shoulder.

"I'm sorry," Sen choked. "I...it...ugh, *gods*." She pulled back slightly, her eyes already feeling red and puffy. She glanced at Narva but, embarrassed for her state, buried herself back in his shoulder. She muttered into his shoulder, something long and drawn out, but it remained too muffled to understand.

"What was that?" Narva whispered back, his voice soft and comforting, a caring tone that she was not particularly used to, not even from him.

Sen lifted her head up slightly, exposing only her lips from the pelt of Narva's shirt, choosing to continue hiding her eyes and tears otherwise. "I said, they must be celebrating back home. Finally rid of me, just what so many of them wanted."

"Hey." Forcibly, Narva pulled Sen's face up, despite her aversion. "Look at me." There was reluctance and hesitation on Sen's part initially, a futile attempt at turning her head away from him. But as his hand rested on her cheek, a coarse and scraped thumb wiping at the stream of tears, she felt more and more compelled to meet him at his glance, and so she did. His brow had furrowed, no shades of doubt visible in his eyes. "Listen to me. You matter. To me, to your family, to more people in our Tribe than you know. Any who would say otherwise can fuck right off. They don't know you. They don't know who you really are, the incredible person you've always been."

For some reason, that only drew more tears from her eyes. She raised a hand and met his on her cheek, clasping fingers around it. "The louder voices always seem to tell me otherwise. The louder voices are the ones harder to ignore."

"Then we need to make the right voices the louder ones."

It was so hard for her to envision what precisely was the "right" voice for her. Too many had intermingled to create a cacophony of noise, of overlapping and overbearing platitudes and condemnations, her existence being labeled interchangeably as a blessing and a curse. Vociferous proclamations of a living blight against ardent assertions of being just another face in a crowd. None made sense, and yet they all made sense. They all screamed at once in her head, echoing in repeated oaths and hateful cries, all conjoining into a singular notion, a singular voice, a singular thought, a singular plea.

Sen, please! Stop! Bang.

She screamed, burying her mouth back into Narva's shoulder. A tremoring quake coursed through her, her eyes forcing open to prevent the return of that grim and shrill shadow. The shadow which looked so familiar, so identical.

Narva held her tighter, firmer than anyone had embraced her before. There was security and comfort within his grasp, something so calming as he softly shushed her, warding away whatever lurked in those depths. Despite everything, she knew that she would be safe as long as she stayed right where she was. The darkness couldn't reach her here, not while Narva was here.

Cautiously, Sen lifted her head back up, every muscle in her body aching and trembling. She slowly looked back to Narva, her lips quivering, teeth rattling. So tense was she that she hardly realized how much her hand clasped at his chest, nails digging into his breast. He didn't seem to object or mind, though. One of his hands held her comfortably in place along the middle of her back, his other resting absently at his side. He did nothing but watch her, wait for her, the pain and concern evident in his gaze upon seeing her in such a state. His eyes glowed with earnestness and kindness in their purest forms, purer than in anything else she had ever seen. And in that moment, as hard as it was, she knew he had earned honesty.

"B...b-back there," Sen started, pausing and contemplating the words carefully. "Back there, it was as though...it was as though I was the monster they all say that I am." Narva opened his mouth to object, but she covered his mouth with her two forefingers, and taking the hint, he let her continue. "The harbinger of death and doom that my kind is so destined to be. The herald of misfortune, the gatekeeper of evil. And when you hear those words thrown at you enough times throughout your life, it just reaches a point where you start to believe it. Now, when I close my eyes, the image of my father falling to the Deatharms...it's not the Invaders at the other end of it. It's me. It's my voice that screamed into the night and became a thunderclap. I keep..." She winced and gritted her teeth. "His *voice*, it still *screams* in my ear, begging me to stop, pleading, praying, everything. And yet, I don't or won't stop because I can't. Because this is what I'm meant to be. This is...I don't know, the *destiny* that nature itself preordained for me. And it's not just enough that it's his voice. There are sometimes two voices, a high and a low, a confident and a timid, but that monster is not satiated with felling only the one voice. It needs to consume both. And despite the desperate pleas, despite the better judgment of who that scared voice belongs to, there is nothing that can stop that monster, that shadow, from engulfing everything.

"If you hadn't broken me from that trance back there, I...I...I don't know. But that wasn't the first time it's happened, and I know it won't be the last. Because it's what I'm meant to be. Deep down, there's a part of me that perhaps just accepts that. That I have no choice in becoming what they all want me to be. Part of me accepts that there's a desire to show those people precisely the monster they wish to see. Because it was always easier to resent the people who resented me simply for being alive, but for as much as they resented me, it was never as much as I resented myself. How much I *still* resent myself. And how in a world that so clearly did not want me around, there was solace and soothing only in cards and drinking myself stupid. That was all that was keeping that looming shadow at bay."

"Sen..." Narva started to say. "But you—"

"And what about you?" she interrupted.

"Sen?"

"You've known what I am for—who knows how long? You were the only one who ever treated me with any dignity or respect. Despite what I became, despite what I've turned into, you remained the same person toward me as when we were kids, traipsing around the Heart, getting into whatever trouble we saw fit, giving our parents heart attacks." She allowed herself to chuckle, but her expression reverted just as quickly to seriousness. "But did you ever mean it? Was it just because you felt sorry for me? You saw me, a broken and hollowed shell never to have any future in this Tribe, and saw me only as someone to pity? Or did you—"

In an instant, Narva took his free hand and pressed his forefingers up to her lips, bidding her to stop. "*My* turn to cut *you* off," he said, warmth in his smile and glim radiance in his eyes, heavy though they were. "It was never just an act. I could never pity you because there's absolutely nothing to pity. Even when I learned—or when we all learned, really—precisely what you were...Eclipseborn, what a title. Even when I learned all of that, nothing changed for me. You were still the same person that day as you were the day before, and no revelation of how you were born would ever change that. I treated you with dignity and respect because you deserved that, and you always have."

Sen's breath caught in her chest. Tears were beginning to well in her eyes. Grateful tears at hearing affirmations she had longed for. The longer she listened, the more they gathered until they cascaded down her cheeks in a steady stream.

Narva took a breath to gather himself, gripping Sen more closely, and continued. "I remained friendly with you because whenever I look at you, I can't help but remember the adventurous and resourceful girl that you were while admiring and appreciating the intelligent and selfless woman you became. And yes, it's been difficult the last few years seeing you in such a state." He sighed, a grimace wrinkling his brow. "I admit my own faults in perhaps enabling that a bit. But even if you resent yourself now, that doesn't mean that you always will, because the person you *truly* are, the one that shines over whatever shadowy creature lurking about in there, she's still in there, and she's coming back. She's the one who would drop anything and everything in the name of familial love. She's the one who would stand up and fight for her family, against whatever she thought was wrong, regardless of the consequences. She's the one who's returning now, putting her own life on the line to save someone she cares so deeply about. She's there, and she's *here*. And I...she..." He paused and looked down sheepishly. "And I...care about her very much."

Sen could feel her cheeks blushing, blood rushing to her head in embarrassment. The impending chill had all but departed, warmth filling her chest once more. Nervously, she looked down, a smile creasing her lips, her brain struggling to formulate anything proper in response and failing miserably. Slow streams, happy streams, continued to flow down her cheeks. And when she looked back at him, his cheeks glowed with the same flushes of red. She chuckled—more than that, really. *Giggled*, even—and said, "Narva, I—"

He wasn't inclined to anything further. Pulling her in closer, his lips locked with hers, supple and soft. Taken initially by surprise, Sen remained wide-eyed as their lips met, knowing not what to do or how to react. But her body tingled and fluttered as she fell into it, her eyes closing, her weight bearing down on his as she rested her hand along the back of his head, fingers running through his tangled mass of hair. She had long pictured this happening—initially with anyone she found cute, but past that phase, almost exclusively with Narva—and now that it did, she felt at peace, warm and calmed and relaxed.

After a minute or three, the motion slowed, and Sen softly pulled back from him, her fingers trailing along his neck and chest, his body leaning back against the tree, a contented smile affixed to his face and hers in kind. Sen's heart was aflutter, her eyes closed as she chuckled softly to herself. She pressed a hand to her chest, feeling her heart beating rapidly, adrenaline coursing through her body. Her lips still tingled, the taste of his rugged mouth still lingering on her lips. She didn't know what precisely to say or what precisely to do next. There was only one thought running through her mind now, pushing away everything else which had lingered and threatened in there. Her eyes opened, and she started to say, "Narva, I lo—"

But just as soon as the words were about to pass her tongue, she realized that his eyes were not open, his head lolled forward. He grunted comfortably, shifting in his seated position, leg twitching as if already in a deep and exciting dream. The sight only made her laugh. Too much excitement for his exhausted body, apparently. The same could be said for Sen, too.

"Narva, I care about you very much, too," she whispered before nuzzling back up to him, pulling his arm around her as she rested her head on his chest. Just as soon as she reached her makeshift pillow, her eyes caught one final glance at the world to the south, and the City that awaited them.

For now, though, there was only sleep to be had. That night, there would be no bad dreams. She allowed herself to be content for the first time in a long while, safe and warm in Narva's embrace, and drifted off into a peaceful rest.

CHAPTER THIRTEEN

The Value of Gardening

Dust kicked into the hues of the golden streets as the sun retreated over the horizon. The bustle of the day had begun to dwindle, citizens returning to their homes to commence evening activities with their families. Merchants packed up their tents for the day, the tolling of the seventh bell warning of the closure of the day's activities as was the custom. Horses snorted and whinnied as their hooves clopped against hardened dirt, beaten paths made hard as iron over years of repeated travel.

With an amber glow shimmering at eye level, Red leaned casually against the front gates. They weren't imposing gates by any means, only the height of an average person, but there certainly was nothing else equivalent that she had seen prior to her coming here.

The summer warmth drizzled sweat down her brow and spine, her uniform top clinging mercilessly to her skin, swaths of dark blue outlining her spine and shoulders within the threads of lighter blue. The ornament around her neck didn't fare much better, radiating warmth along her nape. Her thick red hair was pulled back tightly, largely a safeguard against this humid air, as much as she was fond of her locks, the shade a rarity amongst the Acrarians. This time of year was always dreadful.

She found herself waiting far more casually than her peers. Flanking her at the gates were three others, alternating in a pattern of keeping watch outside and inside the city. She was at the far end, meant to be keeping her eye to the northern horizon, but she was much more relaxed, leaning on the gate by her shoulder, arms crossed beneath her breast and lined against the heirloom hidden beneath her shirt, one foot casually folded over the other. Her rifle was propped up to her side, standing near to the same height as herself, a smaller flintlock resting in her thigh holster, as was the standard array.

Her peers did not look upon her with high regard, but that didn't bother her. She was just happy to be serving this city. Glancing over her shoulder, past the burl and vigor of her male companion's arms, she smiled at the wealth of stacked wooden buildings, the promise of families living in good graces and company often juxtaposed with the more raucous crowds gathered by the adjacent watering holes, often frequented by the same married men beholden to those good graces. Every once in a while, she was interested in visiting one of these taverns because there was always a musty smell and rousing sound that she could pick up that went beyond flowing drinks and drunken banter, but damn it all, she could just never find the time.

The seventh bell had just finished ringing. In two hours' time, those establishments would be brimming and pulsing with life and vigor.

It was an impressive city that they had managed to build over the last decade. She could not help but admire it in the time since she moved here. There was just such a rich and vibrant lifestyle that seemed to spring up so quickly, a livelihood so comparable to a home away from home. Acraria was not a home well known to her, but she had to imagine that, given some more time, this city, whatever they would deem to name it, would thrive in the same manner. There was still plenty of work to be done: plenty of shops, houses, priories, schoolhouses, and the like were being built on the regular, seemingly daily as more and more people made the journey westward. She certainly couldn't blame them for wanting to start anew. That view to the south, just past the city limits, where the ocean shined and glittered in the golden kiss of the setting sun? It was worth its weight in gold.

Stood to reason that the General was the one who got the best view of it every day, what with that impressive manor he built for himself here. Well, *he* didn't build it. He had help. Labor was easy to come by around here.

The thought of the labor? Well, she had certain feelings on the matter.

As far as she saw it, this city was the heart of progress in a stagnant land. The smokestacks peeking above the houses, heralding the arrival of industry, was proof enough of that.

Amazing, what can come to pass, given time.

She arced her gaze back and forth, once to the city, once to the wilderness beyond, amused at the disparity, entranced by the progress, and enamored with the possibilities. The possibilities, namely, seemed to excite her more than most. The only one who could claim to have garnered more excitement?

The one whose host was poking its head out from the knolls beyond the northern horizon.

"Stand at the ready!" called the guard furthest from where Red stood, whose name she didn't particularly care to learn. His voice was far louder than it needed to be when addressing just the four of them present. "The General has returned!"

In unison, her three peers stood to attention, feet clacked together, chins puffed outward, rifles at their sides, butt end down. She mimed the same motion in due course, too, though perhaps a splinter of a second slower than the others. Not enough to call attention to herself, though she had not exactly built a reputation to get fussed over, regardless.

What an exciting week it had been in the General's absence. Well, truthfully, nothing of particular note had actually happened in the city itself—the standard fare of tavern brawls, proclamations of infidelity to the night skies, fishmongers being outed as not necessarily offering the "freshest" selection. No, what intrigued her the *most* was the wait.

The wait for the return. The wait for what came next. She always looked forward to what came next.

The host came into closer view, a coterie of soldiers fronted by one of a lordlier stature. The followers seemed so irrelevant, so insignificant, mice in the wake of a giant. They seemed woefully self-aware of their own insufficiencies, such to the point that they held back a handful of paces, allowing the man of the hour to shepherd his people back to the flock of the city. It never failed to impress her. Red had never known someone of such a higher station, so iconic and individual as the General, especially one so eager to accomplish deeds by his own hand rather than leave it to some no-name lackey. His features grew clearer as he drew closer, those wavy locks of auburn hair, drenched and matted from the week's journey, dried blood spattering his sleeves and neck, whiskers of hair grooming into his normally smooth face. All with the confidence and swagger befitting a man of his station, his strength, his determination.

Only when the General drew nearer did she notice the two captives sandwiched between him and the other soldiers. One would have thought that they were to be last week's runaways, their freedom short-lived and far from worth it. But quickly, she recognized that they were two different people entirely. They were both wearing face paint, which may have been enough of a disguise to those who elected not to pay closer attention. But she was quick to note that they were of a lighter complexion, a more trimmed and proper appearance, as though they had been living a cleaner existence for the past decade-plus.

All the same, though.

She and her peers stood at salute as the General approached, arms clasped diagonally across their chests. For his part, the General brushed them aside with his hand, laying bare the red stain across his arm as his sleeve came undone. He seemed unbothered by it. If anything, he appeared satisfied, relieved. There was no wear and tear on his face, no signs of hardship or struggle. He came back with the same group in tow, but she never got the impression that he was one to mourn losses. She had to respect that in a leader, one who sees the realities of loss but does not get caught up in the numbers. A reality to which she could relate.

The supporting cast of soldiers hung back as the General walked confidently past the gates. The two captives stared at the city, bewildered. One was a middle-aged man, streaks of red paint melting off his face. There was still an air of defiance in his gaze, a hateful and wild expression, untamed though all the more familiar to her. She had seen eyes like his plenty. Far more intrigued was she by the young boy they brought back, maybe a boy bordering on a man. He was scrawny and weak, knees knocking, arms trembling. His eyes were red and puffy from a couple days of tears, no doubt, and with those tears went the last vestiges of hope in his heart. She looked forward to this one. She thought she'd like this one.

"Are these…" started one of the gatekeepers, turning his head coolly over his shoulder in the direction of the General. There was, admittedly, some confusion on his part, perplexity flashing in his eyes, though Red could tell that he could not quite place the source of his confusion. He shrugged instead.

Without turning, the General scoffed and nudged his head further into the city. "You all know where they go. Take them home."

Another one of the gatekeepers—the one who had been stood next to her previously—stepped forward voluntarily, left hand resting upon the grip of his flintlock. He walked toward the more defiant one and grabbed him by the scruff of his neck, hurling him forward as though he were an animal. "I'll take this one," he said uncaringly.

They fashion themselves like animals, Red thought, *then we may as well handle them as such.*

There was a subtle pause, an uncertainty at who would grab the other, the boy. Granted, the pause was only so that she didn't appear too eager for the task. "I'll handle the boy," she said, some note of smugness evident in her voice. She took a handful of steps forward, dragging the butt end of her rifle along the ground, leaving a trail of dirt in her wake. Forcefully, she "nudged" him with her knee, the boy crying out with a whimper as she did so. "Such a baby," she muttered to herself, though to tell the truth, she could feel some sore heat in the bone of her knee already.

The boy flexed his backside as best as he could with bound arms, but to little avail.

"I'll leave you to it," the General said calmly before walking away.

Where he was going, she had no clue, since it was not in the direction of his manor, but it wasn't up to her to question his comings and goings. This *was* his city, after all. She had no issue with him doing as he pleased.

Slowly, Red pushed the boy along into the depths of the city, only as quickly as his fearful little legs would allow them. Nothing in his body language indicated assessing a potential escape—he seemed a bit too forlorn and distracted for something such as that. Instead, he was obviously relishing those last vestiges of his previous life before he was assimilated into his new one. She took an even greater interest in his bewildered expression at his surroundings. Clearly, this city was nothing like he had ever seen before—or would ever hope to see in his previous life.

"I remember my first time in the city," Red whispered to him, a broad smile across her face.

He offered no reaction, apparently because he, strangely, had no knowledge of the Acrarian tongue. How could he not? It was not a difficult tongue to learn.

She picked it up easily enough. What was *his* excuse?

The boy, instead, could respond only in fearful whimpers, wide-eyed like a frightened puppy, tail stuck between his legs, waiting for a wolf to rescue him from the wild when all he could ever hope to see any longer was pristine seas and forward progress.

She met his gaze with her own, meeting fear with satisfaction, and gestured her arm in a wide arc. "Just take a look around you, boy," she said. "You'll get to be part of the growth of a great civilization. A higher calling, a better path. You'll just have to work for it a bit to get there." She took in the vacating streets laid hewn in gold of the setting sun, the world falling to sleep against the day but remaining awake toward the future.

Shuddering tears began to trickle down the boy's cheeks in earnest. If ever he had a shred of defiance in him, it was gone a long time ago.

"If you think about it, you're one of the lucky ones," Red continued. "You'll have a place in this society. A better society, a fairer society. Don't you want to be part of something more? Just look over there." She grabbed hold of his head, unwilling though he was, and forcibly turned it to the west, where smokestacks sat atop the city's factory. "*That*, right there, that is progress. That is the future. The Homeland is filled with factories like this, but *this*, this is what will shape your little island into what it can be. Jobs, industry, production, all of that." She paused, before adding, "And there's something special there reserved for other occasions, but I'm sure you'll behave well enough that you won't need to worry about it."

The boy remained verbally noncommittal.

How annoying language barriers could be. If only there was a way that she could have better communicated with him.

The General's manor loomed large before them, but they were off to a different location, a humbler abode. Something more tucked away from the eye, past a series of fences and in the shadow of some adjacent taller buildings and structures. Her peer had already taken the defiant one in, leaving her with the boy by their lonesome in the thinning streets.

"'Course, that's what they tell themselves," she admitted. "Me? Ah, who knows. I'm just along for the ride. And if I learn a thing or two along the way? Well, where's the harm in that?" She smiled slyly, patting his back with a strong hand. "Maybe we'll both learn a thing or two through all this. One can never be sure what the night will bring, no?"

She passed a final gate and nodded to another fellow guard before stepping into the pen.

In rows, scores of people from those Tribes sat chained at the ankle, dull and silent, hardly acknowledging the comings and goings of the new people, old people, dead people. It was all the same to them after a while. What was another new face to them? Much like how, to her, she had seen enough dark faces to not feel the need to remember all of them. Just the select few who piqued her interest.

With her peer already having chained the defiant one to his spot, Red was feeling a bit generous. "You know, I'll be a little nice. As a little housewarming gift, I'll give you a slice of your old home and put you with your friend there." More eagerly, she pushed the boy along, nearly tripping over his feet. "And just remember, you play a larger part in all of this than you know." She sat him down, kneeling before him knowingly. She winked.

Without resistance, he held out his leg, not meeting her gaze or that of his kinsman, the full array of dejection strewn across his face.

Her grin unfading, the woman wrestled the clamp around the boy's ankle, positioning it in a closing position...and then left it slightly open. Before the boy could realize it, she leaned in closely and whispered a word to him. "*Uaa'c-sunic.*"

And just as quickly, she rose back to her feet and turned away, unconcerned whether he even acknowledged or registered that she said something to him. Something that he should have been able to understand.

Her job done, she set her sights back on the streets, the remnants of golden hour calling her name. But as she fished and weaved her way through the succession of fences and gates, she did not expect the General to be standing in wait for her. To his credit, he actually managed to startle her, which was difficult to do.

"All goes well in there?" he asked. His hands were folded behind his back, his chin puffed out with knowing importance.

"Ah, General, sir," Red stammered, caught off-guard before haphazardly throwing a salute together, to his notable amusement. "Yes, sir. All is well. I'll have a mind to ensure they make themselves right at home."

"Your enthusiasm is appreciated. As you were, then." And he turned and walked away, just as soon as he arrived, off to his manor to do whatever it was a General was to do.

She nodded in the General's direction, but really to no one in particular. "Yes, General Aritz. As I was, indeed." *Much still to do this evening.* She tugged at the chain around her neck, the heat that was radiating at the nape of her neck acting in much the same manner within her.

It was unlike anything she had ever seen before.

With the arrival of the setting sun came the view of the City, something so much larger and more expansive than any sight Sen had set her eyes on. She thought the view of the Forest from deep within the mountains was a sight to behold, but this? It was...

Conflicting.

She and Narva stood atop a rolling hill, the downward trend soon to lead them to land that had once belonged to the Tribes. A Land that *still* belonged to the Tribes. Much of the day's journey had been set in comfortable silence, far from the anxious quiet which had led them through the Forest the day before. While there was significant importance in being this far south, in territory no longer in control by its rightful owners, something about the openness and freshness of the air set her mind at ease.

It could also have been that something about her companion had put her at greater ease, as well. They hadn't spoken of the moment they shared the night previous. Frankly, Sen initially was under the impression that it was a falsehood crafted by her exhausted mind. But given that they did not wake until midday, there was not much in the way of discussing stories of what something may or may not have meant.

So, they set off in silence, electing not to acknowledge the moment. But at the same time, Sen noticed a different air about Narva throughout the day. A slyness in his gaze, stolen glances visible in her periphery, a soft and candid grin replacing the exuberant one he always had plastered on his face.

If she didn't know any better, she'd have thought he intentionally grazed her hand with his own a few times.

The playfulness held the anxiety at bay for much of the day. Even wordless acknowledgment was enough for her to go on.

But as Sen and Narva stood atop that grassy hill, witnessing the fruits of their culture's expulsion from its home, smoke and metal against tall wood impeding the view of the shimmering water beyond, the anxiety returned. And along with it anger.

"Well, this is disheartening," Narva said of the sight.

Sen scoffed and grimaced. "You can say that again." She raised a hand to her mouth, masking her shock at the sight. "I can't even imagine what it was actually like here with the southern Tribes."

"If I was to guess? Probably nothing close to this."

Her heart sank. "And somewhere in all this?" She gestured her hand forward, limbs trembling with fury and pallor. "Brin's there."

"We can only hope." Narva drew a deep breath through his nostrils, exasperated and elongated. Sen faced him, seeing the fire flickering in his gaze. His shoulders tensed, his fists balled. Distinctly, she could hear the wood of his bow crunching in his grasp from the force at which he angrily squeezed it. "I wish we could burn it all to the ground and build it back up to what it is supposed to be."

"There'll be a time for that," Sen said, though she wasn't quite sure if she believed that herself. The words felt hollow, even if there was a hopefulness to them. "But now is a different time."

"Then we should come up with a plan for 'now,'" he said. "Ran said the slave camp was right next to the biggest building in the City, right? Well, I think I can see it from here." His index finger directed toward the center of the settlement, toward an imposing sight more defined and elaborate from this distance than anything else in view. "If we're going to walk right up there, then we're going to need to come up with something."

"Do we, though?"

Narva shot her a sharp and questioning look. "What do you mean, 'do we?' We're not exactly the spitting image of the Invaders, Sen. Pretty sure they don't dress in northern pelts."

"They also look like they don't go out in the sun very often," Sen quipped.

"This is serious, Sen."

"I know. They should go outside more often."

"Sen." His voice was grave and stern.

Softly, Sen smiled. "I know, Narva. I know. Don't think I'm not taking this as seriously as I should be. I just..." She breathed in deeply, letting her words trail off. Her eyes quivered, teeth gnawing at her lower lip instinctively. Part of her wanted nothing more than to run through the City with all the bravery and strength of the folkloric heroes in the stories Brin always told her about. Would that she could house those qualities within her and give them to her little brother, who was always in need of them both. Especially now. *Especially now.*

"So, what are we to do, Sen?" Narva asked again. He gently put a hand on her shoulder, his thumb caressing the frightened skin beneath. She leaned into him, arm resting on his lower back, head against his shoulder.

"I figure," she started, pausing for dramatic effect, "that we should get disguises."

Quietly, Narva maintained his gaze toward the City. Sen could hear his breath startle a moment before resuming its normal flow. Taking her suggestion into silent consideration, he at last said, "You don't have a plan at all, do you?"

Admittedly, she didn't. But she felt none the worse off for it, strangely enough. "Have you ever known me to work up a plan? I've never been much of a gardener. I just pluck the seeds of a plan as they come to me."

"I'd say that's not always gone well for you."

"This'll be different," she said with confidence. "Luck's on our—"

"Don't even say it," he interrupted, half in disbelief, half in amusement. "Luck isn't on *our* side—it's on *yours*. And chancing it all on that right now is a bit of a stretch."

"We've chanced our way *this* far," Sen affirmed. "What's one more turn of the card?"

"Luck's gonna run out for you eventually," Narva warned, his eyes peering down at her from his periphery.

She tugged more tightly at his lower side, fingers wrapped snugly around his hip bone. "Today's not going to be that day. Not as long as Brin is chained up somewhere in that City. By the time we get there, it'll be nightfall. Then we can hide our faces, find some clothes, and track down the largest building in town. Easy."

"I think we have different definitions of the word 'easy.'"

She let go of him, flashing a smile towards him as she made her way down the hill. When she turned back to the road ahead, the smile grew more unassured. "I think we have plenty of time to go over our interpretations. Maybe we might even come up with one of those 'plans' you so earnestly love. You can always be a gardener if you want."

The road ahead was rife with discussions of the verisimilitude of the analogy and whether it was apt to do so with regards to such a momentous occasion. Those discussions, and still nothing resembling a plan.

The City stood in wait, tall billows of smoke fading into a horizon bereft of its gold and glimmer.

INTERLUDE

The Last Syllable of Recorded Time

The Year 1581 Anno Salvatoris
40 Years After the Settling

A chill ran through his veins as he scanned through his chamber. The room stood calm in silence. Trophies and memorabilia alike stared at him, dancing in mockery to the wind's touch. Gulls cawed in the distance, the crashing waves clapping harmoniously against sandy shores and rock faces. The warmth of the sun radiated against his neck, specks of sweat setting into his bare skin. Nature, in turn, spoke its objections to him—the wind, the sea, the skies—but he did not care to listen. This was not some clever jest by the hand of Savior and all he created. This was something more.

It was a threat. The Founder would be loath to stand for threats.

Aritz looked at the letter in his hand once more. The words rang in what were, to him, bold and hollow transgressions. Claims and accusations so audacious that they were ridiculous. *A disease?* he thought, repeating the words to himself over and over in his head. *A monster? How obscene. By what right does this person claim such? I am far more than that. I am far more than a man. I am a country's breath itself.* Scoffing, he crumpled the letter in his hand, but something deterred him from tossing it aside. The call to remember. The drive to forget.

We remember the Harvest. Do you?

The Harvest. That term had dogged his steps for twenty-five years. Nothing but slander and lies, all of it. The words of those living in envy of the society that he had built upon fractured earth. *I remember not the Harvest, because it did not exist. I remember only the Founding, the birth of a nation from nothing.*

And yet.

That chill continued to run through his veins. Aritz gritted his teeth as he gently placed the crumpled letter back on his desk, his eyes drawn to the pendant which had acted as a paperweight. Those runes which indicated Memory, the remnants of an inferior culture and idolatrous people. The sight of it disgusted him. To him, each reminder of those people was a failure, a mistake of his own hubris. A mistake which bore little and offered less, true, but the knowledge of it all was less than ideal.

"Perhaps I needn't rush off just yet," he muttered to himself, eyes still affixed to the pendant. "Perhaps one final expedition to the mountains is needed to rid myself of this memory." He looked at an open palm, flexing his wrinkled fingers. The trophies and memorabilia no longer danced in mockery at his sight; instead, they stood at attention, silent in regard. An open space sat wide open, seeming to plead to him for an addition to close the gap. "I suppose I'll have to figure out what—or *who*—to put up there to complete the collection."

In a furor, Aritz grabbed a letter opener from his desk, which had been collecting dust for who knows how long while sitting next to years upon years of unopened letters and unheeded summons from no-name upstarts from the Homeland. *A Founder does not heed summons,* he would often say to his carriers. *He only summons.* That said, he was at least fond of the letter opener, which took the shape of a small dagger. He had it made by special request to resemble a favorite of his, lost long ago. A scaled replica, as there was not much need for defending himself anymore. He only wished that he had tended better care to it in recent years; the edges were rather dull, the steel marred by specks of rust. But he didn't need it to be a weapon. He needed it only for one thing.

His old war map glowed in his vision. Memories flickered in his mind—fond memories, the ones he relished in his revisits to this land—of the days when this island was an unknown to him, when the borders of the land were as yet unfilled. The image of a greatly detailed southern half amused him, resultant of years of situating themselves in the territory south of that forest until, at last, they realized it was not quite the hard border they thought it was.

The north, by contrast—which now housed the twin provinces of Arnao and Luzia, named for his son and daughter, respectively—was humorously under-detailed, the excitement of bringing the island into the Acrarian embrace too extraordinary to focus on drawing in a map. There were general landmarks drawn, naturally, namely that large lake just to the north of the forest, but little else was drawn but provincial borders.

But the biggest impediment to his peace of mind was the one expanse which he begrudgingly filled in. That wide range of mountains in which those heathens continued to live. He looked at the markings with disgust, little triangles stacked on top of one another, encompassing more than a third of the northern half of the map. Twenty-five years it had been since Ferranda became his in earnest, and he wasn't one to share what was his.

Gripping the letter opener tightly in his hand, Aritz snarled and drove it into the heart of the beast, the tip only barely sticking into the thick wood of the map and the table beneath. The tool wavered and wobbled in place, but *he* stood firm. "Memory need not be a fickle thing," he proclaimed to no one in particular, "when I choose what is to be remembered."

Resolutely, he balled a fist, holding it up to his face, a multitude of scars blending with the wrinkles upon his fingers. His arm quivered as he tightly gripped the air, his eyes ablaze with the intent of seeing the remnants of a culture in similar straits.

But still.

Something called to him from that pendant. Cautiously, he peered back to his desk and to the blue skies and shining oceans beyond. The beckoning of the unknown, cry of something beyond his understanding. Decry it as he would, he could not resist its allure. Call it curiosity.

His chambers remained sat in silence, shadows wavering and curtains dancing. Aritz found himself trapped between two visages: the vast ocean beyond his window, a world beyond his comprehension or knowledge; and the land which he had created from its infancy, on the other side of his door, rife with familiarity and filled with people who had worshiped him as a god.

The world he knew was a good world, one that—despite his annoyances and grievances with those who groveled at his feet merely for the honor being graced with his spit—he was wholly satisfied with. But at the same time, there was an intrigue to what was still unknown to him. He had seen much in his sixty years, and there was still much he had yet to see.

Along with the curiosity, however, lingered residual anger. In a huff, Aritz headed for the door and jerked it open, finding no one but the downstairs servants stop in place and await his beckon. Many dropped whatever it was they were holding immediately, some items including filled buckets of water, glass dinnerware, and other breakable things. Gladly, they strewed themselves against broken glass and porcelain, paying no heed to the slashes and gashes they were receiving, for they had the honor of receiving the Founder's angered glares.

But they were of no consequence to Aritz. He only craned his neck around the corners of both sides of his door, finding neither of his posted guards. He knew they weren't there, but that hardly meant that he did not want answers as to how or why someone snuck into his chambers in the first place.

His presence caught the attention of one servant in particular who, even from far away, he could tell was knelt in a pile of broken glass, stains of red already seeping into the crystalline shards. "My Lord!" he cried out. "Have you need of any—"

Aritz slammed his door without further fanfare. "Nothing that you can hope to help with," he muttered. Angrily, he stepped toward his desk, cautiously keeping his attention to his periphery. Were he a weaker man, he would have considered calling for a guard. He would have considered leaving the island altogether, returning to a loving family. His life was no longer here. But he was not a weaker man. He was as strong as ever.

As he passed the war map once more, the dedication and resolution strewn into the mountaintops served as a reminder of his resolve and drive. "I will see this through to the end. I am not a man of half-measures. They have lived in freedom for far too long. I will see to it that their remnants are wiped from the pages of history."

But there was still the matter of the pendant. He had seen how they worked. *Experienced* it, in a manner of speaking. Perhaps it made him heretical or hypocritical, but who among his flock would ever dare to speak up and say otherwise? Whatever was held in this pendant, he had to know, and he had to be rid of it. One thing after another, one step at a time.

He sat at his desk, his eyes transfixed once more on the crumpled letter. The final words stared at him directly, unblemished from his wrath. *"Memory need not be a fickle thing."* He shook his head, knowing he had nothing to fear from a memory. He lived his life regretting nothing. Everything he did, everything he achieved, it was all for the purpose of bringing him to where he was now. Whatever was in that pendant, it couldn't harm him. He wouldn't allow it to hurt him. How would his memories even be stored within, at any rate?

Drawing a deep breath, Aritz reached out, past the crumpled letter. His fingers grazed the base of the pendant. A sudden warmth jolted through his arm, traveling up the limb, through his shoulder and neck, and into his head. A flash of disjointed sights burst through his vision. All nonsensical, incomprehensible glimpses of lights and colors, vibrant hues and obstructive noises. Immediately, he pulled back, startled. His chair scraped across the floor, nearly flipping over with the force at which he flew back. His heart pounded in his chest with the rhythmic intensity of the execution drums he remembered from his childhood.

"Savior's breath," he muttered. He could already feel the color draining from his face, a wave of everything and nothing hurtling through his body. Momentary and intermittent tremors gripped his limbs such to the point that he had to grip the armrests of his chair just to center himself. A man who feared nothing eventually fears something, and Aritz a Mata found himself fearing what would happen next were he to submit fully to that pendant.

In an attempt to regain his composure, he blindly caressed the whiskers on his face, half to put himself into pensive thought, half to ensure that what was before him was real. His hands still bore the same wrinkles and scars, his chambers the same collection of trophies and memories as before. Everything around him was just as he left it a moment prior. He drew another deep breath and rose to his feet. He was not going to be deterred by a piece of Tribal jewelry. *I am the goddamned Founder*, he asserted to himself.

And he picked it up by the chain in one hand, regarding the rune of Memory inscribed upon it. And then, with a sneer, he gripped the emblem tightly in his hand. Between the slits in his fingers, he could make out a slight glimmer of light. The surge of warmth jolted more ferociously through him, coursing through his arm and back up into his head. Digging his heels more firmly into the floor, Aritz felt his entire body flex with the energy passing through him. The shades and hues flashed before his eyes, colors becoming shapes, shapes becoming sceneries, sceneries becoming landscapes, landscapes becoming...

Home.

No longer was he in control of what was before him. Part of his mind felt as though it was motioning his hand in front of him, but there was no reflection of that within...whatever this memory was. He didn't know when it was. But he knew exactly *where* it was.

The vibrant greens were an immediate indicator. Far more verdant than anything the tainted land of Ferranda had to offer. The path before him was flanked by tall trees, a brick-laid walkway leading forward ornate with intricate carvings. Beyond the trees, the countryside stretched for miles and miles, hills and pastures painted in varying shades of green, sectioned into squares of farmland and plateaus. Further still lay a stunning lake of pristine blue hues, and even further than that, a wondrous range of snowcapped mountains. Often those mountains would provide a refreshing breeze on those warm summer days. Refocusing on the path ahead, the memory stared upon a remarkable façade of splendid engravings, set expertly into molded clay and stone. High above that, a palace reached up to the heavens, all the more easily attainable for the Savior's healing touch. The path led to an interior courtyard, the centerpiece of which was a grand fountain spurting water from one tall faucet flanked by four smaller ones. Stone doves and swans sat along the perimeter of the fountain, itself encased in a vibrant fence of green hedges.

It felt like ages since last Aritz had seen this place, even though it was not long ago at all. It was home. The Mata estate in southern Acraria.

He could feel the chills running along his arms even outside of the memory. But something struck him as odd. Specifically with the fountain. It looked more...complete than when he saw it last. The columns of water featured more intricate carvings than he remembered, a project that he had ordered to have started upon his departure with the anticipation that it would be completed on his arrival. Maybe he just hadn't paid close enough attention to it, or maybe it was quicker work than he realized it would be. After all, he *did* only hire the best craftsmen for these purposes. And the completed work did look marvelous. He looked forward to rewarding the craftsman handsomely upon his return. Unlike in Ferranda, the people of Acraria did not grovel for his attention; they knew their place and they knew their worth, which Aritz was always respectful of.

There was an eerie calm about this memory, though. It was strangely quiet about the Mata manor. Normally at this point of the day—by the sun's positioning, it was near about midday—the birds were chirping and feeding at the fountain. But today, there was nothing. They could have been goaded elsewhere while the mason performed his work, though. Perhaps it was nothing, then.

Slowly, the memory moved along. Forward it carried toward the fountain, stopping to appreciate a reflective glance in the water. The water always had a clear and mirrorlike quality to it, and Aritz's reflection shone clear as day in those pristine depths. How curious, though, that he managed to look a bit younger in that mirror, maybe by a couple years at most. The magic of the fountain, apparently. Nothing for it, though—any illusion of youth was always welcomed at his age. There was a smear on his face that he gratefully washed away, something red as though from a berry. *Was I indulging in the strawberries again?* he thought. *I knew those would be dangerous.*

As he straightened himself out, washing away berry juice from his hands, Aritz's memory continued into the depths of the estate. He took in the expertly landscaped carvings of hedge and bush, paths flanked by short trees and amorous scents. The liberty at which he was able to spend these sums of money to achieve this appearance was wonderful; Their Royal Highnesses were remarkably generous with the rewards they bequeathed him upon his return from the Founding. Everything he ever wanted was in this grand palace. A palace that was his birthright and his alone. One that he had to wrest away from his unworthy younger brothers, who now were off galli-vanting in some elsewhere squalor. One that he had to fight for as the days of his inheritance were growing more and more doubtful. Everything changed with Ferranda. And it all changed for the better.

He entered his hallowed halls, strangely also whispering away in silence. It was curious that there was no sentry posted at the entryway, but it could just have been that Aritz had dismissed them while he was off in the garden. Up in this remote area of the Acrarian countryside, there was hardly any danger to fear. He was perhaps more untouchable here than in Ferranda.

The walls were adorned with portraits of the heads of the Mata fortune, going back generations, back to his grandfather's grandfather. Back when the Mata name was built upon the spice trade. Over time, the family expanded into grander ventures—farmstock, housing, land…even some less than savory ventures into dealings with courtesans, though that was kept more under the rug.

The row of portraits ended with his own, completed a few years prior after he had put it off for decades. He had long expressed disinterest in his physical image, as the legacy of his deeds would have carried more weight. But there was an allure in being immortalized by the brush, and so, he insisted on his other great legacy—his family—being included. For some reason, he seemed very intent and appreciative of the portrait on this day. Of his two auburn-haired children, Arnao and Luzia, who carried not the blonde locks of his wife Lucrecia but at least had her blue eyes and warm smile. He appeared intent on studying them, memorizing them, immortalizing them in his own memory for one reason or another. Sometimes, a good piece of art is its own reward.

But the longer he remained in the memory, the stranger it all seemed. *This can't be any longer than a few months ago. So how are my memories even…*

"Ah, my Lord!" a voice called out from down the hall. "We were not expecting you to return so soon. The Lady Lucrecia will be thrilled!"

Aritz turned to see a sentry approaching, all garbed in the solid blue of the palace guard, the sleeves set with a flourish and frill, the top trending diagonally downward to reveal a part of the man's chest in a V-shape. The uniforms were light fitting and flexible, often appreciated in the warmer days of the Acrarian summer. A cutlass lay at the sentry's hip, the cross-guard set in deep gold as was the custom of the Mata palace guards—mainly as a display of Aritz's own status. Aritz wordlessly nodded to the sentry in acknowledgment and turned back to the portraits.

The guard fell in beside him, appreciating the artwork in equal measure. "Admiring Messer Camora's handiwork again? He did a wonderful job as always, my Lord."

Aritz grunted an agreement, a strangely toned grunt at that. *My voice sounds...odd.*

"Did you change your mind on returning to Ferranda, my Lord?" the sentry continued to ask. "You did not seem thrilled to be heading off. After two days, though, I assumed you'd have committed to it. It was strange not to see your caravan return with you, I must admit."

Wait, what the hell? Aritz thought. *I didn't return to the estate once I left. Who the...*

Continuing, the guard looked down to Aritz's hip, a curious expression on his face. He chuckled before asking, "Since when do you arm yourself, my Lord? You have *us* for that!"

Aritz looked down to the cutlass at his own hip and rolled a shoulder. *I never carry a sword. What is this?!* And just as quickly, he drew the sword from its scabbard, and in one motion, cut the throat of the guard before he even had a chance to react. Even if he had the opportunity, he clearly was far too stunned at the sight of his own Lord brandishing steel against him. Helplessly, he squeaked out an objection, hands clasped to his throat as blood gushed out between his fingers.

And Aritz did nothing but swing away the remnants of blood and return the sword to its scabbard.

Blood pooled beneath the collapsing guard. As Aritz looked down, he noticed crimson splash stains against his trouser leg, fresh intermingling with old. Turning back to the fountain, he could still barely see the motionless body of another guard, an arrow protruding from the back of his head, a red pool trailing its way to the fountain. Outside the vision, Aritz felt his heart catch in his chest. The guard's eyes froze in stunned panic, and Aritz's memory cared little for it. Lazily, he brushed away the smears of blood on his trousers, doing little but to spread it further across the cloth. Passing a final glance at the family portrait, he nodded and proceeded on.

Savior's breath! What…I don't…what is this sorcery?!

"Lord Aritz!" another voice called from deeper in the hall. A female guard came into view, concern plastered about her face. "I wasn't expecting…to…what?" Her tone and expression shifted dramatically as she saw her peer and colleague motionless about the floor, and the red-handed tell clear for her to see on her Lord's figure. "My…My Lord," she stammered, nervously reaching for her cutlass. "I don't…please don't make me…"

He was kind enough not to force her to choose. Drawing his cutlass, he rushed forward and drove it through her chest, red coursing out from her as her heart burst with the attack. Without a care, Aritz kicked her off the blade, pushing her hurtling down to the ground, meeting the floor in a splash of red. So pristine these hallways had been, cut in white marble, now painted in a crimson abstract. Messer Camora was not the only artist in the Kingdom. Aritz could be quite the painter himself.

The sound of drawn steel had alerted further guards. Footsteps echoed down the hallway, leather boots pounding against the hard marble. Swords were held at the ready in the hands of four guards who were gradually and more visibly no longer at the ready at the sight of their Lord. One dropped the steel entirely, the clang of metal resonating throughout the hollow halls. Two others struggled to even hold their steel steady. The fourth maintained a manner of resolution in his face, but his eyes screamed of fear and betrayal.

Words were not necessary. The brave one charged forward, yelling out some indistinct battle cry, eager for a day of glory that had never arrived on a battlefield. Meeting the challenge, Aritz held his cutlass out, blocking the guard's vertical strike with a horizontal parry, knocking the steel away. He spun away from his opponent and slashed across his back, cutting a swath from shoulder to shoulder, removing a significant amount of cloth and silk from the guard's uniform. The man grunted, falling to the ground from the impact, but still feeling brave enough to return to his feet. He called out another challenge, his motioning far more stilted and stiffer. Aritz remained firm on his feet, holding his blade out, pointing to his opponent once again. The guard charged at half the speed of before, wincing with every step as he brought the blade up high. No longer seeing the point in the challenge, Aritz sidestepped the blow with ease and swung through a large chunk of the man's arm before removing him of his head. Adding insult to injury, he kicked the loose head off to his companions, who remained still too frightened and stunned to deign to move forward.

The one who had dropped his steel previously fell to his knees, then to all fours, pleading to everyone and no one in particular for "this nightmare to end." Aritz could see tears streaming down the lad's face and couldn't help but wonder if he met every challenge with the same candor or if it was just this one instance of betrayal.

Either way, as he stepped closer to the three remaining guards, they cowered in greater and greater fear. He turned his wrist to twirl the cutlass about, specks of blood flying every which way as he did so. A soft chuckle rumbled in his throat, something that felt and sounded so artificial, so forced. His opponents were too dumbfounded to notice anything amiss. They only wept with steel wavering, legs shaking.

"Why, my Lord?" asked the guard in front, kneeling down in deference to him. His sword was planted tip down, hands resting atop the hilt as though in prayer. "What have we done to anger you?"

Aritz offered no response but to continue his approach.

"Please, my Lord," the guard continued. "Have we done you wrong? Have we done your family wrong? I don't understand."

"My Lord!" cried the guard still on his feet. "Please don't make us do this."

He had already offered an escape from that choice. He was more than happy to do so again. Calmly, he continued forward, allowing the sword to trail along the ground, scraping against the marble in a shrill but subtle shriek.

Tears still in his eyes, the kneeling guard leapt back to his feet and nearly flew through the air to close the gap between him and Aritz. "Forgive me!" he shouted as a battle cry, readying himself to swing in a diagonal strike.

Just as quickly, Aritz arced his blade upward, scraping further against the marble and swinging with increased velocity upon escape from the impeding earth. The blade's path cut upward from balls to brain, blood erupting up and raining down. The guard's blade landed elsewhere, the steel echoing against the hard marble. There was hardly a face remaining to ask for further forgiveness. Regardless, apology accepted.

"Ignacio, to your feet!" commanded the standing guard to his quivering companion. The one called Ignacio did not comply. "Ignacio, please! Get Lady Lucrecia and the children to safety!" Aritz tilted his head and raised his eyebrows, smiling broadly as he calmly approached the one brave man remaining. The commanding guard was aghast as his companion continued to grovel on the ground while his Lord continued to approach him with drawn steel. "Ignacio!"

Seeing no hope in the sniveling swordsman, the man snarled and screamed, managing to meet Aritz's steel. He was of greater skill than his previous opponents, able to parry his Lord's blows and riposte with his own. It was clear and evident that he had spent longer hours with the master-at-arms than others had, but there was still no matching Aritz's own aptitude with the blade.

For two minutes, they met steel for steel in quick succession, firing at each other with the fury of an angry wind. Aritz felt no exhaustion at the exchange, but more and more, it was clear that his opponent was tiring, but pushing through it. Spittle and sweat intermingled on his face as he shouted with every telegraphed move, his movements laborious yet ferocious. His arms were clearly weighing on him, every subsequent attack weaker and more sluggish.

Deciding that he humored the man for long enough, Aritz elected not to block the brunt of the steel, but instead catch the guard's wrist, maintaining it high up as his opponent had not the strength nor willpower to push forward. He was tired, betrayed, exhausted, and most importantly, saddened.

Slowly, and almost sadistically, Aritz brought the point of his steel into the man's throat, opening it up wider and wider. Crimson pools welled in the man's mouth, dribbling out from the corners in an inundating flow, until the entirety of the steel had passed through his throat. And with a final jerk of the wrist, Aritz flung the sword out the side of his neck, his head only barely connected to the rest of his body.

Splatters of red further painted the room, coloring the whites of the wall and nearby statues and sculptures. As the guard met the ground, eyes still wide open, his head nearly came undone from the remains of his neck. The floor was viscous and sticky beneath Aritz's stained boots.

His final opponent offered no further objection to the conflict. His eyes were very nearly pink from the tears, his sniveling face glistening with saline. Part of Aritz wanted to offer pity to the lad and allow him to live, but he was unsure whether it would be better for him to witness this and live or return to his feet and die. Either option was not ideal for the lad.

"I've failed you, my Lord," Ignacio sobbed. "However it was, I failed you. I cannot cross swords with you. So, please...allow me to end this on my own terms." He awaited an objection from Aritz but found nothing in his silent face. Rising back to his knees, Ignacio nodded and rose his sword up by the hilt. "Please forgive this coward, my Lord. And I pray to the Savior that you find your way again before it's too late." And thusly, he drove the sword through his chest, blood shooting out from his back. He grunted once, and then collapsed to the ground.

Savior's breath, Aritz thought once more. *No...please, no. What in the Savior's name?!*

His white canvas gave way to the sight of further green as interior gardens loomed vibrant against the bloodshed. The rustling of hedges was his only accompaniment as his feet clapped against the now-slick marble, red pools dampening the otherwise rhythmic taps. As his cutlass scraped back home to its scabbard, Aritz continued onward, taking in the pristine and sterile view before him while leaving the decadence and carnage behind.

A stairway led up to a balustrade, adjacent platforms decorated with ornate sculptures of creatures from Acrarian folklore—blazing avians of resurgent life, imposing canine guardians, boreal watchers. With each handful of steps up the stairs, Aritz delighted in nudging the sculptures from their pedestals, toppling them to the ground in an explosion of white marble and carved stone, each drop louder than the last. He wanted his arrival to be broadcast. He wanted to be heard. He wanted to be remembered. Clouds of soft dust puffed into the air, carried along in the playful breeze which had danced in from the countryside.

Curious birds flew in and sat atop the rows of hedges, chirping their own respective astonishment at the sight of a man laying waste to his own home. When Aritz turned to face them, a smile broad on his face, the birds immediately took flight, wanting none of the same fate which had befallen those in the painted hallways.

Each step preceded a crash, each crash preceding a distant cry. Silently, Aritz continued to smirk to himself, fingers playfully rapping along the hilt of the cutlass. At the toppling of the final sculpture, he stood satisfied at the mount of the stairway, taking one final glance at the world he had built, and the same that he had returned to blood and dust. Calmly, he looked down to his hands, stained in crimson, a river running in similar hues down his cheeks. His blue petticoat gained equal and additional coloring from the return home, his hair slick with viscera, but holding little in the way of sweat. Even in this heat, this hardly proved a challenge to him.

He turned about-face, eyeing the ornate door before him. Everything detail of the door was designed according to his instructions—every craft of wood, every intricate carving, every material, and every technique. He had a unique vision for this imagery of valor and creation, of sweat and tears. Qualities emblematic of what he himself felt synonymized him. A herald of who and what exactly visitors and guests should be apt to expect when entering these chambers.

How lovely it all looked as he bore his shoulder through, splintering the wood as the door flew open. Distantly, frightened screams and whimpers became more distinct, clearer, more defined.

Oh, God, no. Goddammit, no. Get...get me...get me out of here! I can't—Stop! Please, stop! Goddammit, stop!

But the memory would not stop. He could not break free from it. A pathway through the heart of the chambers was presented in the form of a long drapery of red carpet, leading to an enormous parlor housing antique musical instruments, crystalline accoutrements, custom-designed furnishings, and all the other necessities symbolic of a man of means aiming to instill both hospitality and envy in potential business partners, suitors, or whomever else. It was here that he had arranged a betrothal for his son, offering the favor of some family to the north whose name he did not bother to remember. And it was here that he found his final marks.

Against the backdrop of a wide array of picture windows—the rich Acrarian countryside rolling distantly in its hills and valleys—Aritz caught sight of a trio huddled in the corner, feet and legs strung together in a collective tremble, soft whimpers and cries echoing from the hollow room.

Dammit, no! I beg of you, stop!

Prayers were audible as Aritz slowly took his time forward. Eyeing the open rooms, he noticed closets rummaged, cabinets flung open, and drawers upended for any sign of hope and defense. Outside the memory, he knew as well as anyone that there was no hope to be found there—he was not one with a need for protection. He no longer carried weapons on his person nor in his possession, for he saw no need of it. But if ever there was a need direr than this...

With every step he took, the huddled mass of feet slinked ever so slightly back, as far back as the walls would allow. Aritz passed the couches, scabbard knocking against the frame of the adjacent grand piano. He glanced one final glimpse at the distant mountains, the skies painted in the richest of blues, the sun bearing down and shining light on an impure and dark scene. With hand still resting on his blade, he stopped, took in the scenery for a further extended moment, and turned to his left.

Arnao and Luzia had buried their faces into Lucrecia's chest, hiding their tears and sobs from their father. Lucrecia's waves of cornflower hair draped down her face, impeding a view of her piercing blue eyes, clear and vibrant as the crystalline oceans. She held their children's heads down, wanting them not to see the sight of Aritz bathed in blood, an expression of smug satisfaction settled into his face. It was evident that there had previously been tears upon her face, but now, there was just nothing. No anger, no sadness. Perhaps only disbelief. A disbelief that had shocked her into a feeling of nothingness.

"Why?" was all she could muster from her lips. "Why, Aritz?" Her voice was rough and scratchy, the words passing through her throat like sandpaper.

Aritz offered nothing in response. He only continued to stare at his family, taking in the sight of them groveling and whimpering, the fading aroma of rich flowers gradually being overtaken with the dominant stench of piss and shit. He considered taking the time to decide who was responsible for what, but he was just as satisfied in witnessing this joyous scene.

"Do you have nothing to say?" Lucrecia whispered. "Nothing at all?"

He did nothing but draw his sword.

No. No! God, no!

At the scrape of steel, the patches of auburn hair burrowed deeper into Lucrecia's breast. Aritz stood quietly, flexing his fingers along the hilt of the blade. He rolled his shoulder, relishing in watching the uncomfortable squirms. He awaited some shift in tone or candor upon his wife's face, but there was no such change. Suspicion narrowed in her eyes, those pools of blue accusatory and investigative, focusing on the area of his neck. He lifted a hand, caressing the red-slicked skin of his neck, traveling a finger down to the cold chain resting around his neck, traveling down his chest. And then he felt for the second chain.

He scoffed. He raised the blade. She winced.

"Dammit, no!" With a burst and a shock, Aritz pulled himself out of the memory, flinging the pendant away from him. Warmth continued to course through his skin, sweat pouring down his face and arms. As he centered and refocused himself, he realized he was nearly atop his desk, leaning over it with so much ferocity and furor that he didn't realize that he had almost knocked his chair halfway out the window. His hands planted firmly on the desk, the dampness of his palms seeping into the rich woodwork. His breathing was heavy and erratic, his skin prickled. Never had he felt so frozen in place, so helpless. "That couldn't be real. Not a chance. Just a trick of light, a devious sorcery. It—it couldn't be!"

Whatever the validity of the vision, whatever the sorcery and wickedness, Aritz a Mata came to the realization of one horrible truth. A truth to which he never thought he'd admit, a truth to which he had never experienced in all his years.

He felt fear. He felt vulnerable.

And he needed that weapon. He needed that flintlock of his.

In a panic, he rummaged through the drawers of his desk, flinging stacks of papers, old documents which probably should have received his attention years ago, ancient memorandums of the nation's Founding, original artwork of his children's designs. But no pistol.

Searching beneath the desk bore little fruit, as well. Nothing but collections of dusty remnants of less-than-satisfactory food. He sprang back to his feet, hunched once more over his desk, head down, sweat dripping down the bridge of his nose and onto the crumpled letter. The words, *"Memory need not be a fickle thing,"* continued to mock him, maintained in unblemished condition. Aritz balled his fist in anger and brought it down upon his desk. Over and over. Again and again. Splinters flew out in iambic rhythm, showering the perimeter with chips and slivers. After beating the desk into submission tenfold, he stopped, gingerly picking the wooden needles out from his blooded knuckles. He was shit out of luck. He was bereft of a weapon beyond a dulled letter opener, one hand bloodied beyond use, the other not his dominant hand. So desperately he wanted to scream out in anger, but he lacked the willpower to do even that. All he could do was stare at the door without a faithful weapon to await a foe's arrival.

He felt something at the back of his head. And then heard a familiar click from behind.

"It is true that memory need not be a fickle thing," warned a familiar feminine voice, mocking and sly in tone. "But, more than that, memory is a *burden*, is it not?"

CHAPTER FOURTEEN

Wild Card

The previous evening was hazy and blurry. Tez's desire for fresh air brought her to the stagnant environs of the tavern once more, accompanied only by stark silence and perfect strangers. Only flashes of the evening were clear, but she at least remembered having a modicum of liquid courage, which explained her waking in an unfamiliar place beside someone she only tangentially recognized. So shattered were the contents of her skull that she didn't have the presence of mind to bid her good morning and goodbye when she stumbled back home.

Much of the day was spent in recovery, sat on the edge of her bed, head in her hands, cup after cup of tea funneled down her throat for some rehydration. Her mother hardly questioned where she had been the night prior. There was enough for her to worry about that adding Tez's comings and goings within the village was somewhat superfluous.

In fact, enough was on Dennalhir's plate that Tez barely saw her emerge from her bedroom. Tez could hear her mother's rummaging throughout the hut intermittently over the course of the day, but she barely had the strength and ambition to shuffle her way across the home. Between the skull-shattering headache, the persistent wave of nausea, and the extreme dearth of strength, she couldn't help but wonder just how it was that Sen did this on a regular basis. It was personally needed for her in the moment, but she just couldn't justify making a living out of it. Still, despite the prolonged recovery throughout the day, she at least understood what compelled her younger sister to seek the drink, the desire to forget everything just for an evening within the haze of an altered state.

Tez had much to think about during her day of recovery. Chief among them was a swearing never to drink that much ever again—strangely, a declaration she often heard from Sen. But, more importantly, there was a persistent worry at the back of her mind. Something that superseded her sister's journey to the south, her brother's wellbeing, her mother's state of mind, the state of the Tribe in the wake of her father's murder. There was a concern for the future, the stability of her people as a collective unit.

And the oncoming of a coup.

The discussion she had had with her mother the previous evening was impetus enough. Koelhe's ominous warning was worrisome, but adding her shit-addled and shit-eating son into that conversation? It was enough to threaten further nausea.

Everything we've built, as a family, as a Tribe...is it all about to crumble? she thought. *Is it to fall in a wave of paranoia and jealousy? Or will we be able to stand for what is right?*

She shook her head, eyes still peeled to the floor, a mess of discarded teacups and misfired vomit staring back at her. With minor difficulty, she pointed her gaze first to Brin's empty bed, then to Sen's. Her eyes remained on her sister's. Deeply, she sighed. *And she's at the center of it all. Our hope and future, and yet simultaneously our fear and despair.* It sent a shudder down her spine. What was she to do in the wake of these odds? She looked up to her wall, at the ornamental twin half-spears hanging above her bed. Would it come to that? Or would it amount to nothing?

More than anything, though, she knew she just needed some air. The ripe and stagnant haze of her room was weighing heavily upon her, and she no longer wanted to face the cleanup she would have to perform in advance of Sen and Brin's return. A worry for another day.

A soft aroma tickled her nostrils from the direction of the crackling flames. At some point, her mother had emerged to lay a meal for her, a bowl containing a basic stew of grains and potatoes. Immediately, Tez felt guilt at not even realizing her mother had waited on her for...dinner? It appeared dim outside, so the entire day had to have passed by already. The stew was kept warm by the fire, and graciously, Tez devoured it, unaware of just how hungry she was.

As she sat by the pyre, she craned her head around the dancing embers, only barely catching sight of her mother sitting cross-legged, her back facing the main hall. Her body was shuddering and trembling, a soft weep audible over the intermittent sparks. Gaze affixed to the empty spot on the bed beside her, it was clear to Tez just what was on Dennalhir's mind. As much as she desired to hold her mother tightly at that moment, there was a part of her that knew that her mother would prefer her solitary moment of grief and mourning, having not been afforded much the chance in the previous day. Instead, Tez bowed her head to her mother's inattentive form and wandered outside into the crisp and biting evening air.

She was unsure of what she needed to do in order to clear her head. A walk through the ranges of the Heart seemed dangerous at this time of day, and the nothingness to the south would only instill in her a desire to try and catch up to her sister. Another evening in the tavern appeared a worse idea, but then her stomach rumbled even after wolfing down that hearty stew. To the tavern it was then. *But only for food,* she promised herself. *Offset drinking my body weight last night with eating it tonight instead.*

The plan after that was beyond her, but stepping into the fresh air, with a crisp breeze rolling in from the mountains, it made her feel better already. Maybe some food and a walk outside were what she needed the most right now. She wondered if Sen had realized the same long ago. On her return, Tez knew she'd have to ask her about it.

With hands stuck in the pockets of the same clothes she had worn the evening previous, Tez slowly walked along the pathways in the direction of the tavern. The beacon of the village square already glowed brightly. Part of her wanted to stare into the flames in search of answers. For when Sen would return with Brin. For what she could offer her mother, and likewise herself.

For what she could do for the Tribe going forward. For how she could mend the bridges ruptured in this village, and mend gaps where there should be none. She wanted to offer a thousand questions to the flames, but they would give no answers in return. They illuminated, but they did not enlighten.

Tez frowned, the aroma of kindling itching at her nostrils. She wondered whether all of this—everything of the past couple of days—was some horrid nightmare. So much had happened. The span of three days felt like a year. And yet she could be expected to do naught else but carry on and hope. But for as long as the previous days had been, she was anxious still for the days to come. Anxious of what was to come from the south and what was to come from within. More immediately, the internals offered more anxiety. But only barely.

She lost track of how long she stood there. It was only the roar of her stomach that broke her from her trance, followed by a subtle tease of nausea. "Food," Tez muttered to herself. "Worry about food now and worry about worry later."

It was odd to hear how quiet the village was. It wasn't completely nighttime just yet, but many seemed to have retired to their homes for the evening. There must have been an impending rainstorm. One of the Owlsigns in the village tended to predict incoming rain around midday just by observing the movement of the clouds, but Tez was still a bit too out of commission to heed that call. All the same, though. Maybe it meant she could eat a meal at the tavern in peace and quiet.

Tez listlessly walked along the path to the tavern, hearing casual conversations in passing. She didn't focus too much on the road ahead. Some stray children were still running about as their parents ordered them to return inside. A few dogs barked at one another playfully, wrestling in the mud over a chew toy. One family was enraptured with raucous and uncontrollable laughter. Must have been a good joke. And, up ahead, there were...*Oh*, she thought. *That's strange.*

Scurrying into a hut up ahead were three figures cloaked with risen hoods. Maybe they were expecting rain and Tez had made a mistake not grabbing her rain cloak. But still, the way they filed into the hut was odd. There was a noted hurry to their motion, a suspicious air to their being there. As far as she knew, there wasn't a particularly large family there; if anything, only one person lived there, though she couldn't quite remember who. Initially, she didn't mind much of it, but as she passed by, she could see the door close just as quickly in her periphery. It was enough to stop her in her tracks. Call it her own paranoia or call it curiosity. Either way, it was suspicious to her.

Despite her suspicion, she carried on toward the tavern. But just as she reached the establishment, something stopped her. That nagging feeling of impending conflict. Those warnings flashing in her mind. Food could wait; she had to turn back.

Tracking along the backsides of the row of huts, she found her way back to the mysterious hut, the question of its ownership still bothering her. Something didn't seem right about those few people gathering inside. She rested an ear to the exterior of the hut, listening intently, and sure enough, there were a host of voices ruminating from inside. And not just the three who had quickly shuffled along inside. There was an entire *gathering* within.

A shrill and biting voice immediately caught her attention. Muffled as it was, the walls to this hut were thin enough that Tez could clearly make out to whom the voice belonged.

Koelhe.

And so it begins, Tez thought.

With a deep breath, she focused her hearing, doing her utmost to draw as little attention to her presence as possible, and listened.

"Enough, enough," Koelhe said over the mixture of voices. "Enough of the racket. We need not draw a noise complaint tonight."

"Who would they even complain to?" an unfamiliar voice quipped. "Isn't that why we're here?"

The comment made Tez grit her teeth. Softly, she couldn't help but growl, but collecting herself, she remained affixed to the earth.

"Quiet," Koelhe continued. "We do all know why we're here, but that doesn't mean the neighbors need to know just yet."

"Fine, fine. Is this all of us?"

"Not quite yet," said another familiar voice. *Fann. Of course, who else?* "There's a new addition yet to arrive."

"A newcomer? Well, we're really bringing in the numbers in the Tribe, then, are we?"

"We are," Fann said, "in our Tribe and beyond. It seems it is not just our own people who desire a change.

"Is that right? Who, then?"

"He'll arrive shortly enough, I'm sure. Now, Mother, shall we…" He paused, the sound of soft rusting against the floor barely audible. "Ah, and perfectly timed. Were your ears burning? We were just speaking of you."

There was a prolonged silence as bodies shifted inside, moving aside to accommodate the new arrival. It appeared that there was great care taken to assure this newcomer's comfort and wellbeing. Tez could hardly remember Koelhe offering that same hospitality to anyone but her own self.

"I apologize for my tardiness," rumbled a deep and commanding voice.

It was so familiar, yet Tez could not quite put her finger on it. She knew she had heard it quite recently, but in what context?

"I hope there are no objections that I brought company of my own. Needless to say, he and I have the same feelings on this matter."

"It does my heart good to know that you are not alone in your actions," Koelhe assured, her voice rife with her customary self-satisfaction.

To think she even has a heart, Tez thought. *I'd be game to dig around in there and pull out whatever it is she calls a heart just to see how small it is.*

"Welcome, to the both of you."

"You do us both a great honor in inviting us," the man answered. "I am curious of your plan of action going forward. When do you aim to move?"

"Soon," was all Koelhe said. "You needn't worry. Even if they were to expect it, there's little they could do to stop it."

"You speak with greater confidence than Fannalhen ever did, though I must admit I've doubts of your success in absence of a plan."

"Please," Koelhe chuckled. "You dishonor me with such words. The pieces have fallen into place, I assure you. But I am quite hesitant to divulge everything so readily, especially when we have you and your companion as new additions to our menagerie. I say this, of course, with no offense given and all due respect."

"I would hardly deign to suggest that you have not planned each step accordingly. I apologize if I've disrespected you in any way. Be that as it may, though, I am putting myself and my people at another's mercy here. I would assume that to mean we can speak as equals, as, soon enough, we will be in name and title."

Name and title? Tez pondered. *Surely, this can't mean...*

"Then, tell me and everyone here," Koelhe continued. "You accepted my invitation with little persuasion. I believe we are all owed the truth of your intentions. Would you not agree that to be fair?"

The man grunted and chuckled softly. "There is a time for a man to admit when he has failed his people. I am willing to admit that. When the Invaders took our lands, after I had so graciously offered a hand in welcoming, I knew I had failed. When I led my people to pastures greener in hope of a new day and a new start, I knew I had failed. When that journey ended in disaster at the hands of those monsters in the Forest, I knew I had failed. But, I at least had the illusion of success amongst my people when we were allowed a new home in the realm of your people. I admit, I thought, at last, my failures had ceased."

Faint murmurs ruminated within the hut. For her part, Tez could only grind her teeth in frustration.

"But," the voice continued, "there was always the lingering desire for revenge. I thought that there would be sympathy amongst your people for the plight of mine. And in finding people of like mind within the Stone Tribe, I assumed those feelings would be mutual with your Chief. I will never deny that my people and I are indebted to the late Chief Fannalhen. Deny that as you will, Koelhe, but that point is not up for discussion nor debate. Though he is beneath the earth, we still owe him what lives we have remaining. But...there's always a 'but,' isn't there?

"He had no sympathy otherwise to our plight."

...Shit, Tez thought.

"He thought we would be content to start anew in these lands. Initially, at least *I* was. But as I listened to our people further and further, I realized that this life is unsustainable for us. We are not a people who can adapt to the cold or live a life away from the sea. And so, for years, I pleaded again and again to Fannalhen, and again and again, he would deny me that desire for revenge. That need for the reclamation of what was rightfully ours. He always brushed it off as 'too dangerous' or some such, that the Forest would divide us from them and that we could live in safety and harmony as a new nation of Tribes. That we could not hope to stand a chance against the Invaders. But how was he to know that if he had never met them before on an open field? They outmatched the Tribes of the south because they caught them off-guard. But with a united force of our extant Tribes, in conjunction with the might of the north? As formidable as a united force would have been, he would hardly give my pleas a second thought, even at third and fourth and fifth insistence."

Various voices shouted their objections to her father's past actions, immediately followed by insistences for silence.

"In those moments, and in these last years, I thought I failed," continued the dejected voice. "I thought our way and people were about to become extinct. But as time wore on, more and more, I knew it was not I that failed my people, but Fannalhen who failed us all when he refused to fight for us. And I see none of that changing in passing along leadership to his wife. They shared too much alike, Fannalhen and Dennalhir, and in this, I know she would not change her stance. I have been forced to start anew, just as my people have, and likewise, there should be no cause which should prevent the people of the Stone from doing the same."

The hut fell silent, a few approving grunts and murmurs all that ruminated within. There was some slight rustling, another affirmative grunt, and little else in the way of noise for the moment.

But at last, Koelhe cleared her throat.

"And do you feel the same as him?" she asked, not to the man and his monologue, but apparently to his companion.

The companion at first said nothing. Perhaps he nodded or offered some other motion that Tez could not see from outside. But there were further affirmative murmurs from within, and finally, he said, "Fannalhen was a coward."

That made Koelhe laugh boisterously. "Ah, how wonderful to find someone on such an agreeable level. What is your name?"

There was further rustling, and the companion said, "I am called Tol'e, hunter of the Sun Tribe." Tez's heart sank, and a cavernous pit opened wide in her stomach.

"And one of our Tribe's best hunters, at that," the other man added. "In my initial years of hesitance, I will admit that Tol'e was particularly harsh on me for not immediately striking back at the Invaders. But the more I listened, the more I realized that his feelings were not just those of a select few; they were the will of an entire Tribe. In your own feelings for your own Tribe, Koelhe, I am sure you can find some mutual ground."

"On that, we surely agree," Koelhe affirmed. "It pleases me greatly that the Sun Tribe stands with us, Chief Han'e. And at the end of this, when I am Chief, I pledge that the Stone Tribe will stand with the Sun with the charge of reclaiming your lands. And that of the Arrow and Haunted, as well, until the Invaders, at last, have been driven from the Land. This I pledge."

"And this, I accept," Han'e pledged in response.

Damn it all, Tez thought. *This is a nightmare. We need to figure out who's on our side, and quick.*

"Are there any objections to our welcoming of Chief Han'e and the Sun Tribe into our fold?" Koelhe posited to the gathering. Hearing nothing, she grunted with satisfaction. "Then, to our plan of action, Han'e." Tez listened closely. "We will—"

Something grabbed at Tez from behind. A firm hand covered her mouth, muffling her protests. She tried fruitlessly to pry the hand loose from her lips, but whoever it was, they were unrelenting. Thinking not to scream as to not draw attention to her eavesdropping, she did her best to silently fight off the assailant, but further and further she felt her heels dragging against the soft ground, pulled off to an elsewhere destination. *Who the hell—how did I not hear...*

Soft and hot breath rang against her ear, and finally, she heard a whisper, "It's quite rude to eavesdrop on the conversations of others, Tezalhat." She knew the voice, cold and stoic as ever.

Rantalha. No wonder she didn't hear his approach. He wasn't one of the best hunters in the Tribe for nothing. It pays to be such an adept Sneak.

His hand still clasped over her mouth, she grunted in muffled disagreement, unable to fight off his strong grip.

"If you wish to spy on others, I can teach you not to do it so poorly. But first, we should have a quick chat." He continued to drag her along to parts unknown.

By nightfall, Sen and Narva had reached the outskirts of the City. The closer they drew to its borders, the more they felt a simultaneous sense of wonder and feeling of anger at what had been built upon stolen land.

Buildings stood taller than anything they had seen before, stretching further than they had ever deemed possible. Sen was under the impression that the Wood Tribe had a tremendous idea of constructing homes in the far reaches of the trees, but she had never thought that wood and stone could be stacked so high on top of themselves like these homes were. It was impressive and sickening all the same.

In the shallow valley of a grassy dune, she and Narva laid in rest, shielding themselves against the cover of night. Peering her eyes around the hill, Sen noticed the main gate, four Invaders standing ready with Deatharm in hand. She winced and ground her teeth, fingers digging deep into her palms. With frustration, she turned back to Narva, allowing her head to fall back against the soft and chilled grass.

"Not as easy as you thought it might be?" Narva quipped, an expression on his face that seemed to say, "*I told you so.*" Gods, she wanted to smack that dopey look off his face.

"You know, you could have voiced an objection," Sen responded.

"That's what I've spent most of today doing, Sen."

"Oh, that's right. I knew there was a reason I tuned you out a while ago."

"I wouldn't expect any different."

"You say that like it's a bad thing."

"Well, right now, I wouldn't call it a good thing, either."

"That, I can work with," she said with a smile. Turning back to the view of the City entrance, she allowed an annoyed growl to escape her throat. "Probably not a great idea to go in through the front door."

"Oh, I wouldn't say that," Narva said sarcastically. "Who knows, you could get—"

"Luck probably wouldn't help the both of us here," Sen interrupted. "This can't be the only way in."

Narva turned around the other side of the dune, examining the City's western side. He hummed thoughtfully to himself, grunting in affirmation, and then motioned Sen to his side with a wave of his hand. "Look over there," he said, pointing to the far corner of the City's walls. "Looks like those walls are pretty low. Think you could scale them?"

Sen could feel the amusement on her face. "You do realize that we spent much of our childhood climbing mountains, right?"

"Hey, I just wasn't sure if you were out of practice, is all."

"I think I can manage. What are you thinking?"

Pensively, he stroked his chin, the remnants of his face paint still dabbed in the stubbled whiskers peeking through his cheeks. "Two options. If that front gate is the only way through, then I doubt there would be any significant collection of guards over there. So, we scale the wall, get to cover as quick as possible."

"And then we find some clothes to blend in, bringing my great plan to fruition," Sen interjected with amusement. She didn't look at Narva, but she heard him groan. "And option two?"

"There *is* another gate with more guards. In which case…" He loosed the bow from around his shoulders and tapped at his quiver of arrows with his forefinger. "You know, Sharrabha taught me a while back how to shoot multiple arrows at once. I've *always* wanted to try it. And what better targets?" He couldn't hide his smile.

Sen couldn't help but grin in response.

"Shall we, then?" she pondered. She held out her hand, meeting the rough and dry skin of her companion's. Collectively, they rose to their feet, hunkered down to a crouch, and scurried along the night-soaked fields, eyes affixed to the western walls.

With each subsequent heavy step, Sen's heart pounded in her chest with increasing fury and anxiety, the constant threat of the Invader stronghold mocking her in her peripheral vision. Even in the dim light, she could have sworn that the City retained an ominous glow, something sinister lurking within those peppered depths. Deep down, she had a hope that the Haunted Tribe's belief of the looming presence of their fallen brethren was entirely true, just for the realization that these bastards would be tailed each step by the souls of the lost. *I hope they never get a clean night of sleep*, she thought, her focus more drawn to the City now than the path ahead, fires stoking in her gaze.

Despite their close proximity to the City, however, the road was eerily calm and quiet. She had expected something akin to the persistent din of the Stone Tribe, given how this place completely dwarfed her home village. But regardless of the glow from within, Sen could scarcely hear a peep from within the City walls. Did they all fall to rest with the rising of the moon? Or were they all truly bewildered by the presence lurking in the ground below? She hoped the latter.

On she and Narva ran, sharing no words with one another and fewer glances. The western wall was turning a corner up ahead, and there lay their opening. Narva ran up ahead, drawing a bundle of arrows between his fingers, carrying them like claws, invoking the Wolf he always was and always would be. The full moon above was gradually being enveloped in sinister clouds, but in what moonlight that remained, Sen would have been remiss not to notice the lupine focus that glowed in Narva's eyes. It was almost as though he was renewed after the ordeal in the Forest, a new man entirely, a man of the Tribes intent on banishing every trace of the Invaders from the homeland.

Another hill stood tall ahead. Narva sped further, leaving Sen several paces behind. Perhaps he was filled with excitement and anticipation; Sen couldn't say for sure. But the manner in which Narva dove and slid behind the face of the hill, evoking every shade of the hunter he was trained to be, it spoke of a man ready for what lay ahead. When at last Sen caught up to him, she found him prostrate on his back, chest heaving up and down, arrows held tightly between his fingers still. It seemed he had already exhausted himself.

"Getting a bit excited there?" Sen quipped. She knelt beside him, ensuring her head was below the face of the hill. Her heart was continuing to pound in her chest.

Peering around the corner of the crest of the hill, Sen could see a wide opening of fencing, a perfect entry point on the outskirts of the City. It appeared much larger an entryway than the front gates. She couldn't help but be curious about what should have been considered a design flaw. Quickly, she realized that Narva was not peering alongside her, evidently having spotted the opening himself already.

Narva exhaled and closed his eyes, a shudder rippling his breath. "Are you ready?" he asked.

Sen nodded.

"We only get one shot at this."

"This whole thing was my idea," Sen dismissed. "Do you think I'd back out right when we're here?"

Narva chuckled. "Just wanted to make sure we're on the same page." He rose to his backside, readying his bow in one hand. Shifting to a kneeling position, he lined three arrows along the bowstring and drew a deep breath. He rolled his shoulder, allowing the bones to crack and unstiffen, and quickly turned on his knee, drawing the string back. The bow's frame creaked with the motion, Narva holding the weapon nearly horizontal with the three arrows ready to fly. Eagerly, Sen awaited the loosing of arrows, but instead, Narva frowned, slackening his hold on the bow.

"What is it?" she asked.

Scratching the back of his head, perplexed, Narva deeply furrowed his brow and said plainly, "There's no one there."

"What?" Sen shuffled over to Narva's position, peering over his shoulder, and furrowed her brow just the same. "Well, that has to be a trap."

"A trap for who?"

She threw her hands up in deference, at a loss for words. "I don't know. But doesn't that seem suspicious to you?"

"Of course, it does. But who they'd be laying a trap *for*, is my question."

Sen sighed. "Just keep arrows at the ready."

Narva nodded and rose to his feet.

Cautiously, they descended the hill, Sen gripping Narva's broad shoulders for purchase and balance. Her skin prickled as each step brought her closer to the City, where somewhere deep within, Brin was ensnared like an animal. She gritted her teeth, fingers digging angrily into Narva's shoulder. He grunted slightly but did not object. If anything, it appeared to keep him focused.

They reached the wall and glued their backs to it. Narva held his bundle of arrows at the ready and ever so slightly peered around the corner. The further he peeked, the more comfortable Sen felt at proceeding forward. Eventually, Narva took a full turn and proceeded down the walkway.

The sight along the walkway was haunting as Sen followed. Even in the darkened alleyway, she could make out the outline of red along the walls, holes the size of what pierced her father peppering the stone. Chains hung from the walls at about head height.

She had a pretty solid guess at what went on in this tainted City. Lowly, she growled, a murmur echoed in greater volume by Narva. "You don't think..." she wondered aloud.

"I think exactly," Narva responded, stuck in a dead stop at the sight. His hands ground at his bow. "Barbaric."

"And they would call *us* the animals," Sen sneered. "I think we found our reason for why this goes unguarded. I'd not want to be the poor bastard stuck staring at this all day."

"Neither would I," Narva agreed. "But that's beyond the point. We're in the City now. What do we do?"

Sen nodded, refocusing on the task at hand. "Same as it always was. Find disguises." She smiled.

"Oh, sweet merciful..." he muttered. "And just how do you intend to do that, Sen?"

Her smile broadened, and just as quickly, Narva shook his head and rolled his eyes. He knew precisely what that grin meant.

His pendant shimmering beneath his shirt, Narva listened closely with his amplified sense of Sound and led the expedition inward. Hearing nothing, he confidently motioned forward with his head, hands still readied at his bow.

The corner they reached was flanked by a tall row of fencing, higher than anything that surrounded the City itself.

Sen couldn't help but back herself up a few paces and stare upward, finding a tall steel column overlooking the City, residual smoke still fluttering out from its opening. "What is that?" she whispered to herself. But recognizing other matters at hand, she chose to ignore it beyond that comment.

As they both peered the corner, they could not help but be caught in wonder at what lay beyond the outer walls. The pathways were more expansive and wider, dirt paved with greater organization than Sen had been accustomed to. There was enough room for two horses to walk side by side, drawing some sort of wagon for people to sit in. Though that sight was far off, it was still clear enough to see. Large homes lined the pathways, some two stories tall, crafted from wood and stone. The craftsmanship looked all too familiar to Sen. There was some originality in their compositions, but it was clear that there was at least some influence from Stone huts in these homes, too. That realization only angered her further.

Continuing along the path, tall metal torches rose from the earth. The flames were enclosed in some sort of casing, illuminating the entirety of the road ahead rather than a singular pyre acting as a beacon. Within each home appeared to be some similar instrument, for many homes had light flickering in greater intensity than she had ever seen.

"As much as I hate to admit it," Sen murmured, "this is impressive."

Narva shook his head but couldn't help but grunt in affirmation. "A shame we'll have to burn it all down."

"I look forward to that one day," Sen smiled. "But one thing at a time. Remember, we're looking for the tallest home in the City, and Brin should be held somewhere near there."

"Can't tell one size from the other," Narva muttered. "Let's cross the street."

Quickly, they scampered along the dirt road, kicking up dust with each quick movement. As they slid behind another building, a cloud of dirt danced into the air, blowing along in the wind. They pressed themselves up against the building, Narva confident that no one dwelt within, and scanned the road from the other angle. Immediately, their target was clear.

"Well, I'd say *that* is where we need to go," Narva said with little humor.

A huge home shot up from the earth, equal parts tall and wide, taking up the same mass as eight normal homes, by Sen's estimation. Even from this distance, she could make out intricate steel gates, the design of which likely rendering impossible the art of scaling. But, if Shara and Ran's words were to be trusted, they needn't head within those gates. Merely to the side of them. That at least instilled some confidence within her.

Narva continued to peer along the road, humming thoughtfully to himself all the while. "Okay, we should probably keep to the sides and alleyways. I still see a lot of people wandering about, and we're going to stick out like a sore thumb. Just as long as we don't draw too much attention to ourselves, we should be...Sen?"

So entranced was he in his observations that he didn't realize that Sen had wandered around the back of the building. Playfully, she waved him over, a wide grin on her face.

"What is it, Se—" Then his jaw dropped. "Oh, you've gotta be kidding me."

A line of clothing stretched from the back of the home to an adjacent fence, clothing fitting for the both of them fresh for the taking. "And, what did I tell you?" Sen chuckled. "Did I not say that—"

"Don't say it," he interrupted, half-annoyed. "Don't even fucking say it."

Quickly, they discarded their Tribal clothing and grabbed the Invader garb, paying little heed to the other's briefly naked bodies. Sen donned a long-sleeved collared shirt, buttoning up to just below her neckline, billows and frills patterned into the dark canvas. To complement it, she picked out a flowing skirt of similar material, which draped down to her ankles, enough to mask the boots she continued to wear, and a dark-colored bonnet that hid much of her face.

Uncomfortably, Narva slipped into a pair of tanned trousers with a similarly frilled button-up shirt. A nearby overcoat completed the ensemble along with a wide-brimmed hat. Just as quickly, they tossed their Tribal garments over the fence into what they hoped was the adjacent field.

"There, that wasn't so hard, now, was it?" Sen joked, continuing to adjust the clothing to her liking.

Narva appeared somewhat bewildered. "I swear, if either of us has to run for it in these clothes..."

"I have no qualms about ruining these clothes if it means being able to run," Sen smiled. "Now, let's keep going."

Despite an annoyed grunt, Narva could not mask his amusement. "Fine, fine. Just stick close and keep your head down. There're still people out, and about and our faces don't exactly scream 'Monstrous Invader.' We should keep out of the light as much as possible."

Sen held out her arm.

"What are you doing?" Narva asked curiously.

She shrugged. "I did see a few people linking their arms like this. Maybe that's just how men and women walk here?" Her cheeks flushed as Narva grinned and slid his arm through hers. "Keep an ear open then, and maybe we'll hear something useful."

Out they went into the darkened streets, walking along the dirt paths rather than the side walkways as other couples had appeared to be doing, though there were a scant few opting to walk along the center roads, so they did not look too out of place. Sen caught wind of scattered whispers which she couldn't make out, hearty laughter deriving from attempted humor, and hooting and hollering from nearby establishments. Out past the veil of her bonnet, though, she had no reason to believe that any of the noise was directed to or resultant of their presence in the City, so she felt some degree of relief at that.

Her feet fell in step with Narva's as they continued to patrol along the road, arms linked at the elbow. "Hear anything useful?" she asked under her breath, ensuring that none would hear her natural tongue.

"Well, I'm hearing plenty," Narva whispered back. "The issue is I don't understand what the hell they're saying."

"Tell them to speak our language instead."

"I'll get right on that."

Sen peered along her periphery, finding little out of the ordinary here. As she examined the people of the City more and more, though, she was surprised that they were just...people. She had expected them to brand that same arrogance and malice which exuded from the pores of the Invader who killed her father. But these people...no. *I'm not making excuses for them. They should not be here. This Land belongs to the Tribes. Their casual conversations and laughter don't make them any more humane.*

She frowned and nudged Narva with her elbow, craning her head off to the side. They walked to an adjacent building, no citizens near to approaching. She leaned against the building, arms crossed, brow furrowed.

"What is it?" Narva asked.

"These people..." she muttered. "Look at 'em all. Laughing and living their lives as though they haven't stowed away right under their noses."

"Who's to say it's under their noses? I'm willing to bet they know already, and they just don't care."

"And yet they continue to live so carefree." She exhaled sharply through her nose. "I thought the soldiers were hateful enough. But seeing these folk just continuing on with their lives, not a care in the world...I'm not sure if it makes them worse or better than the fighters."

"Who's to say it's either?" Narva grunted, ears still scanning the immediate vicinity, the glow of the pendant far less noticeable beneath the canvas shirt. "They're all just as evil as the next, the lot of them."

Sen looked down to the ground, frown still prominent. She wanted to accept that, but there was a part of her still struggling with who she should detest more.

Narva's brow furrowed, his neck craning with interest. He narrowed his eyes and turned back to the corner, arms crossed to maintain a casual air about him. Despite the language barrier, there was clearly something that had piqued his interest.

"What?" Sen asked. "What is it?"

"I mean, I don't know, specifically," he said. "But the *tone* of the voices. It says more than the words themselves."

Peering around Narva's shoulder, Sen stared into the shadows, catching sight of several people stopping along the walkways.

Many pointed accusatory fingers, others whispered to their respective partners. But their attention all universally appeared drawn to the same thing. Someone was wandering through the streets, dirt-stained and ragged, an air of exhaustion and loss affixed to his gait.

And as the form of the person became clearer, Sen's heart skipped a beat. "Brin," she whispered with a gasp.

When Tez was finally being dragged no longer, she realized that she was indoors. It was a hut unfamiliar to her. Unceremoniously, she was dropped onto the floor, the imprint of Rantalha's hand still radiating around her mouth. She rose off her backside and to her knees to find her assailant kneeling before her rather comfortably, a cup of tea somehow already prepared and a deck of cards before him.

She rolled her eyes. "If you wanted to invite me over, all you had to do was ask, you know."

With amusement, Rantalha actually managed to chuckle. Those rare moments where that happened never failed to unsettle her. "And here I was thinking your sister was the only one with wit and candor."

"Where do you think *she* got it from?" Tez offered in annoyance. Her neck was tight and stiff from being held at such an awkward angle, so she massaged the back of it with a wince. "What are we doing here, Rantalha?"

"I did say that we should have a nice chat together," he said. "And here we are. Tea?" Generously, he held a small cup out to her.

Tez refused the cup, not wanting to know its contents. "Fine then. Let's chat. We can start with your betrayal of my mother."

Raising his eyebrows, Rantalha actually smiled. "Betrayal?"

A sneer creased her brow. "Are you truly going to play dumb now? You and I both know what gathering Koelhe had brought into that hut. We both know that you were there. So, let's cut all the bullshit and talk about your plotting against my mother."

A deep chuckle rumbled in Rantalha's throat. Gingerly, he sipped at the tea cup, sighing calmly. "Ah, Tezalhat," he said softly. "I wish you would not place matters into such binary right-and-wrong. There is no betrayal at play here, nor is there taking a side. Only acting in the best interests of the Tribe."

That actually made Tez scoff. "And you think that *Koelhe* is acting in the best interests of the Tribe? Her, of all people?"

"You allow your distaste and anger towards her to cloud your judgment of her."

"My *judgment*? She's godsdamned insane!" Her arms flew out to her sides to illustrate her frustration. "She made my family's lives a living hell simply because she hated us! Turned half the village against my sister! Raised an absolute shit of a son! And you think that *she* is in the Tribe's best interests? And here I thought you were a practical man."

"I *am* a practical man, Tezalhat." That trademark stoicism returned in full force, his expression stern and piercing. "We stand in unprecedented times. The loss of a leader is tragic, but there are greater concerns at play. There have long been greater concerns about the manner in which your father watched over our Tribe."

"If you of all people are going to bring my sister into this—"

"I *am* going to bring your sister into this," he interrupted. "Believe me when I say that I have no intentions of 'siding' with Koelhe. However, I will not entertain the idea of maintaining the current rule of the Tribe. Your parents brought shame upon our Tribe's customs by continuing to allow the *farce* of Sennalhat's existence within the village. Long has our custom decreed—the decree of *all* Tribes throughout the Land—that those born under the Eclipse are to be banished from our borders. They hold no place in our society. History has long recorded the pox brought unto the Tribes by the Cur—"

"Do *not* call my sister that," Tez warned, pointing an accusing finger in Rantalha's face.

He paused a moment but then finished his thought. "Curseborn."

Tez growled but did nothing. "If history truly recorded the Eclipseborn as a pox, it's the first I've heard of it. If that were the case, I'd sooner expect Tawa to be the one preaching that hatred than you. Our histories are entirely blank on the subject, but clearly, civilization never collapsed. And you still deign to call yourself a practical man. I'm sure you've seen enough in your years that you should know that speculation and hearsay don't indicate the truth. Different perspectives offer different histories. And nothing that Sen has *ever* done has *ever* proven some *curse* of the Eclipse."

"Hmph," Rantalha grunted. "Likewise, nothing she's done has *dis*proven it."

"I never would have envisioned such arrogance in you, Rantalha." Tez's fists balled up, nails digging into her palms. It took the suppression of her every urge to avoid launching herself at him. She knew that she could take him—if she had her spear with her. But he was a hunter who often did not even make use of his bow when the need arose. Instead, she just shook her head. "Are you just another who wants to hold that rockslide over Sen's head and call it your proof? She was ten years old when that happened. Nothing was damaged, and no one got hurt."

"Fann was hurt," he said plainly.

"Who gives a shit?"

"Koelhe."

"I mean, who that actually matters in this Tribe. Don't tell me that *you* actually care for that shit's wellbeing."

"My own feelings towards him are irrelevant. The fact remains that—"

"There *are* no facts remaining here, Rantalha," Tez interjected, her teeth grinding more fiercely. "Only your own prejudices towards someone who never deserved it."

"Perhaps so," he admitted. "But customs are customs, as traditions are traditions."

"Fuck tradition," she said, rolling her eyes. "If customs dictate that my sister should be considered less than human, then our customs are wrong."

"And yet, still, they are our customs." He held out the deck of cards, drawing a few from the top of the pile. "Perhaps a demonstration will illustrate the point more clearly. I'm sure your sister has forced this game unto you several times." He held up a face card. "Let us posit that this face card is the Chief of our Tribe. When a face card is played, do you know the first card by which to topple it?"

Frustration flashed in Tez's face, but she decided to play along with the farce. "Yes, of course. Another face card."

Rantalha nodded. Drawing a second face card, he placed it atop the first and drew it back to himself.

"What point does that prove? A rival Chief capturing a Tribe? That has little to do with Sen. If anything, we saw that with the Wood Tribe decimating the Sun."

"You're correct on that point. But there is more still." Next from the deck, Rantalha drew a six and placed it on the ground before them. Next came the first face card. "Second to topple a rule. There are those numbers below the face. Any face card would supersede the value of the numbered card. But if an equal card were to be drawn next…" On his next draw, he pulled another six, sandwiching the face card between it and the first six. "Victory is still claimed. A strength in numbers. A gathering of like-minded individuals joining together. Many outweighing the few."

"Again, you're—"

"*But*," Rantalha continued. "There's one card which would trump them all." He drew a six, then a three, a nine, and a face. "A Chief, looking upon all the differences of his subjects. Unless another Chief rises up to strike him down, there is nothing standing in the way to stop the Chief from claiming victory. However…" Slowly, he smirked as the next card slipped into his fingers. With almost sinister intent, he placed a zero atop the pile, calmly withdrawing his hand from the illustration. "When you place a wild card into the field, nothing is as it should be. Everything falls to the wild card." He drew the cards back towards himself.

"And you think that *Sen* is this wild card?" Tez scoffed, admittedly amused. She was almost in disbelief at the claim. "I don't know if you've noticed, but Sen isn't aiming to topple much of anything beyond a drink."

"But yet, she still remains as a wild card in the field of play. Perhaps not as a threat to the immediate rule, but instead to our way as a people."

Her blood began to boil, heat rising in her face. There was anger enough rising that her arms began to shake. "And you continue to push that false narrative. All as some flawed justification to usurp the title of Chief away from whom it rightfully belongs. You're no better than Koelhe."

Again, Rantalha smirked. "I do not aim to be better than Koelhe. I know my role. And I also know that there is much more to consider than the narrow-sighted focus upon your sister."

"Really," Tez deadpanned. "Please tell me, I'm just bursting at the seams to learn."

There was a long, drawn-out pause, the wind moaning against the straws and wood of Rantalha's hut. "There *is* an Invasion happening currently. I'm sure you realize that."

She threw her hands out to her side, more annoyed at the unneeded reminder than anything else. "You know, I *did* forget that the Invaders killed my father two days ago, but thanks for reminding me."

"Of course," Rantalha said. "And I respect your father for standing against the Invaders when they came to our village, even if it did cost him his life. But it was the *only* stand he ever took against the Invaders. His adherence to the Stone Tribe's long-standing tradition of neutrality cost more lives than was needed. So intent was he on remaining outside of other Tribes' affairs that he repeatedly ignored the pleas from Chief Han'e. To that point, it was not an intertribal affair. Or perhaps it was, given the direct impact the Invasion had on three separate Tribes. He maintained that it was not worth the loss of Stone lives. But what about the lives of the Tribes Sun, Arrow, and Haunted? There were already countless lost—should that answer have provided them solace? His stance on the response to the Invasion sullied his reputation more than you've been led to believe, Tezalhat."

There was part of her that wanted to agree to that point. She often felt remorse for her Tribe's inability—or rather, unwillingness—to assist the Sun Tribe upon Han'e's repeated and unheeded requests. But there was a larger part of Rantalha's argument that irked her. "You decry my sister's remaining in the village as counter to our traditions. And yet, you decry those same traditions when they dictate our stance on neutrality? You can't pick and choose which traditions to keep and which not to."

"Why not?" Rantalha answered. "Have you not done the same? Opting to 'fuck tradition' to ensure your sister's place in our Tribe while simultaneously adhering to a neutral stance."

Tez found herself bereft of a counterpoint. "I...I..."

"Perhaps it makes me hypocritical," he continued. "But that would mean the same for you, as well. Tell me, Tezalhat. You were born under the Sign of the Bear, and as such, you are expected to take up arms with the honor of a warrior. For the wellbeing of our people, our way, our culture, and our Tribe. The Invaders *will* come, eventually. They've proven to themselves that they can withstand the Forest. But what about what's shortly to come? Where will you stand for the heart and soul of our Tribe?"

Fumes rose from Tez's body. She looked up and met Rantalha's stare with fire, a pyre blazing in *her* heart and soul. "I will not betray my family," she said sternly.

"That's well and good," Rantalha said, "but need I also remind you that the Tribe is equally your family? Are we not one people, a collective? Do your feelings of the few outweigh those of the many? Should one family not be greater than the other?"

Rising to her feet, Tez's fury contrasted with Rantalha's calm and collected posture. Her limbs continued to shake from the anger. Every voice in her heart and whisper in her mind was screaming at her to bash in his skull. But she reminded herself what he could do with just his hands, and again thought against it. Something else was far more urgent. "When is Koelhe going to attack?" she demanded.

Rantalha looked up at her, face hard as the stone he defended. "I never said Koelhe was going to attack." He drew the zero card from the deck once again, twirling it in his fingers. "I said that your sister was a wild card in the field of play. But there *is* more than one wild card in each deck. It's fascinating, the wild card. An unnatural birth beneath an unnatural phenomenon is among the wildest. But an element of surprise only sweetens the use of the card. One day, it may be calling to you for help, only to drive the knife in when you least expect it. A tremendous fraternity. A legion of the lost, as it were."

"The lost," Tez muttered. "*Shit.*" She moved to run, meeting no objection or barring from Rantalha. Bursting through the door to his hut, she met the cold nighttime air in a rush and bolted in the direction of home. She could only hope that she'd return to her mother in time. Before the Haunted offered her a chance to join the voices of the lost.

It began to rain.

CHAPTER FIFTEEN

According to Plan

The Year 1556 Anno Salvatoris
15 Years After the Invasion

"Brin."

Uttering his name once more didn't make it feel any more real. Sen was stunned beyond words. There he stood, her dear little brother, an expression of disorientation and confusion strewn across his face, exhaustion deep-set into his posture, fear flaring in his eyes.

Every voice in her head urged her to run to him, embrace him in her arms, and carry him off to where he belonged. But her body was so shocked that she couldn't will herself an inch forward.

"N-Narva..." she stammered, blinking in rapid succession, her hand blankly feeling for her companion's shoulder to enforce that this was reality. "Is this real? Is that really him?"

As Brin continued to pace through the torchlit streets, gait and coordination far from balanced, Narva equally struggled to develop the words necessary. "Ah, I...yes..." He shifted in place, unable to produce anything beyond a hardened gasp.

It had only been a couple days, but Brin had looked so different. So much wearier, more rugged, the weight of a hundred lifetimes bearing down upon him. Even from this dimmed distance, Sen could make out a line of cuts along his face and arms. If anything, it appeared he maintained enough grit and bravery to stand up for himself during transit, unlikely to have been taken with any kindness.

Sen took a half-step forward before finding herself held back by Narva's firm hand, gripping her shoulder like a vice. Sharply, she turned, her eyes cutting daggers into him. "Let go of me," she demanded.

"Think about this, Sen," Narva warned. "We're not exactly alone here."

"I don't care. None of these people are in a rush to do anything either." There was truth to that. All of the onlookers were in similar states of shock, though some more in the grips of curiosity than anything else. From their collective posture and expressions, they were entreating the situation as almost a rarity, something otherworldly and impossible. That only made Sen's blood boil further. "They're looking at him like he's a stray animal."

"And what will it look like for us if we suddenly try to 'corral' him?" Narva asked pointedly. "We need to think this through carefu—shit, Sen! What are you—"

She didn't care to listen to another word. Breaking free from his iron clutches, Sen walked through the main road, a light sea breeze blowing the veil across her face. She had tucked her braid beneath the fabric of her pilfered shirt, but it still caught in the wind and tickled the skin of her back in a rhythmic caress. Brin's eyes widened as she drew nearer, the onlookers gripped in shocked and flabbergasted murmuring beyond her understanding. It mattered little to her. Somehow, Brin had gotten out, and she wasn't going to let this opportunity slip through her fingers.

"Brin," she whispered despite being the center of attention for these night walkers. "Brin, hey."

Jerking to a stop, Brin trembled in place, his lip quivering and head shaking in denial. The closer Sen drew to him, the more his eyes cried with panic. He backed away, nearly tripping over his own feet, his chest heaving up and down.

"Brin, it's me," Sen assured. "I'm bringing you home." Her arms remained at her waist, but she turned her palms to him, holding her hands open in some attempt at reassurance that it wasn't a trap. Beneath her veil, she managed a wounded smile, trying to exude kindness and warmth with her eyes as best as she could.

It didn't work. Brin continued to back away, uttering only stuttered grunts and ragged gasps.

"Do you not recognize me?" she continued to question. "It's me, Sen. Your sister."

Her words failed, and Brin quite nearly fell in a heap as he turned tail to run back the direction he came.

The action immobilized Sen just for the shock of it. Dumbfounded, she raised her eyebrow, perplexed at just what happened on the open road that led him to forget her entirely, or just be utterly terrified of her.

It was enough that she didn't even recognize Narva's looming presence beside her. "Apparently, our disguises are just that good?" he said, watching Brin stumble away into the night.

For a brief second, Sen considered that point, looking down at the clothing she had procured, discomforted by the idea that she would ever wear an outfit like this on the regular. Just as quickly, though, she shook the thought off and followed.

The murmurous onlookers remained curious as Sen sped up, kicking up packed dirt and hopeful patches of grass alike, her heart pounding rhythmically in her chest as the urgency of reaching her brother coalesced with that of drawing the crowd's eyes elsewhere. Dimly, she could hear Narva cursing behind her before his reluctant footsteps followed suit.

"Sen!" Narva barked softly and harshly. "This is reckless! What are you—"

Never gonna get a chance this good again, she thought. *If I have to be reckless to see it through, then, oh well. I'm gonna be reckless.*

Where Brin was going was a mystery to her. He maintained a healthy speed but simultaneously was zigzagging like a drunkard, unable to keep a straight path as he balanced keeping an eye on the road ahead and looking back to find his pursuant sister.

"Dammit, Brin," she growled haltingly. "Where—are—you—"

The chase led them into the heart of the City, where buildings gradually loomed taller and the chorus of its denizens grew louder. There must have been a tavern nearby; the aroma of ales tickled Sen's furious nostrils.

Brin continued to look back periodically, nearly falling over feet each time. With each about-face, the fear in his eyes grew, yet at the same time, there was something else flashing. It was strange, but Sen could almost hear a laugh escaping his lips. She highly doubted that he held any amusement in this chase. Her heart sinking, she could only come to one conclusion.

Here he was, thinking he was escaping all of this, only to think he's been found out by some upstanding citizen Invader.

The chase slowed as Brin finally fell to the ground, his body erupting in a puff of dust and dirt.

Emotions flared in Sen's heart as the anger and frustration at this pointless chase conflicted with the exuberant relief that her brother was still alive. She nearly dove to him, caring little for the state of her borrowed clothing as she impacted with the hard dirt. She misjudged the distance and fell short a few feet, opting instead to inchworm the remaining distance. "Brin," she whispered once again as she crawled after him. "Hey, look at me."

But Brin could not offer her even that. In a panic, he balled a clump of dirt and hucked it into his sister's face, sedimentary grains seeping through the minuscule slits in the veil and obscuring Sen's vision.

It was enough to startle and blind her temporarily, and Brin saw the opportunity to run off to the side, down a close leading further into the dark. As she furiously massaged her eyes, irritated tears escaping down her cheeks, Narva once again knelt beside her, hand on her shoulder. Part of her knew that he would offer some response filled with snark and admonishments, so she jumped back to her feet before he got the chance, vision still half-blurred from the tears and dirt, and ventured into the darkness beyond. Narva's heavy and frustrated footsteps were close behind.

The alleyway was tight and narrow, dim light escaping from a nearby window. Massaging the final specks of dirt away from her inner eye, Sen stepped forward equally with caution and urgency, proceeding a bit too expeditiously for such tight quarters. The darkness reeked of piss and depravity, different than that of the north, that of the Tribes. She felt her way along the walls, trying not to be disgusted at the grimy texture of the wooden exteriors. The end of the close loomed ahead, but it met perpendicularly with an adjacent passage, both directions stretching into a vast unknown.

"Which way?" she demanded sharply of Narva.

"What?" His tone was testier than she presently had time for.

"Shut up, be useful, and *listen* for him."

"There's a bit too much noise around here for—" He stopped, his ears perking up. Annoyed resignation settled into his face as he pointed a thumb off to the side. "To the left."

Apparently, they had drawn enough commotion to warn Brin of their approach. Sen was unsure if that was a good thing or a bad thing, but she turned the corner just the same.

There was a series of approaching entryways. Sen scurried along in a crouched run, eyes peeled to her left as she looked for Brin's shadowed form against an approaching light. The first two adjacent alleys bore little fruit, but by the third, she found Brin slowly making his way down a slightly wider close riddled with broken glass.

He was far more focused on the path ahead than behind, such that he did not recognize his sister's cautious approach. Each step was laborious and drawn-out as though he was taking extra precautions not to step upon broken glass.

Noticing this, Sen took the same precautions, charting each step carefully and quietly, doing her utmost not to frighten away a brother who suddenly had a strange aversion to getting rescued. Much to his ignorance, she was quickly closing the gap. Just a few more paces and an outstretched arm should—

Something loudly crunched from behind. Brin turned, locking eyes with Sen once again, and sprinted off, nearly barreling straight into the adjacent wall as he continued to regain his sense of balance before exiting off to the right.

Frozen in place with hand outstretched, Sen sharply turned around, finding Narva sheepishly raising his foot with bared teeth, face reddening with shame. Sen snarled, not even dignifying it with a remark.

A strange odor lingered nearby. It was more than just the customary alleyway piss and shit. Sen couldn't quite place it, but it just smelled off. A concern for another time, though. Kicking up scattered shards from the ground, somewhat with intent, she skidded out into the open main road, nearly knocking over a couple passersby in the process. A cloud of dust trailed behind her in a puff. Her chest pounded as she rested a hand on her hip, sweat trickling down her brow.

The passersby stared at her with raised suspicion but paid her little mind as they walked across the street, apparently wanting to be as far away from her as possible. One of them muttered something under her breath that Sen couldn't understand but could sense had malicious intent, nonetheless.

Narva caught up to her, his own breath heaving. "Where did he—"

He turned to face the same direction as she and saw exactly what she did. Nothing.

Sen frowned. He had undoubtedly turned right, but there were no adjacent alleyways as the next row of buildings were built almost on top of one another. He easily would have been spotted had he run across the street given how quickly she had exited the alley and how wide the main street was. There was only one passageway within that brief of a distance that she could have missed him, but there was a greater concern with that.

Looming high in her field of vision was the tallest building in the City. Remembering the Haunted's words, she bit her lip as she pondered just what was down that alleyway. "There's no way he..."

"Sen?" questioned Narva.

Frowning deeper, she cautiously stepped forward, the incessant drumbeat continuing in her chest. Waving her hand forward at her side, she urged Narva onward, walking nearly side-face to the road, her eyes narrowed to the passageway.

At that moment, Narva clearly had the same realization, and for the briefest of moments, he raised a cautionary hand to Sen's shoulder before wisely withdrawing it from consideration. They approached the turn, a wide gap, unguarded and unprotected.

Sen drew a deep breath, turning in all cardinal directions—to the road from which they came, to the road ahead, to the main City gates—and found a guard nowhere in sight, only gawking everyday folks who were keen to just turn a blind eye to whatever she was doing.

Narva started to voice an objection, but Sen turned the corner before he even had the chance to let the words escape. The runway was empty, hollow. Each step was met upon soiled ground, almost sinister to the touch. The hair stood up on her arms as she ventured deeper, meeting an opened gate, and behind it, another gate. Behind that, another, until at last, a clearing stretched out, masses huddled deep within.

That mysterious odor grew more pronounced as she took step after step forward, Narva's wordless objections following close behind. She reached a crossroads before the final gate as long stretches of passageways ran along the perimeter of this innermost gate, leading into the inviting darkness. She felt the urge to pursue down either direction, with Narva electing the opposite, hoping to corner Brin somewhere in the middle, but something called to her in this clearing. Something...else.

And when she allowed her curiosity to pull her forward, she gasped at the sight. Rows upon rows of unspeakables. She rose a hand to her lips, eyes widened at such a horrendous sight. Hunched together in almost mimetic unison laid an absence of hope, a loss of will. Though individually, they each bore distinct differences, there was a unity that bound them all together. They were Tribe, each and every one of them. And each and every one of them was chained at the ankle, immobilized beyond the length of the chain. Her eyes scanned the yard. In her heart, she expected a degree of horror judging from the runaways who settled in her village, but there was no preparation suitable to anticipate this.

Sallow and empty faces stared blankly ahead, some so bereft of livelihood that Sen couldn't help but wonder if they were still alive at all. Others bore a stark cognizance in their face but a hopelessness in their gaze. Some stared back at her, and she found not a renewal of dignity in their faces but rather a pronounced indifference to her presence. Whatever they thought it was she provided by her being there, they clearly wanted no part of it. More than anything, those who still held firm to their wits seemed to pretend she wasn't there at all.

A firm hand rested on her shoulder. "Come on," said Narva's voice. "We don't need to see this."

Resolutely, Sen shook her head. "Don't we, though?" she posited, her gaze unbreaking from the throngs of lifeless faces. "This is what the Invaders want to do to us. Animalize us, break us...and then just leave us to rot."

Narva said nothing, only a faint growl rumbling in his throat. His fingers flexed on Sen's shoulder before he turned back to the gate entrance. "Let's check along the perimeter. Brin could be hiding somewhere along there."

Sen nodded and chanced a final look at the broken expressions, but one immediately stuck out to her. So distinctive, so recognizable, and so...perplexing. Furiously, she tapped at Narva's shoulder, nearly jerking him back by the shirt collar to stop him. "No," she whispered, still not breaking her gaze from the huddled mass. She pointed to a boy sat with head down, fading swaths of yellow still visible upon his face. "Look. He's...he's right there."

Sure enough, there he was. There was Brin, sullenly sat with ankle chained down, paying no heed to the world around him.

They were both perplexed at the sight. Dumbfounded, frankly. "The hell's going through his head?" muttered Narva. "'Oopsie, they caught me. Better go back and pretend like nothing happened.'"

"Narva." Sen's voice toed the line between admonishing annoyance and fractured grief.

Still, the point was valid. Of all the places to run upon escaping, why even go back? What would that even resolve? Granted, she had never known her brother to be the bravest boy, but he was likewise not so craven that he would so suddenly and sullenly give up as such. She frowned, and breaking the confuddling freeze holding her, she stepped forward.

Many of those they passed didn't even spare a passing glance. Truthfully, Sen questioned whether they could muster even that. Even while chancing a quick look, she could easily see just how sundered from their heritage many of these folks truly were. Cultural emblems remained separate from this crowd; no aesthetic signifiers such as body paint or hairstyles, no Tribal markers of clothing or jewelry.

And, for many, no pendants. No mark of their passage into adulthood. So much to grieve, so much to mourn. It was little wonder how despondent many of them appeared. Sen couldn't even fathom how long this had felt to them, these torturous and agonizing years.

Not all bore that appearance of grief. Brin didn't. True, he was just as battered and bruised as he had been whilst wandering the City streets, but he was attentive, alert. And when he, at last, raised his head, those piercing eyes once again laying upon his sister, he reacted not with fright, nor joy, nor hope. More than anything, he was…

Just confused.

"Sen?" he whispered sharply. "What…what are you doing here?"

Sen knelt beside him, lifting her veil discretely. "Oh, so *now* you recognize me."

Brin raised an eyebrow. "I…what?" He shook his head. "I don't understand. Why are you dressed like that?"

"Oh, this?" She motioned a hand down the length of her blouse and skirt, looking forward to switching back to her standard Tribal attire. "Just a little something I whipped together for you. Do you like it?"

"Sen," groaned an exasperated Narva.

"Right, right, no time," she muttered, shaking some sense back into her head. "Brin, why'd you come back here? Think we made it pretty obvious it was us chasing you."

Again, Brin raised an eyebrow. "Are you alright in the head, Sen?" His eyes narrowed, a small sliver of their father's ferocity shining through the darkness of his nervous and fearful gaze. "I don't…"

Sen sighed and looked at Narva, who only shrugged and shook his head. She furrowed her brow, running an inattentive hand through the loose pockets of dirt. Turning back to her brother, she heaved her shoulders and slightly rolled her eyes. "A conversation for later, then. We've gotta move."

"Move?" Brin asked. "What are you—"

"Oh, you're right, dear brother. We just came for a visit." It was hard to hide the exasperation in her voice. "Come on, we're getting you out. Narva, help me out with his chain." Awaiting no objection from Brin, she leaned in closer to his ankle, closely examining the chain's locking mechanism, stroking her chin thoughtfully. She turned to face Narva at her side, only not to find him there at all. With frustration and confusion, she sharply turned around, finding him still standing tall, a blank yet focused expression glued to his face, eyes staring out into the middle distance. "What, looking to go for a swim in the sea of grief? Save it for afterwards. Come on, help me."

A thoughtful hum buzzed out from his frowning lips. "Are we really not going to help them?"

For a brief moment, Sen froze in place, almost perplexed at his words. As she turned around, expecting his comment to be some weird jest, she realized just how earnest his words were. "You're serious," she deadpanned in disbelief.

"Were you not just fuming at how the Invaders are *animalizing* our people?" Narva hissed.

"And how are we gonna get them out, Narva?" she retorted with equivalent venom coating her tongue. "I know you managed to hide a bow and quiver beneath that jacket, but do you think you can hide a couple hundred people in there, too? Do you have a *plan*?"

Narva couldn't help but raise his eyebrows at that. "*You're* lecturing *me* about not having a plan? You're right, Sen. I *don't* have a plan. But look at them! They're being treated like animals and left out to rot, just as you said. Knowing that, how can we just leave them to rot while we only save your brother who hasn't even been here a day?!"

Sen hunched her shoulders, flexing her fingers out. She breathed deeply through her nose, frustration and annoyance fuming out in equal measure. As she turned to face Brin, she was met only with her brother's awkward posture. Here he was expecting a rescue, only to be caught as the third wheel in a lover's quarrel.

"Is this *really* the place for this?" she snapped, struggling more and more to keep her voice to a dull roar. "Of course, I want to help all of them. But I can't right now. *We* can't right now. We set out to rescue Brin—now we've found him. And now you expect us to be equipped for even more than that?"

Narva knelt, his eyes filling with a morose hue that so recently was instead a vengeful fire. "Do you not think I realize that?" he said. "But we both know that this is more than just Brin. As much as I want him back, do you really think it's fair that only he gets out while the others just watch?"

Tears started to pool in Sen's eyes. Angry tears, frustrated tears. "It doesn't matter," she growled. "I just want my brother back, and now we have him. We can bring him back, and it's one less horror to remember from that night, and—"

"But he's not the only one who was taken that night," Narva reminded her.

Her heart stopped and sank.

"Do you even remember the other Stone Tribesman who was taken that night? Their name, what they even look like?"

A fog engulfed her mind. So desperately she wanted to prove otherwise, but in recalling just who that person was, she could only come up empty. With a shudder, she shook her head.

"Then you need really need to ask the question," Narva asserted, his tone still hushed but pressing. "Are you doing this for the Tribe, for your brother, or just for yourself?"

Turning completely away from her brother, Sen subdued a violent hiss and instead just shuddered with anger. "I don't care. I just want my brother back." It took the suppression of every urge for her not to lash out at Narva, to raise her voice, to call attention to any and everyone. "If you're that concerned about their plight, then you're more than free to stay behind with them. You can come up with a plan with them then. But I came down here for one reason, and that was to save Brin. Regardless of whether just solace for myself, to prove my worth to our Tribe, or whatever. It doesn't matter. If that makes me selfish, then so be it. But you knew exactly what this journey was when we set out, so either help me or don't."

A long silence passed between them, maybe a second, maybe a minute. But the absence of words was cut only by the clearing of Brin's throat. With a snarl, Sen turned back to face her brother, nose flaring, teeth snarling.

"If you're spurring me loose, can you just get on with it already?" Brin was leaning back, propping himself up with his hands, almost lounging while sitting in on this argument.

Sen gritted her teeth and dove in to the anklet, running her hands along its perimeter. She felt the slit where the two sections of iron met, a slightly larger gap than she expected. More than that, the cuff was a bit loose along Brin's ankle, strangely enough. As she narrowed her eyes, she slipped her two front fingers into the gap between the cuff and her brother's ankle and tugged ever so slightly.

It came undone.

"...Oh," Sen scoffed with surprise, her eyebrows raised. She eyed her brother further, attempting to find something to say.

Something seemed to click in Brin's head. "I...think when the guard put me in here, she—"

"Amazing, let's go," Sen interrupted, pulling her brother up to his feet, completely free of the chain. His posture was a bit more rugged, his gait unsteady, his balance uneven. But there he was, the little brother she had so desperately wanted back. Just a bit more to go, and they would be home free. She tugged at his arm, pulling him back the way they came in, toward the gate and towards freedom.

Weakly, Brin seemed to resist. He was pointing nondescriptly back near where he was chained. "But, what about—"

"No time!" asserted Sen. "We need to leave now! We're never gonna get a chance like this again."

Brin offered no further resistance, but Narva was not in any rush to follow. Instead, he eyed Sen and seemed focused on the same area Brin was pointing to.

"You coming or not?" Sen bit sharply at her companion.

His gaze remained affixed to whatever it was for a brief moment longer before he finally frowned and turned back to Sen. He seemed to do so with difficulty, regret, as though the act tore at him completely. "I'm with you," he said softly. "Let's get out of here."

She needed no further prompting. The three of them at last reunited, Sen took Brin by the wrist and ran, Narva following closely in tow. Part of her was still frustrated and angry towards Narva, after traveling all this way, only to nearly go separate ways at the end, but...

She was still relieved to have him with her.

They weaved through the layers of gates, still left unopened and unlocked as before. The coast clear, Sen took a quick scan of the City streets, the torchlights starting to dim around her. Finding nothing but drunkards and lechers, she ran ahead, motioning Narva and Brin after her. Immediately catching her eye was the front gate.

Left completely unattended.

"Come on, let's go!" she half-whispered, half-shrieked. She sprinted out into the open, seeing her window of opportunity and not allowing anyone to take it from her. Heavy footsteps followed behind her, the exasperated and heavy breaths of her companions carrying along with her. The front gates approached closer and closer, an impossible beacon of hope, of exhalation, of freedom.

And when they crossed the threshold, the lights of the City disappearing from their periphery, they finally had it. Freedom. Sen was so relieved she thought she might cry.

"Come on!" she called after them, waving her arm onward. "Don't stop until we hit the Forest!"

Narva sprinted up closer, nearly dragging Brin by the collar just to keep up. "Am I the only one who finds it suspicious and convenient that there were no guards *anywhere*?"

Scoffing, Sen managed a sly smile, maybe even a small chuckle. "What can I say? It looks like we had a little bit of—"

"Oh, don't even say it," Brin and Narva groaned simultaneously.

She didn't need to say it. She felt it all the same. The fabric of her skirt tearing with the force of her sprint, Sen forced herself on faster and faster, intent on not stopping until those looming trees crested over the horizon once more. Somehow, that thought felt less daunting the second time around.

Sea winds abounded from atop the rooftop. It was comforting and cooling on this warm evening. Just a nice additional reward to a plan gone perfectly.

Red lounged along the slats of the roof, one leg crossed over the other, hands interlinked behind her head. Amidst the raucous entertainment in the house below, she found her own entertainment out in the fields.

For all the time they had taken in the pit, she had wondered whether they would have decided to make camp and hole up there. She didn't think it would take *that* long.

But sometimes, patience is its own reward. She knew that, eventually, they'd have to come out. Eventually, they'd take the bait dangled in front of them, that illusion of freedom, that cradle of liberty.

And, eventually, she'd get to have some fun.

With a crack of her knuckles, she slid down the shingles of the roof, nearly floating to the ground effortlessly. A few of her fellow guards were waiting for her, all dressed in the same regalia as herself. They all bore equal nonchalance as her, too. She had to respect that about them.

"Ready to go?" one of them asked, a stocky man of regular build, sporting the same complexion and auburn hair as most Acrarians.

"Almost," Red said. "I think we can give them a couple more minutes of a head start, no?"

They all nodded.

"And, you know what? Let's get a couple others in on the fun." She pointed to one of her people, a tall and lanky lad with a strong jaw and stronger beard. "You, with me. Let's grab a couple other guards and mount the horses. The rest of you, just back to the barracks. We've a long day ahead of us tomorrow. Best get some rest."

Each step forward was agonizing. Each breath only more so.

Sen's legs were turning more and more to mush, the exhaustion greatly outweighing her ambition to continue. Though her mind ordered her to maintain a sprint, her body just gave the finger and swayed from side to side, mustering little more than a snail's pace.

"Shit," she muttered with broken breath, hands affixed to her hips.

"How much longer?" Brin pleaded, in much worse shape than she. For what little rest she and Narva had managed, Sen could only imagine just how much worse it was for her brother. Not only being forced along a march to a slave's end, but also watching helplessly as an entire Tribe was indiscriminately slaughtered. That there may be solace in their depths was a strange thought indeed.

Sen shook her head vigorously. "I don't know. We—We just gotta—go." Each word was a struggle, each breath a labor, each step a nightmare. But still, she pressed on, the sight of Brin all she needed to go forth.

She pushed through the pain, up that steady incline of grassy and damp terrain, evening dew glistening the earth and making their tired steps all the more treacherous. There was always something.

It could very well have been the first time anyone looked forward to the Forest looming before them, but such was their plight.

Her legs gave out, and Sen collapsed face-first into the grass. "Okay, two-minute break," she relented. The earth was so comforting, so relaxing. Tears started to well in her eyes, and she couldn't tell whether it was due to the extreme exhaustion or the sheer relief of being off her feet.

But relief should never be taken for granted when one is on the run. As Sen turned her face in the grass, cheek soaking in the dew, she managed to point her gaze up to Narva, still on his feet. Or maybe he had just gotten back to his feet—she couldn't really be sure. His body was tense, his fists shaking, his attention drawn back to the south. Back to the City.

"Narva?" Sen said sleepily. She was too exhausted to convey any other emotion.

In a sharp and swift motion, Narva slid down and pulled Sen to her feet. "We need to move. *Now.*"

"Wh...what?"

"Listen."

She did, and, at first, heard nothing. But the wind carried a shrill cry on its waves. Something melodic yet haunting, powerful yet warning. A bell. And not just one ring of a bell. A quick succession, each ring becoming clearer with each toll that preceded it.

"*Shit*," Sen growled, staggering back to her unsteady feet with Narva's assistance. "They know." Grabbing Brin by the shoulder and shoving him forward, she screamed, "*Run!*"

Suddenly, all trace of exhaustion was irrelevant. All that mattered was making it to the Forest. Adrenaline coursed through Sen, the sheer panic propelling her forward. Her heart was ripping through her chest, her lungs ablaze, each breath a dagger tearing at the lining of her throat. Air rasped out from her mouth, so dry that she choked with each attempt.

The Forest wasn't getting any closer. But it was becoming clearer and clearer that their pursuers were. Sen didn't need Narva's enhanced hearing to know they were coming. She couldn't hear their voices, but she could hear their mounts. Horses. The very horses pilfered from the Arrow Tribe, now being used for hunting down the very people who tamed them in the first place. She didn't dare look behind her, but there was enough of an echo over the hills of hooves clopping on the wet earth to send the appropriate wave of panic through her.

Forcing every last inch of strength from her muscles, Sen pushed forward, up that never-ending hill, hoping and praying for the sight of a Forest that was never going to appear. She looked at Narva, teeth grinding and arrows fluttering out from his quiver as he pushed himself to the limit. Then she turned to Brin, all pride and ferocity exuding from his thin and lanky frame. None of them were built for this. None of them were ready for this. They tried. And they were about to fail.

"Deatharms!" Narva yelled in a rasp. His pendant was flickering, his panic and lack of focus not providing as ample of assistance as it usually would, but still able to pick up what it needed to. Time was running out. The Forest was nowhere in sight.

Just a little further, Sen told herself. *Just a little further. We're almost there. Please, please, please, we're almost there. We're almost—*

"Get down!"

Narva's voice pierced her ears as she complied without a second thought.

Sen reached out and grabbed Brin, pulling his body in front of hers, intent on not allowing anything to hurt him, no matter what, right to the end. Her body tingled, less a sensation and more a full flare, and she dove to the ground, taking Brin with her.

She barely heard the thunderclap of the Deatharms. But she heard the groaning and coughing next to her. It wasn't Brin.

Her brother was lucid and unharmed, his face stark white. But as she fruitlessly examined him for any wounds, Brin shook his head and tearfully pointed off to the side. Sen's skin prickled as she slowly turned, not wanting to entertain the sight, not wanting it to be true. But the tears came regardless, and the inevitable proved true.

Crimson streams were already flowing out from Narva's back and chest, four entry points in total, his mouth stained in red. Sen crawled over, turning him on his back. He was still alive, but barely. His eyes flickered with strain, his hand twitching and tremoring uncontrollably. It appeared he was trying to reach his arm up, up to her face, but already was he lacking the strength. And despite all that, he still managed to flash her a brave smile. "Hey," he said, his voice a vicious rasp.

Sen was bereft of words. She took his hand, clasping it in both of hers. She brought his fingers to her lips, softly caressing the tips with a kiss. Violently, she shook her head, tears pouring once more down her face. "No no no no no no no no," she repeated over and over. Not him. Not Narva. She couldn't lose him, too.

Blood was flowing and spurting at a steady pace, his breath becoming a pained, heaving wheeze. "H...H-hey," Narva said again, the words even more of a struggle. "Y...Y-You're—gonna be o...o-o-okay." His eyes winced from the pain, his body beginning to seize a bit.

Dropping his hand, Sen collapsed into him, holding Narva's head in her hands, resting her forehead on his. "Please, oh Gods, no," she whimpered. Brin had filed in next to her, his hand resting on her shoulder, offering nothing but accompanying sobs. "I can't...I can't do this." She opened her eyes, tears falling from the bridge of her nose down onto Narva's face, rain collecting in the red river. "Please don't leave me."

Narva seized and coughed some more, blood spurting out from his mouth and onto Sen's face and neck. She felt his weakening hand rest on her knee, about as far as he could lift it now. He struggled to keep his eyes open, the pierce of his gaze growing weaker, more tepid. "I'll...I'm...w...w...with...y-you..." he managed to say. His teeth gritted, and his breathing grew more intense, fiercer, more shrill and pained. "Al...Alw...Always..."

His eyes closed, his head lolled. And his pain stopped.

Sen screamed. Something inhuman and bestial, some attempt to channel the Wolf that Narva was always meant to be. But he did not answer the howl. In that endless grove of glistening green, the fields were once again stained in red. She blankly held his head in her hands, not wanting to let go, not wanting the nightmare to be real. Brin's urging did nothing to break her from that trance. She needed this moment to last. Because if this was the last time she was ever going to see Narva, it needed to be her last moment.

But she was never that Lucky. Her Luck never extended to herself.

Would that the ropes they tied around her would have gone about her neck, but she didn't have that great fortune. It was only her arms and legs which were bound. A red-haired bitch saw extra attention to that. And when she didn't comply any further, the horses dragged her along, Brin watching over her mournfully. She couldn't do it anymore. Nothing mattered. She failed.

And letting Narva get dragged into it made her failure all the worse. His body was left to rot on that slope. And as for herself? She didn't really care anymore.

Eagerly, General Aritz picked up his pencil and walked toward the center-piece of his chamber: the war map. For fifteen years, he had filled in the southern half of this Savior-forsaken island in tremendous detail, more for his own sanity than anything else. He knew everything there was to know about the lands south of that forest—the resources, the crops, the climate.

But the north. That was always a mystery to him.

No longer, though.

He began to make his first sketched marks on the map, those misty moors providing the first inspiration. Until the bell rang. Calmly, he looked over his shoulder and waited for the succession of bells. An alarm. Not so unlike the last one from the week prior.

"Another escapee," he muttered to himself, shrugging. "Can always get more."

A loose outline of the path he took with his men to that savage village was charted. He didn't need the greatest level of detail—he just needed a bit of a visual aid.

Aritz's eyes wandered to the pieces resting on the location of this city, small circular tiles bearing the Acrarian coat of arms. He moved three pieces northward, through the forest and into the north. And then followed those three with several more.

He grinned.

MEMORY

LADY LUCK

For years, she had looked forward to this moment, and yet there was an air of uncertainty surrounding the occasion.

Sen stood at her family's fore, the brisk mountain peaks of the Heart of the Land standing tall before her. The day's trek had been starkly silent, and what was usually a call for celebration and excitement instead delved into a sullen march toward the unknown.

Her parents, who had brimmed with enthusiasm when it was Tez's turn, had remained focused solely on the road ahead, saying hardly a word the entire journey. Her sister, already a capable warrior of the Bearsign in her own right, retained a knowing frown. Her brother, oft frightened into further reclusiveness than he was as a younger boy, seemed only to see the trek into the mountain as a means to escape the punishment of those stronger than he.

It had been four years since Sen savaged Fann's face. From that day on, things had started to change for her. More and more people had begun to treat her with animosity, and it took hardly a moment's thought at all to know that Koelhe was the reason behind it. Sen never quite learned why—she knew that the witch was spreading some ill manners about her, but her parents never divulged explicitly what it was. Nor did she ever come closer to understanding what that label of "Curseborn" even meant. Those who freely accosted her with that term would say little else to explain themselves; those who seemed more on her side merely brushed the term aside as hogwash while still neglecting to divulge.

And her family? Stark silence on the subject, continuing as though nothing was the matter. There was a pretension that nothing had changed, that everything was the same, and though outwardly her parents and siblings treated her with the same regard, Sen knew deep down that there was something different about her.

Even Tawa, often a font of Knowledge and wisdom, was tight-lipped on the matter, only letting something about an eclipse slip by before disregarding the conversation entirely. Village scholars refused her their knowledge—ostensibly because much of their tomes were reserved for Tribal leadership and Owlsigns, but otherwise, there was some restriction specifically for her.

She didn't have many friends left. Only Narva, really. Though he also went about their friendship like nothing changed, he appeared far more earnest about it than her family. She was always appreciative of that. She couldn't help but...*feel* something for him because of it.

The days would come and go, each day growing lonelier than the last. But there was one day to which she looked ahead, one moment that was keeping her going. She was eighteen now and ready to pass the threshold into adulthood. Today was the day. Today was her Trial.

Whatever secrets that had been kept from her were irrelevant. Today, she would be a full member of the Stone Tribe, and as the daughter of the Chief, she could, at last, do so much as a representative of her people to other Tribes throughout the Land.

Despite the cloud which hung drearily over her day, she only looked forward with excitement. As she crested the final mount, her family in tow, Sen laid eyes on the ceremonial circle, a flat clearing overlooking the depths of the Heart, the innermost sanctum just barely in view. Ready for her arrival already were the Keepers, the guardians of the mountains and officiators of the Trial. It had been four years since she was here last for Tez's Trial, but she recognized these Keepers as the same ones who stood by during her sister's passage. Immediately recognizable was the assured and prominent An Rhan, who, at her (relatively) young age, was the youngest ever to conduct a Trial when she presided over Tez's. Sen had heard tell that she was perhaps the most capable warrior in the Heart, though that was not necessarily difficult given the Keepers were not exactly adept fighters.

To Rhan's left was Ko Zaran, a stoic and weathered man with a long and flowing mane of white. He was something of an idol and mythical figure to Brin, who had longed to see the man's libraries one day. He *was* born an Owlsign, after all, so she was sure he'd get his chance once he passed his Trial in four years. Trailing Zaran, as always, was his steward, Ko Endra, still looking every bit as flustered as he did four years ago, and still cradling an impossibly high stack of books, which perplexed Sen. Why he didn't just put them on the ground instead of wrecking his arms was still a mystery to her.

And, finally, to Rhan's right was Ne Shanne, one of the most well-respected Wolfsigns in all of the Land. She was fiercely renowned as an adept hunter, the patron saint of an entire generation of Wolfsigns. All her life, Sen was told she would be joining those ranks one day. As she took step after step, Shanne's flowing grey hair shifted in the wind, strands caught in the fibers of her leopard pelt. At the sight of it, Sen's heart fluttered with anticipation. Soon, she would kneel at the woman's feet, and sooner still, she would finally undergo her passage into adulthood.

Sen looked back to her family, to her parents, who finally managed to crease a smile in her honor. Really, that's all she wanted on this day.

The wind slowed as Sen stepped into the ceremonial circle, the imposing glares of the Keepers bearing down upon her. At first, her heart stopped—surely, momentary heart attacks were part of the Trial—but she drew a deep breath and pushed onward. Nervous beads of sweat collected on the nape of her neck, strands of her loosening braid sticking to her skin in greater number. Her hands began to twitch, and a cavernous pit opened in her stomach. But with her family trailing behind and a bright future ahead, Sen managed to smile to herself and face the Keepers with bravery and contentment.

She stopped at the center of the circle, just as she remembered Tez doing four years ago. The Keepers approached in unison, stopping several paces in front of her. The sound of her family's rear approach echoed in the thinning air.

A final shudder passed through Sen as she closed her eyes, envisioning for the final time what the future held in store for her. Seeing nothing but excitement before her, she allowed a tear to pass her eye and looked firmly at the Keeper elders. "My name is Sennalhat, daughter of Fannalhen and Dennalhir, of the Stone Tribe." The words nearly fumbled out of her mouth, her tongue suddenly five times too large, but they seemed to get the gist of what she was saying. "I have come to complete my Trial."

Collectively, the Keepers nodded, Ko Endra furiously transcribing the proceedings in a hefty tome the size of his entire wingspan. He didn't seem too bothered about its weight—he frankly had more significant musculature than any other Owlsign she had ever seen and enough to compete with some of the more competent warriors in her village.

Ko Zaran heavily cleared his throat. "Welcome, Sennalhat of the Stone Tribe," he said graciously. He diverted his attention past Sen's shoulder to her parents. "And under which Sign may I ask your daughter was born?"

Sen smiled as she awaited her father's response. The typical proceedings were an introduction on the part of the Trial participant followed by a Sign confirmation on the part of the parents, after which the officiator would commence the Trial in earnest. Sen anticipated her father's confirmation to rupture the foundation of the mountains as his voice boomed with prideful exuberance. But a moment became a second, and a second became seconds, and her smile became a frown as the pause drew on longer than it needed to.

"Chief Fannalhen?" repeated the exalted Owlsign. "Under which Sign was Sennalhat born?"

Maintaining her forward stare, Sen craned an eyebrow, uncertainty rippling through her as the pause became more intense and more uncomfortable. The wind burst at her sight in a sudden gust, almost in a taunting manner. She gritted her teeth, hands folded behind her back, and she could feel emotions well up past their breaking point. Hushed whispers ruminated behind her, almost prodding onward for a response until finally, she could hear the deep rumbling of a cleared throat.

"Wolf," her father's voice said. And nothing else.

A relieved sigh passed Sen's lips, though the relief only begot further questions. She'd insist upon them after all this.

At the confirmation, Ne Shanne took a few large steps forward, meeting Sen's eyes with an assured vigor. There was a feeling of judgment passing into Sen with the gaze, as though the legendary huntress could see into her soul and fish out every ill and wrongdoing and display them in grand array for all to see. Her hands were a river of nervous sweat, glistening with anticipation and freezing against the brisk breeze.

"Kneel," Ne Shanne commanded, authority booming in her voice. Sen did as she was bid, resting both knees upon the mountainous earth. From within her leopard pelt, Shanne withdrew a small tin. As she unscrewed the lid, Sen could see a thick, viscous liquid stuck in place, not quite a war paint, but not quite a paste, either. She remembered it from Tez's Trial, as well, but what precisely was in it, she could not say. All she could say for certain was that there was some degree of power to put people in enough of a trance to see the Otherworld.

"Sennalhat, daughter of Fannalhen and Dennalhir, of the Stone Tribe," Shanne continued, her voice echoing over the horizon. "Here, under the eyes of gods and family alike, we charge you to the completion of the Trial and oversee your passage into adulthood. Under the watchful and keen gaze of the Wolf, you will be judged, and only through the strength of your attunement to its intuition and cunning shall you prevail. Do you understand?"

Sen breathed deeply and nodded, her gaze resolute against the huntress's piercing eyes.

Ne Shanne dipped her two forefingers into the mysterious goop, massaging the tip of her thumb along the smudges, and leaned in close to Sen. There was an unexpected warmth radiating from the substance as it was smeared across Sen's forehead, something beyond the realm of her understanding. "And so, I speak unto you your task, your charge, and your goal as one born under the Sign of the Wolf." The elder huntress paused, her watchful eye still not breaking from Sen's, her expression betraying nothing. "Observe, adapt, and overcome. And you will succeed."

The words echoed in Sen's mind as she drew another deep breath, her entire body quivering equally in anxiety and anticipation. So entranced was she in what she had to do next that she barely registered when Ne Shanne leaned in once more and pressed her thumb hard into Sen's forehead.

A jolt coursed through Sen's body. A frightening and searing jolt, radiating an intense sensation throughout her very soul. Reality quivered before her eyes, wavering in intensifying distortions, her sense of sight going in and out as though a torch was being lit and extinguished over and over. Her spine arched back, spasming against the force of Shanne's touch. She wasn't quite sure, but she may have been screaming. In those moments of clarity, she could make out the growing concern upon the huntress's face, and yet she could not pry her thumb away from Sen despite the pain—only success or failure would remove the link.

Agony and nothingness flowed through Sen's limbs, the odd duality of pain and absence waging war under her skin. Something nagged at her that, maybe, this wasn't quite how her Trial was meant to begin.

When she closed her eyes, it was a release and a relief.

When she opened them again, there was nothing.

In those initial days after completing her Trial, Tez simply would not bother shutting the hell up about how wondrous the Otherworld was. She had described it as ethereal yet defying description at the same time, pleasant yet horrifying, calming yet anxious, a toed balance on the walk between life and death. The last part at least made sense to Sen, given the promise to meet loved ones once again in the Otherworld after you pass on, but all the other stuff just sounded like gibberish and insanity—even more so the longer Tez droned on about it.

That being said, she had expected to understand it even a little better once she finally crossed over to the other side upon her Trial. She looked forward to walking those empty, haunting, beautiful landscapes that she had promised the Otherworld contained. And yet, when she opened her eyes, she found none of that.

There really was just *nothing* before her.

No darkness and no light. No swirling mists or hollow landscapes. No feeling of dread or hope. All that spread before her was a featureless and unending void of nothingness and endlessness, encompassing all that there was and all that ever would be.

Sen fell to her knees, bewildered and bemused. "This is wrong," she muttered. "All of this is wrong. It's not supposed to be like this."

An intense frown stretched across her lips, the prospects of the future she saw as realized as the contents of this void.

This wasn't what her challenge was meant to be. This was never to be the Trial she'd face. She reached out and grasped at the nothingness, hoping to find something—*anything*—that would pull the covers out from this horrid trick and reveal to her the contents of her true Trial.

Ne Shanne's instructions to observe, adapt, and overcome rang once more in her ears, but against this backdrop of nothing, they rang hollow and empty. There was nothing to observe, nothing to adapt to, and nothing to overcome. She had been played for the greatest fool of all, and already could she hear the naysayers of the Stone Tribe laughing her back into obscurity, into reclusiveness, never to again emerge from the sanctity of her parents' hut.

But then, the laughter became tangible, audible. A thousand echoes of amusement rained down upon her, the weight of it all crushing her against the nothingness below. She struggled in the void, grunting and cursing as she grasped at the absence and found nothing for purchase from which she could prop herself up. The laughter only continued to pour upon her, the bestial frustration and anger within howling for release.

Look at this damned Curseborn, a voice called out in her head. So helpless and lost. Perhaps she'll stay in that void forever.

Tears welled in Sen's eyes as she growled in a fury, pushing against the weight with all her might.

Oh, what struggle! What determination! To live with such adamance when you never should have been born to begin with!

"Sh...shut up..." Sen grunted, her face straining as she pushed herself unsteadily to her knees.

Come now, Curseborn. Give it up. You're nothing. Just as the void before you. This is the hope of your future, and this is

THE BLACKNESS YOUR KIND HAS CAST UPON OUR WORLD. YOU DESERVE NOTHING, SAVE FOR THE NOTHINGNESS BEFORE YOU!

"What the...hell are you...talking about...?"

HOW AMUSING, THAT SHE STILL REJECTS WHO SHE IS, the voice said, as though to another.

MORE LIKELY THAT THEY NEVER TOLD HER! another said. OH, WHAT A SAD FATE SHE LEADS! EVER FORWARD INTO THE BLACK, KNOWING NOT WHY SHE TREADS THAT PATH! OH, ILL-FATED CURSEBORN, HOW I PITY YOU!

Straining still, Sen pushed herself further, finally breaking free of the weight and bursting forward in a dead sprint. "Shut up, shut up, shut *up*, shut *the hell up*!" Her voice became shriller with each exuberant command, an ear-piercing shriek on the final syllable. Her tears fell away from her, maintaining their position in the air, falling to nothing and remaining in nothing. Sen had no idea where she was running or if she was going anywhere at all. But though the weight of her burden had long since been escaped, the laughter and mocking tones remained with her, affixed to her with torturous and sadistic persistence.

PITIFUL FOOL, the second voice continued. YOUR IGNORANCE WILL NOT SAVE YOU, NOR WILL YOUR INSISTENCE ON RUNNING FROM THE TRUTH! FACE WHAT YOU ARE!

Sen stopped, breathing heavily. "What...what I am?" She shook her head. "Who gives a shit? I...am...I'm me. I'm a woman. A woman of the Stone Tribe! What more is there to know?"

The first voice giggled giddily, almost inhuman, at that. OH...SO MUCH MORE, DEAR CHILD. FOOLISH WOMAN, SO BLIND. HERE YOU STAND, SO DEFIANT, AND YET YOU DO NOT UNDERSTAND WHY. ENTERTAIN US, IF YOU WILL! ENTERTAIN US THE REASON FOR YOUR EXISTENCE!

A brilliant light shone in Sen's face, blinding and fierce against the endless nothing. She shielded her eyes with her arm for a moment before slowly lowering it, training her eyes to the sudden reappearance of light. As her eyes adjusted back to gazing upon something other than sheer darkness, she starkly realized just what it was she was looking at.

"...The moon?" she questioned.

The moon, it was, closer than she ever would have hoped to be to the stellar evening beacon. It was a full moon, bright and brilliant, itself almost ethereal in its sway and grasp. She almost wanted to reach out and touch it, discover what wisdom the moon held within its faraway form, itself for the first time attainable by human hands. But the closer she stepped, the more the moon shied away. She had to wonder if there was a reason why the moon lived so far from the grasp of humanity.

BEAUTIFUL, ISN'T SHE? the second voice murmured. Such wonder and such power. ALWAYS LOOKING DOWN UPON YOU EVEN AS IT FALLS TO SLEEP ALONG THE HORIZON. BUT HAVE YOU EVER WONDERED WHAT LAY WITHIN HER?

Sen had to scoff at that. It was the moon. It lived amongst the stars. What more was there to know?

I WOULD ASSUME THAT TO BE A NO. NO MATTER. THAT KNOWLEDGE IS THERE FOR YOU TO KNOW, SHOULD YOU WISH TO ATTAIN IT. BUT REGARDLESS OF THAT, YOU MUST STILL MAKE A CHOICE. YOU ARE THE POWER OF THE MOON UNLEASHED, AND TO SOME, TO MANY, THAT IS A CURSE.

"The moon unleashed?" Sen questioned incredulously. "The hell are you talking about?"

The first voice encircled her, something so near to claiming corporeal form. TELL US, POOR LITTLE IGNORANT CURSEBORN. WHAT DO YOU KNOW OF THE ECLIPSE?

The question made little sense to Sen, so pointless and arbitrary. "What eclipse?" she said. "I know what they are. I know they're rare. What of it?"

The voice chuckled once more, almost sinister with its knowledge. AH, TO OPERATE IN SUCH OBSCURED WONDER. YOU DON'T KNOW WHAT THE ECLIPSE TRULY IS, DO YOU, CHILD?

Sen raised her hands with confusion, unable to find the words necessary.

A separate sensation floated before her, the essence of the second voice. DOES THE TERM "ECLIPSEBORN" MEAN ANYTHING TO YOU? Hearing nothing in the way of confirmation from Sen, the voice continued. THE ECLIPSE IS MUCH MORE THAN THE NATURAL FLOW OF THE WORLD. IT IS UNPREDICTABLE, UNCONTAINABLE, AND, IN THE EYES OF MANY, DAN-

GEROUS. THE MOON ON HER OWN HOUSES GREAT POWER INDEED, THE WILL OF THE OCEAN SHAPING TO HER FAVOR. BUT THERE IS GREATER POWER WITHIN HER STILL, SOMETHING RAW, FEROCIOUS, AND VISCERAL. BUT WHATEVER DIVINE PLOY YOUR GREAT DEITIES HAVE UPON HER KEEPS IT SHACKLED WITHIN HER, NEVER TO EMERGE, NEVER TO UNFOLD.

EXCEPT...FOR THOSE BRIEF MOMENTS OF FREEDOM, WHEN THE SHACKLES UPON HER ARE RELEASED, AND HER POWER IS FAR TOO MUCH FOR THOSE PITIFUL ANIMALS TO CONTAIN. ON THOSE EVES OF PURE DARKNESS, SHE IS ALL-POWERFUL. THE NIGHTS OF THE ECLIPSE.

Sen blankly stared forward, grasping not the meaning and intent of their words. "Then, what's that to do with me? I was born un...der..." She trailed off, the stark realization hitting her hard. The life and expectation built around her for so long were crumbling in an instant.

NOW, DO YOU SEE, WHAT YOU REALLY ARE? the first voice taunted. WHEN YOUR PEOPLE ARE BORN, THEY ARE BORN UNTO A STAR SIGN ASSOCIATED WITH ONE OF THOSE PITIFUL ANIMALS. BUT YOU? WHEN YOU WERE BROUGHT INTO THIS WORLD, THE ECLIPSE SHONE IN BRIGHT DARKNESS, HIGH IN THE SKY. THE MOON ROARED WITH HER APPROVAL, ELIMINATING THE POWER OF THE SIGNS AS THEY TRIED SO HELPLESSLY TO SHINE OVERHEAD. YOU, SENNALHAT OF THE STONE TRIBE, ARE ECLIPSEBORN. YOURS IS THE POWER OF THE MOON, AND NOW, THE CHOICE IS YOURS TO MAKE.

"Choice?" Sen stammered, turning this way and that, trying to make sense of it all. "What choice? What does this have to do with *anything*? What is this *curse* that everyone claims I'm part of? Answer me!"

The moon before her began to tremble in place, an aura emanating from its radiant glow. A shadow began to impede the light, taking the shape of a moon gradually waning in its cyclical motion.

YOU SEE, the second voice proclaimed happily. IT IS THROUGH ONE OF US THAT YOU WILL ATTAIN HER GREAT POWER. SOMETHING BEYOND THE MEAGER POWER THAT THAT MANGY WOLF COULD EVER HOPE TO GRANT YOU. IT IS YOURS THAT HOLDS THE POWER TO SUBJUGATE AN ENTIRE PEOPLE TO ITS KNEES, AND THAT IS WHY THEY WOULD FEAR

YOU. THAT IS WHY THEY WOULD CLAIM YOU TO BE A CURSE, DEFILED BY THE WORST TEMPTATIONS OF THE HUMAN HEART, BUT WHY SHOULD SUCH POWER BE CALLED A CURSE? WHY SHOULD YOU NOT BE REVERED? BUT ALAS, SUCH IS NOT TO BE. IT IS HUMAN NATURE TO FEAR WHAT ONE DOES NOT UNDERSTAND. IT IS WITHIN YOUR RIGHT NOW TO MAKE THEM UNDERSTAND, BUT THE PATH YOU WALK ALONG THAT ROAD IS YOURS TO TAKE.

Again, Sen shuffled in place, wholly bewildered and panicked. "What…I don't…*power*?!" she exclaimed, flabbergasted beyond words. "I don't *want* power! What…I just…why me? Why was it me?"

WHY, SENNALHAT, said the first voice. THERE'S NO NEED TO ACT SO HIGH AND MIGHTY. YOU WERE NOT CHOSEN BY SOME DIVINE RITE OR CHANCE OF FATE. NOR WERE THE OTHERS BORN UNDER THE ECLIPSE. YOUR MOTHER JUST HAPPENED TO TEMPT NATURE AND BIRTH YOU DURING THE ECLIPSE. SHE KNEW WHAT IT WOULD MEAN FOR YOU. AND YET, HOW STRANGE THAT SHE DID NOT TELL YOU.

STRANGER STILL THAT SHE DID NOT CAST YOU OFF, HIDE YOU AWAY LIKE SOME UNSPEAKABLE DEMON, ADDED THE SECOND VOICE. SUCH IS THE FATE OF FAR TOO MANY BORN UNDER THE ECLIPSE. PERHAPS, THEN, IT WAS YOUR OWN GOOD FORTUNE, THE BIRTH OF YOUR STATUS, WHEN FACED WITH THE STATUS OF YOUR BIRTH.

Her hands trembled in place. In disbelief, Sen stared at them, fearful of what power she now held in her grip. She wanted to lash out, remove the voices from existence, but as the moon continued to wane before her, the imposing dread grew only more intense, the need for action tantamount to everything else.

IT IS TIME TO CHOOSE, SENNALHAT, reminded the first voice. WILL YOU WALK THE PATH OF LIFE?

The essence of the second voice quivered before her. OR TAKE THE HAND OF DEATH?

"What?" Sen asked incredulously. "*That* is my choice? *That* is my power? To decide right now whether to live or die?"

In unison, the voices laughed. The first danced along as if to indicate its intent to speak. AH, THE IGNORANCE OF YOUTH. TO SEE THE WORLD

IN SUCH BLACK-AND-WHITE, LIVE-OR-DIE BINARY CHOICES. NO. YOU BECOME ONE WITH THE MOON, BUT AS SUCH, YOU ARE BEHOLDEN TO HER AND WHAT SHE PROVIDES. AND AS THE MOON GIVES RISE TO LIGHT AND LIFE, SO, TOO, CAN SHE TAKE IT AWAY. BUT, AS SUCH, NATURALLY, THE FOOLS WILL DECRY YOU AS THE CURSED ALL THE WHILE.

AGAIN, SENNALHAT, THE CHOICE IS YOURS, the second voice assured, almost attempting to take a reassuring and motherly tone. WILL YOU WALK THE PATH OF LIFE, THE LIGHT OF THE CURSE FOLLOWING YOU TO THE END OF YOUR DAYS, WHENEVER YOU CHOOSE YOUR DAYS TO END? OR WILL YOU BE THE MOON'S JUSTICE, METING OUT PUNISHMENT IN HER NAME?

"The *hell* are you talking about?" Sen continued to scream, her hands continuing to flare in anxiety. "I want *none* of this! To hell with both of you! I refuse!"

HMPH, the second voice grunted. HOW UNFORTUNATE.

UNFORTUNATE FOR *YOU*, THAT IS, the first affirmed. THE CHOICE IS YOURS, BUT YOU'VE NO CHOICE OTHERWISE. YOU'VE UNTIL THE LIGHT ENDS, AND FROM THERE? I AM AFRAID I CANNOT SPEAK TO YOUR SANITY. TIME IS SHORT. GOODBYE, SENNALHAT.

The essences vanished, and the moon continued to wane. Pacing in place, Sen panicked, angry tears flowing from her eyes and spittle frothing from her mouth. She understood still precious little, and yet she was charged with deciding the trajectory of the rest of her life based on what, to her, amounted to a binary decision.

She screamed endlessly into the void, cursing the moon and the stars and the Deities and all the rest. She cursed the bastards of her Tribe for allowing the circumstances of her birth to be the defining characteristic of their blind hatred. She cursed Koelhe for leading them to that well from which to drink. But most importantly, she cursed her parents, not only for bringing her into this world during the Eclipse, but also for keeping that from her for all her life, lying to her about what she really was for as long as she could remember.

"I...what's even the point?" she muttered as the final bastions of light began to dwindle. "I *am* a curse. Doling out life or death? Why should anyone have that power?" She fell to her knees, the rivers still flowing down her cheeks.

"I can't do it. I can't do either. Whichever it is, they'll all see me as a curse who never should have been born. More than they do already. I can't...I just can't."

And yet.

The fate of other Eclipseborn began to gnaw at her. That off-hand mention that they were cast out just for being alive. So many in the Stone Tribe wished that fate for her. But not her parents. Despite it all, despite all the lies and deceit, they still gave her a life. And a life worth living, at that.

She contemplated that in her final moments as the final slivers of moonlight began to disappear behind the threatening aura of the Eclipse. "I could have been thrown to the wilds like an animal. And yet, they knew exactly what I could turn to be, and they kept me anyway. I had a life, a family, valuable friendships, and even more valuable experiences. I can't even imagine what's become of those of a less fortunate station. I don't know how I can even look them in the eyes right now, and yet, I can't help but realize just how lucky I am to be alive and to have led the life I've led. And so..." Sen breathed one final breath, consigning and relenting that it may be her last. "In choosing Life or Death, I choose neither. I want to spend my final moments reflecting on just how lucky I was to have the parents I had."

Sen closed her eyes as the Eclipse finally took over the moon. She felt a strange tingle throughout her body, an odd sensation, and what sounded like a voice distinct from the others.

The aura overtaking the moon vanished, and Sen's vision exploded into a burst of white light.

When the flare quelled and her vision restored, Sen locked eyes with those of Ne Shanne, at last able to break free of the link intended to send her to the Otherworld. Instead, Sen could not say where precisely it had taken her.

Wherever it was, the Keepers looked upon her with the same shocked and fearful regard. Ko Endra had dropped his tome of records at some point. Ko Zaran's jaw was slack, his hand gripping his mouth and wide wonder. An Rhan had drawn a spear, ready to strike at the earliest provocation.

And Ne Shanne exhibited a fear in her eyes that Sen did not deem was possible from the legendary huntress. Whatever she felt from that link must have been enough to drive her into brief insanity, unable to break away, unable to stop what was happening.

Sen found herself nearly prostrate on the ground, her entire form leaning backwards as her knees remained firm on the ground. Pushing herself upright, she saw in greater clarity just how shaken the Keepers were by the sight and yet how cognizant they were that something of this nature may happen in greater numbers. Reluctantly, she turned herself around, wanting dearly to see just what her parents felt at the sight of whatever it was that was happening on the outside.

Her parents couldn't even be bothered to look at her. They looked away entirely, shame evident in their faces, eyes diverted from any acceptance of responsibility. For their part, Tez and Brin at least could look upon their sister, but Tez's expression of sadness was matched only with Brin's shaking eruption of...anger? Sen couldn't help but wonder if even *he* knew, too.

"Y...y-you!" Ko Zaran said, pointing a finger at Sen's parents. "You knew this would happen, and yet you said nothing!"

Dennalhir sighed deeply, shaking her head all the while. "We...didn't know what would happen. We couldn't have known that..."

"Ne Shanne could have been killed!" An Rhan asserted. Sen thought that the claim was a bit of a stretch, but they *were* the experts, she supposed. "You don't know what your daughter could have done to her!"

"You're saying *could have*," Dennalhir retorted. "But you don't know for certain. None of us knew. None of us remain who would have seen the last Eclipse four centuries ago. We had no idea that—"

"Precisely!" An Rhan interjected. "You had no idea. We're lucky that we're all still alive!"

Sen rose to her feet, bewildered that even the mighty Keepers, guardians of the way of the Tribes and protectors of the Deities, would also be as prejudiced against her as those in her village. She thought them better than that.

"Keep away!" the warrior continued, spear at the ready. "We don't know what she'll—"

"Rhan, enough," Ne Shanne said, holding an arm out to deter Rhan's advance. "What's done is done. And I see no harbinger of doom arising out of her just yet, do you?"

That at least made Sen feel somewhat better, but not by much. Truthfully, she didn't feel any different than she had when she went under. Stranger still, she chose neither path laid before her. She still felt...normal. Part of her wanted to celebrate that, that there was no cause for alarm, that her sanity remained intact despite those voices' warnings.

But there was something greater still that prevented her from doing so. She turned back to her family, to her parents. To her father, who still had yet to lift his head and look at her. She had never seen him exhibit such wild, untamed shame, and yet, here he was, the great Chief of the Stone Tribe, a man of unbridled and unmatched courage, now unwilling and unable to meet eyes with his eighteen-year-old daughter.

"Were you ever gonna tell me?" she said softly, trying desperately to mask her anger. "Or did you just hope that I'd be long gone before even getting the chance to learn the truth?"

Still, Fannalhen kept his head down, but at least now he managed to speak. "Sen, this changes nothing. You're still the same—"

"I am *not* still the same person!" she screamed, her voice echoing throughout all the valleys and hills, surely soon to rouse the Bear from his hibernation. "You knew all this time just what I was, that I would never be welcomed into our society! Everyone who's ever called me 'Curseborn' now has all the confirmation they'd ever need! And those who didn't, they'll see me only as someone who failed her Trial because she had no right to one! How can nothing change when my life up to now has been a lie?!"

"Sen..." Fannalhen muttered. "You'll *always* be—"

"Save it, I don't give a shit." She walked off, barreling through her family, shoving her father aside with her shoulder. He offered no objection. "Go home. I'll find my own way back."

She didn't bother turning back to see if anyone was following. Ostensibly, she wanted to give the illusion that she was too furious to even look at them, but truthfully, she just didn't want anyone to see her tears.

After walking along the downward trail aimlessly, Sen caught sight of a small enclosure, a dull din of frivolity ruminating within. It had grown a bit too cold for her liking, and she could see from the orange glow in the window that it was probably much warmer in there. She realized upon entering that it was a tavern; the smell immediately gave it away. She hadn't had alcohol before but, damn it, she was an adult now, regardless of a Trial to declare one way or another.

"Evening, miss," said the man behind the bar. He had a gentle exuberance on his face as he inattentively cleaned out a mug with a stark-white rag. "You seem a bit far from home, don't you?"

Sen was still a bit too forlorn and wistful to fully register the man's comment at first, and by the time she did, she could say only, "Huh?"

He chuckled. "Stone Tribe, right? I can tell from the braid." He pointed at Sen's hair. "My name's Seln. Ko Seln. I run this tavern."

Rubbing her arms for some warmth, Sen managed to push aside some of the grief in her heart and offer a half-smile. "Sen," she said plainly.

Ko Seln appeared to want to ask her further questions, but he seemed to save them for another time. "Pleasure to meet you, Sen. Why don't you grab a seat somewhere—we have cards set up at a few tables. I'll bring you one on the house."

She nodded her thanks and weaved her way through the occupied tables, not wanting to meet eyes with some of the rougher crowd staring at a young—and frankly, lost—girl. Ultimately, all of the tables were occupied, which perplexed her, this being a remote tavern in the middle of nowhere, but the Keepers did seem to make their home wherever in the Heart and be comfortable doing it. Regardless, she stayed on the prowl for somewhere to sit. Eventually, she found a young man—probably no more than a few years older than she, by the look of him—sitting alone, blankly flicking cards this way and that to no one in particular, dragging them back to himself when he had a winning stack.

"Mind if I sit here with you?" she asked him.

He smiled and held out his hand to the seat. "By all means, be my guest," he said. "Would you like to play cards? The name of the game is—"

Sen held up her hand. "I think I know the game. I've played it a couple times here and there with my sister. It's been a while, though—she always used to trounce me at it."

"Ah, well, there's always a degree of luck and chance with this game, isn't there? Maybe this'll be your day."

Shrugging, Sen half-smiled and flipped her card over—a seven. When her opponent made to flip his, a tingle ran along Sen's arm, a strange sensation unlike anything she had felt before and yet felt somewhat familiar. When the man flipped his card, he wound up with a three. At Sen's next play, the sensation returned, and she locked eyes with another seven, winning the cards for herself.

As the game went on, Sen found herself in a fortunate streak of plays, claiming small bundles and large, drawing face cards where she needed to, sandwich draws at other junctures, and a wild card whenever the need arose. It wound up being a quick round, but still the first she ever won.

"See?" the man said. "Sometimes, you get lucky."

Lucky. Huh. "Yeah," Sen said, something about that ringing a bell in her head. "I guess so."

Ko Seln weaved through the tables and provided a tall mug of ale for Sen. "Apologies for the delay, Sen. Here you go."

Again, Sen nodded her thanks and then turned back to her opponent across the table. "Another round?"

He voiced no objections.

It wasn't much, but it was the only solace she could find at the moment.

CHAPTER SIXTEEN

NEEDS MUST

The ground had turned to mush quicker than Tez thought it could. The rain poured down in buckets, an unexpected torrent blinding her, soaking her from head to toe. Mud splashed against her trouser legs, caking much of the length up to the knee, filling her shoes with a soft layer of it all the while. Stark darkness enveloped the village as torchlights dampened to nothing, the howling of the wind and pattering of heavy rain all that guided her home.

Her skull rattled, her throat ached, and her stomach churned, but she couldn't let it slow her down. Frantically and futilely, she wiped the rainwater away from her brow, attempting in vain to restore some line of sight. She needed to be ready. For whatever awaited her back home. Her heart pounded in rhythmic blasts, threatening to burst from her chest at any given moment.

It was a rare occurrence indeed, but Tez was frightened. If not for the sludging through the muck, she'd have found herself paralyzed to her fear and anxiety. She couldn't lose her entire family in a span of days. She had already lost one family member for good, a possibility for three, and now a threat of four. She couldn't allow it to happen. She had to stop it.

The family hut grew clearer in the dark storm. The interior glowed a delicate orange hue against the darkness. In her drenched clothes, she felt twice as heavy, the pelts absorbing an overabundance of rainwater while the rain drenched her braid with enough force to undo it entirely. As she helplessly wiped away another river of precipitation from her brow, a flowing stream of red came up with it, a path of washed-away red paint trailing down her neck and to the earth below.

Tez was mere paces away from the door to the hut. Part of her wanted to scream out, alert her mother to the danger that approached. The wild card in the deck that Rantalha had so graciously warned her of, and the mob of opportunists sure to follow. But another part of her accepted that there just may be a host already waiting, a host already accomplishing their evening's task. In that split-second decision, she elected the former. She burst through the hut, soaked hair crashing through and covering her face entirely.

And her mother was sitting silently by the fire, startled out of her good graces, a shocked hand pressed firmly to her chest as she tried to catch her breath.

"Goodness, Tez," Dennalhir gasped. "What on earth—"

"Where are they?" Tez demanded, nearly shouting in a singular word before she found herself bereft of the necessary breath. She tried to remain attentive, but she couldn't help but hunch over with exhaustion.

Raising an eyebrow, Dennalhir plainly raised her hands out to her side, a confused shrug passing her face. "Who?"

"The Haunted." Her breath was still heaving, lungs pure fire. In her haste to return home, it didn't dawn on her to draw in her Endurance, her pendant hanging dormant around her neck, dangling loosely above her breast. "Are they...where...did they—"

"Calm down, Tez." Her mother's calm expression betrayed nothing, but if she was this collected, then it was clear that nothing had happened. Yet. She rose to her feet and approached her daughter, wrapping a reassuring arm around Tez's drenched shoulder. "What's this about the Haunted? The runaways, do you mean? What about them?"

Tez gritted her teeth, finally collecting herself enough to restore some of her lost energy. Her pendant glimmered, and the fire in her lungs dissipated as she drew in Endurance, a pleasant cooling swimming through her tired muscles. "Were they here? *Are* they here now? We need to—"

"You need to explain, first," Dennalhir warned, pushing Tez in front of her, holding her by the shoulders at arm's length. "They're not here, at any rate. You know we haven't been lodging them here. Why would today be any different?"

Pacing off to the side, to her bedroom, Tez pushed the damp hair out from her eyes and scoured the room, checking the dark corners and searching beneath the beds. The coast was clear. "Something's happening, and tonight. They're gonna be involved, and...*shit*, where did I leave my spear..."

Dennalhir remained unamused, but with concern piqued. "What do you mean, 'something's happening?'"

Tez maintained a panicked silence as she scanned her room for her spear before at last finding it propped against the wall. Firmly grasping it, she turned and faced her mother, hand nearly grinding into the shaft for the force of it. "Koelhe. Whatever she's doing, she's doing it soon, and those two Haunted are involved somehow."

"Come now, Tez, do you really think that—"

"Rantalha just dragged me off and told me as much."

That caught her mother's attention. "*Rantalha*. You don't mean to say that *he* is siding with—"

"He's siding with no one," Tez grunted. "In his own words. But Koelhe's gathered a whole host of folks loyal to her—who knows how many?—and if anything's to happen... well, we need to be ready."

The rain continued to pound outside, deafening against the hard stone of the hut's exterior. Dennalhir paused, hands on hips, sighing deep into the ground. "Didn't think she'd move so quickly, if I'm honest."

"But you expected it." The possibility was all that Tez could think about over the last day, but that that woman would be so bold already? She could have at least had the decency to wait for her father's body to turn cold beneath the earth.

Dennalhir nodded. "But I expected it. And so here we are."

Sweat intermingled with rainwater as Tez's grip on her spear grew tighter and tighter. Faintly, she could hear the wood of the shaft begin to splinter, the butt end burrowing into the ground. The flames of the fire pit crackled and popped, the only response to the storm's call. Tez looked to the door, the unknown beyond that wall of water filling her with dread. Growing up, she had often dreamed of rushing out of the hut with spear in hand, heeding the call to battle with a warrior's honor. But she had never once considered the possibility that that call would be extended by her own kinfolk.

"Here we are," she repeated to her mother. "But how do we stand? We two, against however many of them."

Grunting softly, Dennalhir retreated to her chamber, the sound of rummaging through this and that echoing in the hollow midst. She returned with spear in hand, intricately crafted and finely honed, runes of Courage inscribed into the steel of the end. A weapon that Tez had not seen drawn in years. A weapon that belonged to her father.

Looking fondly upon the spear, Dennalhir allowed one tear to pass before regaining her resolve. "We stand...as we stand," she said softly. "And if we fall, we will do so on our feet rather than our knees."

If we fall. They weren't words that Tez needed to hear, but words she needed to accept. Knowing not who to trust, she felt it was her and her mother against the world. But if the world were to rise against the might of two women, it may as well have been a stand worth taking.

"Our plan, then?" she raised to her mother, acceptance in her tone.

There wasn't even a hesitation in Dennalhir's step. "Find the Haunted. Go from there."

"Go from there," Tez chuckled. "Sen's more like you than you think."

A sly smile creased her mother's lips. "Then I pray that she inherited her luck from me." She made for the door, ready to pass into the watery unknown. "To the safehouse, then. We'll get it out of them."

Tez didn't have to press further to know what that meant. *Haven't they suffered enough?* she wanted to ask, but this was no time for being delicate. She joined her mother at the threshold, spears brandished, and as mother and daughter shared one final glance into each other's eyes, they nodded in unison and pushed forward into the storm.

They just didn't expect that the storm had arrived already to greet them.

"Well, good evening, ladies," Koelhe shouted over the torrent.

Her voice only made Tez grip her spear tighter. The usual accompaniment was to the woman's side—Fann, as smug as ever with that self-satisfied glimmer in his eyes, scars and scabs already settling into his face. The rain shined against the steel of his spear, the rune of Strength glimmering as he allowed it to preemptively pulse within him. Koelhe, for her part, carried precious little in the way of weapons—only a small knife. Fighting was never her niche; granted, she was only a Futureseer, but she was also one to ask others to fight her battles for her.

Given the host at her back, it appeared she had quite a few volunteers to champion for her. Frankly, far more than Tez ever realized. Many she knew from passing encounters, some by name, some not. A hulking presence behind was evident as being Han'e, Chief of the Sun Tribe, the sight of which only deepened the pit in Tez's stomach. After all her father had given him and the Sun Tribe, to see him turn away from it all in the pursuit of vengeance was disheartening, to say the least.

The dim lighting bid them the appearance of something malevolent, a host amidst the darkness. Only the glint of weaponry and the flash of gritted teeth could be made out from this distance, but Tez didn't need a headcount to be able to fully appreciate just what it was they were up against. There were a *lot* of spears and arrows primed and ready to let loose.

As sobering as the sight was, it paled in comparison to the final knife drawn in the form of two bodies standing next to Koelhe. Even in the dim light, it was clear just who they were—Shara and Ran, the two runaways.

"Lovely weather, isn't it?" Koelhe called. "A pity that you don't get to look into the eyes of each and every person desiring a change in our Tribe's direction."

From the corner of her eye, Tez could see her mother twitch in place, all the Courage radiating through her bones willing her desire to charge forth into certain and assured demise. Thankfully, she held back. "A pity, indeed," Dennalhir called out. "A pity that my disappointment is not visible to you all."

Koelhe bared her teeth, a wide smile visible, but barely so. "I'm happy that you meet your end with an honest sentiment in your heart. Perhaps you can lock eyes with someone sharing that same conviction."

Dennalhir grimaced, slightly snarling at the woman. "What's your plan here, Koelhe?" She pointed her spear out and craned it in a wide arc, outlining the half-circle which had encompassed the clearing before her hut.

"What do you promise these people, that they would risk their lives for your schemes?"

"My *schemes*?" A gross chortle escaped Koelhe's throat at the accusation, streaks of her gray hair burrowing into the wrinkled valleys of her face. "Ah, such arrogance, Dennalhir. It was your husband's downfall, and likewise, it is yours in the end. Truly you both were meant for each other in the Otherworld." She motioned an arm to her host of champions, satisfaction stark in her expression. "Look at all who stand before you. Each of them has been failed by you and yours, by your husband's incompetence, by the taint upon our Tribe borne from your misguided leadership. Look at them all, and then look me in the eyes. What could you possibly offer them that your husband could not?"

The game amused Tez and Dennalhir both, whatever the endgame was. Tez shifted in place, feet digging into the mud below, seeping in through the fabric. She had her doubts initially about raising a spear to her kinfolk; listening to Koelhe was enough to assuage those doubts.

"And you believe that *now* is the ideal time to play your game?" Dennalhir scoffed. "If you've not noticed we have a crisis to the south, and an imminent threat returning to the north. I hardly think this is the time for any of this."

To that, Koelhe could only laugh, turning her head up to the heavens to voice her amusement. "But therein lies the important question," she said. "Who truly represents the greater threat to our Tribe and our Land: the Invaders, or your family's incompetent leadership?"

If this was some attempt at a joke, Tez failed to see the humor. "Your leap of logic is astounding, Koelhe," she quipped, "and I *cannot* wait to hear your justification for it."

"Be quiet, child," snapped Koelhe. "The grown-ups are talking."

To his mother's side, Fann chuckled.

"Shut up, Fann," Tez called. "The grown-ups are talking."

"Quiet!" Koelhe shrieked, oblivious to the irony as she lay a comforting and warm hand on her son's shoulder, knife still drawn in the other.

"My daughter speaks true, Koelhe," Dennalhir called out, taking a broad step forward. "Neither I nor Fannalhen were responsible for the Invaders coming to our Land! We did not displace countless people from their homes, murder countless more, and force even more into slavery! Equating us with those monsters is not only irresponsible; it's entirely moronic and baseless!"

Feigning offense, Koelhe struck a hand to her chest and pretended to swoon with shock. "Oh, I'm moronic!" chirped she, her voice rife with sarcasm. "Do you hear that, all? Our claimant Chief would decry me, a member of her own council—"

"*Former* member of my council," Denna tried to say, her voice doing little to impede Koelhe's.

"—as moronic?! Is *this* who you would stand to back as your Chief? Hah! No, see, dear Dennalhir, you do speak truthfully that you did not displace our brothers and sisters to the south. I would *hardly* be so crass as to suggest that, despite what you may think. But as we move forward, who *truly* will cause our Tribe the most harm? Will it be the Invaders who would claim land they see fit? Or will it be the Tribe so staunchly steadfast to its tradition of neutrality that it would allow such a theft to happen? You don't have to object otherwise—your past and present actions have been loud enough. Your reluctance and outright *refusal* for retribution on behalf of the despondent Sun Tribe says it all. Is that not right, Chief Han'e?" She turned to the imposing form behind her, a fire glowering in the man's eyes. "Tell me, just how many times did you express to Fannalhen your wishes to reclaim your own lands?"

Han'e did not break his gaze. He remained affixed to the sight before him—Tez and Dennalhir, the sole remaining reminders of an era apparently threatening to pass. Tez had always known him as amiable and pleasant, despite his raw size. But, for the first time, she looked upon him and saw sustained resentment and anger. It was ill befitting him. After a prolonged silence, Han'e shook his head and spoke softly, "Too many times." His voice only barely carried over the din of the storm.

"Too many!" Koelhe repeated for all to hear. "And have you even considered extending any similar offer to the Arrow Tribe and their leadership—whatever passes for leadership for them, at any rate? Of course not. You believe that you've given these people enough by allowing them purchase of our lands, Stone lands. Perhaps that's not enough for them—have you thought on that? Have you given consideration that there is much more at stake than just our own people's safety and well-being? Have you not stopped to consider that of other Tribes? They are *suffering* in our lands, stagnant to the point of self-extinction! And you would deny them that chance to reclaim their livelihood?" She spat, joining it with the pounding rain. "Unforgivable!

"And none of this is taking into account your greatest sin of all. Allowing—"

"Do *not* bring Sen into this," Dennalhir threatened, holding her spear parallel to the ground. Tez was equally ready to charge at a moment's notice.

Crouching down, giddiness stretching across her face, Koelhe nearly howled into the storm, enjoying the sight. "Look how feral she becomes when faced with the harsh truth of how she doomed our village and our Tribe! Feral and dangerous, just like the Curseborn she brought into the world and allowed to wander about, *spitting* in the face of our traditions and customs all the while! Perhaps it was only right that her husband met a violent end, thanks to these *wonderful* little offerings who arrived on his front door!"

"How *dare* you, you hateful *witch!*" screamed Dennalhir, her feet digging into the mud, resisting every urge to charge into an assured death. "It was of no fault to Sen, or these two for that matter, that—"

Quickly, Koelhe wrapped an arm around the boy, Ran, knife held to his throat, a grin upon her smile. "Oh, I think they play *some* part in Fannalhen's death, do you not?" There was a sinister earnestness to her voice, something almost agreeable. "You can't tell me that you don't think your husband would still be alive had these two not arrived in our midst, can you?" The boy was still as stone, his expression betraying nothing. The woman, Shara, offered no objection, either. After everything they had been through, Tez could only imagine that what Koelhe threatened could have been a release. "Would it not give you some satisfaction to see their blood spilled, Dennalhir? I can give you that. If I'm honest, it would please me as much as you. Your husband was flawed, but even *he* didn't deserve an end because of these two."

"Release them!" Dennalhir shouted, waving an angry arm in a horizontal arc. "They are far from responsible!"

"They're nearer and nearer to the scent of death than you would think, I assure you," Koelhe sneered. "Should their hands not be considered stained red even if they themselves did not spill the blood?"

"We are neither murderers nor executioners, Koelhe," called a sudden voice.

Tez turned her head as emerging from the storm and shadows came an immensely welcomed face.

Tawa. And behind him, a host of dozens more, spears and arrows glinting against the residual light emanating from the hut.

Wouldn't you know it, Tez thought. *Mother did say she expected this.* Even Tawa himself brandished a spear, an unusual sight for the calm and reserved scholar that he was.

"Ah, Tawa," Koelhe chuckled, steel still pressed against the boy's throat. "Ever the voice of reason. But alas, sometimes, needs must. I had only hoped you'd have seen the light of things and choose the side befitting your talents."

"You need not worry about me," Tawa answered. "I already have. Now, release the boy!"

Eyes brimming with curiosity, Koelhe smirked again, the grip on Ran's throat tightening and loosening with fleeting and momentary interest. "And so, this is your stance. To think, I held you in such high regard, Tawa."

"I hardly wish I could say the same of you."

"Hmph," she grunted, considering the barbed words. She stood in silence, the rain continuing to pelt down upon her. There was a sullen consideration in her expression, thoughtful contemplation glimmering in her eyes. And as the stalemate drew ever longer, spears and bows drawn on both sides of the field, each side ready to charge at the slightest of provocations, Koelhe relented and removed the knife from Ran's throat. "Fine, then. Perhaps you're right. We don't need to be executioners, do we?" She placed a hand on Ran's shoulder from behind and her other on his other after a brief pause. She appeared deep in further thought, and Ran, for his part, continued to betray nothing, regardless of whether his mind was filled with solemnity, fear, anger, malice, or come what may. With a gentle shove, Koelhe urged Ran out from the darkness, and Shara along with him, nudging her head to the opposing side. "Go on, then. You welcomed them into our midst. It is your responsibility to decide whether they deserve punishment or if they should be free to go on as they will."

With suspicion, Tez eyed the two Haunted as they silently traversed the narrow no-man's-land between the two parties. They filed in behind Dennalhir, her mother hardly breaking gaze with her foe. Shara and Ran appeared to be muttering to themselves—it was hard to tell if they had been doing so beforehand due to the grim darkness of the stormy night. Still, Tez couldn't help but wonder if they were apologizing to some dead friends that they were keeping from a reunion. Despite her mother's insistence to the contrary, it was hard not to feel some residual resentment toward them for her father's death. She couldn't blame them, truly, but the feeling remained, nonetheless.

Beyond the rain, the village was gripped in stark silence. The storm continued to pound upon the stone huts, echoing in a monotonous and repetitious chorus. Koelhe stood silently—a rarity for her—content in the show she had put on this evening. She passed a satisfied smile first to her son, then to her expansive cadre, before finally exchanging it with Tez and Dennalhir. "I will say, Dennalhir," she started, "I must admire your conviction. You've chosen your hill to die upon, it seems, even if that hill means you have to stubbornly adhere to your flawed ideas of morality rather than examining the larger picture. If you wish to spare these lives, then that is your prerogative. But remember this: honor and dignity are all well and good in peacetime. However, in wartime, I must warn that it's best to keep watch for the things that go bump in the night."

Tez narrowed her eyes at Koelhe's words before noticing something amiss about the woman. She examined her more and more closely, and then the thought hit her. *Where's that knife she was holding?*

Before the issue could be pressed any further, the air and rain were broken by a dart in the atmosphere, a wind crushing and zipping by. A soft thud sounded from behind, accompanied by a viscous spurt and pained cough. Tez turned around immediately and saw an arrow protruding from Shara's throat, blood erupting from her mouth as she helplessly tried to remove it. There was no panic in her eyes, however, only an acceptance, a raw and expecting acknowledgment of her fate. The Haunted woman collapsed to the mud, off to join the lost, wherever they may roam.

Tez and Dennalhir both looked from Shara's dying body and the direction from which the arrow came. So distracted were they by that mystery that they hardly noticed something else going bump in the night.

"No!" Tawa screamed, and before Tez could fully register what was happening, she watched as her surrogate uncle barreled into Ran, knocking the boy off his feet. But before he could hit the ground, Ran continued the forward momentum of his arm, a knife driving forward and down, missing what was surely an intended target, but instead finding a home in Dennalhir's thigh.

Her mother gasping and howling from the pain, Tez had a realization of the knife's origins, but before she could pass a fleeting glance back to the bitch smirking across the no-man's-land, she watched Tawa rise back to his feet, spear in hand, and drive the end of the weapon into Ran's throat, blood spurting in a fiendish burst.

The air was still. And then it erupted.

In the passage of mere seconds, Tez fell into an offensive position. Crouching at the knees, spear held out to meet anyone fool enough to challenge her, she scanned the field, faces painted in blurred darkness against an obscured wall of rain. To her left, Tawa withdrew the tip of his spear from Ran's throat, screaming a battle cry to the opposing force with ferocity quite unbefitting of him.

Further still, Dennalhir was still in the process of falling to the ground, the knife protruding from the fleshy center of her thigh, a grimace and snarl flashing across her face behind a splash of pained spittle. And beyond that scene, beyond that span of a handful of seconds, beyond the dead and dying forms of two who, despite their brief taste of freedom, quite probably found greater release in a painful death, Tawa's host roared into motion, a wall of spears aiming to converge with those of a separating resistance, arrows primed to join the falling rain.

Time had slowed, only to regain its bearing once more.

Tawa continued to roar and howl like a wolf, something compelling him to channel his son, and Tez likewise channeled her father's bellow, one portion of host braving the storm to lock steel against steel, spear against spear. A gang of three set its sights first on Tawa—the weaker and less battle-hardened of the menagerie of he, Tez, and Dennalhir—knowing full well that Tez could take them all on with ease and Dennalhir, even immobilized with a knife in her thigh, remained as fierce as ever, perhaps even more so, as though she were a wounded beast.

Tez saw their gambit and charged forth, blocking their path to Tawa, and, in an act of raw impulse, felt her spear jut forward, finding its mark in soft and viscous organs. The initial shock was startling—she had spilled the blood of one of her own kin, one of her own Tribe. *May the Deities forgive me a thousand times over*, she thought initially, her arm frozen in place as her foe was held in equal stasis, steel and wood protruding out from his back. But just as quickly, Tez shook her head. *Forgive me, for a thousand times over, these people are no longer of our Tribe.*

She growled, kicking her opponent off her spear tip with a snarl, knocking his dying body into the onslaught of several more oncoming. As Tez regained her footing—beheld to a brief moment of vulnerability—Tawa saw a clear opening as another charged ahead, seeing enough purchase to drive their spear through Tez's defenseless form. Just as the tip drew nearer to Tez's side, Tawa found his mark in the enemy's arm, sending their weapon wide of the target, lurching it away and grazing one of their own, their hubris greeted with the passage of arrow through skull, a return to the earth sure to follow.

There was hardly any time to look back in gratitude. Tez weaved from foe to foe, Endurance surging through her body, her muscles reinvigorating with each thrust and slash, running through one after another, blood coating the mud and filling footprints in shades of crimson. Puddles became streams became rivers as she met each would-be slayer with completely outmatched skill, the shaft of her spear growing stickier and stickier as more blood trickled down its length. Wind and rain competed against the war cries of warrior and hunter alike, death rattles and scraping steel screeching into the night in a span of minutes.

So willing was she to sprint ahead to drive cold steel through Koelhe's black heart before she scurried away—she was already beginning to disappear against the throng of separatists—that she very nearly neglected to pay attention to the clash of spears immediately to her left, to the ferocious grunts and growls of a woman in pain, of a woman enraged, of a woman protecting not only her own children, but her collective children. Backing up enough to catch a sight in her periphery, Tez made out the image of her mother knelt to one knee, her wounded leg outstretched, still holding off the wave of Koelhe's forces, piling up the bodies with ease. How Dennalhir did so was an art form—freed from the shackles of diplomacy and goodwill, she unveiled what a life of marriage to Fannalhen had wrought, a marriage built upon the backs of two equals, not just in status, but in prowess as well. Her father had received all the glory, but so easily ignored was just how adept her mother was with a spear.

Loyalists falling in beside her, Dennalhir continued to thrust and slash, despite remaining immobile, blood continuing to trickle out from her wound. Her head at chest height, she was a prime target for an overconfident combatant, but not even Tez could have predicted her mother's prowess as two simultaneous thrusts arrived at her face, to which she coolly pushed one aside with her spear and the other with her arm, holding both on either side of her head long enough for her entourage to drive counterattacking spears through their foes' chests.

Clearly seeing the opportunity before her, Dennalhir dropped her husband's spear to the ground, drawing both of the fallen spears instead. In a swift motion, she snapped both on the ground, turning them to makeshift half-spears, maintaining one in each hand. She screamed a challenge to any who would listen, the words indecipherable over the rage of storm and man, but the meaning understandable just the same.

Tez wished she had more time to appreciate the sight, but more of Koelhe's forces took the chance to charge toward her. Several of her own had flanked her, protecting her at her sides and rear, herself at the head of what became a circle of spears. Arrows whipped through the air, felling friend and foe alike, whether charging challenger or protective guardian. Tez's menagerie caught a gradual swath through the oncoming throng, moving further away from her mother's furious defense and her family's home. Blood rushed against her arm, intermittent spurts finding their way to her face, painting it in the shades of the markers previously washed away in the rain earlier in the evening. Her pendant shimmered and shimmered, very nearly a bright radiance underneath her shirt as Endurance continued to pulse through her arms, her muscles every bit as full and angry with each subsequent thrust as the last.

The problem was, she wasn't the only one drawing in the power of the Bear. Strength and Endurance alike shone beneath the shirts of Koelhe's forces, raw brute force rupturing several spears and sheer determination outlasting others. Others drew in Restoration to close wounds, despite the initial shock of vital organs being ruptured. Tez wouldn't give up, though. She couldn't give up. As long as she had life in her veins, she would fight on.

As more of her menagerie fell, others fell in, filling in gaps and holes as Tez fiercely pushed forward, slaying more of her previous kin and marching further away from the sight and sound of her mother. Howls of pain and furor continued to pierce her ears, the storm screaming in the night sky, lightning flashing in brief illumination of the bloodied and battered faces before her.

A clearing was but a few bodies further.

"*On!*" she bellowed, a wave of spears bursting outward in rhythmic efficiency, a cascade of red rainwater meeting the earth in measured response.

Five heads to the clearing, then four, three. Arrows continued to fell her flanks, others falling into place to close the gaps. Two heads, one. A meek and gangly face, all wild anger in gaze but poor dexterity in arm, meeting the mud in shuddered gasps as steel kissed his windpipe.

Tez pushed forward, clearing the throng, her arms rattling as the wave of clashing spears and buzzing arrows became indistinguishable. She had no recognition of who was who against this backdrop of storm and darkness, but now she found herself on the other side of it all, ready to cut another swath into the rebelling force.

At least, until she caught sight of that sneering face, caught wind of that ugly laugh. His spear unbloodied, his face unblemished beyond the normal blemishes, Fann stood watching and ready for any brave enough to challenge him. Tez didn't need a reason further—his cocky eyes were reason enough.

Fann caught sight of her in equal measure as she froze for the briefest of moments. His pendant of Strength flickering beneath his shirt—more than that, really, perhaps even acting as a beacon in the darkness—and the rune upon his spear glinting simultaneously, he began to voice some spiteful challenge to Tez, inaudible over the cries of battle and the rapturous storm.

Tez couldn't care less what mockery escaped his lips; she fell into a sprint, kicking up mud and muck as the battle raged on to her left, and leapt at Fann, hoping the spear would strike true.

His defense was visually awkward, his misshapen arm holding the end of his spear unconventionally, but he turned aside Tez's strike with ease. With enough force, mind, that it very nearly knocked her off balance.

Falling off to the side, Tez turned on her knee, rolling in the muck, and kicked up the grime with an upward slash of her spear, hoping to immobilize him with the splash. Deftly, Fann evaded the mud, the dirty stream instead finding its path to the eyes of some unfortunate and hapless bastard who then had a spear driven through him on one end and an arrow on the other. Tez couldn't tell which side he was on.

Still smirking, Fann feinted to the left before striking from the right, a move clearly telegraphed as Tez pushed the spear into the mud, rising up to land a kick to the chest. With Strength continuing to course through his body, Fann brushed off the kick like it was nothing, his chest akin to stone.

Tez spat and repositioned herself, jumping over the grounded spears and swinging her own with a wide arm, finding that Fann's prowess was greater than she expected as he ducked his head, the slash doing little but clipping a few hairs from his soaked head.

The din of steel continuing to ring into the night, Fann mirrored Tez's own move, waving his spear with his good arm, cutting a large swath through the falling rain. Tez turned it away, meeting his spear in a crossing pattern, their respective steels sparking and grinding together in the darkness. Grimacing, she felt the weight of his inhuman Strength coursing through his arms, his arms wavering from the intensity. But for all the Strength Fann held in his body, Tez had a better advantage—he couldn't maintain that sheer force without tiring.

Her heels digging into the mud, the force of Fann's strike pushing her closer to the vicious crowd of spears, Tez drew in more and more Endurance, her muscles willing against the diminishing power of his strike. She retraced the path of dragged mud, forcing her way back to her initial fighting position, and knocked his spear back, offering a mighty thrust in retaliation only to miss by the slimmest of margins as Fann fell to his backside.

The bastard shook his arms, trying as best as he could to release some of the accumulated tension. He chuckled, that ugly gap-toothed grin glimmering in the storm, and jumped forward, spear descending like a bolt of lightning. Tez side-stepped, deflecting the blow only to feel the weight of an enhanced punch take her in the shoulder. Pain coursing through her bones, an intense heat radiating up the length of her arm, she winced and slashed her spear upward with a single hand, missing Fann's face as he ducked and slid beneath it, mud accumulating up the length of his trouser legs. He was panting from the sheer force of effort, to which Tez held the advantage, but she knew just as well that any simple punch could crush her bones if she wasn't careful.

Still, her foe was tiring, and she was not. Drawing in enough Endurance to cast a beacon of her own across her chest, Tez screamed and charged with spear held out, eager to meet the gush of Fann's blood. But just as her mother had turned away a surely fatal blow with a deft turn of her arm, Fann channeled as much Strength as he could into his functioning arm and caught the spear, holding it inches away from his chest. The shaft of her spear wavered, the wood beginning to splinter. Tez grimaced, noting the weakening integrity of her weapon, and dropped it from her hands. Moving with as quick of reflexes as she could muster, she zipped through the air, pushing off the muddy earth and aiming a rageful fist at his face.

Fann took the bait, raising a spear in his weaker arm to skewer her on the fly. Flashing a slight grin of her own, Tez redirected, pushing her body off to the side. The feint, however, knocked her off balance, positioning her poorly for a free-flowing strike. She was inside his guard for the briefest of moments, but her shoulder was still ablaze, and now Fann had *two* spears. With no time even to curse, Tez kicked out, planting the ball of her foot against his knee, buckling it.

As Fann stumbled to the ground, she could feel the wind shift, the rain part, as both spears came hurtling toward her. She ducked, the spears passing her by on both sides, and held her arms against his, her shoulder screaming bloody objections and her voice matching the call. Holding Fann's strong arms back, she raised a knee up to his face, bloodying his nose, rebreaking it as partially healed bones shattered back into disrepair.

He grunted and snarled and rose back to his feet before Tez could plant another strike. His arms unperturbed by the continued drawing of Strength, he pushed his limbs against Tez's, her wrists giving way against the boulder crashing down upon her. Her knees buckled in turn, her ankles rattling and creaking like a tree finally about to give way.

Despite the Endurance running through her, Tez could feel the limits of her own strength approaching. With immense strain, she pushed against Fann's force, budging him back upward by the slightest and slimmest of inches. Slowly, her ankles felt less like they were ready to snap in half, her knees no longer battered timbers, and a forceful groan and grunt evolved and evolved until it was a fierce scream, a mighty roar, a channeling of the Bear itself ready to rupture the foundations of the earth itself. She was regaining her footing, little by little, and the more she pressed, the more Fann's Strength began to deplete.

Harder and harder, he tried to shove Tez back to the earth, the palms of her hands objecting with every fiber of their being. But Endurance prevailed over Strength, the grip on the spears depleting as Fann dropped them both to the earth. At last seeing the opportunity, Tez dove to the side, Fann following suit. Each grabbed a spear, swinging wildly and meeting in a harsh screech of steel.

Tez's eyes turned to the throng still in the throes of battle, it growing more and more difficult to make out individual sides. Frankly, she couldn't help but wonder how anyone distinguished the other. But beyond it all, her family's hut still stood, and with it, she could only hope that her mother remained standing. Or kneeling with spear still in hand, as it were.

The sparks flew as steel ground against steel, neither side giving an inch. This struggle should have been all she focused on. But warriors were beginning to fall with increasing regularity, with almost rhythmic efficiency. Arrows flew out from behind her, picking off fighter after fighter, such that Fann did not even need to look at what lay behind him to see just what was responsible.

Snarling, Tez broke away from the stalemate, sliding over to the side, partly to reposition herself after digging herself into a muddy rut but partly also to find the source of the arrows. It was hardly a squad of people, judging from the rate of fire, but whoever it was operated with incredible accuracy. Turning away Fann's spear as she broke into a half-slip, half-slide, Tez looked past and saw a form in the shadows, bow drawn, arrow loosed, one after the other with remarkable speed. Her own astonishment freezing her, Fann, almost knowingly, stopped his pace and smiled.

A smile that seemed to say, *"You know you've lost."*

Truthfully, when the shadows parted and Rantalha's face became clear against the rain, Tez had a sinking feeling that he wasn't lying. Stoic as ever, the hunter seemed to pull arrows out from nothing, having such a feel for the trajectory of his shots that he wasted no time at all perfecting his aim; it was perfect enough as it was. Each shot found its mark, and Tez had to guess that, even in this stormy darkness, he knew perfectly well who it was he was aiming for.

Despite knowing just where Rantalha stood, the sight only instilled further anger in her. So remorselessly he moved, regarding nothing but the thrill of the hunt. A hunter to his very core, he saw his prey and marked it as quickly as he killed it. There was nothing in his face, nothing in his eyes, nothing in his soul. Only a desire to come out on top.

Fann remained motionless in open challenge, his arms outstretched so as to beckon Tez forward. Her rage voicing no resistance, she held her spear out and charged. Just over the roar of battle, she could hear Fann chuckle. He met her spear with his own, clashing against it once, twice, thrice, his face amused but his eyes disinterested. Tez sought to offer a fourth strike, aiming to strike true at his chest, but something knocked her back, clanging against the tip of her spear. Enough to knock her strike off-balance, missing her mark entirely. The forward momentum of her missed strike led her right into Fann's guard, shouldering him back in the chest instead. Repositioning herself, she aimed another thrust, only for it to be turned away, too.

An arrow clattered to her feet, and by the slightest of glances, she realized that Rantalha had turned his gaze to her. And yet strangely, she still lived. *He doesn't want to see me dead. He's just toying with me.*

With a growl, Tez made to push one final attempt at her foe. But this time, Rantalha's shot hit her, if only a graze. Though it drew only a sliver of blood along her arm, it was enough for her balance to be thrown off entirely.

Attempting to regain her footing but failing, Tez slipped in the muck and rolled to the ground, spear falling out of reach, just another arm's length from her grip.

Fann waved confidently behind him, not even bothering to look at the defecting hunter, and playfully rattled his fingers along the shaft of his spear. He was two steps away from Tez, one step, half a step. He rose his spear, ready to strike down. Tez looked up, mud and blood and much raining down on her in equal measure, realizing time was less than short.

The spear trailed down. A blur, and Fann grunted.

The spear planted in the ground beside Tez's face, and her opponent took a couple ragged steps back.

Clumsily returning to her feet, she felt a forceful tug at her shoulders, one side protesting from where Fann punched her, the other from where Rantalha's arrow grazed her. There was a familiar touch to whoever was behind her. The din of battle had grown stagnant and indistinguishable, but a man's voice behind her brought her out of the fog.

"Tez! Tez!"

She blinked, brushing away the rain and mud, and barely made out Tawa's face, marred by streams of blood and splashes of mud—a stark contrast to the calm and reserved visage she'd always associated with him. The night's fray knocking any remaining words out of her, she looked back to her foe, past the spear planted in the mud, and saw that Fann was pulling an arrow out from his shoulder. From the *front* of his shoulder. No games from Rantalha here.

"We need to go, now!" Tawa screamed, pulling Tez along before she had a chance to protest.

Out from the darkness, evading a wave of arrows, Sharrabha appeared, a trio of arrows drawn to her bow, drawn and ready to fire. She had remained relatively unharmed, only some splashes of mud here and there marring an otherwise pristine image. She nodded knowingly to Tez and loosed her shot, the barrage pushing Fann back. As Tez was pulled further away by Tawa, Fann spat at the ground and drew his spear out from the earth, returning instead to observing the evening's fight now that his foe had departed. The coward.

Exhausted beyond what her Endurance would permit, Tez followed along in a daze, her head a fog as the battle continued to rage in the village square. "Wh…" she started. "Wh…where…?"

"The battle is lost," Tawa stated matter-of-factly, making no effort to hide his disgust and disappointment. "It was over the moment Rantalha showed his hand. We need to regroup, reconvene, and—"

Tez was only loosely listening, but the sight of her home restored a will to fight. Her home, and her mother. Bodies continued to pile in the square, Dennalhir still visible and still fighting strong against a significantly over-matched force. Breaking free of Tawa's grasp, she stumbled, then ran, back toward the fray, weaponless though with a determination to protect what was rightfully hers and her family's. But just when she was within ten paces of the fray, a hand pulled her back, jerking her to safety.

"Where are you going?!" screamed Sharrabha, turning Tez around to face her, her other hand still gripping bow and arrows alike.

"My…my mother!" Tez said, only barely managing to piece the words together. "I…I have to save…!"

"It's suicide, Tez! We've lost!"

"But!"

"Tez!" Sharrabha slapped her, trying to knock some sense into her. "There will be another time, but now is not that time."

Tez growled and found herself dragged away by the huntress. The din was still constant, but it had begun to quiet. Not breaking her sight from the view, she watched as one of the half-spears that Dennalhir had made was shot out of her hand, and then the other. Motion ceased within the throng as a wave moved to the side.

Out from the depths walked Koelhe, hardly a speck of blood on her, Rantalha not far behind. Though Tez could not hear her, she had to imagine that Koelhe was laughing that horrendous laugh of hers. With Rantalha aiming an arrow, holding Dennalhir in place, Koelhe knelt beside the Stone Chief—*former* Chief, it now seemed—and jerked her knife out from the woman's thigh, Dennalhir's head craning back in a howl of pain.

There was a ruminating consideration to Koelhe's posture, and after a moment's pause, she made some gesture to Dennalhir and then to the hut.

On command, two of the traitors grabbed the warrior by the arms and dragged her into the hut—into Tez's *home*—and from there, everything else disappeared into the dark.

"We...we could have..." Tez muttered listlessly as Sharrabha continued to pull her back.

"We could have done nothing," Sharrabha repeated, returning her to Tawa's side.

Tez found her footing again and turned, seeing Tawa's distraught expression, despair glowing in his eyes. Behind him stood a small contingent of loyalists, a stark few who took up arms to defend their village and Chief and managed to escape with their lives.

A shudder coursed through Tez; anger mixed with fear mixed with loss. "And so, *this* is your plan?!" she nearly screamed at them, her whole body shaking. "We're just giving up? Turning tail and running? What kind of—"

"There is nothing that awaits us there but death right now, Tez," Tawa asserted, calm hands resting on unwilling shoulders.

Tez tried to brush him off, but this man, perhaps the closest thing to family she now had remaining, was insistent.

"Had we Rantalha on *our* side, this may have been different. But their fighting force outnumbers ours, and that is without even taking the Sun Tribe into consideration, and Rantalha fights as twenty men besides. No, it would be suicide to stand and fight there now."

That hardly seemed acceptable to her. "I'd rather suicide than surrender," she growled. "To see our village in Koelhe's hands is—"

"Then what would you do to see our Tribe and village restored to proper hands?" Tawa pressed on.

His words gave Tez pause. "I...what do you mean?"

"Would you not fight to the end for the good of our Tribe?"

"Of course, I would. You know that."

"Good," he nodded. "Then, in knowing that we are outnumbered as we are, we are going to need help taking the village back. The Sun Tribe is clearly a lost cause, but there are greater forces still which roam about her in the north."

Tez raised an eyebrow. "But...the Arrow and Lake Tribes? I mean, sure, you could say the Arrow owe us, but they have no leadership with which to organize. And the Lake Tribe? Are they not too busy fighting amongst themselves to worry about our problems?"

"Do you have a better solution?" Tawa insisted plainly.

Tez thought on it a moment, but, finding nothing, she kept her mouth shut.

Sharrabha stepped forward, depositing her loose arrows back to her quiver, a broad hand pushing rainwater away from her brow. "We bank this on the hope that our allies in the west hate us far less than they hate each other. No better odds than that, I'd say."

Wordlessly and without further options, they nodded and departed to the west. Chancing one final view of her home village, obscured by storm and darkness, Tez's breath quivered. Her mother was trapped in there, probably fending for her life one final time, if she hadn't been killed already. It shouldn't have been so sudden. It shouldn't have been so easy. And yet, here she was, here *they* were, a handful of survivors, a Tribe previously so unfractured by the outside world, now fractured from within. In closing her eyes for a second longer than a standard blink, Tez bid a temporary farewell to her home and rejoined what remained.

Everything they were and everything that they could be rested upon the hope of an alliance with a diasporic people stripped of home and livelihood and a warring people seemingly always on the threat of civil war.

But sometimes, needs must.

CHAPTER SEVENTEEN

Neither Victims Nor...

What more was there to say?

The taste of victory, of freedom, they were now but distant memories, fleeting voices upon an angry wind. The Forest never once broke the plane of view, and now it grew further away still. Somewhere in those rigid hills, a dune of verdant green was staining red, the life of flesh mixing with the life of earth. Somewhere up there, a past, present, and future were ripped clean from the book, a chapter written in ink only to be dashed in broad strokes of blood.

Sen was numb. Dirt, rocks, and blades of grass alike tore at her stolen garb, at her skin, but she felt none of it. When the Invaders grew tired of her body battering into non-use, they threw her onto the back of one of the horses, belly down, and though the bumps in the road knocked the wind out of her again and again, she felt none of it.

All she could focus on was the final spark of life she ever would see, the hills burrowing into a freedom she would never again have, a home she would never again see, and a rose that would never bloom for her.

Her tears had stopped a while back. She couldn't say for certain if it were minutes or days since Narva departed this plane. There was no coming to terms with it. She had failed.

And Brin returning to the City alongside her, bound at the wrists, was proof enough of that.

Her hazy head only barely registered that her brother was walking alongside her, saying nothing but what needed to remain unsaid. Sen had expected that there would be resentment in his eyes, anger, hatred. But, in truth, there was nothing. Perhaps it was the déjà vu of reliving this march to his own end. Or maybe it was the realization that a darker fate likely awaited him. Awaited them both.

Whatever it was, Sen had not the capacity to experience it. The thunderclap played in her mind over and over, the pleas for cessation, the calling of her name. Her form upon a shadow in the Forest, a screeching inhuman, a darkness always at one with her now finally at the fore. For all they had asserted she was whilst growing up, she had long tried to run from it, to prove otherwise. But who was she to argue to the contrary now? A path of death had followed her at her own touch for days now.

Her father, struck down.

Narva—*her* Narva—struck down.

Brin? She didn't want to think on it. She couldn't.

But herself? Maybe that would be the merciful end to her story.

Faintly, she heard the distinctive voices of the four Invaders who had wrangled her and Brin up. One voice was most talkative—she noted it as that red-haired woman who had taken a special interest in her while she felt her heart tearing asunder. Not that she could understand what any of them were saying anyway. Nor did it matter by any means, either.

Sen could tell by the approaching smell that the City drew near. It was only then that she could break her gaze away from the north, to what she hoped to reclaim. She looked to the side, finally seeing—truly seeing—the look in Brin's eyes. So lost, so helpless. Like so many times before when they were kids. So much had he to endure because of her, because of who she was. This was hardly a fate he deserved. It was a fate that should have been bestowed upon *her* a thousand times over. But here he was, trying with every inch of bravery that dwelt within him to be strong in the face of what was to come. Though the intent and effort were there, the quiver in his lips deftly spoke in different inclinations.

As they passed the main gate to the City, the kick of dust blinding her eyes, someone threw Sen down from the horse, the union of body and earth sending shockwaves through her side. Her elbow throbbed from bearing the brunt of the impact, but the Invaders hardly cared enough to check on her wellbeing. One dragged her to her feet, pulling up from the binding ropes at her wrists. He did so effortlessly, this Invader, a hidden strength betraying his less-than-imposing frame.

In their own tongue, the Invaders conversed amongst themselves, leaving Sen and Brin to contemplate their fate in silence. Sen exchanged a look with her brother, or at least attempted to, as he maintained his gaze due forward. What he was looking at, she couldn't say for sure—that giant building at the center of the City was an impressive sight, to be certain, but not one worth gawking at, nor was its adjacent slave camp where she could only hope they were going next.

Desperately, she wanted to say something to him. Even just an apology. But, what good would that do at this point? It's not as though the promise she made for him had bid them any good fortune. It had been nothing but ill fortune since the day of Brin's Trial. It was a day meant to change the lives of both him and the family for the better, but since then, everything had fallen to shit.

The Invaders, at last, wrapped up their conversation, with two of them dragging the horses along elsewhere while the other two dragged Sen and Brin forward by their bindings. The red-haired woman pulled Sen along personally, while another woman took Brin. With each step, the collective pain in Sen's body started to mount—the cuts and gashes along her legs roared with each step, her ribs protesting each movement, both voluntary and involuntary, the throbbing in her hands resultant of bindings tied a tad too tight. Not that those mattered at all to this Invader. The woman kept looking back at her, back at both of them, for one reason or another, though for what purpose, Sen couldn't say. It's not like they were able to go anywhere.

Stains and tears littered Sen's skirt, male drunkards stopping in their tracks to whistle at her for her exposed legs, the act of which was the one matter distracting her mind from what was to come, as though exposed skin was something worth getting excited about for these people. The red-haired woman waved her hand at them, saying something that probably meant to disperse, which the men begrudgingly did.

The gates to the slave camp loomed ahead, now with a guard posted. Sen cursed under her breath, at once thanking the stars that they had the most golden opportunity for escape while also cursing those same stars that the opportunity was squandered. The guard paid them no mind whatsoever, only nodding to the two dragging her and Brin along.

Passing through the gates, the collective stench of a people regarded and treated as wild animals attacked her nostrils, more so than it had previously that evening. Few paid her any regard as she entered, nor did they with Brin, just as had been the case earlier. They were uniformly blank, listless. But despite that, the red-haired woman was content enough to stand in front of them, hands on hips, a broad smile across her devious little face. She flashed a smile to Sen and Brin both, taking each of their bindings in one hand, and pulled them along with her. Sen readied herself to be sat at the empty space where she had found Brin, next to a familiar-looking man with a lingering splash of blue on his face.

But as that vacant spot approached and Sen prepared to stop, she found herself only being dragged along further, Brin alongside her. A flash of emotion came to life in his eyes; surely, he had the same thought.

Rather than a return to a new home, this woman had something else in mind. She started parading Sen and Brin up and down the rows of Tribespeople, softly chuckling to herself. As though it were a performance, something to entertain a lost people. But when she tolled a nearby bell, the chime ringing loudly in Sen's ears, the show was about to begin in earnest.

"Pay attention!" the woman screamed, speaking the Tribal Words perfectly, much to Sen's shock. She narrowed her eyes to the red-haired woman, no hint of struggle or consternation in her eyes as she searched for the next words to say.

Just who is this woman? Sen thought. *Since when do the Invaders speak our tongue?*

With a sharp jerk, the woman pulled Sen and Brin closer by the bindings, raising their arms up high. Again, she rang the bell, louder and fiercer, drawing further attention from the bewildered gathering of enslaved Tribespeople. "Pay attention, I say! Look at these faces! Remember them, recognize them!" Individually, she forced Sen's face toward the crowd, then Brin's, holding them both at the cheek as though she were trying to pry food from their jaws. "It appears we must now make examples of those who think they are above the work we provide for you. Already we've had to make two separate hunts to bring *this* one back," she continued, gesturing distinctly to Brin, even though he wasn't even a runaway to begin with, "and worse still that he clearly had *help* this time! Do not think yourselves beyond this life we have given you here, for if you attempt such a folly, then you will soon know what will become of you. Listen closely for the sounds soon to come, for then you will know the fate that awaits you."

Sen gulped and looked at Brin, whose face was now stricken beyond just pure shock. His limbs trembled, his eyes glistening. For her part, Sen accepted the fate as a reality—especially after seeing the fate that befell both her father and Narva. But for it to become real...what more was there to say, really?

The woman smiled some more, looking in the eyes of each collective face as, once more, she paraded Sen and Brin around the camp, forcing them all to look upon the faces of their perceived runaways.

Despite it all, despite Sen merely trying to return her brother to the land from which he was unjustly stolen, they were still regarded as runaways from the Invaders' sense of justice.

At that moment, Sen felt even greater animosity toward those two Haunted escapees for what they brought unto her and her family. As she closed her eyes, she remembered the night of her father's murder, when she nearly throttled that woman into the Otherworld. When she was stopped, it seemed a mercy, a justified mercy at that, but now, as she was, staring down the prospect of a death paraded as ceremony and justice, she wished only she could return to that time, to that place, to finish the job and extend the same good graces to that boy, as well. Maybe she could have acquiesced to the Invaders' demands, to hand them off without objection. Then, perhaps, she would still have her family, her life, her future.

But no. Because of them, because of those runaways, she and her brother were held in their place, prepared for a death that should have been reserved for someone else. And where was the justice in that?

The mock ceremony finally concluded after a humiliating length of time. Blank and listless eyes continued to watch them, or at least the space in which they were occupying, but beyond pained groans or sickly coughs, no one voiced any objections or pleas for reprieve. There were only their eyes, ever watchful and ever fallen, which spoke the volumes necessary.

Out the front gates they were dragged once more, to the streets of the City. Chancing one final glance beyond the main gate, Sen took in the last vestiges of greenery and livelihood that she would ever see, the rolling hills which teased the false promise of home. As much as she wanted to look to her brother, as much as she wanted to beg for his mercy, that it was only she and Narva who sprung him free and that it should only be her that should be cut down, it felt futile and pointless. These were not a people capable of reason. They were not a people capable of mercies, hollow though they may be. They were a people of monsters, of true animals.

The red-haired woman seemed hardly interested in potential mercies, anyway. Almost playfully, she continued to tug along the bindings, now joined by the other female guard. Onlookers watched in silent regard as Sen and Brin marched to their end, dirt and dust kicking up as the sea breeze intensified. A chill presided over the air, a distant rumbling in the heavens threatening oncoming rain. The air smelled of it, too, mixing distinctly with the aromas of salt and drink.

More and more people began to file out from their homes, from their taverns and eateries, to watch this solemn and silent parade. Many had surely been roused by the tolling of the bells which alerted the attempted escape, and some pointed fingers directly at Sen, likely recognizing her from her jaunt through the streets just a short time ago. Why they were focusing squarely on her rather than Brin, who had been running around just the same, made little sense to her, but what good was it to dwell on it now?

Finally, after a march lasting for a seeming eternity, they reached the end of the road, a familiar sight to Sen. Just to her right was where she and Narva had borrowed the Invader garb, and just over that adjacent wall was where they had deposited their Tribal clothes.

And to the left, where they entered the City. The wall painted red. And the paintbrushes stood at the ready.

As Sen and Brin were dragged silently into that large alleyway, they encountered the other two Invaders who had captured them in the fields, each holding a long Deatharm, similar to the ones held by those who attacked her village. They looked upon Sen and Brin with disgust in their eyes and eagerness in their fingers. Sen knew what awaited, knew what to expect. She had seen it enough already just in the last couple of days to last a lifetime. But at least the remainder of her lifetime was not long at all.

Dragging them over to the wall, the red-haired woman unfastened the bindings on Sen and Brin's wrists, circulation thankfully returning to Sen's hands in full, throbs of delight filling her digits as she flexed and unflexed them. The freedom of it all was short-lived, however, as she was pressed against the wall, the hanging metal chains fastened first to her wrists, then to her ankles. With a loud and rusty *click*, they were bound into place, her range of movement very limited. To her right, Brin was locked in just the same, and as she stared at her brother for the last time, she felt fear, anger, sorrow, remorse, and most of all, regret. She thought of a thousand things to say to him but could barely even get one across. The words caught in her throat, a desperate croak equivalent to absolutely nothing, and Brin could not be roused to say a thing.

The red-haired woman and her companion returned to their comrades, taking hold of their respective Deatharms, and turned to face these proud two of the Stone Tribe. Sen turned her head toward them in equal measure, breathing in deeply and trying with everything she had not to be afraid. Though, desperately and horribly, she was terrified.

"Sen," a soft voice whispered to her.

She turned slowly to her right as the sounds of preparation and discussion ruminated across the way.

Brin stared at her with open and fearful eyes, mouth moving but the attempted words barely escaping his tongue. He tilted his head back, choking back tears, drawing in a ragged and uneven breath. "It's okay, Sen," he whispered.

Such simple words, and yet, they had a greater impact on her than she could even fathom. So often was it that *she* had said those words to *him*. Back when he was sickly and could barely rouse himself from bed, Sen had always told Brin it would be okay. When he had faced ridicule for not being as strong or as brave as his father, Sen had always told Brin it would be okay. When faced with the uncertainty of his future with the Tribe upon becoming an adult, Sen had tried to tell Brin it would be okay. But now, as they both faced the impending strike of the Deatharms, the embrace of the longing and lost sure to follow, it was *Brin* who needed to comfort *Sen*.

"I...but I..." Sen muttered, stumbling over her words, not aware of how even to respond to those simple words when she knew that it most certainly was *not* going to be okay.

Brin shook his head, seemingly prescient of her intended meaning. "You did all that you could. Then...and now. Always."

She drew another sharp breath, the words stinging more than their intent. "I did all I could, and I still failed," Sen said, pushing back tears. "I always did what I could, but it never did anything for anyone."

"You're wrong," Brin asserted, bearing more resemblance to their father in that moment than he ever did previously. "You never failed. The only ones who failed were the ones who failed you. Maybe I'm to blame for that, too. But it was never you. *Never.*"

There was so much sincerity in Brin's eyes, so much warmth, that for a brief moment, Sen was able to focus not on the line of Invaders awaiting their chance and their shot but on this shared sequence of final seconds. This final moment that neither the victims nor executioners could take from her or them.

"We won't be long, now," Brin continued. "And we won't be apart, either. We'll see Father in the Otherworld soon. Together."

Chills ran down Sen's arms at the mention. Somehow, that put her at greater ease. The knowledge that the suffering will be but a handful of drops in the vast ocean that awaits them. That, despite it all, their father would be awaiting them with open arms in the Otherworld, just as they were always taught when faced with the embrace of death.

"You always *did* know the right words to say," Sen murmured, just audible enough for Brin to flash a nervous yet sincere smile.

Struggling against the chains, Brin shimmied along the wall, fighting with the limits of his range of movement to put his head in close enough proximity to his hand. He rubbed his chin against the chain around his neck, it being loose enough to pull against his skin. The pendant came free from out of his shirt, and with enough momentum, he managed to swing it over to his hand, pulling the chain free of his neck. He held the pendant by the chain, holding it out toward Sen as far as his arms would take him. "And if this is a final Memory, then at least it should be shared."

The Invaders had stopped conversing and preparing amongst themselves and appeared ready. There wasn't much time left. Seeing the pendant held out before her, Sen battled the chains, trying desperately to reach out and grab the dangling medallion, its inscribed rune calling out to her. As the Deatharms were raised, held in a firing position, Brin and Sen equally struggled toward each other, grunting and straining against the resistant pull of their bonds. Sen could feel the bones in her wrists crack in protest, the sensation of her arm being ripped out but an afterthought beyond the touch of this final moment.

The Deatharms cocked into position, one of the Invaders shouting something unknown to Sen's ears. Closer and closer the pendant was, Brin doing his part to swing it by the chain toward her. Another word was shouted, feet settling into place. As Sen uttered one final scream, she could feel the cold sensation of stone and ore graze against the skin of her fingertips and then closed her eyes and felt something run through her.

The thunderclap roared.

Over and over, the thunderclap echoed in her mind. The pleas for mercy once more rang out, the faces changing but the words remaining the same. The shadow stood over the form with two voices, one of aged strength and the other of youthful knowledge. At one shot, the two voices became one, and the youthful voice tried to scamper away. The shadow embraced it, wanting not to let it go, screaming words indistinct into its corporeal form but finding no comfort or welcoming in the embrace. The shadow called again, and this time, it was accompanied by the thunderclap. The youthful voice faded away to nothing, and the shadow turned back toward her, the only accompaniment in a world of nothingness.

When Sen opened her eyes again, she felt nothing. Not in the sense that she was numb from the world around her.

No, she felt no pain at all. The world around her still existed, the acrid smoke from the Invaders' Deatharms billowing up to the skies, itself intermingling with the rain that had now begun to fall. But in that brief moment of regathering, Sen could not help but notice a frown on the face of a couple of the Invaders, a readjusting of their Deatharms shortly following. And then, pained and ragged breaths rasped out beside her.

Sen turned and nearly screamed out at the sight. Two streams of blood poured out from Brin's abdomen—one from the chest, one from the stomach. Foaming crimson eruptions burst from his mouth as he groaned and screeched with discomfort, looking for solace in his sister's eyes and finding none of it. As Sen looked down, she realized that both shots fired at her missed entirely, the resultant holes finding homes above one arm and underneath the other. That mattered little to her. Desperately, as two of the Invaders stepped a couple paces closer, Sen reached for Brin's bloodied form, the light flickering from his eyes, the strength fading entirely. She screamed something indistinct, wanting only to embrace and comfort him in his final moments but finding not the ability to do so. The Deatharms clicked into place and fired as a familiar tingle greeted her once again, and as the thunderclap faded into a resounding echo, Sen felt nothing, the shots again passing her by.

In her periphery, she could see one of the Invaders spit on the ground and approach even closer, but again, it mattered little. Her bones cracked with greater intensity as she tried to force her way to Brin, but it was for naught. Helplessly, Brin mouthed something, but only blood passed his lips, the pained breaths ceasing, and as his pendant fell from his weak fingers, his eyes closed at last.

The Deatharm was held at point-blank range, aimed right at her head, but Sen could not break her gaze from Brin's fallen form. Even when it clicked into place, she did not turn. And even when a familiar sensation ran through her, she did not turn. She could only stare at the symbol of her failure, the resounding reminder of just what she always was told to be. Curseborn.

She awaited the thunderclap, but it did not come. She heard a faint clicking, a mutter of frustration, but nothing to bid her to the warm embrace of her family in the Otherworld. It wasn't supposed to be like this. She wasn't supposed to watch him die like that.

And then two more shots roared into the air, a spatter of blood splashing across Sen's face and chest. The Deatharm in front of her fell to the ground, and along with it, the Invader who held it. Slowly, she turned, her breath heavy and arms chilled, thick and viscous crimson running down the left side of her face in streams. A second Invader lay dead upon the ground, but the tools of their demise were held by their own comrades.

The red-haired woman and the man of hidden strength.

Writhing in place, Sen breathed heavily through her teeth, tears intermingling with the blood. The red-haired woman approached, dropping her weapon to the ground. There was a calm strut to her walk, something sinister yet assured. Pushing aside her dead comrade with her foot, she placed a hand against the wall, the spilled blood soaking into her skin, to which she paid no mind.

"You are a Lucky one, aren't you?" the woman whispered to Sen, again speaking the Tribal Words perfectly.

Sen was shocked and stunned beyond words, instead only managing to grunt and growl at her captor, both for the toying with her and for her dead brother.

"Ah, so raw and bestial. If I were to hazard a guess, your Tribe has regarded you as something inhuman all your life, is that not right?" The red-haired woman smiled. Something faint shimmered beneath her shirt, only barely recognizable beneath her uniform. "We're of the same flock, then, you and I."

Before Sen could voice any opinions to the contrary, the light shone brighter beneath the woman's shirt, and her form changed entirely. Where once she was a young woman with the hair of fire and skin of an Invader, she now bore the appearance of an old woman, aged beyond anything else, hair painted in long streaks of white, and the complexion of…kin. Of Tribe. An Illusionist? Or…no. Barely, Sen could make out three individual chains along the woman's neck.

"You may think your powers a curse, or have been informed as such," the woman continued, "but nothing could be more to the contrary, my child. Who could be more fortunate than you, to hold the power of Luck?" She paused, backing away from the bloodied wall, from the smell of death radiating both from Brin and the now-brainless Invader before them both, and smiled. "My name is Kamataa. And I offer you an opportunity to learn. From a fellow Eclipseborn."

EPILOGUE

ALL OUR YESTERDAYS

THE YEAR 1581 ANNO SALVATORIS
40 YEARS AFTER THE SETTLING

As the hair stood on the back of his neck, Aritz could feel the familiar touch of his flintlock rummaging along the surface of his head, his assailant slowly walking around him, their pace deliberate and methodical, still hiding from his line of sight.

"Who are you?" Aritz demanded, his blood running cold in his veins. "Do you understand who it is you're dealing with? Do you realize just what it is you've done? Do you—"

"Save it," the voice commanded, flintlock now back at the rear of his skull. "Sit."

Breathing heavily through his nose, Aritz complied, returning to his chair with fingers digging into the cushioned armrests, elaborate and intricate as everything else here. "What do you want?" he said sharply.

"Did you not enjoy my gift?" the sly feminine voice mocked, a warm chuckle escaping her throat. "Perhaps now everyone can know the true Aritz a Mata."

Aritz growled, eyes still pointed directly ahead. "That was *not* me. Whatever vile sorcery is behind that, I swear upon—"

"Upon what, *your* authority?" the woman sneered. "It is unfortunate how long it takes for word to travel across the ocean, but I can assure *you* that your authority is quite dwindling given your crimes in the homeland."

"Crimes?" Aritz barked. "There were no crimes. That wasn't me! I wasn't there!"

The woman paused but then chuckled once again. "Amazing the tales that people will craft, though, isn't it? The idea that Aritz a Mata, one of the most brutal murderers of our age, would turn his rage against his own household, against his own family? How heartbreaking for all except those who truly know you."

A brutal murderer? Him? Hardly. His fingers were nearly tearing at the cushions of his armrests, the stuffing coming out from the seams. "A devilish trick by someone more devilish still. I killed no one."

"Did you not? It's all right in there, by many who recognized their assailant as you. Did you not watch my gift to you?"

"I watched enough to know how preposterous it all was."

"But you didn't finish."

He growled, almost ferally. "No."

"Then, finish. Now."

Aritz snarled, his nose wrinkling like an angry hound ready to strike. "No."

Something sharp grazed his throat, his eyes widening at the cold kiss of steel. He didn't have to look down to know that the woman was holding a knife to his throat. "I'm afraid I must insist that you finish."

Gently, the knife was eased from his throat so he could lean over to his desk and grasp the pendant once more, to which he complied, seeing no other option. The flintlock remained hard against his skull, every step bringing him greater dread of what lay on the other side of this pendant. Had he something—*anything*—in this blasted desk with which to defend himself, he could have fought her off. But by whatever misfortune bestowed upon him by the Savior, he had nothing, and he had no choice.

Gingerly, he reached for the pendant, and at its cold touch, the Memory surged through his arm, up through his shoulder, and into his mind, resuming just as he had left it.

A resumption of blood and horror.

He scoffed. He raised the blade. She winced.

And steel met bone and flesh, the soft crush of brain matter and blood oozing out as Lucrecia collapsed in a heap. There was no hesitation in the next act as Arnao and Luzia's voices screamed in a bloody chorus, horrified at the sight of their mother lifeless and wide-eyed on the ground, the expression of shock permanently frozen upon her face. The kids shook her violently in an attempt to restore some semblance of life into her, but it was for naught. They both knew that, but try as they might, nothing was bringing life back to that caved-in head.

There was a wince of motion, a slight twitch, that sent Aritz back into action, and before the children could go in whatever direction they had elected to next, whether to run away, to fight back, or whatever the case may have been, their heads rolled along the ground, blood splattering in a wide arc against an otherwise pristine room, the crimson wave on the windows interrupting the view of the mountains and countryside beyond.

Aritz grunted and spared no further thoughts to his wife and children. He merely turned heel and walked back toward the door, sword still drawn and dripping with the blood of countless people, his clothing stained further still.

He exited his large chambers and sauntered down the steps, past the slaughterous carnage he laid in his wake. Further down the corridor, at the end of the line of portraits, a handful of cleaning staff stood in shock at the sight, pointing at one dead body in the garden and at the other in front of the portrait of Aritz's family. When they caught sight of Aritz himself, all bloodied and emotionless, they surely assumed they were to be next.

"L-L-Lord Aritz," stammered one woman, an older maid who had likely served this household for much of her life, from the look of her. "W-w-w-what's happened? P-please, sp-spare us!"

There were three of them, all huddled together and holding onto each other for dear life. The other two didn't even spare him a fearful glance. No matter. They weren't getting in his way, and so he merely passed them by, grabbing a cleaning rag from one of their skirts to wipe the blood and viscera from his face, at least to some degree. Walking past the fountain, he found the first guard he slew, an arrow stuck in him, and returned his bloodied sword to him, no longer having a need of it. Hidden amongst the hedges, a bow and quiver lay, still unfound by those unsuspecting. A grin stretching across his face, Aritz retrieved the weapons, the familiar weapons, and retreated into the countryside.

The surge left him, and Aritz found himself back in his chambers, his Ferrandan chambers. He could already feel his face paling and released a wave of nausea, the floor below and part of the desk covering in that smatter of what remained of his seafaring breakfast. He felt a jerk at his collar, and before he could register it, he was thrown back into his chair, flintlock still held firmly to his head, but knife no longer present.

Shock had momentarily paralyzed him but quickly was replaced with anger. "Do you...*realize* what you have done?"

The woman was silent for a moment before at last scoffing at the assertion. "What *I* have done? It's quite apparent who it was that your household and family recognized you as."

"By some horrid trick!" he screamed. "That was two days after I departed for Ferranda! It could not have been me!"

"And yet, they don't know that, nor do they much care," she answered with amusement. "I'd have to imagine that word traveled to your King and Queen. It's a believable story and all, given some of the stories I'm sure that older maid can attest to."

He had nothing to say to that. Nothing to say to this murderer. "You killed my family in cold blood," he growled plainly.

"Just as you killed mine."

That gave Aritz pause. His nose wrinkled, again bearing that of a rabid and vengeful hound. "Who the hell are you?"

The flintlock lifted from the back of his head, and slowly, the woman circled him, coming into view just before the puddle of vomit. "Was I not your favorite student?" It was that girl from the lecture earlier, the one who so ardently labeled him a monster. Who else?

Rolling his eyes, Aritz looked down the barrel of the gun with annoyance and distaste. "Let me guess. Yours is some sob story about how your family couldn't afford to—"

"Not exactly," the girl interrupted, not even attempting to humor him. A light shone underneath her shirt, bright and radiant, so familiar and haunting. In an instant, the girl was someone entirely different, yet so recognizable. How could he forget that face, that wild and untamed face? She hadn't aged a day in twenty-five years, but there was something greater bothering him.

"You..." Aritz muttered. "How are you even here? You're supposed to be dead."

His assailant smiled, a grin that said everything and nothing all at the same time. "A people and culture do not cease to exist simply because your eyes have shut."

<u>End of Book One of</u>
<u>The Spellbinders and the Gunslingers</u>

GLOSSARY

Tribes, Cultures, and Dramatis Personae

The Stone Tribe: Occupants and landholders of much of the territories bordering the southern ridge of the Heart of the Land, the Stone Tribe has been considered the gatekeepers to the Heart. The most populous Tribe of the Land, they are a melting pot of multicultural roots due to the large number of adept warriors, hunters, and scholars who dwell within the Tribe's borders. Since the Invasion of the Acrarians, the Stone Tribe has offered land to the displaced peoples south of the Forest, most prominently the Sun and Arrow Tribes. Physically, they are easily identifiable by the braids they fashion at the nape of their necks and the face paint they adorn in adulthood in correlation to the Sign under which they were born: red for the Bear, blue for the Wolf, and yellow for the Owl. An adult bearing no face paint is considered an outcast not to be interacted with.

- **Sennalhat:** Also known as Sen. Second daughter of the Stone Chief Fannalhen and Dennalhir. Considered an outcast but is allowed to remain in the village.

- **Tezalhat:** Also known as Tez. Firstborn daughter of the Stone Chief Fannalhen and Dennalhir, eldest sister to Sennalhat and Brinnolhat. An adept warrior Bearsign who was granted the Boon of Endurance.

- **Brinnolhat:** Also known as Brin. Youngest child of the Stone Chief Fannalhen and Dennalhir, younger brother of Tezalhat and Sennalhat. A bookish and shy young man who recently completed his Trial as an Owlsign and was granted the Boon of Memory.

- **Fannalhen:** Also known as Fanna. Chief of the Stone Tribe, husband of Dennalhir, and father of Tezalhat, Sennalhat, and Brinnolhat. A revered Bearsign granted with the Boon of Courage.

- **Dennalhir:** Also known as Denna. Wife of the Stone Chief Fannalhen, mother of Tezalhat, Sennalhat, and Brinnolhat. As equally revered a Bearsign warrior as her husband, her talent with the spear is unparalleled.

- **Tawandhar:** Also known as Tawa. A member of the Tribal council, a close friend to Fannalhen's family, and the father of Narvarho. An Owlsign of the highest order and a master of Knowledge.

- **Narvarho:** Also known as Narva. Sen's closest friend. A Wolfsign imbued with the Boon of Sound.

- **Rantalha:** A member of the Tribal council and one of the Tribe's most accomplished hunters. A Wolfsign granted the Boon of Stealth.

- **Sharrabha:** A member of the Tribal council. An accomplished Wolfsign imbued with Packmind who makes frequent trips through the Heart on behalf of the Tribe.

- **Koelhe:** A member of the Tribal council. Mother of Fannadhan. An Owlsign bearing the rare Boon of Foresight.

- **Fannadhan:** Also known as Fann. Once a close friend of Sen, now a bitter rival. A Bearsign granted the Boon of Strength.

- **Grafhar:** A mute Owlsign granted the Boon of Language.

The Keepers: Dwelling within the mountainous ranges of the Heart of the Land, the Keepers are the conductors of the Trial and the guardians of the Bear, the Wolf, and Owl. They are the only Tribe not to be displaced by the Acrarians nor have their territory occupied by displaced Tribespeople. The Keepers are the most prolific of the Owlsigns, with many of the Land's greatest scholars being born a member of this Tribe. They are bestowed an honorific dependent upon which Sign they were born under after they complete their Trial: Ko for the Owl; Ne for the Wolf; and An for the Bear. The Tribe is home primarily to Owlsigns and Wolfsigns, with very few Bearsigns.

- **Ko Zaran:** An Owlsign with the Boon of Knowledge who conducts Brin's Trial. One of the most learned scholars in the Land with an enormous collection of tomes in his personal library.

- **Ko Endra:** An Owlsign with the Boon of Memory. Ko Zaran's direct steward.

- **An Rhan:** A Bearsign with the Boon of Strength. One of the most adept fighters in the Heart by virtue of being one of the only ones. Tasked with guarding the True Heart where the Animal Deities sleep.

- **Ne Shanne:** A well-respected Wolfsign bearing the Boon of Pack-mind. One of the few Keepers who has ventured beyond the Heart.

- **Ko Seln:** An Owlsign granted the Boon of Language. Runs a tavern that can be found on the ascent through the mountain ranges of the Heart.

- **Ne Arsah:** An embittered Wolfsign with a Boon of Stealth. Spends much of his time at Ko Seln's tavern.

- **An Nara:** A Bearsign with the Boon of Restoration who spends much of her time at Ko Seln's tavern.

The Sun Tribe: One of the Tribes displaced by the Invasion of the Acrarians, the Sun Tribe once dwelt along the southeastern coast of the Land, making a living off of fishing and other seafaring activities. They were the first to be displaced by the Acrarians after their arrival. At first resettling in the Forest, they were then further attacked by the zealously territorial Wood Tribe, leading to lingering animosity between the two Tribes. They have since settled in the Stone Tribe's territory at Stone Chief Fannalhen's offering, but many in the Sun Tribe are eager to retake their homeland. Members of the Sun Tribe are distinguishable by their hide garb bearing only one shirtsleeve, their long hair tied in two vertical buns at the back, and their tribal paint of two red lines crossing vertically over the eyes.

- **Han'e:** Chief of the Sun Tribe. A Bearsign with the Boon of Courage, toeing an uneasy alliance with Stone Chief Fannalhen.

- **Tol'e:** A Wolfsign bearing the Boon of Movement. One of Han'e's most trusted hunters.

The Wood Tribe: The de facto guardians—or rulers—of the Forest, the Wood Tribe is fiercely defensive and territorial, such to the point that they attacked the displaced Sun Tribe merely for trying to settle within their lands. Many Tribesfolk from the south who were merely passing through to the Heart to complete their Trials considered passing through the Forest a trial unto itself. The Wood Tribe makes its home high in the trees of the Forests in order to hold a strategic position against any would-be infringers of their territory. Leadership of the Wood Tribe is denoted by their makeshift crowns crafted from tree leaves and branches. Rarely is their skin kept bare; normally, it is painted in greens and browns to camouflage themselves amongst the trees.

- **The Elder:** A fierce old Bearsign with the Boon of Fear.

- **The Matron:** An Owlsign healer bearing the Boon of Knowledge.

- **The Chieftain:** A Wolfsign often accompanied by a contingent of yeomen with Boons of Packmind.

The Haunted: Perhaps the most mysterious Tribe of the Land, the Haunted Tribe bore the worst of the Acrarians' assault, and the few who remain have been forced into servitude by the Invaders. "Haunted" is not the true name of the Tribe, but rather a somewhat derisive term used to address the Tribe's fascination with the plane of existence after death, particularly believing they could commune with the souls of the dead.

- **Shara:** An escaped slave from the Acrarian City.

- **Ran:** An escaped slave from the Acrarian City. Has never known freedom due to the Acrarian Invasion happening when he was only a year old.

The Acrarian Kingdom: Labeled merely as the "Invaders" by the Tribes, the Acrarians hail from a continent far to the east. They laid claim to the Land after mistaking it for the mythical Great West before deciding to formally settle the island while displacing the native population. The Acrarians are subject to an industrial age with steam power driving innovation and exploration forward. To an extent, Acrarians are also religious zealots who follow the teachings of an unnamed Savior figure in whose name they have claimed the Land with the idea of spreading his will unto the world.

- **Aritz a Mata:** Leader of the invading Acrarian forces. The son of a lord in tremendous favor with the royal family.

- **Master Hernan:** A sycophantic Scholar.

<u>TRIBES NOT APPEARING IN THIS VOLUME</u>

The Lake Tribe: Settled upon the Big Lake north of the Forest, the Lake Tribe is a warlike group often more at odds with each other than with the matters of the outside world. There is wide infighting amongst the Tribe, specifically on opposite ends of the Big Lake. They are skilled naval fighters if only because they've constantly warred with each other on boats along the Big Lake, leading to the body of water to be nicknamed the Lake of Bones by other Tribes.

The Arrow Tribe: Hailing originally from the Plains encompassing the southwestern regions of the Land, the Arrow Tribe were a once-proud group of nomadic wayfaring horselords until the Acrarians displaced them and stripped them of their horses. Comprised almost entirely of Wolfsigns, they have since been allowed resettlement in the north within the Stone Tribe's territories.

<u>RELIGION AND BOONS</u>

The Tribes revere the will of nature, and more specifically, the three Animal Deities: the **Bear**, the **Wolf**, and the **Owl**. Each Deity is represented in the fields of strength, community, and wisdom, respectively.

When a Tribesperson is born, they are born under a celestial "Sign" that correlates to one of the three Deities. When a Tribesperson comes of age at eighteen, they go on a pilgrimage through the mountain ranges of the Heart to receive a Trial from the Keepers, which tests their acumen in the fields relevant to their Sign. If a Tribesperson fails their Trial, they are exiled from their respective Tribe and considered an outcast. If they succeed, however, they are granted a specific Boon which enhances certain physical or mental capabilities. This Boon is later carved as a rune into a pendant or a weapon, such as a spear. Once inscribed, this object will hold the power of that specific Boon. In theory, this means that any who holds the object will be subject to those abilities, but this is a strict taboo, and those who break it are immediately banished.

Each Animal Deity offers five possible boons.

Boons of the Sign of the Bear:
- *Strength*: amplifying power and force. Also called Strongarms.

- *Endurance*: increased stamina. Also called Lasters.

- *Fear*: masters of intimidation. Also called Instillers.

- *Restoration*: quicker recovery from injuries. Also called Restorers.

- *Courage*: heightened bravery. Also called Strongsouls.

Boons of the Sign of the Wolf:

- *Stealth*: muted footsteps. Also called Sneaks.

- *Packmind*: thought sharing within a group

- *Scent*: heightened sense of smell. Also called Trackers.

- *Sound*: heightened sense of hearing. Also called Listeners.

- *Movement*: can more easily detect movement in the earth. Also called Sensors.

Boons of the Sign of the Owl:

- *Knowledge*: high intelligence. Also called Learneds.

- *Memory*: storage of the history of the world. Also called Rememberers.

- *Illusion*: masters of disguise. Also called Illusionists.

- *Language*: quick to learn any foreign tongue. Also called Linguists.

- *Foresight*: can observe glimpses of what is yet to come. Also called Futureseers.

ACKNOWLEDGMENTS

I would first like to thank my editor, Michele Perry, for her sound advice and assistance in bringing this story to life and for helping guide it to being the tale I wanted it to be. I would also like to thank my cover artist, Felix Ortiz, and graphic designer, Shawn King, for creating a wonderful cover that I can't help but stare at all day.

To my close friends Adam Maguire and Samantha Smith, this story would never have happened without the ample encouragement I received from both of you over the years. Without the two of you, I would not have had the confidence to go forward with this whole writing thing.

To Dr. Naomi Appleton, I'm sure it wasn't your intent to sway me away from academia and instead pursue storytelling, but if it was not for your course on studying the Mahabharata and the Ramayana, I would not have discovered just how much more I loved narratives than I did academic study. If this finds its way into your hands, thank you for redirecting me towards a much happier path.

To you, the reader, thank you for taking a chance on this book. I hope I've convinced you to stick around for the next one.

And finally, to my rock, my support, my loving fiancé, Annie. Thank you for everything you do—with regards to this book, and also just in general.

ABOUT THE AUTHOR

Joseph John Lee has lived near the Boston area for most of his life, except for the years when he didn't. He pursued a career in academia and received a Bachelor's degree and two Master's degrees in history before realizing his true passion lay in creating new worlds rather than studying old ones. Currently, he works in higher education and spends too much time looking at dog accounts on Instagram.

THE BLEEDING STONE is his first novel.

Twitter: @joelee__
Instagram: @joelee__